## Also by Sharon Bolton

*Sacrifice*
*Awakening*
*Blood Harvest*
*Little Black Lies*
*Daisy in Chains*
*Dead Woman Walking*
*The Split*
*The Night Train*
*The Pact*

The Craftsmen series
*The Craftsman*

The Lacey Flint series
*Now You See Me*
*If Snow Hadn't Fallen*
*Dead Scared*
*Like This, For Ever*
*A Dark and Twisted Tide*
*Here Be Dragons*
*The Dark*

# THE
# BURIED

## SHARON BOLTON

ORION

An Orion paperback

First published in Great Britain in 2022 by Orion Fiction
This paperback edition published in 2023 by Orion Fiction,
an imprint of The Orion Publishing Group Ltd
Carmelite House, 50 Victoria Embankment
London EC4Y 0DZ

An Hachette UK company

1 3 5 7 9 10 8 6 4 2

A CIP catalogue record for this book is
available from the British Library.

ISBN (Mass Market Paperback) 978 1 4091 7417 2
ISBN (eBook) 978 1 4091 7418 9
ISBN (Audio) 978 1 4091 7552 0

Typeset by Input Data Services Ltd, Somerset

Printed in Great Britain by Clays Ltd, Elcograf S.p.A.

MIX
Paper from
responsible sources
FSC   FSC® C104740
www.fsc.org

www.orionbooks.co.uk

*For John Sawyer . . . wisest, weirdest, most wonderful of men*

# PART ONE

## 1999
### *Larry Glassbrook's last days*

Lancashire Morning Post
9 July 1999
By Abby Thorn, guest editor

Human remains found in land above Laurel Bank in Sabden are to be cremated in a private service later this month, according to a short statement released today by the Lancashire Constabulary.

Black Moss Manor Children's Home, formerly known as Black Moss Manor Orphanage and Foundling Hospital, dates back to 1893, when it was opened by the town mayor using money raised by local benefactors. It closed in 1969, following a police investigation into alleged neglect and cruelty.

The remains found are believed to be those of four children: news almost certain to raise hackles among those residents of Sabden with long memories. It may be three decades since Larry Glassbrook's reign of terror caused all parents in the town to fear for their children, but dark memories linger, especially in Lancashire.

According to the official police statement, the four deceased children probably died of influenza or tuberculosis, two diseases prevalent in Lancashire throughout the late nineteenth and early twentieth centuries. Local historian and retired librarian Daphne Reece told the Post that Victorian orphanages typically had their own patches of consecrated ground, though there had been no burials at Black Moss Manor that she could recall. 'I would expect headstones,' she said, 'even very simple ones, although it's possible they were removed years ago.'

Police Superintendent Tom Devine told the Post that no formal investigation would be launched. 'These are old remains,' he said, 'dating back to when, sadly, infant mortality rates were much higher than they are now. We have no reason to believe a crime has been committed.'

The identities of the deceased children are not known and there are not believed to be any living relatives.

# 1

## Florence

Monday, 26 July 1999

'Black Moss Manor,' I say, across the rickety, Formica-topped table in the visitors' room. I'm picturing the steep, laurel-lined drive on the outskirts of town, the soot-blackened stone, the pointed gable in the centre of the slate roof. I can see large square windows, those on the ground floor barred.

Behind us, an argument breaks out. A whistle is blown; someone barks out an order.

I remember peeling red paint on the front door, the rusting drainpipes and the ferns that sprang from crumbling mortar. I can almost smell the crisp air of the moor, the boiled vegetables, the stink of urine that formed an evil-smelling cloud around the rear of the building.

Conscious of Larry's eyes on me, I quickly reread the article from the *Lancashire Morning Post*: human remains found, four children assumed dead from natural causes. I register the byline of the journalist and the references to the local historian and the police superintendent. I tell myself that it is nothing to do with me.

'That place saw a lot of children through its doors,' I say, when I look up.

Larry's black hair has turned snow white, and his skin has coarsened. His nose has been broken more than once, and there is a puckered scar above his right eye where someone tried to remove it with a dinner fork. He is handsome for all that. Anyone wondering how Elvis might have looked had he reached the age of seventy, and kept his weight under control, need only look at Larry.

'Some of them would have died,' I finish.

Larry lowers his voice. 'Oh, they did. I buried 'em all, and not on the premises.'

'What are you saying?' I ask. 'Did you do this? Did you kill them?'

Larry pulls a face, an expression of surprise, of disappointment. 'Hell, no,' he says.

'You can hardly blame me for asking.'

'Florence, I killed Susan Duxbury, Stephen Shorrock and Patsy Wood. I owned up to it, and I've served three decades for it.'

I do not need him to tell me this. Thirty years ago, in 1969, three young teenagers disappeared from near their homes in Sabden and were never seen alive again. I was a lowly WPC, still on probation, but I tracked down and caught the killer. Larry.

'I'm not getting out of here alive,' he says. 'What have I got to gain from lying?'

He has nothing to gain. Nothing at all.

'I remember every coffin, every casket I ever made, Florence. Does that surprise you?'

Larry, before his imprisonment, was a master carpenter and a part-owner of Sabden's only funeral directors, Glassbrook & Greenwood. His partner, Roy Greenwood, ran the business and walked before the cortège in black tailcoat and top hat, carrying a silver-topped cane. Larry made the beautiful, satin-lined, hardwood caskets.

'In all the time I worked with Roy, I made eight children's caskets for Black Moss Manor,' Larry tells me. 'Three were for babies. There was never any budget, but I made 'em nice because I had two kids of my own.'

I cannot help the raised eyebrows. A devoted father who killed the children of others. He either doesn't see it or ignores me. He starts to cough and pulls out a handkerchief. A bloodstained handkerchief.

'Ten minutes, ladies and gentlemen,' the officer on duty calls. Around us, we hear people making their preparations to leave. Some have a long way to travel and are impatient to be out. Behind Larry's head, I see a couple embrace.

Larry and I never touch. Larry and I are not lovers, spouses or partners. We're not relatives, or even friends. I have no idea what Larry and I are.

'My point is,' he goes on, 'they weren't buried at Black Moss. They went to St Augustine's, the nearest churchyard.' He taps his finger down on the cutting and says, 'So where did this lot come from?'

'They predate you,' I suggest. 'When did you start work at the firm?'

'In 1946.' He's anticipated the question. 'Roy came into school looking for an apprentice good at carpentry.'

I glance back at the cutting. Four small skeletons. 'So these remains go back further. It says here the home dates back to the nineteenth century.'

Larry sighs, a damp, unhealthy sound. 'Florence, I know a thing or two about dead bodies and what happens to them in the ground. The soil up there is acidic. And wet. Small corpses wouldn't last fifty years.'

'You're saying these are unofficial burials?'

'Yep. And recent ones at that. Last twenty years. Thirty at the absolute outside.'

'Then they'll be investigated.'

'Does it look to you like they have an investigation planned?'

I look once more at the newspaper cutting. *The remains are to be cremated following a private service.* 'I can't get involved.'

'Doesn't sound like the WPC Lovelady I remember.'

I'm the last visitor sitting. The officer in charge is looking at his watch.

'Larry,' I say, 'we closed the children's home down. The people who ran it served time.'

I'm trying to remember the name of the two people in charge. Ashton? Aston?

'A couple of years,' Larry says. 'Then they were out again. You might have closed the children's home down, but you didn't stop what was going on.'

I'm shaking my head.

'You know there's something wrong in that town, Florence,' he says. 'You could feel it all those years ago.'

Thirty years ago, in Sabden, Larry was my landlord. I lived in his house, along with his wife, teenage daughters and a couple of other lodgers. It wasn't the easiest of times: I was struggling to find my feet in a rough Northern town, wondering if becoming a police officer hadn't been an arrogant mistake, feeling out of place and out of sorts from the moment I woke up in the morning. Larry had been decent to me, his wife kind, almost motherly, his daughters friendly albeit in the self-absorbed way that teenagers have. The Glassbrook family and their home had been one of the few positives about my new life.

Until I found out too much; until Larry kidnapped and tortured me; until he left me for dead in a freshly dug grave.

The third finger on my left hand is hurting. Phantom pain, of course: I lost that finger years ago, but it hurts me all the same, especially when I'm anxious. Normally I tuck it into my armpit and the pressure helps, but I won't do that in front of Larry.

*Something wrong in that town.* I could almost laugh. I raise my eyebrows again. This time he sees it and he smiles. 'More than just me,' he says.

'I'm not going back there.' I mean it. I am never going back to Sabden.

Larry pulls out his bloodstained handkerchief and I notice again how grey his skin looks, how his flesh seems to have dissolved. I shouldn't be shocked. And yet I am. For the first time in decades I have to face the thought of a life without Larry.

'How about for my funeral?' he says.

# 2

## The Poisoner

The poisoner is weak.

The poisoner is your servant, child, spouse, the powerless chattel for whom you barely spare a thought, except when your convenience is disturbed.

The poisoner walks beside you, barely noticed, rarely considered. He knows that you are a fool, blissfully unaware of the patient assassin who cooks your food, plays at your hearth, sleeps in your bed. You are never safe from the poisoner because he is always by your side.

The poisoner has endless patience. He will bide his time, counting out his wrongs and his grievances the way a miser counts his gold, knowing that all will be played out. The poisoner can afford to wait.

The poisoner has skill and craft, the like of which you never dream, because he feels no need to attract either your praise or your attention. The greatest danger is the one you never see coming.

I say 'he' and 'him', but of course the correct pronouns are 'she' and 'her', because poison has always been the weapon of choice for those who otherwise have no power. The poisoner is a woman.

The poisoner is me.

# 3

## Cassie

Never underestimate another witch's power. That's what my mother always told us, and so I don't, even when the witch in question *is* my mother. In her day, Sally Glassbrook was a powerful practitioner of the old craft, and I watch myself when I'm around her.

I say a prayer for strength as I get out of the car, imagining a thin silver cord running from my core right down to the centre of the earth. When I'm calm – God, it pisses me off that she can still do this to me – when I feel calm enough, I head for the door.

The old bitch's nursing home is a few miles out of Sabden. It's not nearly as old as it looks and, once inside, might be any modern medical facility. The old stone exterior is fake, like the filial devotion that picked the most expensive home in the area for my mother. I don't give a monkey's about her comfort. I chose it for its location.

I never use the front door, preferring to slip in unnoticed through a side entrance. The floor isn't carpeted, but she never hears me approach. I'm about to turn the door handle when I hear voices inside.

'All the signs say Larry will pass soon.' The woman speaking has a rich voice, with Lancashire overtones. 'Maybe even the day of the full moon.'

My mother gives a faint laugh. 'He always had a flair for the dramatic.'

My mother? What the fuck? My mother has barely spoken in years. She has early-onset dementia, exacerbated by chronic depression. She lies in bed with her eyes wide open or sits in a chair and stares out at the moor. Sometimes she wanders the room in bare feet and pulls at her hair. Occasionally she mutters to herself. She doesn't talk to people.

The strange voice says, 'Cassie has been making enquiries. She wants to hold the funeral in Sabden.'

'She's back?' my mother says. 'She's been in town?'

I hear the panic in my mother's voice. I have been forbidden to set foot in my home town for nearly thirty years: forbidden by Larry, but Sally went along with it. At sixteen years old, shortly after his arrest, the two of them had me sent away to live with relatives, told me that under no circumstances was I to return. I went along with it. I had no choice.

'No, no, I don't think so,' says the other woman in the room. 'Not in town as such. Just phone calls. It's not a good idea, Sally. The funeral, I mean. Even ten miles down the road would be better.'

I can hear traces of a West Indian accent. We knew a West Indian family years ago, but I can't quite bring their name to mind.

'What difference does it make now?' my mother asks. 'People will get excited for a few hours and then they'll all go away, including Cassie.'

Hearing her say my name feels like an old sore being scratched. It's been years since she's even acknowledged my existence.

'She wants to sell the house,' says the West Indian woman. 'She wrote to Avril.'

Avril Cunningham is my solicitor. So much for client confidentiality.

'So do I,' my mother says. 'I'd have sold it years ago. I owe her that, at least, after what I did to her.'

'Will you go to the funeral?' asks the woman.

'No.'

*After what she did to me?*

Even in the corridor I hear the sigh that comes next. 'Sally, we need you to come back to us. When it's over, when he's really gone, will you leave this place?'

There is silence in the room for several seconds. Then my mother says, 'What can I do? What can any of us do?'

'You must have seen the news? About the children's bodies found at Black Moss Manor.'

I have a subscription to the *Lancashire Morning Post*. I remember that story. Meanwhile, from inside the room comes a heavy sigh. 'I did,' my mother says. 'So what?'

'They're going to cremate them. Not bury, cremate.'

'It's the cheaper option.'

'And it destroys all the evidence.'

I press a bit closer to the door.

'There's talk of it being the same day, Sally. All the attention will be on Larry's funeral. No one will pay any mind to what they're doing on the other side of town.'

No response that I can hear.

'They're trying to hide something, Sally.'

*They?* Who are they?

'Sally, you knew that place. That girl you helped, she came from there, didn't she?'

'Marigold?' There is warmth in my mother's voice. 'Florence and I delivered her baby.'

I remember Marigold. She appeared in our house shortly after my father was arrested. And then vanished, just as suddenly.

'We tried to save her,' my mother is saying. 'We did our best. Why don't you ask Florence?'

'No,' the woman snaps. 'We're all agreed. Florence must not come back.'

*Tried to save her? Did their best?* What are they on about? Marigold went back to her family.

'The Craftsmen are our curse, Sally,' the woman says. 'No one can face them but us.'

The Craftsmen? I've never heard this before, and yet it is resonating somewhere deep inside me, like an ancient fear awakened after a long sleep.

'Long-dead corpses, Marlene,' my mother says. 'What can we do?'

The woman, Marlene, says, 'What if they're not so long dead? What if it isn't over?'

I wonder whether I heard talk of them as a child – disturbing talk – whether I let it slip into my subconscious, never to be thought of. *The Craftsmen*. I find my mouth forming the words silently and realise that I'm unnerved, maybe even – afraid?

There is movement in the room. I backtrack several paces until I can slip round the corner. I find myself breathless.

My mother has been lying to me. Oh, I know, she never actually said, 'Cassie, my love, my mind has fled, leaving me empty and useless. This paper-thin walking corpse is just a bad memory made flesh.' She never actually said it, just— Bloody hell, I had no idea my mother was such an actress.

And Marigold? The Craftsmen? What the actual fuck?

And what was it, exactly, that she did to me?

I hear a door close and footsteps walking away. Fortunately for me, Marlene – of course, I remember now – she is Marlene Labaddee, an old friend of my mother's and the owner of the flower shop on Sabden's main road – does not share my habit of sneaking in by the back door.

I move quickly towards my mother's room, hoping I'll catch her in the act of . . . I'm not sure what – some act of the living – but she's back in her usual chair by the window, staring out at the moor.

She is wearing a shapeless wool skirt that's too big and too warm for the day. Above it is a blouse I remember from when I was a child and a thin pink cardigan. Her hair, once long and fair like mine, is shorter and thinning now, more grey than silver. She has a habit of twisting strands round her fingers and pulling at it. Her cardigans are always littered with loose hairs.

For several seconds I watch her reflection in the glass of the window. Only when her eyes lift and meet mine do I walk to her bookshelf and kneel. As I start to pull out the books, I watch her out of the corner of my eye, waiting – hoping – for a reaction. She stays still in her chair, shrunken and dull, her eyes on her lap.

Every time I come in here I mess around with her bookshelves. Sometimes I leave books under the bed, or outside on the window ledge, or soaking up a spill beneath a coffee mug.

'Your husband is dying,' I announce. I have a sudden brainwave and put the books back with their spines facing inwards. 'Any day now. Lung cancer that's spread to the pericardium. Sorry for your loss, blah, blah, blah.'

I stand and cross to the wardrobe. Last time I came, I turned everything inside out. I have my hand on the door when I realise it's pointless. My mother is never going to come out of her stupor and snap at me to behave myself and leave her things alone. She knows exactly what I'm doing, and why, and she doesn't care.

Weary now, I take the other armchair, just as we hear noise out in the corridor. The trolley is approaching. There is a brief knock on the door and it opens immediately.

'All right, Sally. Ready for a brew? Oh, hiya, Cassie, love. I didn't know you was here.'

I've never learned the names of the staff, but this woman's face is familiar enough. Creased and bloated, red-veined and sweating with the effort of pushing a wheeled trolley. They all know me, of course. I pay the bill every quarter.

'Has my sister been recently?' I ask her.

'Not as I know of, love.' She pours tea and leaves.

'I'm going to see Dad on Wednesday,' I say when Mum and I are alone again. 'I've got special permission, seeing as how he's dying.'

My mother doesn't reply.

'Any preference for funeral flowers?' I say. 'Who was that friend of yours? You know, the florist on the main road, Marlene someone or other? Do you see much of her?'

Not an eyelid flickers.

'I was thinking of asking Marigold to the service,' I say. 'You remember Marigold, don't you? Lived with us for a time. Don't suppose you can give me an address?'

Again, Sally doesn't move, but I sense a difference in her breathing. She will know, now, that I was listening outside the door.

'Maybe the Craftsmen,' I say, thinking *in for a penny*. 'Are you still in touch with any of those old guys?'

Almost. She gives a start and a half-glance in my direction. She and I make eye contact for a split second, then she slips back into her stupor.

'What did you do to me?' I ask. 'What was it, exactly, that you feel you need to make up for?'

Nothing. Absolutely nothing. Giving up, I get up to leave, but at the door, I stop and turn back.

'I'll be staying in town for the funeral,' I say. 'I've booked a room at the Black Dog,' I say. 'With John.'

Finally, a reaction. Her head jerks upright, her eyes wide with fright. I'm smiling as I leave the room.

# 4

## Florence

'Florence! Florence, wake up. It's not real.'

I'm entombed. The blackness is all around me and creeping ever closer is—

'Florence, come on. Wake up.'

Movement beside me and then soft light brings me back to my own bedroom, my husband leaning over me. I am wrapped up tight in the bedclothes. Sweating, I pull myself free. Nick hands me a glass of water.

'You OK?' he says.

I nod. 'Did I wake Ben?'

When the dark dreams come, I scream. I've been known to wake neighbours if the windows are open.

'Can't hear anything,' he says. 'I'll go see in a minute. Are you sure you're OK?'

'Fine. Check on Ben.'

I'm not fine. It will be hours before I'm anywhere close, but I want Nick out of the room. If he stays, I know exactly what will come ne—

'Usual dream?' he asks me.

I nod again, although strictly speaking, there are three recurring dreams that we dread. The first, that the hands of dead children reach towards me from the earth of their own graves. That's pretty bad. The second, that a man without a face is cutting pieces off me, one by one. I really don't enjoy that one. The third, and worst, is that I'm still alive but trapped in a coffin deep underground. A coffin made by Larry.

I've been having these dreams for thirty years.

'Every time you go to see him,' Nick says as I head for the bathroom.

This isn't strictly true, but close enough that I don't even try arguing.

'How much longer?' he asks me.

My face in the mirror is corpse pale. 'Maybe not long at all. He's ill.'

I start counting, a therapy trick to control my breathing. 'He's dying,' I add, before I reach four.

'Good,' says Nick.

Nick goes back to sleep eventually. I never can after the dreams – so I don't try. Instead, I climb to the top floor and release the loft ladder. Hidden behind a box of Ben's baby toys that I can't bear to throw away, I find a cardboard box, dull beneath a veneer of dust, shrink-wrapped in cobwebs and with missing, nibbled-away corners. The woman I used to be wrote SABDEN on the lid.

I skim past the file on the Glassbrook murders – I need no more of those memories in my head tonight – and find my file from August 1969. Sure enough, there are newspaper cuttings of the Black Moss Manor case. Working back in time, I find a follow-up story of what happened to some of the children after the home closed down. I find court reports, summaries of the trials of the people who worked there. Aster was the name I couldn't remember. The two people who ran the home were Drs Frederick and Judith Aster.

And then I find the one I'm looking for. On Thursday, 14 August 1969, the front page of the *Lancashire Evening Telegraph* was given over entirely to a story about the fire that swept through the home the night we closed it down.

The accompanying photograph was taken shortly after nine o'clock the same morning. I know that for a fact because I'm in it. Tom had driven us both up there, screeching to a halt some distance from the blackened building. There had been too many fire engines in the way to get closer.

In the photograph, I'm looking at the manor. Tom, perhaps sensing that we were being watched, has turned to face the camera. I don't really need to read the accompanying story. I remember every detail of that day: windows blown out by the heat; the sodden ground littered with broken furniture, books, even children's clothes. I remember the soot that seemed to hang in the air, the charred walls, the fallen chandelier.

I remember the fire chief showing us round, indicating two distinct points of origin in the staff offices.

'Fires don't start accidentally twice,' I'd said.

'No, they don't, young lady,' he'd replied.

I remember the heat-buckled filing cabinets, their contents reduced to ashes. They'd been left open, those cabinets, so the fire could destroy their secrets.

I'm not going back to Sabden, but I can make a phone call or two. I can put Larry's mind at rest before he dies. I owe him that much. I turn to leave the loft and stop dead.

I owe him? *I owe Larry?* Now, where the hell did that come from?

# 5

## Cassie

Larry is dying. In a few days, maybe even hours, they tell me, he will be gone. He will take his secrets to the grave.

And I will be free.

The rising moon has woken me, as it often does. It's a waxing gibbous moon, a day off full, a time when human energies are at their peak. I do my best work when the moon is nearing fullness. My loft flat has floor-to-ceiling windows on three sides. Moonlight floods in. It gets hot, especially in summer, but I usually sleep during the day and work at night.

A few years ago, one of the rare magazine interviews I've ever agreed to made a big deal of my nocturnal habits, calling me a 'silver-haired vampire'. Daft twats. My hair is ash blonde, not 'silver'. And I'm not a vampire. I'm a witch.

I get up. I have a piece to finish – an opening score for a new musical – but I'm not sure I can work tonight. So I stand at the open window, looking down at the sparkling lights and deep shadows of Salford at night, and I have a sense of my life opening up like a flower. Everything I've dreamed of for so long has slipped a little closer, will soon be mine for the taking.

A little over thirty miles north is the town I grew up in. Sabden. And in Sabden lives the only man I've ever truly loved. As long as Larry is alive, I can't go back, and yet I've never been able to leave it completely. From my mother's nursing home, miles away across the moors, I can sometimes see its rooftops. I hover at its edges, obeying the terms of my banishment, but close enough to get there quickly when the time comes.

That time is coming. I can feel it.

I can picture Sabden's lights in the distance, its endless rows of dirty terraced streets, its factory chimneys like blackened fingers clutching at the sky. In my head, I can see the great black mass that is Pendle Hill at night and our old house on the edge of the moor. I hear my mother's bees humming their songs around the apple trees and the sound of hammering in Larry's workshop as he bangs and saws and nails in time to the Elvis Presley music he loves so much.

A sudden pain. As though someone has hit me hard in the stomach. I gulp in a breath, and when I let it out again, it greets the world as a sob.

My father is dying.

No, I will not cry. Not for Larry. And yet that's exactly what I'm doing. Tears are streaming down my face, I'm gulping in breath, and I'm crying for everything I once believed to be true and the life that should have been mine. And yes, I admit, I'm crying for my father, who is leaving me for ever. Where is this terrible grief coming from? I've waited thirty years for this. I'd have killed him myself had it been possible.

I can't stop, so I let myself cry. After a time, when the moon has risen higher, I feel calmer. There are no clouds in the sky tonight, but I can see the silver lining behind my pain. I remind myself that I've waited for Larry's death. This misery is simply the price I have to pay. My tears are the sacrifice.

Perhaps they'll be the only one needed. But I can be flexible.

I'm getting cold, but I don't close the window. Instead, I walk to the stereo and press 'play'. The track is one of my favourites and it seems appropriate for tonight. Paul Simon's 'Fifty Ways to Leave Your Lover'. I have my own lyrics, of course.

The music starts. 'Stab her in the back, Jack,' I sing. 'Throw her 'neath a bus, Gus.' I'm feeling better already.

I look out, towards the blackness that I know is Sabden. Towards the place where *he* is, and I send my words out into the night.

*I'm coming, my love.*

# 6

## Florence

It's late afternoon before my schedule frees up and I have a chance to make the calls that I've been thinking about all day. I start with the easiest of the three, to the water company.

'What can I do for you, Assistant Commissioner?' says the gruff Northern voice of the company's managing director. Were I anyone else, he probably wouldn't have taken the call, but most people, even hundreds of miles away, prefer to keep on the good side of the Met's senior ranks.

'Not much to say, really,' he tells me, when I've explained why I'm calling. 'We've a reservoir up at Astley Bank, bit further up the moor. Long story short, we've been losing more water from it than we should, even at this time of year, so I had the lads check for leaks. The equipment picked something up just outside the manor so we dug that section of pipe up. That's when we found the bodies.'

'Did you see them yourself?' I ask.

'Aye, I went up there. Something like that, we take it seriously.'

'Can you tell me anything about the condition they were in?'

A short pause. 'Well, I rather think that's a question for the local police, love.'

I give him a second or two of silence, hoping he might fill it. He doesn't.

'Are there plans to search the rest of the grounds?' I ask. 'How do we know there aren't more remains to be found?'

'Already done.' His voice takes on a note of satisfaction. 'The entire back garden was dug up. Nothing else. Case closed.'

Case closed.

For a moment, I try to give myself permission to believe it, to put it behind me and move on. But I'm still reeling from the thought that sprang into my head in the small hours: that I owe Larry. The idea is absurd. I owe him nothing. And yet . . .

Nick has asked me, many times, why I have stayed in touch with Larry over the years, why I visit him, receive his letters, send him gifts in return, even fight his corner when he is being ill-treated. I think my husband suspects, although he has never voiced as much, that I had feelings for Larry thirty years ago, feelings I've never managed to leave behind.

He's wrong. I don't, and never did, have feelings of that sort for Larry. Nor am I one of those women for whom sadistic killers hold a grim fascination. Larry's crimes revolt me, enrage me, even after all this time.

The truth is, I cannot explain the hold Larry has over me, why I keep going back. I'm not sure I ever will.

The press office supplies me with the telephone number I need next, but only after repeated assurances on my part that it's a personal matter and nothing to do with the Met.

Abby Thorn, who wrote several of the stories about Black Moss Manor in 1969, was a cub reporter in Sabden at the same time I served my probation there. Like me, she moved away as her career took off. I've caught glimpses of her over the years. She's been the Middle East correspondent for several of the national papers and at one time had her own radio show with the London Broadcasting Corporation. Now, like me, she seems to be winding down. She's the Northern correspondent for *The Times*, writes occasionally for her old paper, the *Lancashire Morning Post*, and presents a weekday current affairs show on BBC Radio Lancashire.

The switchboard at the BBC in Blackburn is answered quickly and I'm put through to the news desk. Ms Thorn isn't available and so I leave my number.

# 7

## Cassie

I should be doing this face to face. People can lie when we only hear their voices. (Take it from me: I've turned lying into an art form.) And she can put the phone down on me if I really piss her off. I should go up there, walk into her shop, look her in the eyes.

I could, at that. Larry has days left. What difference can it make now?

Except it does. It's been drummed into me for so long I can't change it now. While Larry is alive, I can't go back to Sabden.

'The Flower Pot,' she says in her low-pitched, sing-song voice. 'How can I help you?'

'Hello, Marlene,' I say. 'This is Cassandra Glassbrook.'

She catches her breath. Good start.

'Well, hello, my girl,' she says. 'Long time no see. How are you, Cassie?'

She'll know exactly how I am. My mother will have told her.

'Your father's time is very close now,' she hurries on. 'I hope he rests in peace at last.'

That is most unlikely. Still, I say nothing.

'What can I do for you, Cassie? Are you calling about funeral flowers? I would be honoured to do a wreath for your father.'

Brilliant opening.

'Yes,' I say. 'Can you do it in marigolds?'

Silence.

'That's not really the sort of flower we get in the shop.' Her voice is guarded now.

'Shame,' I say. 'Marigolds shouldn't be forgotten about, should they?'

Nothing. Then, 'I know you were at the home yesterday, Cassie. Your mother called and told me.'

So, she can use the telephone as well.

'Why is she pretending to have dementia?' I ask. 'What the hell is she playing at?'

'She is not pretending—'

'I've seen her medical notes. She's a fraud. I want to know why.'

'Then you must ask her yourself.'

I walk to the window of my flat and look out, north, to where Marlene is. I should have gone. I should be in the shop with her right now, facing her down.

'She won't talk to me,' I say. 'She hasn't talked to me for years.' I hear the weakness in my voice and know I'm losing.

'Then you must ask yourself why.'

I fight the urge to slam down the phone.

'Does she talk to Luna?' I hate myself for asking.

'I couldn't say.'

I try a different tack. 'What happened to Marigold?'

She says nothing.

'I heard you yesterday. You said my mother and Florence Lovelady tried to help her, tried to save her. What does that mean?'

'Cassie,' she sighs, 'it was a long time ago.'

'Luna and I thought Marigold had gone back to her family. That she'd made up with her parents and they were going to help her bring up the baby. Florence told us and Mum was there. Were they lying?'

Marlene doesn't reply.

'Tell me what happened to Marigold.'

'I don't know. Nobody knows. She vanished. The night the children's home burned down. There was a row at your house and she ran away. At least, that's what we think.'

Of course there was. A terrible row. I was the cause of it. Am I to blame for Marigold too?

'You must have looked for her?'

'Of course,' Marlene says. 'But she'd gone.'

'Who are the Craftsmen?'

Another sharp intake of breath.

'You said they were your curse, that only you could stand up to them. Are they witches too?'

'Don't go there, Cassie, I'm warning you.'

'You said they were hiding something, something to do with the old orphanage, and dead children. What's going on, Marlene?'

'There's someone in the shop,' Marlene says. 'I have to go. Do you want me to do some flowers for your father?'

'No,' I say. 'Absolutely not.'

# 8

## Florence

The third phone call is the one I'm dreading, the one to Sabden Police Station. As I wait to be put through, I get up and walk to my office window. I'm on the fifth floor and have an uninterrupted view downriver towards Waterloo Bridge. Lying flat on the water, waiting to be raised for the celebrations at the year end, lies the giant Ferris wheel that will become the London Eye.

'Collins,' the female voice says. My left hand starts to hurt as though the town still has the power to harm me, even down a telephone line.

'It's Florence Lovelady,' I tell her. 'How are you, Perdita?'

'Ma'am, good afternoon. What a surprise. I'm well, thanks. You?'

Detective Sergeant Perdita Collins and I met when she was a child, and then came across each other again several years ago at a conference aimed at encouraging more women into fast-tracked police roles. Chance had assigned us to the same discussion group, and I'd liked her. She'd worked in Manchester at the time. We'd kept in touch since, mainly through emails and the odd phone call.

'Congratulations on making sergeant,' I say.

'Thank you. I'm enjoying it. I'm leading a team investigating domestic violence.'

I listen for a while, and when the conversation lulls, I say, 'Can you talk?'

I mean, of course, can she talk freely.

Her voice drops. 'Give me a sec.'

When I hear birdsong and traffic down the line, I know she has stepped outside and I remember the car park at the rear of the building. If she climbs onto the perimeter wall, she will see a river too, but one that is narrow, with steep banks, that runs underground through much of the town. Very different to the Thames.

'I'm all ears,' she says, at last.

I glance down at the cutting from the *Lancashire Morning Post*.

'Can you tell me anything more than I've read in the paper?' I ask when, without mentioning Larry, I've told her the reason for my call.

'It's not something I've been involved with,' Perdita replies. 'One of the DIs is dealing with it. Is there a problem?'

'I'm sure there isn't. But it reminded me of something that happened a long time ago. You know those niggling feelings you get sometimes?'

'What do you need?'

Trying not to feel guilty about putting her in a difficult position, I tell her.

# 9

## Cassie

This is a mistake. This shrivelled old creature in the high-sided metal bed is my grandfather. I turn to the guard who escorted me into the prison's hospital wing, but he's scarpered. And then the husk on the bed speaks.

'Sal? Sal, is that you?'

His head is off the pillow, he's holding out a shaking, yellow hand, and there is joy in his eyes.

'It's me, Dad,' I say. 'Cassie.'

I want him to be disappointed, but when the smile plays at the corners of his eyes, I find my cold heart softening. I'll have to watch that.

'Cass,' he says. 'Good to see you.'

I move closer and sit. There are handcuffs attached to the side of my father's bed, but they hang loose and empty. This man is never getting out of bed again. He is no danger to anyone. Not even to me.

'I saw that write-up in the paper,' he croaks. 'The assistant governor saved it for me. About that film score you wrote.'

'Not all the papers were that kind,' I say, although I'm touched, more than I want to admit, that he's seen it.

'You've done so well. I'm that proud, love.'

His breathing quickens and pain screws up his face. Wires and tubes, not chains, are keeping him in place now.

'Have you seen Luna?' I don't know why I ask that. I don't want to talk about my sister.

'No,' he says.

I wait for him to go on, but it seems he has nothing more to say on the subject of Luna. Suits me.

'How's your mum?' he asks.

Million-dollar question. I haven't a frigging clue, is the only honest answer. 'Improving a bit,' I decide upon. 'Better than she has been.'

He nods, pleased, and I'm pissed off that I've given him any sort of good news. *You killed Mum*, I want to say. *She never got over what you did. Everything shit that happened, everything I did, everything we lost, was because of you.* I open my mouth to begin, but his body seems to convulse on the bed. His head rocks back and he gasps. The heartbeat monitor at his side picks up.

'Dad? Dad, what's wrong?'

He can't answer me and so I get up and rush to the door. A little way down the corridor is a nurses' station.

'My father's in pain,' I tell the woman behind the desk. 'He needs help.'

'He's been refusing pain relief,' she tells me, as we hurry back. 'We can keep him hydrated, but that's all.'

'Why? Why does he want to be in pain?'

I'm wondering if it's some weird form of penance.

'The drugs we give at this stage are very strong,' the nurse says. 'He wanted to keep a clear head.'

We stop at the door of his room and she lowers her voice. 'I think he has something to say to you.'

After the nurse has left us – my father has once again refused pain relief – he seems to drift into a light doze and I wait. Then his eyes flicker open again.

'I don't need to make a will,' he says. 'I signed everything over to your mum long ago. And I've written a letter of wishes. It's in the cupboard.'

I follow his eyes to the small bedside cabinet. The letter inside is addressed to me in a scrawling hand that I wouldn't have recognised.

'Open it,' he tells me.

Only a paragraph long, it contains instructions for his funeral.

He is to be cremated, at the prison, without a service of any kind. His ashes are to be disposed of anonymously. There is to be no headstone or memorial.

He watches me crumple it.

'You're going to be buried in the family plot at St Peter's,' I tell him. 'I've spoken to Dwane at the old firm. He's given me some dates, although he was a bit reluctant, while you're still alive. Sentimental old fool, isn't he?'

Larry shakes his head. 'Not Sabden. I don't want you going back there, any of you.'

'There's something in Sabden that belongs to me,' I tell him. 'I'm going to get it back.'

He's getting agitated, actually trying to sit up. 'No,' he says. 'You need to stay away from that place. You need to stay away from that lad.'

'Not a lad anymore,' I say. 'Thirty years have gone by. Thirty years you stole from me, Dad. Well, it's over now. I'm going back.'

His hand clutches mine before I can pull away.

'You can't stop me,' I tell him. 'Not anymore.'

A sly smile sneaks over his face. 'I can,' he says. 'I have. I've written to Florence.'

*What?*

'What?' I say. 'What have you written to Florence?'

All the breath seems to leave his body as he gives a heavy sigh. 'I served thirty years,' he says. 'I paid for my crimes, Cass. When are you going to pay for yours?'

And then he dies.

# 10

## Florence

I'm driving home when I hear the news. I'm listening to LBC, a phone-in about police numbers in London, when the half-hour strikes and there is a brief news bulletin. The lead story is the death, in Wormwood Scrubs, of serial killer Larry Glassbrook.

'Glassbrook was convicted in 1969,' the reporter reads, 'of the abduction, torture and murder of three teenage children. Throughout his thirty-year incarceration he maintained a close personal friendship with the police officer who arrested him, Assistant Commissioner of the Met Police Florence Lovelady. She was unavailable for comment this evening.'

A car horn sounds behind me. The lights have changed. Another horn sounds. A cacophony strikes up around me. London drivers at rush hour have no concept of patience and yet I cannot move.

It's over, then.

Doesn't feel like it.

# 11

## Cassie

He's written to Florence.

I'm sitting at the nurses' station, a cup of tea cooling in front of me. I'm anxious to leave, but there are forms to sign, empty condolences to receive from the prison staff. I'm taking nothing in and they stupidly put my numb state down to shock. Maybe not so stupid after all. I am in shock.

The old bastard has written to Florence. He's told her.

It was no idle threat. I knew that the second he said it. She's been visiting him, all these years.

In the seconds after he breathed his last, when the dancing lines on the machine by his bedside fell still and the high-pitched alarm took their place, I searched his room. I worked fast, knowing the alarm would bring nurses within moments.

I rifled through cupboards, pulled open bags, looking for an unposted letter, anything that might let me know whether he was telling the truth or making a last desperate attempt to keep me in line.

In the drawer of the bedside cabinet, I found a notepad. The top page had the faintest indentation of his handwriting. I could make out *Dear Florence*, but nothing more. I found a book of first-class stamps and a faded, torn address book. Under 'L' for 'Lovelady', I saw her London address. He wasn't bluffing. He's told Florence.

Shit, shit, *shit*!

What the hell do I do now?

# 12

## Florence

Nick has booked a table at Umberto's, a small Italian restaurant within walking distance of our house in Clerkenwell. Wednesday is the night in the week I most look forward to. Nick picks Ben up from swim club at eight, by which time I've usually finished work. We eat late, go to bed late and spend most of the next day a little tired. I wouldn't have it any other way.

While we're waiting for the food to arrive, Ben says, 'We did snorkelling and freediving.'

Nick says, 'I thought you were speed-training.'

'We can do sub-aqua when we're sixteen.' Ben's hand creeps across the table towards his dad's wine glass. 'Coach was trying to find out who might be interested. Can I do it? It costs two hundred quid.'

'How can you do freediving in a metre and a half depth?' I ask.

'We used the diving pool. I was the best at holding my breath underwater.'

'I'm sure your mother and I are very proud.' His father retrieves his glass after a small tussle. 'But the point about sub-aqua is you have a tank on your back. You don't have to hold your breath.'

'The air in your lungs acts like the air in a life jacket,' Ben tells us. 'Just taking in a deep breath will make you rise up in the water.'

'More air in your body makes you less dense,' his dad says.

'Exactly, and do you know how to get maximum air into your body?'

'Enlighten me.'

'You pant for a few seconds to expand your lungs. Then you take one God Almighty breath and hold it.'

Ben starts to pant, as though his father and I might need a demonstration, then puffs his cheeks out like a hamster. I watch him for a while, then turn to Nick.

'I missed your call earlier,' I say.

'Just had some time on my hands,' he says, which is our code for 'Not in front of Ben'.

The air bursts noisily out of our son. 'Over a minute,' he says, looking at his watch. 'I need the loo.' He gets up and walks away, panting. As soon as he is out of earshot, Nick pulls an envelope out of his jacket.

'This arrived,' he says. 'Posted yesterday.'

The letter is from Wormwood Scrubs. From Larry.

'If you're going to open it, do it before Ben gets back,' Nick says.

I read the two short sentences, check inside the envelope to make sure there's nothing more, then hand it to Nick.

'What's it mean?' he says.

'I'm not sure.' I look down at the letter again.

*I've kept them safe for thirty years. Over to you . . .*

'He wanted me to look into some remains that have been exhumed from an old children's home,' I say. 'I told him no. I'm not about to interfere in another force's case.'

Nick says nothing.

'Maybe he means his family,' I say. 'Sally and the girls.'

'You haven't been in touch with them for years,' Nick says. 'Florence, tell me you haven't.'

'No,' I say, truthfully. I only know what Larry told me about his family. Sally stayed in Sabden; the girls went to university and left the town. Cassandra, whom we called Cassie, became a successful songwriter and lives near Manchester. Luna, christened Elanor, is a corporate lawyer somewhere in London.

'Will you go to the funeral?' Nick asks me, and because I don't want to answer, I throw it back at him.

'Do you think I should?'

'No,' he says.

Nick and I rarely argue. No one ever really argues with Nick.

But my ongoing relationship with Larry has led to rare but regular exceptions.

'Why are you being so aggressive?' I ask.

'Larry Glassbrook has been the other man in your life for a long time. I'm glad he's gone. But this' – Nick stabs a finger down on the letter – 'this looks to me like he's trying to manipulate you from beyond the grave.'

'That's ridiculous,' I say, but I'm thinking, *Not Larry. If there was ever a third person in this marriage, it wasn't Larry.* I'm picturing someone else, a tall, dark-haired young man dressed in the fashion of the late 1960s. A man I have never spoken to Nick about, because he would hear it in my tone. A man who might look a little like my husband does today, because I've always stuck to type, and it was in Sabden that I discovered my type.

'You're off to Paris at the weekend,' I say. 'I have leave booked, and Ben is off school.'

'I don't want Ben anywhere near that place.'

'What's up?' Ben says. Neither of us noticed him coming back. Moving slowly, because he's as sharp as nails, I slide the envelope from Larry into my bag. 'What place?' Ben says.

'Sabden,' I reply, because we both know Ben won't let it drop.

'Where the witches live?' His eyes light up; Nick's darken.

'No,' I say. 'Where the witches lived. A very long time ago.'

Nick's eyes meet mine. He says nothing. His eyes say everything.

# 13

## Cassie

Sabden. I see the sign as I drive down from the moors. I imagine the rusting chains that stretch across the road, the rotting 'Keep Out' signs written in my father's handwriting, and I pick up speed. The town boundary, which I haven't crossed in nearly three decades, flashes past. The chains shatter, their splinters flying into the air around my car, and I'm home.

The spell is broken. The princess is free.

My home town has changed. So, so much. The mill chimneys that dominated the skyline in the old days, guiding us in when we were still miles away on the moors, have mostly been felled like unwanted trees.

The cottage hospital where I was born is a Chinese restaurant now. As I drive further into town, I see that the tramlines have been ripped out and the cobbled streets tarmacked over. The record shop where we hung out on Saturday afternoons has become a Barnardo's charity shop.

It's raining hard and the wind is getting up. The weather never changes. Raindrops run down the windscreen and my wipers can't keep up. Inside the car, tears spill over and fall down my face. I've missed so much.

Towards the centre of town, the elusive familiarity I've been chasing seems to draw within reach. Here are the grand old Victorian buildings: the library, the town hall, theatre, masonic lodge. The outdoor market has gone, though, and in its place is a 1970s monstrosity of concrete and multicoloured plastic hoarding. I drive through an amber light, turn the corner into the market square, take another left and I'm here.

St Peter's, our old family church, is the largest in town. Stone-built, with a great clock tower, it overlooks much of the town centre. Mum, Luna and I were pagans, of course, and Larry didn't have a religious bone in his body, but his job as the town under-taker meant we had to keep up appearances. Back when we were a family, we came here most weeks.

As I leave the car, the wind hits me. It's always so bloody windy in Sabden. The few times in the year when it drops, we get nervous. For us, calm weather means something worse is on its way.

The great front door is open. Few churches are as big as this one, but I guess we'll need a big church. Larry had a lot of enemies who'll want to make sure he's really dead. The gallery will be useful. I'll be able to sit in it. I'll see everyone, and no one will notice me.

'Cassie?' says a voice behind me. 'Miss Glassbrook?'

A man in his mid-fifties, in the uniform of a senior police officer, and carrying a huge black umbrella, is coming towards me. He is tall and dark-haired, classically handsome. My heart hasn't been my own since I was sixteen years old, but I've never been averse to a casual shag. I'd shag this one. He holds out a large, warm hand and I register the lack of a wedding ring on his other one.

'Tom Devine,' he tells me.

I should have known. Tom Devine was a young detective con-stable when Larry was convicted. Several girls at school had a crush on him. I think Luna and I might have done too, until he came to the house that night. Shivering in my nightdress, peering over the banister, I watched him put handcuffs on my father and push him out of the door. He wasn't the most senior officer present, but I always think of Tom Devine as the man who took my father away. No, I decide. I will not shag this man.

'You look a lot like your mother,' he says. 'How is she?'

'Advanced dementia,' I say, because the truth is too complicated. 'Not the woman she was. How's your wife?'

Tom Devine was married in the old days. To a woman with long, thin legs and a huge blonde beehive.

'Eileen and I divorced ten years ago,' he says. 'Far as I know, she's fine. Will your sister be joining us?'

'I haven't the faintest idea.'

His eyes cloud over as he labels me potential trouble. 'I want you to think about having the service somewhere else, Cassie,' he says. 'Another town ideally, but even another church where your family wasn't so well known.'

'Every church in town knew Larry,' I say. 'He buried the town's dead.'

And a few of its living. We're both thinking it. I remember that Devine was present when two of the bodies were found.

'And a few of its living,' I say, to see his reaction.

'We can still bury him here in the family plot.' Devine isn't giving up easily. 'Just hold the service somewhere else.'

'This was our family church,' I say. 'Some of my earliest memories are of sitting in the front pew, looking up at the beautiful stained glass, listening to the choir. I was hoping to sing with them one day, but . . .' I sniff.

Devine's face is unmoved. 'OK, then. If you can supply a list of people you expect, we can have a constable on the door making sure no one else comes in. I assume you want the press kept out? And here's Dwane.'

We turn to greet the newcomer. Dwane Ogilvy, who runs Glassbrook & Greenwood now, is less than five feet tall, with the disproportionately short arms and legs of dwarfism. He has a prominent brow, deep-set eyes and thick grey hair. He stops a short distance from us and plants both feet apart like a child. He is wearing a black suit and tie, and green wellingtons.

'Cassie,' he says. 'How do?'

'I'm good, thanks, Dwane. Have you dug the hole yet?'

It is mean of me, I know, to remind Dwane of his humbler origins as the town sexton, but he takes me seriously. 'I will dig it, for Larry,' he says. 'I wouldn't for most, but for Larry, I will.'

I remember that Dwane always took a ridiculous pride in his sexton skills, claiming his graves were perfect and unique to him. All these years and I'm still surrounded by idiots.

'Luna phoned me,' Dwane says. 'She's in New York. Can't get back till next week. She said she'd go along with anything you decide.'

It is typical of my sister to leave all the hard work to me. It does, though, make things easier.

'We should go and look,' suggests Devine. 'Make sure you're happy.'

I couldn't care less about the exact piece of ground they put Larry in. This funeral is not about Larry; it is about giving me a legitimate reason to be in town for several days. They can throw his body on the town dump for all I care, but I pretend interest and we leave the church.

'You can pop down t'shop after,' Dwane says, as I walk slowly to accommodate his swinging, lurching gait. 'Choose the casket. I've got some nice cedar in. It was always Larry's favourite. I can have it done in time – it's no bother. You can choose the trim, and the lining.'

'Kind offer,' Devine says. 'Dwane's become quite the craftsman over the years. His caskets are famous.'

I hear a sharp intake of breath from Dwane, as though he's actually insulted by Devine's compliment.

'I want the cheapest you've got,' I tell him. 'One hearse, no cars, absolutely no flowers. I don't want him embalmed, because nobody is going to look at him ever again. And I don't want anyone doing that ridiculous thing where you walk in front of the coffin with a top hat and a silver cane.'

Dwane stares up at me. 'Do you want a headstone, or have I to stick a plank in t'ground and write on it with a felt pen?'

'Yes,' I say. 'Do that.'

We leave the path and my heels stick in the mud. Dwane offers me his arm, just as something occurs to me. What did Devine just call Dwane?

'Happen I should talk to your mum about this,' Dwane says.

'You might have more success talking to Larry himself, but up to you,' I say. 'Barring interference from anyone else, you've had your instructions.'

I'll give Dwane his due, he never sulks. He comments upon the dreadful weather and the damp ground as we approach the site of the Glassbrook family plot.

'Have either of you heard of the Craftsmen?' I ask, when he finally stops talking.

'No,' snaps Dwane.

'Can't say as I have,' Devine adds. 'What are they? A pop group?'

I watch Dwane's face closely. 'I'm not sure,' I say. 'But something local, specific to Sabden. I thought perhaps some sort of guild.'

'You mean like the Rotary?' Devine says. 'Doesn't ring a bell. How about you, Dwane?'

'No,' says Dwane again, keeping his eyes on the ground.

I'm getting nothing more from these two. We inspect the patch of turf. I acknowledge that there isn't room to add Larry's name to the headstone that was erected in my great-grandfather's day. Plank of wood and a felt pen it is, then.

# 14

## Florence

It is three days before Perdita calls me back and she waits until the evening. Now it's my turn to take the call somewhere I won't be overheard. I walk out into the small garden behind our house. It's raining and I have to shelter beneath the eaves. Around me, the patter of drops on strong, broad leaves sounds like percussion.

'The four remains were all of children,' Perdita says quickly, as though wanting to get this over with. 'Aged between about three and fourteen years old. Sex unknown, although clothes suggest at least one of them was female.'

'Official burials? Were they in coffins?'

'Hard to say. Some fragments of wood would suggest so.'

'Can you use the clothes to date them?'

'To an extent. Natural fibres, most of which have rotted away. Some buttons which suggest pre-war clothing. Hang on, I made a note.'

I watch a cluster of yellow flowers bowing their heads in protest at the relentless downpour.

'Celluloid,' Perdita says. 'It looks like plastic but is actually a plant derivative using wood and cotton fibres. The buttons are small, backed with metal. They were common from 1900 to about the 1920s, but by the 1940s other materials were taking over.'

'Cause of death?' I ask. 'Range of decomposition?'

'Impossible to say about the cause, but they were all in a very similar condition, suggesting they died at roughly the same time. Some sort of epidemic seems likely.'

I feel a familiar mix of disappointment and relief. There is no case here. The remains seem to be old. Pre-war at least. The children appear to have died of an illness. Larry was wrong.

'I don't have access to the files, so I had to have a sneaky peek on someone else's desk,' Perdita says. 'Does it help at all?'

I'm getting wet. At my feet, one of the marigolds springs up, throwing off its burden of rainwater. It seems to look directly at me. I bend to pick the flower to take it indoors with me.

'It puts my mind at rest,' I say. 'Thank you, Perdita.'

Perdita hangs up, eager to be away. A breeze blows a flurry of raindrops into my face, but I make no move to go inside. Once I do, I decide, it will be over. Larry is dead. Whatever unhealthy, inexplicable hold he had over me is broken and I can safely ignore his fake concern over the discovered remains and his cryptic last letter. Both were nothing more than attempts to mess with my head, something he's been doing successfully for thirty years, and that I have to bring to an end for my own sanity. I cannot let Larry's influence stretch beyond the grave.

'Hello, Florence.'

I start. The voice is as clear as if the speaker were standing beside me, and yet I'm alone. The voice is that of a young woman, and there are no women in our house other than me.

I step away from the shelter of the eaves, into the rain, and follow a short gravel path into the garden. It thrives, as many London gardens do, and the vegetation is thick and high. Even so, I cannot believe anyone is hiding in it.

'Hello?' I say. I am still holding the yellow flower in my hand.

In response, I hear a high-pitched, childish giggle.

I wake in the night with a name on my lips that I haven't uttered in thirty years. Marigold McGowan.

Beside me, Nick is fast asleep. I lie in the darkness, listening to the sounds of traffic, to the occasional shout or scuffle, to the distant scream of sirens, and I think about Sabden in the 1960s, when the nights were silent.

A glance at the clock tells me it's nearly four in the morning.

Beyond the clock is the vase with the yellow flower I picked earlier. A marigold.

I have no idea what happened to Marigold, why she disappeared the way she did, where she went. I only know where she'd come from. Marigold McGowan fled Black Moss Manor Children's Home, where she claimed she'd been held prisoner.

I remember the giggle I heard earlier in the garden, the childish voice calling my name. And I know that it isn't only Larry calling me back to Sabden. Marigold is doing it too.

# 15

## Cassie

Florence's house in London is a turn-up. Large, Georgian, in one of the fancy Clerkenwell squares. There's no way she can afford this on a police officer's salary. Jammy bitch must have married a banker.

I check it out from the other side of the square, like a burglar casing the joint. Three storeys high with a solid front door. There are ground-floor-level windows, but they sit above a high basement void and I'll never reach them.

The door opens, but it isn't Florence who comes out. Instead, a tall man in his mid-fifties appears, standing to one side to let a teenage boy past. I feel a twist of jealousy with the realisation that Florence has a family. I've always thought of her as damaged, some-how, like me. As the boy runs down the steps, the man – obviously his father: they are alike as two peas – locks the door.

They climb into a parked estate car and drive away. If Florence is home, she's probably alone. I could ring the bell, confront her, but once I do that, I'll have forced her to act. Any accusation Larry might have made about me in his letter will be only that. An accus-ation. She will have no proof – Larry had no proof – and if Florence is still the woman I remember, she'll want proof. She'll do nothing in a hurry and I'd be a fool to provoke her.

I approach carefully. She is a senior, high-profile policewoman. She will be security-conscious, and there may even be CCTV cam-eras watching me now. I walk right up to the tall black railings that prevent idiots and drunks from tumbling into her basement void and look through the ground-floor windows. Can't see a thing. It's dark inside.

Beneath me are three chained bicycles and two refuse bins.

I walk away, down the street and round the corner, to find that access to the house, while difficult from the front, is impossible from the rear. Florence's terrace backs on to another row of houses and any gardens can only be reached through the houses themselves. This house is a fortress. I cannot get to her here.

She'll have to come back to Sabden.

# 16

## Florence

After Nick and Ben leave the house, I find my Black Moss Manor file again. I spend longer than I should looking at the image of Tom and me outside the blackened building, and then, on page eight of the newspaper, the last page before the classified ads start, I see a picture of Marigold and her young baby.

*Missing?* says the headline. The story is short, simply mentioning that the police are interested in the whereabouts of young mother Marigold McGowan and her baby boy. Anyone with information should contact Detective Constable Tom Devine at Sabden Station.

I asked to head up the hunt for Marigold and was told it wasn't appropriate for a constable on probation. Instead, I was assigned to another case, one that had taken a lot of my time, and it had never occurred to me that that might have been deliberate.

A subsequent issue of the *Lancashire Morning Post* covered the court cases. Both Frederick and Judith Aster were sentenced to two years for child neglect and actual bodily harm. Both were medical doctors, and the story, written by Abby Thorn again, speculated that they'd be unlikely to practise medicine again. The three staff members had shorter sentences.

I'm distracted by a noise outside, in our basement void, where we keep the rubbish bins. I wait but hear nothing else and put it down to foxes, even in the middle of the day.

A third story I find is about some of the children being rehomed after the manor closed down. Three photographs show the blackened manor, some children playing in a primary school and one little boy with short dark hair and big brown eyes. The story, very briefly, states that all the children formerly resident in Black Moss Manor have been found loving and supportive foster homes. A happy ending.

I'm not sure that, in Sabden, there was any such thing.

# 17

## Cassie

It's late when I get back from London and I'm knackered, but I don't drive home. I head towards Sabden, not quite as far as the town. I turn off the road before I reach its boundary and make for Pendle Hill.

The road gets narrower, winding. It's not an easy drive, especially in poor light, but the Hill acts like a signpost, drawing me in. When I'm so close that the Hill seems to be soaring above me, I turn off the road along a farm track. I slow down, take my time, until I can see the black gleam of a moorland lake ahead of me. A little way from the water's edge, I get out and walk to the shore.

'This lake is the Black Tarn,' Sally told us when I was about eight, Luna six or seven. 'Also known as the Black Mirror, and the baptism pool of Pendle Hill. When you were both just a few days old, I brought you here and submerged you completely in the water. Years ago, my own mother did the same to me. We are women of Pendle, baptised twice.'

I've come prepared. I've brought an old-fashioned fishing reel, made of holly, dull with age. Sally used it countless times for winding spells and it will have absorbed some of her power. The thread is silk. Not as strong as I'd like, but natural fibres work best. The lure is something I found in Florence's London bin. An old Dior perfume bottle. Not as good as something from her body, such as hair or nails, but she will have handled it hundreds of times. It will do.

I tie the bottle to one end of the silk and unwind about twenty yards of it. Then, envisaging Florence, I toss the bottle as far as I can out into the lake. Its splash disturbs some birdlife nesting around the edges and I wait for the flapping to stop before picking up the reel. I take up the slack, feel the resistance of the bottle and give it a little tug. It edges closer to me across the bottom of the lake.

I wind slowly. The last thing I want is for the silk to break. If that happens, my spell will have failed.

'Come back to us, Florence.' I picture the roads, first the M1, then the M6, that will bring her north. 'Come to Sabden.' I envisage Larry's letter in her hand, imagine it pulling her back here.

I wind the black thread round the reel, praying and picturing as I go. Spells do not have to be elaborate. Sometimes the simplest ones are best.

The bottle slides and bumps its way along the mud of the lake bed. When it's close enough that I can see it beneath the surface, I step into some reeds and anchor my reel, digging it deep into the mud. It will hold there.

Florence will come back to us now. I've never known a winding spell to fail. And when she does, I'll be ready.

# 18

## Florence

After we've eaten, Nick and Ben switch on the TV in our living room. I take a mug of mint tea into the garden and light a fire in our firepit. Once the flames have taken hold, I let myself stare deep into the embers, trying to find some measure of calm.

Since my last visit to Larry, especially since the news of his death, I haven't been myself and my health problems have taken centre stage this evening. I'm alternating between being cold and so hot I start to sweat uncomfortably. Regularly throughout the day, I've made myself do my breathing exercises. When I don't, my breaths start to get faster, shallower; a feeling of light-headedness steals over me. More than once, I've been afraid to stand up in case I faint.

Learning that the remains found at the children's home were old after all has done little to put my mind at rest, and my unease is all the greater for not understanding its cause.

I can't find Marigold McGowan anywhere. There is no record of her on the electoral roll or the Police National Computer. A marriage was unlikely in her case, and there's no record of an official name change. She hasn't died, at least not officially. She may have emigrated, but again it seems unlikely. I should not be surprised, I suppose. Some people can't be found.

One of them, it seems, is Abby Thorn, erstwhile reporter at the *Lancashire Morning Post*. I've called her three times, leaving messages with the same male colleague. She still hasn't got back to me. It probably means nothing and yet Sabden, I remember, has a way of closing in on itself when it has secrets it needs to keep hidden.

The night is clear, and even in London, light pollution can't completely dull the stars. The waning moon hangs low in the eastern sky. The dark moon is getting closer, and this always puts me on edge. I add more wood to the fire and watch stray sparks dance above it. On a sudden impulse, I release the chain round my neck that holds my wedding band and hold it up to catch the light. I have never worn this ring in the way normal women do. There is no third finger on my left hand. It was cut off, taken from me, the most brutal theft I can imagine.

Thirty years ago, in Sabden, I went through an ordeal comparable to what soldiers experience in combat, and so it's entirely understandable that I suffer from post-traumatic stress disorder. My employers, most latterly the Metropolitan Police, have always known and made allowances. Secretly, I think they're rather proud I can function as well as I do, and that they can accommodate me. It helps them tick a mental health diversity box.

Of course, I've never told anyone, not even Nick, the whole truth. The physical symptoms – escalating breathing, nausea, sweating, the nightmares – are not the worst of it.

Worse even than the nightmares is the knowledge that I have a damaged soul. I love Nick, of course, and I adore Ben, but that's about it. I cannot emote. I cannot be moved by stories of other people's pain or distress. I am cold, entirely logical, and that is almost certainly one of the reasons I've progressed so far in the police force. My decisions are never affected by my feelings.

Still not the worst of it.

'Hello, Florence,' says a voice, and I turn to see Marigold McGowan sitting in the chair beside me.

'Hello, Marigold.' I've learned to be polite to ghosts. They stay around for longer, become more confiding. 'You look well.'

The worst of my post-traumatic stress disorder, by far, is the psychosis: the fact that I sometimes see things I know cannot be real. People from my time in Sabden visit me – the dead ones, I mean now, especially Larry's young victims. They sit beside me in my car, lean against the window ledge in my office, even join Nick, Ben and me at the dinner table, and they talk to me. I know they are not real.

I don't believe in ghosts. And yet they often seem more vivid, more relevant than the real people around me.

It's been going on too long now for me to form any conclusion other than that the balance of my mind has never recovered from what happened to me thirty years ago. In simple terms, I suppose you could say that I'm insane. I am the most senior serving police-woman in Britain and I am insane.

Tonight, Marigold's strawberry-blonde hair is clean and shining. She is wearing a dress I remember Sally giving her, pale pink cotton with white daisies. She is small and plump, pretty in her own distinct-ive way.

'You're dead, then, Marigold,' I say, because only dead people appear to me in this way. 'I was afraid you might be.'

She looks directly at me. 'Are you coming back?' she asks.

'No.'

She says nothing, just looks at me with her slanted blue eyes.

'The bones are old, Marigold,' I say. 'Decades old. There's nothing for me to do even if I went back.'

'Are you sure, Florence?'

Of course I am. I've seen the post-mortem report. Or, at least, spoken to someone who has. I don't say any of this to Marigold, of course.

'Why didn't you look for me?' Marigold asks.

This stings. 'I did. We all did. Me, Sally, Tom. We all looked. You'd vanished.'

Her fair eyebrows draw closer together. 'It was your job, Florence. You were a police officer. And my friend.'

She is right.

'Maybe they're mine,' she says.

'What?'

'The bones.' She smiles sadly. 'Maybe they're mine.'

# 19

## Cassie

Long ago, Sally taught me that plants used in magic need to be harvested as the moon is rising. If that moon is waning, or black, even better. She also taught me that plants growing close to the subject of the spell will have more power. And so, once again, I am back in Sabden.

I pull over in a street I barely recognise, so crowded is it with parked cars. The terraced houses have been painted and pebble-dashed; they have satellite dishes on the roofs and PVC window frames. The river, though, still runs where it always did. Flowing underground through much of Sabden, it emerges, wider and faster, at this edge of town, feeding one of the reservoirs.

Getting to the bank is harder than it used to be. Metal fencing stops reckless children and drunks from littering the water with their frail bodies and rusting shopping trolleys. Likewise, a concrete wall has been built round the reservoir.

I leave the street behind and step onto the rough land that edges the river. I'm looking for bindweed, hawthorn and cowslip – which I can find anywhere – and one particular plant that only grows here.

Some of the plants I will use, the exotic ones, I already have. Chinatown in nearby Manchester has a ready supply of fresh cardamom, cinnamon and ginger.

Other things I need – basil, silverweed, bay – I can get from our old garden. As I near the bridge, I remember standing in the outer kitchen in our old house – the witches' pantry, Dad called it – usually with Luna, Mary, our old housekeeper, and Mum, pulling off petals, chopping leaves, peeling roots. We sang to each other as we ground, pulped and boiled, transforming the plants we'd gathered into jewel-coloured tinctures. My mother turned us all into witches.

A few more yards and I see it, growing over the stump of an old sycamore tree. Some late flowers, purple with a yellow centre, nestle amid the mass of broad leaves. Its berries are still green, but they will do. *Solanum dulcamara*, also called scarlet berry, snakeberry, violet bloom and bittersweet nightshade, is one of the most versatile and dangerous plants I know. Fun fact – one of its many uses is to protect against witchcraft.

It won't work against me.

# 20

## Florence

On the first floor of the Natural History Museum, the visitors peter out. The exhibits up here lack the appeal of the dinosaurs and stuffed mammals downstairs. By the time I reach the east wing, my footsteps are the only ones clicking their way along the polished floor. I pass display cabinets full of human skulls and come at last to an unobtrusive wooden door labelled 156b. I wait for a moment, wondering if I'm doing the right thing.

The bones found at Black Moss Manor were those of children. Marigold was at least seventeen years old. And yet she was small for her age.

I knock.

'If you're not a Girton girl, piss off,' calls a voice.

I push open the door. 'Guilty as charged,' I say to the woman sitting behind the crowded desk.

Caroline Trickett looks me up and down. 'You've put on weight,' she says.

I wait.

'Pre-emptive strike.' She shrugs, glancing down at an ample form that is clad, most unscientifically, in a very loose floral dress. Tricksy was never a slim girl. Thirty years on from when we met at university, she seems as wide as she is tall. Her hair is about two inches short now, dyed an astonishing shade of lilac. It stands upright from her head, giving her the look of a purple hedgehog.

She doesn't get up, to kiss me or shake hands, but instead leans back in her chair. 'What can I do you for?'

'I need an expert opinion on the rate of decomposition in human skeletons buried on the Lancashire moors,' I say. 'Good to see you, by the way. How's Dennis?'

'Dennis is a git. You have the Met's finest to call upon. Why bother me?'

'This is unofficial,' I say. 'And I don't have a budget.'

She stands up, revealing that she is wearing pink Doc Martens. 'In that case,' she says, 'you can buy me lunch.'

Tricksy's choice of restaurant is a great deal more formal than she is, gleaming with polished silver and fine crystal. Table linen like fresh snowfall and forest-green curtains seem to absorb all sound above a gentle whisper. For several minutes after we sit down, we exchange social pleasantries about our families, our jobs, other alumni we've kept in touch with.

'So,' she says, when our food arrives, salmon for me, rare steak for her. 'Shoot.'

I hand the newspaper cutting across the table. 'Four small skeletons, probably children, found by accident when a water pipe burst,' I say, although I know she'll be reading and absorbing the information faster than I can speak. 'I need an idea of how long they've been in the ground.'

She looks up. 'Post-mortem report?'

I shake my head.

'Photographs? Anything?'

'Some unofficial info from an officer who sneaked a look at the files. According to the post-mortem, the bones are of a consistent age, meaning they probably died at the same time and were buried together.'

Blood runs across the plate as Tricksy slices into her steak. 'Yes, I know what "consistent age" means.'

'Officially, the remains are several decades old, probably early twentieth century, probably the result of some sort of epidemic. On the other hand, I have' – I stop and think how best to describe Larry – 'an ... acquaintance who believes that can't be the case. That bones wouldn't last that long.'

Tricksy lifts both hands and makes a beckoning motion. 'You're going to have to give me something more to work with.'

'According to my source, the remains were largely skeletonised, with some fragments of tissue and some scraps of clothing that helped hold them together.'

Her eyes narrow. 'What sort of clothing?'

'Natural fibres. Old-fashioned. Buttons that suggest the 1920s or earlier.'

'Were they in coffins? Any sign of embalming?'

'There were wooden fragments that suggest the possibility of coffins, but nothing conclusive. Embalming seems unlikely, given that this was an orphanage.'

She nods her agreement.

'So?' I prompt, after a moment.

Tricksy pulls a pen from the pocket of her dress and flattens her napkin on the tabletop. She draws the numbers one to four on it in bright blue ink.

'You do know that napkin is linen?' I say.

'Four stages of decomposition,' she goes on. 'You probably know this. Stage one, autolysis or self-digestion. The body starts eating itself. Stage two, bloat, as gases cause the body to swell.'

'How's the steak?' I ask.

'Stage three, active decay, when tissue starts to liquefy. Stage four is skeletonisation, when only the bones remain.'

I catch a waiter glaring at us and make a mental note to double the tip. Tricksy, meanwhile, is drawing a wiggly line to connect the four bullet points.

'The time taken from stage one to stage four depends on whether embalming took place, how deep the bodies were buried and the surroundings,' she says. 'At the outside, I'd say you were looking at fifteen years maximum from death to skeletonisation.'

'Mid-1980s,' I say. 'They were buried at least as long ago as that or they wouldn't be skeletonised.'

Tricksy chews for a moment. 'But what you really want to know is whether I can date skeletons,' she says.

'Can you?'

'Course I bloody can. Show me the bones and I'll tell you to within a decade.'

'I can't do that.'

In response, she turns the napkin over to its clean side and starts numbering again. One to six this time.

'Bones are a fibrous matrix of collagen fibres,' she says. 'Over time, bacteria and fungi will attack the collagen and the bones will crumble. There are six stages of bone decay.'

By the door to the kitchen, two waiters are watching us.

'Stage one, fresh bone, the sort you might give to a dog,' Tricksy goes on. 'Two, it's all getting crunchier. At this stage, the bone has dried out but still has a smooth outer cortex. Stage three, the bone looks normal from the outside but inside is starting to recrystallise. Are you following?'

'Very closely.'

'Stage four, it's all getting a bit mushier. The outer cortex has gone, and the recrystallisation is complete. The bone has a crumbly texture and will fall to pieces if you manhandle it. Stage five, you've basically got the consistency of a biscuit dipped in hot tea.'

'Six?' I prompt, as she breaks off to finish her steak.

'At stage six, only a chemical analysis of the soil will tell you whether there was ever a body there in the first place.' She puts her knife and fork down on an almost spotless plate.

'And this takes how long?' I ask.

'Depends.' She pulls a face as though trying to loosen something from a back tooth.

'Don't be annoying.'

'Lancashire, right? Wet and warm? Peaty, acidic soil?'

I nod.

'Twenty years at the outside. Very likely less.'

I do a quick calculation, adding together the time needed for bodies to skeletonise, and then for the skeletons themselves to disintegrate. 'Mid- to late-1960s,' I say. 'They could not have been put in the ground earlier than that. And given that there are still visible and tangible bones, it would likely have been later. There is every chance these children died in the 1970s.'

'Looks like your . . . er, acquaintance was right.'

I put down my knife and fork.

Tricksy says, 'I'm guessing I haven't given you good news?'

Larry was right. The four children could not have died prior to his starting work at Glassbrook & Greenwood in 1946. And his firm handled the funerals of all eight children who died officially at the home between that time and its closing in 1969. The post-mortem report that Perdita sneaked a look at and relayed to me over the phone was deeply flawed.

'Not remotely,' I agree.

# 21

## Cassie

I can't stop thinking about Marigold and what could have happened to her.

Saving Marigold was the one good thing we did that summer. After dad was arrested, the whole town turned against us. They called us scum, threatened to rape us and burn down our house. They spat at us in the street. I even had black ink thrown at me by one bitch. All our friends vanished. We'd become pariahs and we felt like it too. We felt corrupted, soiled, guilty of crimes someone else had committed.

And then Marigold came along, with her bright hair and shiny blue eyes and her fat, giggly baby. She was so frightened, at first, and then so grateful. Marigold and her baby didn't judge us. They needed us. They loved us.

Mum saved Marigold. Luna and I helped. And in a weird way, she saved us back. Marigold was our redemption.

And now, it seems, that was all a sham.

# 22

## Florence

Larry was right. He may have had his faults – possibly the understatement of the century – but he was no fool. The four bodies could easily have been buried behind the home after we closed it down. That should not be possible.

One of them could be Marigold. Something dreadful could have happened to Marigold and I didn't stop it. I could have looked harder. And if one of them is Marigold, what on earth happened to her baby?

It is years since I've led up a major murder investigation, since I've been a detective; years since I've done anything more than management and strategy planning. I don't have the skills for this anymore.

My PA interrupts via the intercom to remind me that a car will be waiting at the front steps in ten minutes. One of several responsibilities that fall into my portfolio as assistant commissioner is protection of the royal family, and I have a meeting at St James's Palace on the hour.

OK, think, Florence. The dead children must have been linked to the children's home and, in theory, every child who passed through Black Moss Manor in recent decades would be traceable. I find the number for Lancashire County Council and ask for the Information Governance Team. The head office is in Preston now.

'What you're trying to do will be quite challenging,' the head of the archives department tells me, after I've explained who I am and why I'm calling. 'If the home was privately run, then even though the council would have kept some records centrally, they might not be complete. A child who was privately referred, for example, might not make it onto the local authority records.'

For some reason, I'm picturing the archivist as the woman I met on my first visit to the council years ago, a pretty, motherly type who'd turned out to be vicious as a stabbed cat.

'Without a central register, you'd be reliant upon individual case files,' she goes on. 'You'd have to know the child's name, date of birth, et cetera. Vaccination records could help, or school records, but it would be quite a jigsaw puzzle you'd be putting together.'

She is sounding pleasant, helpful, but so did her predecessor. Until it all turned mean.

'The authority kept a central register,' I say. 'I remember being told at the time. I'd like to look at it, if I can, to go back several decades if need be and trace the children who came in and who left.'

'It will take some time,' she tells me. 'And the survival of early records isn't guaranteed. You're likely to find some gaps.'

'I'd have to come up, wouldn't I? This couldn't be done over the phone.'

She agrees that that would be practically impossible, and I wish her a good morning.

I don't put the phone down. Instead, I ask my PA to join me.

'Can you get on to the GMC for me?' I ask when she appears. 'Strictly off the record for now, but anything you can get me on Drs Frederick and Judith Aster.'

She gives me a look. As she closes the door, it occurs to me that twice in two weeks I've asked subordinates to bend the rules, and that really isn't like me.

It is, though, very like the woman I used to be.

# 23

## Cassie

Friday evening is still bell-ringing night and in the tower of St Peter's, the ringers are practising their peals and changes as I pull up in the pub car park. It's still a godforsaken fucking din, but I barely register it as I switch off the engine. This is it. No more waiting. Thirty years of torment end tonight.

From the outside, the Black Dog hasn't changed – a huge building with finials and gables on its black slate roof. A door opens at the back of the pub, but the man who appears is a stranger. I find my bag and walk round to the front. The door is heavy, and the hallway beyond dimly lit.

'With you in a sec,' calls a voice from below the reception counter. His voice. The universe holds its breath.

I hear rustling of paper, a sound of boxes being slid, a grunt of exasperation. I've heard that grunt before, although not in exasperation.

'Sorry to keep you,' he says, and this amuses me. He has kept me waiting for thirty years. What do a few more seconds matter?

'No problem,' I reply. Behind the counter, all sounds stop. He stands up.

'Hi.' I am the one who speaks. John's mouth is open, but nothing is coming out.

Thirty years older and still the most beautiful man I ever saw. Six feet tall and much broader at the shoulder than I remember. His forehead is higher, but his hair is still mainly the dark glossy brown I loved. He has lines round his mouth and eyes, and I feel a stab of pain – although it could be rage – that I wasn't here to see them appear. He has a short beard and it suits him.

I've played this first encounter over and over in my head. I'm more than ready for a Black Dog twist on the *Casablanca* line: 'Of all the run-down pubs in the arse-end of Lancashire, she had to . . .' Or he might go for a nonchalant, 'What kept you?' Maybe he won't speak, just set off towards me, and I'll leap into his arms as we meet, Cathy and Heathcliff-style, halfway along this faded, beer-sodden carpet.

'What are you doing here?' he says.

Not quite what I was expecting. 'Checking in,' I tell him. 'I reserved an attic room. Is our old one free?'

He stares a second longer, then looks down at the register.

'Miss Glass,' I prompt. 'You must have known it was me?'

He knew it was me. I've called myself Cassie Glass for over twenty years. All my songs are published under that name. This show of surprise is because he thinks someone might be listening behind the kitchen door.

I hope she is. I'm starting as I mean to go on.

*Hang her from a tree, Lee.*

*Drown her in the lake, Jake.* I like that one. I know just the lake.

'It's not a good idea, Cass.' He picks up the phone with a shaking hand. 'I'll find you somewhere else.'

I step behind the counter and reach for the key to room seventeen. 'I know the way,' I tell him. 'Will you bring my bag?'

The stairs are to my left, and I'm glad to get out of his sight for a second. I'm breathless and my hands are shaking with a nervousness I can't let him see.

As I reach the first floor, I realise he isn't following me and that I may have made a mistake leaving my bag behind. I will be harder to throw out if I've unpacked.

He won't throw me out.

She might.

I walk the length of the hallway to the second flight of stairs.

The carpets are different. The walls have been papered in a soft gold stripe. They used to be painted a pale yellow.

I remember everything.

My hands are still shaking when I put the key into the lock, but the creak that I remember, that used to have us both holding our breaths in gleeful suspense, has gone. The door opens silently.

Not the same. The elaborate florals his mother favoured have gone. This is *her* taste. The style is simpler, even verging on elegant. The twin beds are close together, dressed in stark-white linen and counterpanes of a moss green. The pine furniture is simple and functional. It's better. I hate it.

Footsteps in the corridor. I've no sooner checked my hair in the mirror and slipped off my coat when there is a knock on the door.

'It's open,' I say.

He pushes the door wide but stays where he is in the corridor. 'I'm sorry about Larry.'

I laugh. 'That puts you in a crowd of one. I was expecting bunting in the streets.'

'People have long memories.'

I smile. His colour rises and he knows exactly what I'm thinking. I have a long memory; looks like he does too.

There is a noise in the corridor and he starts before stepping away from the doorway to let her past. She walks into the room as though she owns the place, which, technically I guess, she does.

'Hello, Cassie,' she says.

'Hi,' I reply. 'Sorry, are you—'

'You remember my wife, Tammy,' John says, and he doesn't intend it to be a question.

I remember her perfectly.

'Gosh, Tammy,' I say, feigning mild embarrassment. 'I wouldn't have known you.'

Only a year or so younger than me, Tammy looks years older. She's gained a couple of stone in weight, her dark brown hair has half an inch of grey at its roots, and her once heart-shaped face has been lost amid an amalgamation of chin and neckline. Her big dopey doe eyes are the same, though.

'I was sorry to hear about your dad,' she says.

'I stand corrected.' I smile at John, like we're sharing a private joke. He doesn't smile back.

'John asked me to do some phoning around,' Tammy says. 'Rose-hill Guest House on Shaw Street has a nice double free for a few days. You'd be closer to your mum.'

'We're going to be busy the next few days,' John adds.

'Lucky I booked a room, then.' I beam at them both.

Tammy folds her arms across her chest, in the way her mother no doubt did before her, and her grandmother before that. 'We've already got one TV crew staying,' she says. 'And several people from the papers coming over the next few days. You won't get any peace if you stay here. Not once they know it's you.'

'So, if I change my mind and hold Larry's funeral miles away, you'll lose a lot of business?'

'We'll cope.'

'So will I. I like this room. It has some very happy memories. But thank you for your concern.'

They stand facing me, wanting to fight on, not quite knowing how. I have prepared for this, they haven't, and it's not surprising that I win the first skirmish. It unsettles me, though, seeing the two of them united against me.

Was I wrong to think John's reaction to my banishment would be the same as mine? Has he not been counting the days, the bloody hours until I come back?

'We'll leave you to it, then,' says Tammy. 'After you, love.' She steps into the corridor and waits, making sure he leaves first, giving me no chance of a last exchange, or even a smile.

'See you later, John,' I call after them.

Unpacking can wait. I check the time and head out.

After all the rain lately, the river is running high and fast. I stumble down the steep bank, almost catching my heel on what looks like an iron grid that has been mortared into the ground. It puzzles me, because it doesn't appear to be a drain. I'm some distance from the pub, but the cellars beneath the Black Dog are old and cavernous, several rooms, each leading one from the other. There are rumours about a secret room, where prisoners on their way to Lancaster Gaol were kept chained in days gone by. I've never seen it. I wonder if perhaps I've found it, but I can make out nothing below the grid.

The River Sabden runs over a bed of heavy Lancashire clay and I scoop up two large handfuls. Finding a dry spot to crouch on, I mix it with drier mud, scooping, squeezing and rolling until I have a pliable substance. I fashion a head, then a torso, followed by arms and legs. I'm making a clay picture, an effigy of my human subject, just as the Lancashire witches did in the old days.

I make my picture tall and slender, spending some time on the hair and face. A clay picture needs some essence of the person it is supposed to depict. Blood, teeth and bone are best, but hair or nail clippings will work. I have nothing yet, but there's time and my picture won't harden until it's been fired.

When it's done, I get to my feet and climb a few yards along the bank. I've already spotted the blackthorn. I fashion thirteen thin slivers of wood and push them into the right places.

I know exactly what shape of moon is above me, but I glance up all the same. Still a few days before the dark moon. I can't cast my spell just yet.

# 24

## Florence

I'm late leaving work on Friday evening, trying to clear my desk before I start annual leave on Monday, and I still haven't heard from the journalist. I decide to try one last time.

'Abby Thorn,' says the gruff voice before the phone has even rung once. I'm so surprised I don't respond.

'Hello?' she prompts.

'This is Florence Lovelady.'

'From . . . ? Oh, bloody hell. *That* Florence Lovelady? Christ, to what do I owe this honour?'

'I've been trying to speak to you for days. This is the fourth time I've called.'

'Nobody told me. Bloody incompetents. What's this about? Larry, I expect. Are you coming up for his funeral?'

'Abby, I need to ask you about the old days. How good's your memory?'

She laughs. 'Try me.'

'Remember Black Moss Manor? The stories you wrote back in 1969?'

'Oh, you're calling about the bodies. I thought they were old remains. Why, is that no longer—'

'Yes, I'm sure they are,' I say, because I'm not about to set any hares running if I can help it. 'I'm just curious. Did the place reopen after we closed it down? Did it ever start up again?'

'Not to my knowledge. It's been some sort of retreat these last few years. For clerical and professional types needing some serious R and R. Look, I'd love to do an interview with you the day of Larry's funeral. You know, your memories of Sabden back then, what that case did for your career. Can you come to the studio immediately afterwards?'

'I'm not planning on coming up. Where did all the children go? There were nearly twenty of them and we found new homes for them all. You did a follow-up story. I'm looking at it now.'

'Hmm.'

'What?'

'I'd forgotten, but it was a bit odd. That story was my idea, and no one was keen. Certainly not the boss at the time. I pushed, though, and managed to find one or two of the kids.'

'Only one or two?'

'Most had left the area. Only three stayed close, and none of them in Sabden. The one I spoke to was fostered in Newchurch. Funny little thing. Couldn't get much out of him.'

'Did he say anything about the home that seemed odd to you?'

'Oh Christ, you're stretching the old grey matter, Florence. It was twenty years ago.'

'Thirty,' I tell her.

'I tell you what did seem odd. His foster parents wouldn't leave him alone, all the time I was talking to him. And when I asked about Black Moss Manor, they jumped on me. Oh, it's all coming back now. They didn't want him talking about anything that might upset him.'

'Interesting.'

'And the climate of secrecy goes on.' Abby is warming to the conversation and I know she'll be making notes. 'When the bodies were found last month, I tried to go up there,' she says. 'Maybe do a piece with the management of this retreat, or whatever's supposed to be there now, but no one would see me. What's up, Flo? What's this all about?'

'I'm not sure. Did you ever come across the two people who ran it again? Frederick and Judith Aster?'

She thinks for a moment. 'They served time, didn't they?'

'Only a couple of years. So did other members of staff. Some of them could have come back to Sabden.'

'I can ask around, I suppose.'

This is more than I hoped for. Although it won't come without its price. 'Could you?'

'What's in it for me?'

And there's the bill. 'Find me people I can talk to, and if there's any story at all, you'll be the first to hear.'

'What about the Larry interview?' she says.

'Good talking to you, Abby.'

I put the phone down, my heart a little lighter. I feel as though I have an ally.

And then I almost pick up the phone again to tell her not to bother, to forget I called. Because I've remembered what happened the last time I made Abby into an ally.

# 25

## Cassie

The next day, I get invited to lunch by Avril, my solicitor, and her partner, Daphne. I've nothing better to do, and John is nowhere to be found, so I accept. They've improved a bit with age, those two, not bad company at all for a pair of old dykes. And both seemed genuinely pleased to see me.

The pub feels like the *Mary Celeste* when I get back. The girl on reception tells me that John is at the cash and carry, and Tammy has taken her elderly mother to a chiropody appointment.

Both of them out?

To get to the staff flat, you have to take a different staircase to the one the guests use, one that leads from behind the kitchen. The door at the top is locked, but I remember the Donnellys' habit of leaving a key beneath a loose piece of carpet. I let myself in and slip the key into my pocket.

The room beyond, the living room, is heavy with Tammy's smell, an unpleasant mix of cheap perfume and female pheromones, as though she's been marking her territory. A sudden growling makes me jump and I spin to see a half-blind black whippet approaching. It stops two feet away, its scrawny body shaking. I look it full in the eyes. It backs away a little but gives a shrill bark.

One of John's jackets is hanging over the back of a chair and I make for it like a cat closing in on a kill, bringing it to my face and breathing in deeply. Last night, I lay awake for hours, wondering if he'd have the nerve to come to me. I should have known she wouldn't let him out of her sight. He wasn't even on breakfast duty this morning and I'm shocked by how much I miss him. Thirty years without him and now even getting through a few hours is hard.

I don't recognise the aftershave he's taken to wearing. I check his pockets and find a handkerchief that isn't entirely clean and a handful of change. I leave the change. The handkerchief goes into my pocket along with the key.

The room is full of family photographs: a family wedding, baby pictures, Tammy's fortieth birthday party downstairs in the pub. The family is everywhere, as though Tammy needs constant reminders that what she and John have is real.

It isn't. It never was. I imagine a bonfire, blazing high and fierce, with every one of these pictures sucked in by the flames, blackening and crumbling.

All in good time.

The small kitchen hasn't changed. It has the same pale blue Formica cupboards, the same rusting venetian blind at the window, the same old boiler. In the noisy fridge, there is a bottle of cheap Chardonnay and several cans of lager. I don't see John drinking either, but I know so little of the man he is now. I can't tell which of these things around me are his and which hers.

I must not get angry. I can't afford to be careless.

The boiler fires up, making me jump. It might be the same one that was here thirty years ago. Who changes a boiler until they have to? A narrow pipe runs from the bottom and disappears into the wall. I look through the window to pinpoint where I am and almost run my fingers fondly down the boiler door. I remember just in time. Leaving fingerprints wouldn't be wise.

I'm done in the kitchen.

Three doors lead off from the living room. John's old room is the first I come to. A woman is lying on the bed, fully dressed but fast asleep. She can only be in her early seventies, but a lifetime of abusing alcohol makes her seem older. Her dyed-blonde hair has a greenish tinge; her make-up could have been applied last night. Or last week. Beryl Donnelly, John's mother, snores gently. I back out and head towards the next room. This one is a double bedroom, painted the cold blue of a mountain lake.

I go to the fitted cupboards that line one wall and find John's suits, running my fingers through my hair until I pull out several loose strands and drape them over the fabrics. I take my perfume from my bag and squirt tiny puffs onto linings. I do the same thing with his sweater drawer and his underclothes. I tuck a strawberry-flavoured condom into the pocket of a pair of jeans and rub a smear of my lipstick on the inside collar of one of his shirts.

I'm having fun, but I came here for a reason, and I can't run out of time. On the dressing table is a large brown comb. I check the few loose hairs to make sure they're his and not Tammy's, and then I pocket them. In the adjoining bathroom, I find a square of toilet tissue spotted with blood. I take that too.

Back in the bedroom, I notice that the bed has been made, but quickly, without care. From the contents on top of the two bedside cabinets, I guess which side is John's and lie down on Tammy's side, moving my head around so that the pillow will pick up my scent.

Footsteps. I've been a fool. If she catches me in here, she'll throw me out of the hotel for sure. The footsteps are heavy, though, and only one set. John is alone. I lie back on the bed and close my eyes.

'Only me, Mum,' I hear him call. I stifle a giggle as I hear him moving around in the other room, the TV being turned on and then the bedroom door sliding across the carpet.

'What the fuck?'

I open my eyes, feigning sleepiness. 'Honey,' I say. 'You're home.'

He shoots a glance behind. 'What the hell are you doing? My mother's in the next room. Tammy'll be back any minute.'

'Sorry.' I let my feet slip to the floor. 'I must have got confused.'

'How did you get in here?'

'Your mother let me in.' I don't want to mention the spare key; he'll want it back. 'She said she needed something from her room and she never came back. Is she OK?'

He steps further into the room but keeps a hand on the door. 'Cass, what are you playing at? You can't come into our flat.'

In the other room, we hear the news begin. The lead story is about an armed robbery in Central London. The volume is turned up quite high and we hear the presenter's words clearly. 'Our reporter is outside Scotland Yard waiting for Assistant Commissioner Florence Lovelady.'

John shoots me a startled glance; together we hurry into the other room.

Our old enemy – according to her Wikipedia page, the highest-ranking policewoman in England and Wales – is in full dress uniform. Her bright red hair has faded to a soft auburn. It curls around her chin now, but in the old days waved halfway down her back when she didn't tie it up for work. Her jawline has softened, and there are wrinkles around her eyes and her mouth. She reads a pre-prepared statement about the robbery, the various leads her officers are pursuing and the Met's appeal to the public for information. When she's finished, she smiles her thanks, but the journalists aren't ready to let her go.

'Assistant Commissioner, have you any comment to make about the recent death of Larry Glassbrook?'

'Do you think he should be buried in the same town where he buried his victims?'

'Will you go to his funeral, Florence?'

'Will you miss him?'

The questions are fired at her like arrows from a castle's keep. For a second, I think she isn't going to respond, that she will simply turn her back and vanish inside Scotland Yard, but she stays.

'Larry Glassbrook paid the price for his crimes,' she says. 'I hope he finds peace now. As for the funeral arrangements, that's a matter for his family, and for the town.'

She turns then, and the programme switches to a new story.

'She'll come, won't she?' John says to me, and I want to bless Florence Lovelady in her absence, because with three simple sentences she has united John and me again. We have a common enemy. We will face her together.

'Larry sent her visiting orders every year,' I tell him. 'She always went. She saw him more than anyone, except perhaps his solicitor and my mother. She'll come.'

I think of the letter Larry sent to her, hours before he died, and of the perfume bottle, tethered to the shore of the Black Tarn. Of course she'll come. Together, Larry and I made sure of it.

John doesn't reply, but I can see his eyes are troubled. He's wary of Florence too.

'Maybe she'll stay here,' I say. 'If she does, give her room seven.'

'The one below yours? What are you up to?'

There! That tiny glint in his eyes, gone in a flash, but I saw it. That was the John I remember. I was beginning to think he was gone for ever.

'We have to meet,' I tell him. 'Somewhere we won't be interrupted. Tonight.'

'I can't.' There is panic in his eyes. 'We've got a family thing. Vicky – my eldest – is coming over with her kids. I said I'd run them home.'

Anger rises up, but I can't fight with him. Not while the chains of family are still strong.

'Tomorrow, then. The Black Tarn. At Daylight Gate.'

# 26

## Florence

I'm running late. Ben will be home soon from athletics training and he's texted to say he's forgotten his key. Again. I've changed and hung up my uniform. A car is waiting downstairs to drive me home. I'm about to log off my computer when I see a new message in my inbox.

It is from the archivist at Lancashire County Council.

With regard to your recent enquiry, I regret to inform you that the records in which you expressed an interest were most likely destroyed by a flood in 1975. Other commitments prevent me investigating further for the time being, but if you contact our offices again in the early autumn, we will try to allocate resources to assist.

By early autumn, the four dead children will have been incinerated.

# 27

## Cassie

The sky is deepening to turquoise when I leave the pub. The few remaining clouds are awash with colour, but the warm light that floods the world at the day's end is fading and colder tones are taking its place. Shadows stretch out, and the shady places become darker and deeper. This is Daylight Gate, a time that is neither day nor night but something in between, when the border between the worlds of the living and the dead weakens. In Lancashire, we believe that most people die at Daylight Gate, that their subsequent crossing into the next world will be easier. Magic can be particularly successful at Daylight Gate, and I have magic on my mind tonight.

I head out of town, leaving behind the Victorian buildings and the terraced housing, then the newer housing estates that have sprung up on the outskirts. The buildings become fewer, more run-down, and then vanish altogether as the great wildness of the Pendle Forest opens up.

I turn off the main road and follow the farm track that will take me to the Black Tarn. I park by the old farm building where we used to shelter from bad weather, smoking and drinking stolen booze. When I climb out of the car, a startled sheep in a nearby field runs away. Somewhere in the distance, an owl hoots, and I can hear an odd barking sound that I think is a fox. I can smell animal dung, pine trees and the bitter, metallic scent of the water.

Luna and I learned to swim in this lake. Sally brought us here often in the summer months, and she never let us wear our swimming costumes. 'We honour the water by swimming sky-clad,' she insisted.

'Sky-clad' means naked. Lots of witches work 'sky-clad' because they believe clothes diminish the power they get from their surroundings.

When I hear a car engine, I pull off all my clothes until I'm quite naked in the moonlight and then step to the water's edge. Out in the middle of the lake, I catch a glimmer of light that makes me pause for a moment. It wasn't unusual, in the old days, to see night fishermen out here, but they never bothered us, and we didn't bother them. In any case, he's too far away to see me.

The cold water takes my breath away.

All colour has left the sky now. The moon has risen and its pale light casts a path across the water to guide me in. When I can see headlights making their way along the farm track, I take a deep breath and fall into the cold, black mass of the lake.

John leaves his car, walks to the lake's edge and stands by my clothes as I move silently through the water back towards him. When I'm close enough to the shore to stand, I call out.

'I'm here.'

He sees me.

'Are you coming in?'

He doesn't move. I step forward through the soft mud as the water leaves my body and the moonlight finds it. Did I plan to be so bold, this soon? I'm not sure, but his eyes don't leave mine as I walk the few steps up the bank to where he is standing.

'Pass me a towel,' I say. The breeze, although gentle for the moors, feels like ice on my skin.

John bends to the ground. I turn my back to him and lift my arms high. I feel the fabric wrap round my skin. His arms stay where they are, encircling me.

'This is insane,' he mumbles into my ear.

'It always was. And at the same time, the only thing that makes sense.'

I twist in his arms. For long seconds we stare at each other. Kissing him would be the easiest thing in the world. All I'd have to do is stand on tiptoe and lean forward. He won't resist. He is holding me too tightly for there to be any fear of that. But I need him to kiss me.

He bends his head, his lips find mine, and the battle is won.

'Mate, I'm sorry. I really am, but you've got to get out of there.'

We break apart. Someone in a boat is shining a torch at us. The beam moves to one side and darkness cloaks us again.

'What the fuck are you doing?' John yells.

'Mate, I'm serious,' the man's voice replies. 'People come here at night. They're doing something in that old shed. I'm expecting them any minute. You do not want to be caught here. Not with a woman.'

The light vanishes and we can see a man in a boat, about twenty yards out on the lake. It's hard to tell but he looks to be middle-aged, dressed for night fishing. He switches on a small outboard engine, turns the boat and motors away. As he fades into darkness, he switches off his engine and vanishes.

'Get dressed.' John is picking up my clothes.

No. I want to scream with frustration. I'd got him.

'Cass, I mean it. I've heard things about this place,' he says.

'No one comes here.'

'Things have changed. Come on, we'll drive up to Greenwell Tor.'

★

I get dressed. John's nervousness and the fear I heard in the voice of the fisherman have got to me. We drive, in our separate cars, away from Pendle Hill. After a mile, we leave the road again and park. A public footpath takes us up to the tor, a rocky outcrop higher up the moor, and we sit, side by side, looking down at the orange and white lights of Sabden. He makes no move to touch me and I know I won't catch him unawares again.

'Never thought I'd see you frightened of a farmer,' I say. I'm still annoyed with him.

'I've learned to pick my fights. And these guys aren't farmers.'

I'm intrigued by this. 'Who, then? Did Sabden get a mafia while I was gone?'

No response. A thought strikes me.

'Have you ever heard of the Craftsmen?' I ask him.

He stiffens. 'No,' he says.

I wait for him to ask if they're a rock group, or a branch of the Rotary Club, or an ancient medieval guild. He doesn't. We're silent for the better part of a minute, and I can feel him slipping away from me.

'I didn't come back here to bury Larry,' I say. 'I came for you.'

'I know,' John tells me, after long seconds.

'Do you still love me?'

For a heart-wrenching moment he doesn't answer. I look down at Sabden's lights and half expect to see them going out, one by one.

'When I see a woman with blonde hair,' he says at last, 'even if it's not your colour, just an ordinary blonde, I have to see her face in case it's you.'

The lights below us start to twinkle again.

'I own every song you ever wrote,' he says. 'I can't keep them in the flat – Tammy would see them – so I have a garage down near the allotments that I've rented for years just so I can go there and listen. I think of you at the piano in your old house and imagine you singing them to me. I listen for meanings, messages in the lyrics like I'm some creepy stalker. Every time a new record comes out, I think, why don't you sing them, just once, just so I can hear your voice again.'

For a moment, I can't speak. Then, 'I want you to leave Tammy,' I say.

He doesn't respond. I wait.

'I can't do that,' he says.

I tell myself I didn't expect it to be a walk in the park. 'Your children are grown up,' I say. 'We can stay close by if you want to play the fond grandad. My flat isn't much more than an hour away. Let Tammy keep the pub if she wants it.'

I wonder if I should mention his mother and decide against it. She is hardly a major concern.

He gets to his feet. 'Cass, we can't.'

'Why not?' I know why not, of course, but I'm going to make him say it. 'Why can't we be together? Larry was the only one stopping us, the only one who counted for anything, and he's dead. We've waited thirty years. We'll be old soon. This is our chance.'

'You know why we can't.'

'It never really bothered me,' I say.

He pulls me up. 'That's because you're a woman without morals.'

'It might not even be true. Have you thought of that?'

'So, let's do a test. Find out for sure. They can do that now.'

Obviously, I don't jump at this. It probably is true.

'I don't care,' I say. 'I don't care whether it's true or not. All I know is, I'm not complete without you and we've wasted too much time already.'

'Have you thought what will happen to your career if we're found out?' he says. 'No one will work with you again.'

He turns to leave.

'They won't find out,' I say, as I follow him down the path. 'There's no proof. Larry is dead. My mother's gaga.' I feel a stab of alarm as I say this. My mother is far from gaga, but I've come too far to stop now. 'Your mother's not much better. Neither of them will have any credibility.'

'You're forgetting Luna,' he says. 'And I'm damned sure Tammy won't keep quiet.'

I take hold of his head and force him to look at me. I say, 'Then we have to find a way of making sure she does.'

# 28

## Florence

Nick and Ben are worried about me. The unusual silences at dinner, the shared looks when they think my attention is elsewhere, the frequent displays of irritability on both their parts; I know the signs.

They're right to be concerned. Something is happening to me that I can't control. I'm now living more in the past than the present. Random memories come from nowhere. I feel myself drifting away, even in mid-conversation. Concentrating on anything is becoming almost impossible.

The pull of 1969 is becoming dangerously strong.

When dinner is over, I light a fire outside and ignore the two serious faces watching me from the kitchen window. I have no need of warmth – the night is quite mild – I use fire to help me think.

Scrying, the ancient art of seeking visions, is something I've practised for years. I look deep into the embers, let my mind drift and, usually, I start to see. Some people claim to see the future when they are scrying, but for me, it's simply an aid to an otherwise rational thought process. Scrying helps me get in touch with my subconscious.

Sparks fly into the air and the embers shift.

It is thirty-six hours, give or take, until Larry's funeral takes place in Sabden and I still haven't decided whether or not to go. Nick doesn't want me to. He knows that my mental health has taken a turn for the worse, might be reaching the point where I can no longer keep it in check.

More worrying still is the fact that I will have to take Ben with me, and Sabden feels like the last place I should take my beloved son.

A breeze rushes through the nearby trees and I look up, half expecting Marigold, or even Larry himself, to be walking towards me.

I add more wood to the fire. I sit in my darkening garden and wait for my ghosts to join me. And I know that when they do, they'll be calling me home.

# 29

## Cassie

Monday, 9 August 1999

I'm woken the next morning by a loud and continuous banging. I've barely pushed myself up in bed before the door to my room bursts open. Tammy almost falls over the threshold. Behind her, John's mother, Beryl, loiters nervously in the doorway. I think I can see a third figure too, but for the moment he, or she, is hidden behind Beryl.

'What the hell is this?' Tammy, in shapeless jogging bottoms and a stained T-shirt, her hair scraped back behind her head, is holding the clay effigy I made of John. I'd left it in a low oven in the pub kitchen overnight to bake hard. I'd meant to get up early to retrieve it. Or maybe I hadn't. Maybe I'd wanted her to find it, to bring matters to a head.

Matters seem to have come to a head. Tammy is furious. She lifts the figure high, as though she's about to chuck it towards me. I check a pillow is in grabbing distance. If that thing hits my skull, it will hurt.

'It's a clay picture,' I say. 'Did it fire all right?'

It has. The clay has taken on a dark reddish-brown sheen and it hasn't cracked at all. Several of the blackthorn spikes have broken under Tammy's clumsy grasp, but that won't matter.

'Is John around?' I add, as I stretch my arms up high. I don't wear anything in bed and the quilt falls low. Tammy's eyes narrow in disgust.

Beryl gives up the effort of standing unaided and leans against the door frame. Her hands roam about her body as she searches for cigarettes. Or a hip flask.

'It's none of your business where my husband is,' Tammy snarls.

'He's playing football if you'd like to know,' says his mother.

'You two need to work on your solidarity act.' I get out of bed, naked, and head for the bathroom.

'Slut,' Tammy mutters under her breath. 'How dare you go into my kitchen? I'm calling the police.'

'And telling them what? Accusing people of witchcraft went out of fashion a long time ago, even here.' I open the bathroom door, reach for my robe and wonder if I can leave Tammy where she is while I have a pee. I decide that would be pushing it. 'And they don't burn us anymore.' When I turn back, I see that Beryl has moved further into the room and is leaning against the wardrobe. The third person is now in the doorway.

'Hello, Mary,' I say. 'How are you?'

Mary was our housekeeper. Looks like she works at the pub now.

'Cass,' she says, without smiling, and I remember that Luna was always her favourite.

As Mary steps into the room and closes the door, I walk to the window and open the curtains. These three have barged their way into my private space and I'm feeling more uncomfortable than I'm letting on.

'This thing is sick.' Tammy is annoyed that we've taken our attention away from her. 'What is wrong with you?'

Come to think of it, Mary didn't like Luna much either. She didn't really like anyone.

'I'm going to smash this sick object.' Tammy moves towards the fireplace and lifts it high.

'Oh, I wouldn't do that,' I say, as I wander back towards the bed.

'Tammy, no,' gasps Beryl at the same time. Even Mary looks shocked.

'That picture is made in John's image,' I say. 'It contains his essence. If you harm it, you risk harming him.'

'Tammy, put it down,' Beryl says.

'Put it down, lass,' Mary echoes.

I step close to Tammy and let my eyes drift to the figure's genitalia. 'What do you think?' I say. 'Have I got it about right?'

She shoves it at me. The blackthorn spikes dig into my hand as I take it.

'Pack your bags or I'll throw your stuff out into the street,' she says. 'I'll have your bill ready when you come down. You've got ten minutes.'

She marches out, leaving Beryl staring stupidly in her wake. Mary glowers at me. I glower back.

'Best pack your bags, lass.' Mary turns away too. Beryl follows her, half stumbling as she crosses the threshold.

I shower, wash and dry my hair, put on make-up and dress. Forty minutes have gone by, but there's no sign of the Three Musketeers returning. When I'm ready, I get my bag from the wardrobe and lay it open on the bed. I've no intention of leaving, but I wouldn't put it past Tammy to carry out her threat to dump my things outside, and I want to throw her off the scent if she comes back. I put some clothes on the bed for good measure.

I find all three of them in the kitchen. Mary is cleaning a coffee machine, Tammy is cubing steak, and Beryl appears to be peeling potatoes. I make a mental note to go easy goading Tammy, or at least keep the kitchen table between us. If she comes at me with that knife, all bets are off.

They don't notice me. I watch the loose skin on the underside of Tammy's upper arms wobble as she brings the knife down hard against the chopping board. I hear Beryl's constant sniffing, as though she has a coke habit rather than a drink problem. Only Mary's movements have some grace, some purpose. She's the one to watch.

I hadn't planned a confrontation quite this soon. John will be angry, I know, that I haven't given him the time he asked for.

'You can keep the pub,' I say, and watch their heads flick round, Beryl's a second behind the other two. Tammy's hand tightens on the knife handle.

I stay where I am, quickly measuring the distance to the back door.

'John will move in with me in the short term,' I continue. 'Until we can sort something out. Money won't be a problem.'

'I told you to leave,' Tammy says. 'I hope you're packed.'

'If I leave, I'm taking him with me.'

In her anger, she falls back on an old teenage insult. 'You're mental.'

'He doesn't love you anymore,' I tell her. 'I'm not sure he ever did. You were . . . useful, for a time. That's over now.'

'You're delusional.' She sneers at me, but her hands are shaking. Worryingly, they're still holding the knife.

'Tammy, put that down.' Mary steps behind Tammy and pulls the knife from her grip. I breathe a little easier.

'Out,' Tammy says. 'I want you out.'

'Out,' echoes Beryl.

'Things have moved on,' I say. 'Do try to keep up, you drunken old whore.'

Beryl comes at me, faster than I'd have given her credit for being able to move. I sidestep; she bounces against the door frame and goes down flat.

'John is mine, you vile bitch. I love him.' Tammy is close to tears. She knows she's losing.

'I don't care,' I tell her.

Beryl makes an odd noise from her position on the floor. When she looks up, I see that she's bitten her lip in the fall. 'You and my son will never be together,' she tells me. 'I'll die first.'

'Not necessarily a problem,' I quip back. 'You're not too steady on your feet and this old building is treacherous. Or had you forgotten?'

Her eyes open wide. Until that moment, I think she actually had forgotten.

'It's wrong,' Beryl says in desperation. 'I'll report you.'

'Oh, I don't think you will,' I tell her. 'Come with me, all of you.'

I turn my back on them as I leave the kitchen. The door to the cellar isn't locked. I hear the others approaching and I step back a little, just in case one of them gets the urge to give me a shove. When I switch on the light, we see the flagstone floor at the bottom of the dark steps. We can smell the damp air, the stale beer, the creeping mould.

'How long was your husband lying at the bottom of those steps before you found him, Beryl?' I say. 'Two days? Three? A busy pub and nobody went into the cellar for three days?'

It was actually just over twelve hours before Ted Donnelly, John's father, was found with a broken neck and a fractured skull, but I'm not expecting her to correct me.

'Did John ever tell you what happened that night?' I ask Tammy, and I see from her confused look that he hasn't.

'Beryl,' I go on. 'Have you ever told anyone?'

'It was an accident,' she says. 'Accident.'

'Such a grim summer,' I say. 'Who'd have thought there'd be so much evil in one town?'

'If you know about it, you must have been there too,' Tammy says. 'Whatever happened, you were involved.'

'I wasn't involved in what happened to those three teenagers, though, was I?' I search Tammy's face for signs of alarm. She's agitated and angry; I'm not sure she's afraid yet. 'Did you never once think that Larry might tell the truth in the end? I saw him right before he died.'

I'm bluffing. Larry told me nothing, of course. I know nothing beyond what I worked out for myself years ago, that John, Tammy and their gang, including my sister Luna, were complicit in leading at least one of Larry's victims to her death. Fourteen-year-old Patsy Wood thought she was heading for a romantic rendezvous with John when she vanished. The gang had planned to lie in wait, to leap out yelling 'surprise' or some other cruel teenage shit. It had been a mean joke gone wrong, and while I doubt the kids would take any blame for what subsequently happened, they'd probably been living with a whole load of guilt for a long time. I'm chancing my arm now, but I've struck a nerve. The anger on Tammy's face is fading.

'So many people could be in so much trouble if I tell what I know about that summer.' I glance back at the tall, stocky woman standing silently behind us. 'Not you, Mary. I've got nothing on you.'

She glares back at me.

'It's funny, isn't it,' I continue. 'People thought my father's arrest meant the bad times were over. They weren't, though, were they? They were only just beginning.'

'Well, what about what happened to Roy Greenwood?' Tammy spits at me. 'You've a few skeletons of your own in the closet.'

Over Tammy's shoulder, I catch Mary's eye and remember what I should have thought of before now. Mary and Tammy are related. I think Mary is Tammy's aunt. Blast it.

'I'd forgotten him,' I lie, knowing I have some recalibrating to do. Tammy won't give up John without a fight, and she has weapons I didn't allow for.

It looks like I'll have to kill her after all.

# PART TWO

**1969**

*Four weeks after Larry Glassbrook's arrest*

Lancashire Morning Post
Monday 4 August 1969
By Abby Thorn, junior reporter

### 'Heroine' Police Officer Back on the Beat

Florence Lovelady, the WPC who brought Larry Glassbrook to justice, is expected to return to active duties at Sabden Police Station today.

Glassbrook, who has been charged with the kidnap and murder of Patsy Wood, Susan Duxbury and Stephen Shorrock, and the abduction and attempted murder of WPC Lovelady, is in HMP Manchester awaiting trial. Further comment is not permitted under legal reporting restrictions.

The injuries Lovelady sustained during her period of incarceration at Glassbrook's hands, while not made public, are believed to have been significant. Her return, following a four-week period of recuperation, is against the advice of many. 'She'll be traumatised,' a police colleague who did not wish to be named told the Post. 'Police work is hard. After what this young woman's been through, well, maybe a quiet, civilian job at one of the bigger stations would be in everyone's best interests.'

To some, Florence Lovelady is a heroine, a courageous young woman who brought an end to one of the worst periods in Lancashire's history. To others, she's proven herself a little too keen to rock boats. Her return today won't be universally welcomed.

# 30

## Florence

I folded that morning's edition of the *Post* and handed it back to the porter; he took it from me wordlessly.

We were both in the entrance hall of the nurses' home – my new home. Outside the knocker-up was making his way down the street. His boots clattered on the flagged pavement and his long pole tapped at upstairs windows as he woke the early shift workers. He'd turned the corner out of sight when the nurses came streaming past, down the stairs and out of the front door, all in full uniform, several smoking, most chatting, laughing or complaining.

I should have followed them, and yet I couldn't bring myself to do it. Four weeks wasn't enough time. I wasn't ready.

The crocodile of caps and sensible shoes set off down the path. The forerunners had reached the road when a couple at the rear looked back. I turned away to go back to my room and was almost at the stairs when I heard the front door opening.

'Come on, Flo! Trams don't wait.'

She was a small, bright-eyed woman of around my own age, twenty-two. I'd never met her, hadn't spoken to any of them in the few hours I'd shared their living accommodation, but they were all waiting for me. I had no choice but to join them. They swept me up and carried me along, down the path, past a row of shops and along the rough, flagged pavement to the busier main road. A distant ringing sound and a buzzing of the overhead lines told us the tram was on its way.

'How you settling in?' the young nurse asked me as we neared the stop.

'Fine, thank you.'

What else could I say? The nurses' hostel, with its beige corridors, noisy plumbing and shared bathrooms felt institutional and cold, lonely in spite of the thirty or so young women who lived there.

'Bit of a change for you? I'm Jenny, by the way.'

'Florence,' I said, unnecessarily. She knew my name. They all did.

Jenny was right. It was a massive change. When I'd first arrived in Sabden, the question of where I'd live had posed a problem. There was no police accommodation for women, and it was unthinkable that I move into the men's hostel. So I'd lodged with a family. The Glassbrooks. My return had given my superiors another headache. I couldn't continue living with Sally Glassbrook and her daughters, given what had happened with Larry. Needing to find a solution quickly, they'd got permission for me to take an empty room in the nurses' hostel.

The hostel was a little over two miles from the town centre. Once I found my bike again, I could cycle to work, and that would be easier, because it seemed every pair of eyes at the tram stop was turned my way. Staring at my feet felt cowardly and so I looked up, over their heads. This far out of town, the buildings were mainly residential houses, two-up two-downs, black as soot, their front doors opening onto the road. Above and beyond them, I could see the western edge of the Pennines, a wild and windswept landscape that surrounded the small industrial town of Sabden. It was my imagination – of course it was – but it seemed the hills had drawn a little closer in the weeks I'd been away. This sense of claustrophobia, of being trapped by the moors and the black stone of the town's buildings, wasn't something I'd experienced before.

The tram arrived and the nurses ran upstairs. As I walked towards a seat at the rear of the lower deck, eyes met mine. Four weeks had passed since Larry Glassbrook's arrest. I'd been away for all of that time, and on the surface nothing in Sabden had changed. Where it counted, though, everything had. This town had given birth to a monster; it would carry the shame of that for decades, and I'd been responsible for unearthing it. They would hate me, far more than they hated Larry. All this had been explained to me by the police welfare officer who'd visited me in hospital and again at my parents' house. An immediate move to another force was in my best interests.

The bell sounded; the man in the seat opposite mine pulled himself to his feet and spat before moving off down the tram. Spitting in public wasn't uncommon in the North. People smoked heavily. It hadn't necessarily been aimed at me.

More people got on and I heard someone mutter my name. The tram set off and I found my left hand throbbing. Four weeks after Larry had mutilated it, I was still taking prescription painkillers. 'It's getting better,' the last nurse who'd changed the dressing had said, but we'd both known it would never get better. The third finger of my left hand, the one that might have worn a wedding ring one day, was missing.

As the tram got closer to the centre of town, I could feel the nervous knot in my gut tightening. I was half expecting him to be at the station, I realised, in a cell. He'd be whistling away to one of the Elvis Presley songs that were constantly playing in his head and flirting with the tea lady.

The idea was stupid. Larry was in a high-security prison in Manchester, pending his next court appearance. And yet so integral a part of this town was he that I was expecting to see him on each street corner.

It was a short walk from the tram stop to the station. I slipped in through the back door and made my way to the ladies' cloakroom, passing two uniformed officers in the corridor. At the sight of me, they turned and hurried away.

I'd been stupid to imagine anything would change. No one had wanted me at the station even before Larry's arrest. A female police officer upset the natural order of things. I'd been ignored, taunted, the subject of endless practical jokes. It would only get worse now.

Another minute and I'd be late on parade.

Parade was the start of the working day for uniformed officers. At the given time, we'd gather in the parade room for an inspection by the duty sergeant. Our whistles, pocketbooks, handcuffs and truncheons, known as our 'appointments', would be handed out and we'd be given our tasks for the first half of the shift. The station seemed unnaturally quiet as I made my way there. I pushed the door open and went in with my eyes down.

Silence. I looked up.

'Attention!' called the duty sergeant.

Normally, the officers on parade would face the duty sergeant. These officers, far more than would normally be present, just about every uniformed officer posted to the station, it seemed, were facing the door. Facing me.

Saluting me.

CID were in the room, standing together at one side. Detective Inspector Sharples, who hated me, who'd called me a 'jumped-up swanker of a schoolgirl' was there. Detective Sergeants Brown and Green, known as Woodsmoke and Gusty, were also there. So was Tom and, for a moment, all the others faded away as he and I stared at each other, and he did a little mock salute with his fingertips.

The civilian staff were there too. Women from the typing pool and the switchboard. Even the canteen staff.

The station superintendent, a tall, dark-haired man in his forties called Stanley Rushton, stepped towards me. 'Welcome back, Florence,' he said. As he took my hand, applause rippled around the room, and I did the worst thing possible in the circumstances. I started to cry.

'Was I hallucinating earlier or did Rushton actually hug me?' I put my tray down opposite Tom on the canteen table.

'Dirty git,' Tom said.

Detective Constable Tom Devine was eating steak and onion pie with chips, mushy peas and gravy, a side order of two slices of bread and butter, and had a waiting dish of jam sponge pudding and custard. He had a huge mug of tea and I knew there'd be at least two sugars in it. Three if he'd had a bad morning.

I'd been nervous about approaching Tom but had found him sitting at an empty table, some distance from his CID mates. I thought— No, I was sure he'd wanted me to join him. I opened my ham sandwich and began scraping off the salad cream.

'That's the best bit,' Tom objected.

'Disgusting stuff,' I told him. 'It isn't even mayonnaise.'

'Mayo-what? And should bread be that colour?'

'It's wholemeal.' I looked down. 'Actually, I think it's just white bread with added dye.'

Tom resumed eating. 'Like my new jacket?'

Tom's clothes, and he had a lot of them, were on the flashy side for a detective, bold colours and patterns, huge collars to his shirts and ties so wide they could have doubled as napkins.

'It matches your eyes,' I told him.

Those eyes narrowed.

'Your hangover eyes,' I clarified. The jacket was maroon.

He grinned. 'Good first morning?'

'PC Butterworth didn't leave my side for four hours,' I said. 'He walked on the traffic side of the pavement and stepped in front of me every time we were approached. I was actually hindering normal police work because he was so focused on looking after me.'

Police Constable Randall, or Randy, Butterworth was a few years older than me. He too had lodged at the Glassbrook house, and for that reason I probably knew him better than most people at the station. Except Tom.

Tom forked up three chips. 'Yeah, well, he's a dirty git too,' he said, chewing. 'How's the home for fallen women?'

'Full of exuberant nurses who have Cinzano parties and play Buddy Holly music into the small hours.'

His grin widened. I glared. We were silent for a few seconds, while Tom ate and I tried to.

And then: 'No one's mentioned the L-word yet,' I said.

Tom gave an exaggerated look round. 'Fair play, Floss, I can't tell you I love you in the staff canteen.'

'Larry,' I said. 'L for Larry.'

He sighed and put down his knife. 'What do you want to know?'

'Everything. What's happening?'

'We've submitted our files to the prosecution department. Last I heard, he's still intending to plead guilty, so we're looking at a hearing, rather than a trial, probably sometime later this month. There are no guarantees, but he'll be expected to serve his sentence a long way from here.'

'They don't want to talk to me again?'

'If he changes his plea, all bets are off. Otherwise, I think they have more than enough. Be grateful.'

'Did he do it?' I asked my sandwich, in a voice I doubt even the dyed white bread could hear.

'Come again?' Tom said.

I risked looking up. 'Is he guilty?'

'Jesus, Floss. Where did that come from?'

The hard stare in his eyes was too much. I looked down again.

'I don't believe I'm hearing this.' Tom's voice had risen and I could sense glances coming our way, other conversations in the room falling silent. 'Do I have to remind you what that bastard did to you?'

He grabbed my left wrist and held my hand in front of me. 'I found your finger in his— Jesus, Florence.'

I heard the sound of a chair sliding along the floor.

Tom let my hand go but leaned forward across the table. 'He was going to bury you alive. What the hell—'

'Everything all right here, youngsters?'

We both looked up to see Detective Sergeant Brown, known as Woodsmoke to the team, for no reason I'd ever been able to understand. He smelled of smoke, most of them did, but it wasn't woodsmoke.

Tom leaned back again, holding up both hands as though in mock surrender. His face was uncharacteristically red and I thought I could see the gleam of tears in his eyes. The Glassbrook case hadn't only been bad for me, I realised then. Everyone was reeling under the weight of it; some were just hiding it better than others.

'Fine, Sarge.' I forced a smile. 'Tom's arguing Leeds United will win the league next season, and I'm saying Everton will walk it. You know Tom and football.'

Woodsmoke dropped a hand onto my shoulder before nodding at Tom and walking away. After a few seconds, conversations around the room resumed.

'We've missed you,' Tom said.

'We?'

We held eye contact for a split second.

'Woodsmoke's been cleaning the ashtrays,' Tom told me. 'He took four dirty mugs back to the kitchen yesterday muttering Florence wouldn't like the mess.'

'I won't be up there anyway.'

While the Glassbrook investigation had been ongoing, I'd been co-opted to CID. That was over now. I was back on the beat.

'I phoned you,' Tom said.

'When?'

'Last Thursday night. I sneaked into Rushton's office and found your home phone number. The butler answered. Said you were asleep and he didn't want to disturb you.'

My family did not have a butler. 'That would have been my dad. He didn't tell me.'

'Obviously doesn't want to encourage gentleman callers.'

I raised my eyebrows. 'Gentleman?'

Beneath the table, I felt something nudge my foot. Tom was looking directly at me, and any second now someone would notice. Then his foot pulled away.

'You have to let it drop,' he said. 'You have to move on now.'

'I know.'

'Look at me, Floss. Promise me. The Glassbrook case is over.'

I promised. I'd have promised him anything.

# 31

# The Poisoner

The poisoner is young but gathers knowledge as she grows.

The poisoner wanders the paths around her home and learns the secrets of the hedgerows. She smiles to see the pale green flowers of the black bryony because she knows she will have a use for it one day, and likes to bring indoors the sapphire-blue columns of wolfsbane because it comforts her to have its power close. She becomes entranced by the deadly beauty of the countryside's poisons.

She walks the woods in spring in search of the green hellebore and rises early as the year grows older to seek out mushrooms. Destroying angel, death cap and Satan's boletus, she finds them sprouting from the dark places and greets them like old friends.

The poisoner learns to gather according to the phases of the moon. She learns to chop and peel and grind, to make tinctures, oils, salves and syrups. She reads books about natural healing and delights in discovering that the same plants appear in the books of both medicines and poisons.

The poisoner watches the wise women and absorbs their skills. She learns an important lesson early: that degree is everything and that what will be beneficial in small amounts will kill quickly and painfully when taken to excess. She discovers that some plants can both save lives and take lives, and that they are the most powerful of all.

# 32

## Sally

It was on his third visit that I really began to be frightened of him – the third visit since Larry was taken away, I mean. I'd never liked him, avoided him whenever I could, and after Larry was arrested, just seeing him gave me the creeps. But I wasn't afraid, until that third time.

I was late getting home. After my shift had finished, the supervisor had called me into her office, suggesting I might take extended leave from my job. 'Not compassionate leave, obviously not compassionate leave, but something along those lines, just till it all dies down,' she'd said.

'That could be years.'

I'd been tired, and my last delivery had been difficult, a lengthy breech birth, on top of the fact that no expectant mother really wanted me anywhere near her anymore. The look of dismay when I showed up on their doorstep wasn't something I was getting used to anytime soon. 'I can't see the county paying full salary for years in return for me doing nothing,' I went on.

My supervisor had made what my mum used to call her lemon-sucking face. 'As to salary, well, that would be another matter. I don't think normal rules of salary would apply in the circumstances, but I imagine you have a bit put away, don't you?'

Not a lot I could say to that. *A bit put away?*

'That young policewoman is back,' she went on. 'She's been seen in the town centre this morning. That will be difficult, won't it?'

'Are you sacking me?'

She'd looked flustered. 'Well, no, that is to say, not at this stage.'

'Then I'll see you in the morning.'

I'd driven home quickly, even forgetting to lock the car doors from the inside, a habit I'd got into after a woman opened the door at some traffic lights and screamed in at me, 'Your husband's a bloody murderer!'

Like I hadn't worked that out myself.

The second I opened the kitchen door, I knew something was wrong. My daughters, Cassie and Luna, were both obviously waiting for my return. Luna's boyfriend, John Donnelly, was with them, but there was none of the subdued excitement I could usually sense when he was around the girls. All three seemed on edge.

Mary, the woman who helped me around the house, was fifteen minutes late going home. Her eyes met mine. 'Greenwood's in the living room.'

'Again?'

Her shoulders twitched.

'How are you two?' I stroked Luna's hair and looked across at Cassie. She'd been scribbling notes on blank sheet music. She wasn't that clever, Cassie, but she had a talent for music. Luna, my younger girl, was the exact opposite. Smart as a brass button, not a creative bone in her body.

John stood up to offer me the spare chair. He seemed to have grown since I'd last seen him. To be honest, he wasn't the boy I'd have chosen for Luna. Even if his mother hadn't been Beryl Donnelly, the woman Larry had been having an affair with before his arrest, there was something a bit too clever about him. He had a way of smiling like he was hiding a secret. And he was just a bit too good-looking – tall with dark hair and an almost perfect face. On the other hand, he was the only one of the girls' friends who'd stuck by them.

'Hello, John,' I managed a smile. 'Are you staying for tea?'

'Mum's expecting me, thanks.' His eyes dropped from mine.

I couldn't blame John for what his mother had done, but it was hard all the same, seeing him in the house. Hard for him too, I guessed.

'Good day?' I asked when neither of my girls spoke to me.

Luna gave a tiny snort. 'Can we swap schools?'

John and Cassie looked at each other.

'What's the point?' Cassie said. 'You think they've never heard of us in Burnley? Or Nelson?'

'It's five weeks before you go back,' I said. 'It'll have blown over by then.'

Luna stuck out her bottom lip. 'There was a gang at the bottom of Snape Street. They followed me.'

'I walked her home.' John gave me a nervous glance. 'I've told her to ring me if she wants to go into town.'

'What about me?' Cassie said. 'Who's going to protect me from the bad guys?'

John smiled at her. 'Me,' he said. 'I'll protect you both.'

'I suppose I'd better get changed,' I said, as Mary put a mug of tea in front of me. I suspected she'd sneaked sugar into it again, although she knew I didn't take it.

'For Lurch?' Cassie said. 'God, I wouldn't.'

'I'd get it over with,' Mary said. 'Look sharp, I have to go home sometime.'

'You can go now. Sorry to have kept you.'

'I'll keep Luna and Cass company,' John volunteered.

'I'll wait till he's gone,' Mary insisted.

I carried my mug through to the living room. As I pushed the door open, Roy Greenwood got to his feet. The girls' nickname for him, after Lurch the butler in the TV show *The Addams Family*, was a bit cruel, but you had to see their point. Well over six feet tall, Roy was thin and prematurely stooped. He was around fifty but looked older. His hair was dark, too long and slick with hair products, while his long face carried a huge nose and a wide downturned mouth. His eyes were a dull, dead brown. I'd never seen him wear anything but a black suit, a starched white shirt and a black tie. His worst feature, though, were his teeth. They were huge and unnaturally white, obviously dentures and probably ill-fitting because when he wasn't speaking, he was always pulling his lips over them and making odd faces.

'Hello, Mr Greenwood,' I said. 'Please don't get up.'

And another thing. While his hands and nails were spotlessly clean, and his clothes always smart and laundered, he smelled bad.

He waved a finger at me with his left hand. In his other, he held an overfilled sherry glass that I knew Mary wouldn't have offered him. 'Now, now,' he said.

'Roy,' I corrected myself. 'Please sit down.'

'Let me get you a drink.' He strolled over to the cabinet. 'You must be exhausted. I hope that woman of yours is pouring you a hot bath. What will you have?'

'Nothing, thank you. I don't drink at home.'

I heard the sound of bottles clinking. 'I'm looking for something sweet,' he muttered. 'This Tío Pepe is a little dry for ladies' tastes.'

I wasn't going to win this. 'Sherry will be fine,' I said. 'A very small one. I might be called out again.'

'I may have to put my foot down on that. Sit down, my dear. I'll bring it to you.'

I took an armchair on one side of the fire and registered that he'd been sitting in Larry's chair. 'How's your mother?' I asked. 'You must worry leaving her alone in the evening.'

He held a sherry glass up to the light, then took out a handkerchief and polished round the rim. 'Tolerably well, thank you.'

'And business? How is the business?'

He stiffened. 'All in good time, Sally.'

He brought the sherry, somehow managing to brush his fingers over mine as I took it from him, then returned to Larry's chair.

'What shall we drink to?' He raised his own glass.

'A not-guilty verdict?'

He actually sniggered. 'Oh yes, very good. How about to brighter times ahead?'

I let the sherry dampen my lips. I would pour it over my head and stick the glass in my own eye before I drank it.

'I thought we might have a little supper together,' he said. 'After the girls have gone to bed. What do you say?'

'You might faint from hunger before those two go up,' I said. 'And I eat my main meal at midday, I'm afraid. Authority rules. They don't want us running out of energy. What did you want to talk about?'

'How are you fixed for money, Sally?'

Roy was Larry's partner. Sooner or later, we would have to talk financial matters. 'Well, I have my wage, of course,' I said. 'It's not much, but more than a lot of families live on. And I have the rent from the lodgers, although . . .' No need to go on. Two of our lodgers, the police constables Florence Lovelady and Randy Butterworth had left the night of Larry's arrest. The third, Ron Pickles, had gone a week later.

'Yes, I thought so.' Roy didn't seem concerned by my difficult financial circumstances. 'Have you thought about how you might pay the mortgage now that you no longer have Larry's wages coming in?'

'We don't have a mortgage. We own this house.'

Roy shook his head. 'I was afraid of this. So many men keep their wives in ignorance of the true state of affairs. It's understandable, of course: ladies and money have never been good bedfellows. Well, except when it comes to spending it, of course.' His lips separated to reveal the full span of his huge teeth. 'Funny how you never need any help in that department. As to managing it, though? As I say, understandable, but should the worst happen . . .'

'What are you talking about?' I hadn't meant to snap, but he'd scared me.

'I'm afraid I own this house, Sally.'

I picked up the sherry glass and swallowed half.

'How is that possible?' I managed.

Greenwood spoke slowly, as though to a child. 'When I took Larry on as an apprentice, I bought it for him and his parents, and any family he subsequently had. Larry paid rent out of his wages, but my name is on the deeds.'

He stopped. I waited.

'He'd fallen a little behind in recent weeks,' Roy went on. 'There's about a hundred pounds owing. But no need to worry about that. For now.'

'How much? How much per week?'

He named a sum that was close to my weekly wage. I finished the sherry.

'I won't pour you another, if you don't mind, Sally,' he said. 'I don't approve of ladies getting tipsy.'

'How old was Larry when he agreed to this?'

Those big, dark brows flickered a little closer together. 'Old enough. If the partnership dissolves at any time, the house reverts in its entirety to me.'

'What about all the money he's paid back already? You've been partners for twenty years.'

The grin was back. His eyes stayed cold. 'I was always kind enough to call him a partner. And it's possible that, had I retired first, I might have made him a present of the business. You know how fond I've always been of you and the girls. But really, you know, he was just an employee.'

My heart was hammering. 'I need to see the loan agreement,' I told him. 'I want to have a solicitor look at it.'

He pursed his lips in mock concern. 'Don't you trust me?'

'Of course,' I said. 'But I have the girls to think about.'

'Actually, it could be a good idea to see a solicitor. You'll need to start divorce proceedings.'

'I'm not divorcing Larry.'

Roy's mouth twitched, as though he was sucking on an invisible straw. 'My dear, you must. Unless you and the girls cut yourselves off from him completely, you'll be tainted. As it is, you'll struggle to throw off the stigma, but, given time, with a new and entirely respectable partner, people will forgive. If not forget.'

Out in the hallway, the phone rang. Roy held up his hand.

'It will wait,' he said. 'Or one of those girls will get it. You do too much for them.'

The ringing stopped and I heard Mary's voice.

Roy got to his feet. 'I've given you a lot to think about,' he said. 'I'll leave you for now.'

The door opened and Mary looked in. 'That was the clinic,' she said. 'You're needed at t'police station.'

'Tell them Mrs Glassbrook is tired and can't go out again tonight.' Roy stepped in front of me.

Mary came into the room. 'Young woman pitched up at t'station half an hour ago. About to drop. They can't get an ambulance out in time and every midwife on shift is busy. You're the only one left. I'll show you out, Mr G. While Sally gets ready.'

Roy turned his back on her and put both hands on my shoulders. 'Don't worry, Sally,' he said. 'I'll always look after you and the girls.' He glanced back at Mary. 'And if you'll take my advice, this sort of thing won't be necessary in future.'

'Your bag's ready,' Mary told me. 'I'll stay with the girls till you're home.'

She backed out of the room and the door closed. I took a step towards it and Roy caught me, grabbing me round the upper arm. I could feel his hard, bony fingers digging into my flesh.

'Do you like bad men, Sally?' His cold eyes drilled down into mine. 'Do they excite you?'

# 33

## Florence

I finished work shortly before six o'clock. My shift had ended hours ago, but when reporters started arriving at the front desk – they'd heard about my return to work – the super asked how I felt about a bit of overtime. He had a report that needed writing about a possible link between late-night violence in the town centre and an extension to the pubs' opening hours, and none of the other numbskulls – his words, not mine – could be trusted with it.

I'd put my handwritten pages away in a folder and locked it in my desk drawer – I'd been touched to see my borrowed desk was still in its place in the CID room – when PC Butterworth, who was also working overtime, poked his head round the door and yelled at me.

'You're wanted downstairs, Florence. Like, ten minutes ago.'

I ran down after Randy to the front desk, where the desk sergeant was leaning over a small female figure. She was doubled over and bellowing like an angry cow. Her hair, fair in colour, hung down almost to the floor.

'Flossie, take over.' The sergeant straightened up, letting me see that the woman was young and heavily pregnant. She'd stopped moaning but was panting hard. Her face was round with plump cheeks and small, slanted eyes.

I hurried to the woman and together with Randy tried to usher her to a seat. No sooner had she sat down than she bucked up again as though something had impaled her and resumed yelling.

'She needs an ambulance.' Shock made me state the obvious.

'None available,' Randy told me. 'The sarge is trying Blackburn.'

Blackburn Infirmary, our closest hospital after Burnley General, was some distance away.

'Then we need to get a midwife here.'

Randy, too, was red in the face by this time. 'Yeah, we thought of that, thanks, Florence. They've a lot on tonight, by all accounts. God knows what was going on nine months ago.'

The woman collapsed onto all fours as the outside door opened. We looked towards it, but it wasn't an ambulanceman, or even a midwife, but two older men, who stared at us in horror.

'No!' screamed the woman on the floor. 'Can't take me. Don't listen to them. They're going to kill me and the baby.'

Behind the front desk, something heavy clattered to the floor and broke. The two men started to back out.

'Get her out of here,' the sergeant called from his position at the phone. 'Cell one is free.'

Randy and I wrapped our arms round the screaming woman's waist and lifted her between us. We ushered her out of reception, along a short stretch of corridor and into cell one. She sank onto the narrow bed and looked, terrified, at the open door.

'Can they get in? Lock that door. Lock that door!'

'Love, them two were here to report the thieving of late-summer veg from the allotments,' Randy said. 'I really don't think they're interested in you.'

She stared up at me, her eyes huge and frightened. 'Not from Black Moss Manor?'

'No,' Randy told her firmly. 'Nobody from Black Moss Manor is coming in here tonight.' He beckoned me to the door. 'Did you know mongols could get pregnant?' he said in hushed tones.

I, too, had noticed the young woman had a condition that was just starting to be known as Down's syndrome. Behind us, she began to moan again.

'Shall I get some towels?' Randy asked me. 'And hot water?'

I stared at him. 'What for?'

'It's what they do, isn't it? When a woman's having a baby. Get towels and hot water. I've seen it on telly.'

'Do you know what to do with either?'

He shook his head.

I went back into the cell and kneeled on the floor in front of the woman. She was very young. 'What's your name, sweetheart?' I said.

'Marigold McGowan,' Randy said from the doorway.

I stole a look at Marigold's left hand. No wedding ring.

'Marigold,' I said. 'Who brought you here? We need to contact your family. Or your friends.'

'No. Don't tell. Please don't make me go back. They lock me in my room all the time. I tried to go home and they wouldn't let me out.'

'Who wouldn't, Marigold? Who wouldn't let you out?'

'They hurt me. They killed my friend and they'll kill me.'

I turned to look at Randy. He shrugged.

'Which friend, Marigold?' I asked her. 'Who killed your friend?'

She was panting. 'My friend Wendy. The Black Moss people. They killed Wendy and now they want to kill me.'

'Nobody wants to kill you, love,' said Randy, in a small voice.

'And my baby,' wailed Marigold. 'They'll kill my baby.'

The sergeant was back. 'Midwife's parking her car,' he announced. 'Randy, go and bring her in. Then get every kettle in the station full and boiling. And find some towels.'

Randy didn't need telling twice.

'Sarge, what do you want me to do?' I said, quietly praying he'd tell me to go and man the front desk.

'Help me get her undressed,' said a new voice. 'Sergeant, can you find us some more sheets and blankets?'

Sally Glassbrook, Larry's wife, was standing in the doorway of the cell, in her pale blue nurse's uniform. Her long blonde hair hung in a plait down her back. Her eyes met mine and I swear I felt a moment of sheer terror. I'd liked Sally when I'd lodged with the Glassbrooks. She'd been kind to me, a hard-working, intelligent woman, devoted to her family, but as her silver-grey eyes grew darker in the poor light of the cell, I remembered that Sally Glassbrook was reputedly a very powerful witch. And given that I'd been responsible for getting her husband arrested, one who had every cause to hate me.

I didn't believe in witchcraft – the idea was ridiculous – and yet this woman had frightened me with a look.

She came in, took the sergeant's place at Marigold's side and began firing questions about contractions, timing, waters breaking. Marigold answered in between moans but managed to convey very little information other than it hurt, it hurt really bad, and was she going to die?

'Sarge?' I said, during a brief lull in the noise. I could not be in the same room as Sally Glassbrook. Even if I hadn't been shaking like a leaf, I'd had specific instructions to go nowhere near the family.

He looked from me to Sally. 'Love, I'm not sure we've much choice in the matter.'

'No, you haven't,' Sally snapped. 'Florence, there's a cotton robe in my bag. Get it. Is someone bringing hot water?'

'In hand,' muttered the sergeant. 'I'll get the sheets.'

He vanished, leaving Sally and me alone. Even then, I couldn't move.

'Robe!' Sally snapped, leading Marigold to the bunk. 'I need to examine the mother.'

I found the robe and, without speaking – I'm not sure we'd have been heard anyway – we undressed Marigold. It didn't take long. The poor girl was only wearing a thin cotton dress, an equally thin cardigan, bra, slip and knickers. She was tiny. I guessed she wouldn't come anywhere near five feet when she was standing upright.

'Towels,' Randy announced from the doorway, a small pile in his hands. 'All I could find. We only use them in the lavatories and they're small.'

Marigold was flat on her back by this time, her knees in the air as Sally examined her.

'I'll see how the kettles are doing,' Randy gasped, and was gone.

'Oh blimey!' The sergeant had appeared, laden with sheets. He too swivelled and turned his back. Braver than Randy, though, he stayed in the doorway. 'Have we time for an ambulance to get here?' he asked. 'Or we could drive you both to Burnley in a panda car.'

'I'm not sure we've time for the hot water to get here,' Sally said. 'Go and chase it up, will you?'

The sergeant scarpered, leaving the sheets behind. Sally pulled on white overalls and tied a cap over her hair.

'What do you want me to do?' I asked.

'I can handle the business end,' Sally said. 'You sit behind her on the bed, let her lean on you, and give her sips of water if she needs it.'

Time passed. Each minute seemed to increase Marigold's agony, and when the pains eased, her mental torment took centre stage. She yelled and sobbed about how much she hated Black Moss Manor and was never going back. She only stopped shouting to resume screaming. Just listening to her was exhausting.

I'd had my fair share of excitement since joining the Lancashire force, but this was something else entirely. Primitive, unpredictable and no less terrifying for being entirely natural. Sally, throughout, was like a robot, emotion-free, entirely in control. Just once did her composure break. As a contraction seemed stronger than most, Marigold's face twisted with pain.

'Don't want a baby,' she yelled at Sally. 'Can't make me, bitch. Get away from me.'

'Call me what you like, love,' Sally snapped back. 'I'm going nowhere, and neither are you until this baby's out.'

Marigold threw back her head, in temper as much as pain, I thought, and yelled to the ceiling. I was concentrating on holding her on the bed, so I didn't see what happened next. I just heard Sally's cry of alarm as a chair in the far corner of the cell, on which she'd left her bag, fell over, scattering her instruments everywhere.

For a second or more, all three of us were shocked into silence.

'Maybe the chair broke,' I said. 'The stuff in here's ancient.'

'I'm sorry,' Marigold mumbled. 'I'm a bad girl.'

The hot water arrived and mugs of tea, which none of us had

time to drink. I made soothing noises and told Marigold she was doing very well and that it would soon be over. I sat holding her up until my own back ached and handed Sally instruments when she couldn't reach them herself. I held a cup of greenish liquid to Marigold's lips and encouraged her to drink it.

'What is it?' I asked Sally, remembering her pantry full of bottles and jars, with stoppered lids and gleaming contents.

'Camomile and catnip tea,' she told me. 'Eases labour.'

More time passed. I hadn't realised how long it took for babies to arrive.

'First labour,' Sally said, when I said as much. 'Never easy.'

Eventually, Sally helped Marigold into a more upright position and told her she had to push the baby out. The terrible scene got worse. Marigold screeched as Sally urged her to push, to stop, to pant. I felt tears rolling down my face but couldn't let go of Marigold for long enough to wipe them away.

'And again,' Sally urged. 'Push, Marigold.'

Push. It became the only word we could say, as Sally and I urged and coaxed and bullied, and poor exhausted Marigold tried to comply. In the end, it happened very quickly. There came a glooping sound like that of a cowpat falling to earth and then Sally was holding a blood-smeared little creature. She handed it up to Marigold while I stared in awe. Everything real humans had this little thing had too, even down to minuscule fingers and toes. It was thin, though, and red, covered in a fine, dark hair. A thick grey rope swung from its middle, pulsating as though with a life of its own. Then Sally clamped and cut it, and the baby was properly born.

'I didn't die.' Through tears of exhaustion Marigold turned her head to me.

'No, you didn't die.' I couldn't help smiling back at her; she had such a sweet face.

'Florence, take the baby,' Sally said. 'Find something to keep him warm, and make sure he keeps breathing. I'll be with you soon.'

I stood on legs that didn't feel stable, saw that blood was pooling on the floor and took the baby gingerly. Terrified I might drop the slimy little thing, I held it close to me as I carried it over to the pile of towels.

*He*. The baby was a he, not an it.

He wasn't crying by this time but panting softly, his eyes tight shut. I stared down at the ugly, wrinkled little face, awestruck at the wonder of it all. I looked at his tiny perfect nose, his ears, his toes and his fingers.

Oh.

I looked again, checked his other hand and then wrapped towels round him. I carried him back to Sally and crouched at her side. Her eyebrows rose when she saw the small, additional finger on his right hand, about half the size of his little finger, and forking off from it.

'Polydactyly,' she whispered. 'It's not uncommon, especially in Lancashire. Nothing to worry about. Surgery can sort it out when he's a bit older.'

The baby might be delivered safely, but our work for the night was far from done because after the placenta was delivered, Marigold had lost a lot of blood and needed stitches. The sergeant found us a strong cardboard box lined with toilet paper and more towels. After we'd wiped the baby clean, we laid him in his makeshift cradle. Randy cleaned away the blood, so that the sickening metallic smell was replaced by one of artificial lemons. As my energy drained away so did my terror of Sally. Of course she wasn't a witch. There was no such thing as witchcraft. She was a clever midwife with a gift for herbalism.

Marigold lay back exhausted as we washed her and changed the sheets. We propped her up with pillows, and when the baby became fretful, Sally showed her how to feed him.

'Marigold, can you tell me what happened to you earlier today?' I asked, ignoring Sally's look of disapproval. My stint as a midwife was over. I was a police constable again.

The young woman stared up at me. This time, though, I thought I saw a slyness behind her lovely blue eyes.

'Marigold, you said you thought you were going to die. Why would you say that?'

She blinked and dropped her eyes. 'Hurt bad.'

'Who is Wendy?' I asked her.

Marigold let out a heavy sigh and her eyes closed. Putting a finger to her lips, Sally lifted the baby gently away.

Randy brought more tea, along with fish and chips for all three of us. Marigold was sleepy, but Sally and I were starving. We sat not two feet from the snoozing girl and pushed food into our mouths.

'How are you and the girls?' I asked, when the immediate demands of hunger had been sated.

Sally's face tightened. 'We're not friends, Florence,' she said. 'Don't pretend you care.'

It seemed our brief fellowship was over.

'What do you know about Black Moss Manor?' I said.

'They have a maternity wing.' Sally seemed willing enough to answer questions that weren't directly related to her family. 'It's small but efficient. I've attended a couple of births there.'

'Any fatalities there recently?'

She thought for a moment. 'No, but I can check tomorrow. Deaths during delivery are all notified to the authority.'

'Are they mainly unmarried mothers at Black Moss Manor?' I'd let my voice drop. I wasn't entirely sure that Marigold was asleep.

'Sometimes older mothers,' Sally said. 'Very poor families who can't cope with another mouth to feed.'

'And mothers with Marigold's condition?'

'I've never come across a Down's syndrome pregnancy before. I think there are fertility issues. And most people like Marigold are in institutions where the sexes are kept separate.'

'Will her baby be . . . ?'

'Will he inherit her condition? I'm honestly not sure.'

We looked across at the tiny human in the box.

'It's hard to tell,' Sally said. 'It'll be clearer when he's older.'

We heard footsteps in the corridor outside and then another midwife appeared in the doorway, her amused eyes taking in the cell, the dozing mother, the infant in a cardboard box. 'Well, this is a first,' she said, slipping off her cloak. 'Burnley can get an ambulance out in about an hour. I'll stay with her till then. Matron thought you shouldn't really be here, Sally, seeing as how . . .'

She didn't finish. She didn't have to.

# 34

## Sally

Word had got round about me being in the police station and several blokes in uniform watched me walk along the back corridor towards the door. I thought I heard the words 'Dumb bitch'. As I turned the corner, a huge man in a sergeant's uniform blocked my path.

'You want to watch those girls of yours, Sally.' He sneered down at me. 'There's folks in town think they're fair game now.'

I glared up. 'Excuse me,' I said.

He stayed where he was for another second, then stepped to one side. 'You too,' he muttered as I walked past. 'You want to watch yourself.'

The back door was being held open for me. Thankful for even a small courtesy, I hurried towards it. It slammed in my face.

I sat for several minutes in the police station car park, desperate to be away, shaking too much to drive. This was a police station. A ruddy police station. If I wasn't safe here . . .

How could he? How could he do this to us? His wife. His babies.

The night of Larry's arrest, I'd been sure there'd been a dreadful mistake. When I heard he'd confessed, I didn't believe it. I carried on refusing to believe it until I sat opposite him in the prison visiting hall and heard it from his own lips.

'I did it, love,' he'd said. 'You need to accept that. Tell the girls I love 'em.'

I'd spent a bloody month accepting it, turning everything I knew about the man I married on its head, and I was almost there. What I hadn't bargained for was the town turning on me and the girls.

The station door opened again and I fumbled for my keys, but it was only Florence and Randy Butterworth. Without seeing me, they walked to a panda car and got in, Randy in the driving seat.

I'd been unfair to Florence. Childbirth is frightening if you're not used to it, but she'd done well. She couldn't be blamed for what Larry had done. Her hand had been bleeding when we'd finished seeing to Marigold. I should go and see her. Make sure she was all right. Apologise.

I started the engine and pulled out onto the main road thinking, for once, not about me and my own problems but about Florence.

When she first came to lodge with us, back in February, I'd taken one look at the awkward, nervous girl and given her three months among us. Her Southern accent and boarding school manners set her apart like a different race. I didn't imagine for a moment she could cope with being a police officer in our rough Northern town, with being vomited over and punched by drunks in pubs, with seeing children raped and beaten by their own families. Of course, back in February, no one had dared to imagine what would actually happen to WPC Lovelady. And yet she'd survived. She was back among us.

Traffic was light and it didn't take long to reach the nurses' hostel. Randy's panda car had gone and there was just one other vehicle in the car park. A Ford Cortina sprayed metallic gold with a black vinyl roof. There were two people in the front seats and I could see Florence's bright red hair. I put the car into reverse and then something made me pause for a second, because I'd realised whose car it was. The young detective who the girls were keen on, the man who'd been at the house the night Larry was arrested, was sitting with Florence in a darkened car park. I saw his head lean towards hers. I saw them kiss. I remembered that he was married, and my heart hardened against Florence Lovelady.

I drove back into town, staying on the main road until I reached the Black Dog. Traffic was light and so I pulled over and sat looking at its huge, fancy black façade. Were it not for the swinging pub sign, it would look like a castle from a dark fairy tale. I saw the back door open and then John Donnelly, whose dad was the publican, carried out an empty crate. He put it down, stretched to ease his back and went inside.

I'd never liked the Black Dog, although it had long been the place Larry went drinking without me. It had taken me some time to realise the attraction was neither the beer nor the male company in the public bar, but the bottle-blonde landlady with the love of gin and other women's husbands. I could imagine no two women more different than Beryl and Florence Lovelady, and yet they were cut from the same cloth after all.

I'd started the car engine when the back door opened again and John reappeared. Not alone this time. The girl with him was slim, with long, fair hair.

'Cassie!' I was out of the car in a flash. 'What are you doing here?'

They both jumped a mile.

'Oh, hi, Mum,' Cassie said. 'Good – you can give me a lift. Did Mary tell you I was here?'

'Why are you out? Who's with Luna?'

'Mary. She's waiting for us.'

'Cass had her piano lesson,' John explained. 'I was going to walk her home, but I had to do something for Mum first.'

Remembering that I would have to cancel Cassie's piano lessons – we couldn't afford them now – I thanked John and wished him good night. As we drove from the pub, I could see him in the rear-view mirror, watching us.

# 35

## Florence

I waited until Randy's panda car had disappeared before crossing the car park and climbing into Tom's car. 'You shouldn't be here,' I told him.

'You shouldn't be spending the evening with Sally Glassbrook.' He leaned over to kiss me, his mouth full of warm smoke.

'Exceptional circumstances,' I said, when we broke away. As I told him about Marigold and the baby, Tom smoked, putting out one cigarette and lighting another immediately.

'What do you know about Black Moss Manor?' I asked, when I'd finished the story.

He pulled a 'not much' face. 'Charitable trust. Takes in kids from all over the North-West. Run by a husband-and-wife team. Perfectly respectable establishment. Why?'

'Marigold claimed she'd escaped. That they'd been keeping her prisoner and that they were going to kill her and her baby. She mentioned another young mother, a girl called Wendy, who'd died there.'

'Sounds a bit far-fetched. Did you report it?'

'The desk sergeant heard it. I assume he's made a report.'

'You can check tomorrow. It'll be a nice distraction from that other case. You know, the one you're not supposed to be involved with.'

I looked down.

'What were you doing with the Glassbrook file?' he asked.

'How do you know about that?' I countered.

'Shelley told me.'

Shelley was Rushton's secretary. 'It's sickening what those girls will do for you.'

'None of them have done what you have.' His hand crept onto my knee and I didn't object.

'I'm pleased to hear it. I just wanted to . . . I don't know.'

'You cannot get involved in Larry Glassbrook's case. If you do, Rushton will send you to another station.'

I opened my mouth.

'And my heart will break,' Tom went on, before I could say anything. 'I don't know how I got through these last few weeks, thinking you might not come back, that I'd never see you again.'

He leaned towards me, his hand inched up inside my jacket, and only the clatter of heels on the path forced us to break apart. We waited until the four women had gone inside the building.

'I'm coming in,' Tom announced.

'You can't.' The rules about gentleman visitors had been explained very clearly by the matron who'd shown me round. Any transgression on my part would be reported immediately to Superintendent Rushton.

'I'm coming up the fire escape,' Tom insisted. 'It's only two doors away from your room. If you unlock the door at the top, I can open it from outside.'

'How do you know this?'

'I did a safety check before you got back. Told the porter I was here officially to make sure reporters couldn't get in to harass you.'

'My blouse is covered in blood,' I said.

'Won't be a problem for long. Now, push off. I'll see you in two minutes.'

He was nuts. We'd both be in such trouble. But I was out of the car and heading for the hostel. I wished the night porter a good evening and ran up the stairs. There were noises coming from several of the rooms on the first floor, but no one in the corridor. I tiptoed to the fire escape. It was an ordinary door with bolts top and bottom and a single key, fastened to the door by a chain. I slipped back the bolts and turned the key. From a distance, the door would look no different.

I ran back to my room, flustered. I hadn't showered since that morning and I really was covered in Marigold's blood. Did I have time to clean my teeth? I grabbed my toothbrush and had just squeezed half an inch of Colgate onto it when my door opened.

# 36

## Sally

I woke, listening – once again – for the sound of screaming. Luna had been having night terrors since she was four years old, but they'd got a lot worse since Larry had been taken away. I reached for the light, waiting for the wailing to start.

Night terrors are bloody awful to witness. God knows what they must be like to experience. The child sits bolt upright, sweating and crying. She might look awake, but she'll be confused and unresponsive. She won't recognise those who are trying to soothe her, may even see them as her enemies. When Luna was tiny, her terrors were miserable to see. Now they're frightening, because she thrashes her arms and legs, and tries to escape. Larry was always strong enough to hold her. I wasn't.

No screaming. The house was silent. And yet something had woken me. Something was wrong. I could feel it in the air around me. The vibrations of the house had changed. Something had happened.

Downstairs, something clattered.

I got up and ran to Luna's room. She was curled up, her arms round an old bear I hadn't seen in years. I tried Cassie's room next. The door was ajar, and when I peered inside, her bedclothes were pushed back and her bed empty. She wasn't in the bathroom.

A familiar beat was pounding in my head. I was never entirely sure which was worse, Luna's night terrors or Cassie's sleepwalking. Whichever I had to deal with at the time seemed the only sensible answer.

Several times a month, usually when the moon was waxing or full,

Cassie would get up and make her way around the house, intent on something we could never understand. Larry had even hung bells on her door so we'd hear her in the night, but she'd made us take them down when she'd turned sixteen.

I hated her doing it. She would hurt herself one day. She might even go outside, sleepwalk her way down the road, and the thought of that made my blood run cold. I couldn't bring myself to imagine what might happen to Cassie if she were found wandering the streets alone at night.

As my bare feet stepped onto the cold tiles of the downstairs hall, I could no longer ignore the unnatural chill in the air. The house was freezing. The waning moon shone in through the glass in the front door and I stepped into its cold light to soak up its protection. Looking around for a weapon, I saw an umbrella of Larry's near the door.

Just Cassie, I told myself, as I crept along the hall, umbrella in hand. I reached the kitchen door and listened. Nothing. I pushed it open and saw Cassie in the dark room, standing with her back to me. I felt a split second of relief before I saw the man.

Tall, dressed all in black, and with his hands on my daughter.

His head was lowered and I couldn't make out his face. I caught a gleam of eyes as he saw me, and then he turned, almost leaping for the open kitchen door. He was through it before I could reach Cassie. One look into her listless eyes told me she was OK. Fast asleep but unhurt.

Shaking, I closed the back door and locked it. Cassie hadn't moved.

'Come on, Cassie.' I took hold of her shoulders and turned her round. 'Time for bed.'

With my arm about her waist – I was shocked at how cold she felt – we walked along the hallway. As quickly as I could, I steered her up the stairs and into her room.

'Night-night, Mummy,' she murmured, as I pulled the bedclothes over her. She only ever called us Mummy and Daddy when she was asleep. We used to laugh about it. A bolt of pain struck me then, so sudden and so deep it was like being stabbed. Larry and I would never again race to our daughters in the middle of the night, to calm their fears and coax them back to a sweeter sleep. We'd never rush back to our own bed, clinging together for warmth and wondering how two girls so smart and beautiful could be so quirky and strange. From now on, it was up to me.

# 37

## Florence

Sleep didn't come easily, even though Tom's brief, and thankfully undiscovered, visit had left me exhausted. I took a bath, made a Horlicks and read for a while. I woke up to find the hostel silent. It was nearly three in the morning.

I'd been dreaming about Marigold. Or rather, myself in Marigold's place, giving birth in a dark cellar while somewhere in the shadows, Larry, Sally and Tom waited to take my baby away.

Poor Marigold. She was probably awake like I was, because new mothers didn't sleep well. I couldn't imagine how she'd be feeling.

*Tap, tap, tap.*

Someone was knocking on my door. Any other time, it wouldn't have been unusual. The nurses were constantly in and out of each other's rooms, sharing make-up, swapping clothes, offering or begging coffee. Any other time, I'd have thought it was one of my hostel-mates approaching with friendliness in mind. Not at three o'clock in the morning.

I lay in bed, listening, and heard it again. *Tap, tap, tap*. Barely audible above the howling of the wind outside, above the sound of the window rattling in its frame.

'Who is it?'

Getting up, I crept to the door and leaned against it. The wood was cold against my face and I thought perhaps it trembled, as though pressure had been applied from the other side.

'Who's there?' I whispered.

No reply came. But I thought I could hear breathing, as though whoever was outside was mirroring me, leaning against the door at the exact same spot. I turned the key, took a deep breath and pulled open the door. The corridor was empty.

'Hello?' I could hear the wind blowing outside and the creaking of the plumbing. Nothing else. But on the side of my face was a draught, and when I looked towards the fire escape door, it rattled in its frame, making a tapping sound. Letting my own door close softly, I stepped along the corridor to the end. Both bolts on the door were closed. It was still locked.

All over my body, sweat drops burst and turned cold in the chill night air. I'd been warned it would take a long time to get over what had happened to me. This jumpiness, this sense of impending dread was entirely normal.

'Perfectly safe, perfectly safe.' I muttered it like a mantra as I walked back along the dark corridor to my room. My hands and the back of my neck were sticky with sweat and so I turned on the hot tap at the sink before wondering if I'd locked my door. I checked. I had. I washed my hands, turned off the tap and looked up.

Two words – *Help us* – were written in steam on the mirror.

The edge of the sink struck the small of my back as I spun round to face whatever had crept into my room while I'd been out.

No one.

I checked beneath the bed, the desk, behind the curtains, in the narrow wardrobe. I even pulled open drawers, as though my intruder could have folded himself up and concealed himself away in one of them. Nothing.

By this time, I was shaking, and not just with fear. The temperature in the room had fallen. I ran to my bed and climbed in. The sheets felt like ice. The light was still on, but I didn't think I could deal with darkness again that night. And so I lay in bed, staring across the room at the plea for help that someone had written on my mirror.

# 38

## Sally

Shivering, I waited for my call to be answered by the police station. There was a long pause after I'd given my name. I almost suspected the sergeant had left me hanging, but after several seconds, he asked why I was calling.

'Did this intruder break into your property, Mrs Glassbrook?' he asked, when I'd explained.

'No, I don't think so. I think my daughter let him in.'

'So, not a break-in? Mrs Glassbrook, why would your daughter – I think you said she was sixteen – why would she open the door to a strange man in the middle of the night?'

'She was sleepwalking. She does it a lot.'

'She opened the door to him in her sleep?'

I reminded myself that to most people, sleepwalking was the stuff of fairy stories.

'And were there any signs of a break-in? Any doors forced? Any windows broken?'

'He came in through the back door. It was open.'

There was a long, heavy sigh down the line. 'OK, Mrs Glassbrook, I'm going to file a report and have someone come round tomorrow.'

'No.' I was being too loud. 'I need you here now.'

'Has your daughter been hurt?'

'No, I found them in time.'

'Have you locked the back door this time, Mrs Glassbrook?'

'It was locked before.'

'Ah yes, I think you said your daughter opened it. Maybe put the

130

key somewhere out of reach. I have another call coming in now. We'll be in touch tomorrow.'

The line went dead. I went upstairs, checked on the girls again and returned to my own room.

I was so cold. When a house is full of negative energy, caused by its inhabitants being afraid or sad, its temperature can drop. It creates a vicious circle because the cold depresses the occupants even more. Natural flame is the best remedy. I couldn't face lighting fires, but I kept candles in most rooms and there were two on my dressing table.

Between them was a photograph of Larry and me on our wedding day. As the candles began to flicker, their light danced over the image of the two of us. He'd been the handsomest man I'd ever seen back then, even counting singers and film stars. As I'd walked down the aisle towards him, I couldn't believe he was marrying me. I'd fully expected him to shake his head and say, 'No, there's been some mistake. I didn't mean you. I meant another Sally. A beautiful Sally.'

At that moment, I didn't care what he'd done, I didn't care who he'd been unfaithful with, I just wanted him back.

# 39

## Florence

'Well, it was quite a first day back you had, young Florence.' Rushton got to his feet, to signal the meeting was drawing to a close.

'Over half a dozen reporters and a news crew outside the front door,' Woodsmoke announced. 'I said you'd talk to them at nine.'

Rushton looked at his watch. 'Just so you know, I'll be saying that we're delighted to have WPC Lovelady back with us, and that she is one of our brightest and most promising young officers.'

'Not that she looks it this morning.' DI Jack Sharples had caught me stifling a yawn. 'Out on the town, were we?'

'Sir.' I stood up too. 'The duty sergeant said I wasn't to go on the beat for the next few days.'

'Just till the fuss dies down. Jack will find you something to do.'

'Sir, I was wondering if I could go up to Black Moss Manor this morning. They'll need to be told what happened to Marigold McGowan.'

Blank looks from both of them.

'The young woman who gave birth last night in cell one. She was making some pretty wild accusations. On the other hand, she does have a genetic condition that suggests impaired intellect and the possibility of misunderstandings. Either way, it needs follow-up. I should also check on her. She's in Burnley General.'

'I can drive up to Black Moss,' Tom said. 'I've got some time this morning.'

'But I was there when she gave birth,' I said. 'It should be me, shouldn't it?'

'If it keeps you out of trouble,' Sharples said. 'Take one of the panda cars. Can you drive?'

He knew perfectly well that I could drive.

'Thank you, sir.'

'Want me to come with you?' Tom offered.

'I need you here, Tom,' Woodsmoke said, in a voice that brooked no argument.

Black Moss Manor lay at the very edge of town. To get to it, I had to turn off the main road and drive to the top of a road called Laurel Bank. There wasn't a laurel bush in sight, or any sort of greenery. The terraced houses, all small, many of them unkempt, opened directly on to the street. I had to drop into second gear to reach the top, where the cobbles ended and a narrow dirt track began.

The track was dark. Sycamore and beech trees grew to either side, and the gaps in between were filled with glossy green shrubs. Here were the laurel bushes, lining the track all the way up to the building at the top. I rounded a corner and saw it. A big, old, solitary manor house. The stonework was stained with damp and soot, the copper piping tarnished. Moss grew on the slate roof, and several of the tiles lay on the overly long grass border. There were six barred windows on the ground floor, three either side of a red-painted front door. Another six sash windows, slightly smaller, without bars, lay directly above them. A single steep gable rose from the midpoint of the front façade.

Parked to one side of the front door was a black Rover.

I'd been to Black Moss Manor twice before, to escort young children whom the local authority had taken into care. A girl of around six with very poor eyesight and a boy of just three with a club foot, who'd whispered to me that his mummy always called him Robbie. I'd held their tiny, cold hands as we climbed out of the panda car and approached the front door. They'd both been scared, poor things, pulled from the only home they knew. The same woman had met me at the door both times and taken the children from me. I remembered her as being middle-aged, stout and low-voiced with a tight perm. I imagined she was the Mrs J. Aster, who ran the children's home with her husband, Dr F. Aster.

She kept me waiting for several minutes, but I'd given her no warning of my visit. After three minutes, I knocked again, louder.

The door opened suddenly. 'May I help you?'

It was not the woman I'd been expecting. This woman was nearly six feet tall, and an age I found impossible to guess. Her face was unlined, her jawline perfect; her black hair had no sign of grey.

'I'm . . . I'd like to speak to Mrs Aster, please.'

'Concerning?'

'Could you tell Mrs Aster that WPC Lovelady, from the police station in town, would like to speak to her?'

'My name is Aster. What do you want to talk to me about?'

'Mrs J. Aster?'

Something about this woman felt out of place. Her hair was a dense cloud of curls around her head, gathered at the back of her neck. Loose, it would be long and flowing. Her face was lovely, if a little long. Her nose was prominent, but her eyes were huge, dark pools and her brows thick and perfect. Her mouth was perfect too, the lower lip full and deep. She was wearing a colour that looked white in the sunlight, although as she moved into shadow, I could see it was somewhere between cream and beige.

'My given name is Judith,' she said in her low-pitched voice. 'I am known as that, or Dr Aster, not Mrs. Now, I will ask you for the third time why you're here, and if I don't get a sensible answer, I'll wish you good morning.'

'I'm here about Marigold McGowan. Is there somewhere we can talk?'

Dr Aster stepped to one side and gestured that I should precede her in. As the door closed behind me, I had a moment to take in the entrance hall. Sunlight was struggling its way in through two of the barred windows, casting a striped effect on the floor and walls, and creating the illusion of an oversized cage. Directly ahead of me, a wooden staircase led to an upper floor, and to my right was a large, empty fireplace. A wrought-iron chandelier that held candles rather than electric light bulbs hung from a hook in the centre of the ceiling. I was shocked by how cold the room felt. A draught caught the ash in the hearth, blowing it up and spreading it around. It hung in the air, forming strange, swaying shapes.

A bell rang, startling me.

'Come with me,' Dr Aster said, before leading the way to a door that was almost hidden in the panelled walls behind the stairs. The short, silent corridor on the other side carried a smell of boiled meat and the unmistakable aroma of young children. (I'd visited a lot of primary schools in my time in Sabden.) Halfway along, Aster ushered me into an office.

Through a single window, I could see that the building had two wings to its rear. Between them, a rough patch of land passed for a garden. I could see several children outside. One of them had a ball. He tossed it, listlessly, into the air. None of the others seemed to be playing.

'Take a seat.'

I did what I was told.

'A young woman answering to the name of Marigold McGowan gave birth at Sabden Police Station last night,' I began. 'Afterwards, both mother and son were transferred to a local hospital.'

Judith Aster continued to stare at me. This time, I let her do it.

'Thank you,' she said at last. 'Which hospital?'

'I wasn't told, I'm afraid.'

I had no idea why I was lying, only that I was certain this woman knew I was doing so.

'Anything else?' she asked.

I took out my pocketbook. 'Yes,' I said. 'She said she came from this establishment. Is that the case?'

Aster got up and opened a filing cabinet as the bell rang again. It went on for five seconds and then silence fell over the building. Aster took her time looking through the various files, eventually choosing one.

'She was resident here for two weeks.' Aster took her seat again. 'Her contractions started at two o'clock yesterday afternoon. She became quite agitated at one point. It's not uncommon with young girls, especially those of a feeble intellect. The experience of child-birth can be frightening.'

'Do you have an address for her next of kin?'

'She was from Nelson, I think.' Aster opened the file. 'I couldn't give out those details without a court order, though.'

'So, what happened last night?'

'She vanished when the attention of the nurse was drawn away,' Aster said. 'Somehow she managed to leave the building.'

I thought of the barred windows downstairs, the heavy front door. I looked beyond Aster to the stone wall that surrounded the outdoor area.

'She told us she'd been kept prisoner here.'

Aster gave a soft, mirthless laugh. 'Absurd. We have tight security, naturally – we have young children in our care, but the older guests can leave whenever they like. Most of them have nowhere else to go. They may feel like prisoners. It doesn't make them so.'

'She said you were planning to kill both her and her baby.'

Aster held up both hands as though the answer hardly needed voicing. 'The girl must be considered a frightened and fanciful child. We were encouraging her to put the baby up for adoption, although the final decision would have been for her family. Are you sure she didn't say, "Take my baby"?'

Yes, I was sure. 'Did you report her missing?'

'We looked extensively. Every member of staff that could be spared spent the night combing the moors.'

'Did you report her as a vulnerable missing person to the police?'

'I imagine so.' Aster's eyes had dropped to the file. I knew she hadn't. I'd checked.

'You didn't do it personally?'

Her eyes lifted to mine once more. 'I believe I gave the instruction that it should be done. If it wasn't, then I imagine everyone thought someone else was doing it.'

'Have you been in touch with the police this morning?'

She gave me a half-smile; her eyes stayed cold as death. 'It's on my list of jobs. Actually, it was next on my list, and then you knocked on the door.'

'What was higher on the list?'

Her big eyes opened even wider. 'Excuse me?'

'It's twenty minutes past nine. What was more important than finding a mentally handicapped young woman in extreme need of medical attention?'

Aster put her hands on her chair's arms, as though to push herself up. 'Was there anything else, Constable?'

I didn't move. 'Yes. I'd like some background on Marigold Mc-Gowan. Can I take that file with me?'

She pulled it towards herself. 'I'm afraid not. What do you need to know?'

Trying not to show my annoyance, I said, 'Tell me everything you can.'

Aster sighed. 'Marigold is seventeen years old, or claims to be. I suspect she might be younger. She's from Nelson and came to us two weeks ago on the recommendation of the local authority there.'

'Who's the father?'

'Marigold's father.'

'No, I mean, who's the father of Marigold's baby?'

She tilted her head back so that she could look down her long, slim nose. 'I know what you meant. My answer is the same. Marigold was impregnated by her own father.'

'That's horrible.'

Aster's right shoulder twitched in an elegant, disdainful shrug.

'Have you reported that to the police?'

'I have not. I have no idea what Marigold herself has done, or the local authority in Nelson.'

I stood up. 'Thank you for your time,' I said. 'Do you mind if I look round before I go?'

Aster didn't move. 'Yes, I do. Visits upset the children if they haven't been prepared for them.'

'Children are upset by visits?'

'Some of these children are very damaged.'

I walked to the door. 'I'd like to see Marigold's room, please.'

'What on earth for?'

'Marigold made some complaints about Black Moss Manor that we're taking seriously. I can come back with a warrant.'

'Then I suggest you do.'

The door was pulled open and a tall man stood immediately outside. 'Sandra told me we had a visitor. Good morning, Constable.' He held out a hand. 'Frederick Aster. I am the manager here. What can you tell us about poor, dear Marigold? We have been out of our minds with worry.'

He smiled down at me, lifting his eyebrows as though encouraging me to speak.

'She gave birth to a son last night,' I said. 'She's in hospital right now.'

'Which one?'

I was going to have to lie again.

'Burnley, I suppose,' he said. 'I will telephone and check.'

His English seemed perfect, but I didn't think he was a native Englishman. He was good-looking and clean-shaven, with short, very blond hair. He appeared to be in his early forties.

'Your wife was about to show me round,' I said.

'I most certainly—' Judith Aster began.

'I expect you're busy, dear,' Frederick said. 'I'll give the young lady a tour. This way, Constable.'

Another bell rang as I followed Frederick Aster back into the entrance hall and up the stairs. As we climbed, the smell of disinfectant and cooking faded, to be replaced by that of stale clothes and bathrooms.

'We're now on the first floor,' Aster said. 'We don't use the attics. The rooms to the front of the building are the private apartments I share with my wife. I assume you're not going to insist on seeing those?'

He was smiling as he said it.

'Of course not,' I told him.

'Those to the rear are our mother-and-baby rooms.'

There were five doors overlooking the back of the main block. The central door was ajar and through it I could see a very sparse bathroom.

Aster produced a key and unlocked the second door along to reveal a narrow room. The floor was bare linoleum, worn to the underlay in places. A washbasin was fixed into one corner, with a rough wooden shelf above it. There was a single bunk, a narrow armchair, a chest of drawers and a cradle. Marigold's nightdress hung on a hook behind the door. From the window, I could see the high surrounding wall and the vast emptiness of the moor. Even in August it was a bleak sight. All the children had gone from the garden.

'The other rooms are exactly the same,' Aster told me.

'Are there any other expectant mothers here?'

'Not at present.'

'Marigold mentioned a woman called Wendy who'd recently had a baby. Where is she now?'

Aster frowned at me. 'I don't recognise that name, I'm afraid. Are you sure it was Wendy?'

'Yes, quite sure.'

He shook his head. 'We haven't had a birth here in three months. Marigold has only been with us for two weeks. She hasn't seen any other mothers.'

Short of calling him a liar, I had no choice but to let it drop.

'The children's dormitories are in the wings,' he said, 'but I don't suppose you have any interest in those?'

I could think of no reason to see the children's rooms and so, reluctantly, because something about this place didn't feel right, I followed Dr Aster back down the stairs. We were crossing the central hall when a voice hailed us.

'Doctor, can I have a word?'

The woman who'd appeared – Sandra, perhaps – was the one I'd seen previously, who I'd assumed ran the home. Dr Aster crossed the hall to speak to her and I heard a high-pitched voice from somewhere nearby. Without asking, I went back into the rear corridor.

Directly opposite Judith Aster's office was a door. Behind it, I could hear the soft tones of a woman speaking. I put my hand on the handle and pushed.

I'd found the classroom. Roughly two dozen small wooden desks were facing the front of the room, and behind most sat a small child in a grey pullover. For a moment, it was hard to distinguish the sexes. The boys' hair was very short, the girls' pulled back in ponytails. Only one or two looked towards the door. The rest continued to face forward. One appeared to be asleep, her head on the desk. Two were in wheelchairs.

The teacher turned to me. 'Can I help you?'

I'd opened my mouth to say something – I'm not sure what – when a small boy pushed back his chair so hard it clattered to the floor. He was on his feet, racing across the room towards me. His left leg was fastened inside a caliper.

'Robert!' The teacher's voice was loud and cold. 'Get back to your desk.'

The little boy, barely more than a toddler, ignored her, pushing his way past desks until he reached me and wrapped his thin arms round my legs.

'Way, way, way,' he began to yell.

'What is going on in here?'

I heard Judith Aster's voice in the doorway as I bent to lift the little boy. He clung to me like a baby monkey.

'Way, way, way,' he sobbed into my ear.

'Give him to me.' Judith Aster had reached me, the other woman hard on her heels. 'Robert, stop this noise instantly.' She held out her hands.

'What's upsetting him?' I could feel his tears against my face. 'I brought this child here, didn't I? A couple of months ago. This is Robert Brown?' I remembered the skinny, trembling boy, taken into local authority care after his unmarried mother had died giving birth to her second child. The baby had died too.

'What's he frightened of? What's he trying to tell me?'

What did 'Way, way, way' mean?

The matronly woman grabbed hold of Robbie. She must have done something to hurt him because he yelped with pain and released me. She whisked him away in an instant. Several of the other children were crying too by this time, the teacher trying hard to restore order, as Frederick Aster appeared in the doorway.

A sudden crash startled us all. A bookcase at the rear of the room had tumbled over, scattering books across the wooden floor.

'Out,' ordered Judith Aster. 'Now.'

'I think it probably best,' Frederick said, as he put a hand on my shoulder to usher me from the room. Even I could see I was upsetting the children, so I went with them. In the hall, I stopped and turned back to face them both.

'Why was that child so frightened?'

Judith Aster glared. 'You had no right to intrude on the classroom. I told you they were disturbed by visitors.'

'That child wasn't disturbed – he was hysterical. What kind of establishment are you people running?'

'Many of our children were taken from their homes by police officers,' said Frederick, in a more conciliatory tone than his wife. 'They associate your uniform with their worst memories.'

In fairness, that did make sense.

'Some of the children take months to settle in here and feel safe,' the other Dr Aster added. 'The sight of a police uniform would reawaken all their old fears.'

'He ran towards me, not away from me,' I said. Suddenly I knew exactly what 'Way, way, way' meant. Not 'way' but 'away'. He remembered me as the one who'd brought him here, and now he was begging me to take him away.

# 40

## Sally

I was rushed off my feet all morning and it was mid-afternoon before I had a chance to check on Marigold and her baby.

The maternity ward was one of the nicer ones at the hospital, on the second floor, with views over the town and moors. There were always cards pinned to the walls, more flowers than we could find vases for, and children's drawings done by the siblings of newborns. The smells of sickness and death, so common in most hospital wards, were replaced by cosmetics and talcum powder.

I pulled open the door and found Florence Lovelady on the other side, holding a small knitted toy in the shape of a mouse.

'Marigold?' I said.

Florence nodded. 'Is this suitable for babies? I got it in the market. I've no idea, really.'

'It looks fine,' I said, as we walked towards bay four, an open space for six beds at the end of the ward.

We passed the day room. A couple of the mothers sat in easy chairs, babies on their right arms, their left hands holding cigarettes. A few more paces and we came round some screens to see Marigold sitting up in bed, one hand reaching out to the cot by her side, the other clutched to her neck. Judith and Frederick Aster were standing to either side of her bed. The girl looked terrified.

'What are you doing here?' Florence demanded, as we neared the bed. 'Marigold, are these people bothering you?'

Marigold's eyes went from one person to the next as I sneaked a glance at the baby. He was fine. Fast asleep, fists clenched tight, his little chest rising and falling. Marigold, though, was anything but fine. She'd been crying. Her eyes were swollen, her face red and puffy.

'We were on our way out,' Judith announced. She turned back to Marigold and stroked an imaginary lock of hair from her eyes. The girl actually flinched. 'Look after yourself, dear. And baby too, of course. We'll be in touch.'

Florence and I watched the Asters all the way back down the ward and out through the doors. Only when they'd gone did we turn back to Marigold.

Her recent upset aside, she looked a lot better than she had last night. Her hair, no longer damp with sweat, was long and curly, a lovely shade of strawberry blonde, and her pale face was sprinkled with freckles.

'Marigold—' Florence began.

I held up a warning finger. 'How are you, love?' I said to the girl in the bed. 'How's baby? Florence, find us a couple of chairs. We can all have a nice chat.'

While Florence tried to locate two chairs – I knew it would take her a while: there are never enough on the maternity ward – I coaxed Marigold through a few routine questions about feeding, sleeping, her stitches. I felt her tummy and told her everything was exactly as it should be.

'He's a beauty,' I said, as the baby stirred and Florence came back with two chairs.

'He's lovely,' Florence agreed, in a tolerably convincing voice. She held up the knitted blue toy. 'I brought him this.' She put it in the cot.

'I wish he was a girl,' Marigold said. 'Then I could call him Florence or Sally.'

'Well, that's a nice thought,' I said. 'But he's going to get bullied in the playground if you do.'

She smiled at that. 'You two choose,' she said. 'What boys' names do you like?'

'I only had daughters,' I said. 'And sisters.' I was struggling to think of any boys' names other than Larry.

'I have three brothers,' Florence said. 'The eldest is Andrew, after my father, the next Charles, after my mother's father, and the baby is Henry. After nobody.'

'I'll call him Henry,' said Marigold. 'Because he's a baby. After your Henry, not nobody.'

'My Henry will be honoured.' Florence stroked a finger down the baby's head. 'Hello, little Henry.'

'You could call him Harry for short,' I said. 'Or Hal.'

'Or Hen,' Marigold said, as she stroked his tuft of dark hair. 'He looks like a hen.'

Florence took a notebook out of her jacket pocket. 'Marigold, I need to ask you some questions about last night,' she said.

Marigold's eyes dulled. 'Baby Hen's tired now,' she said.

'It won't take long,' Florence promised her. 'But the sergeant on duty and Sally and I heard you say that you'd run away from Black Moss Manor. That they'd been keeping you prisoner.'

'I was con-confused.' Marigold's eyes were fixed on her baby.

'Confused about what?' Florence asked.

'The bars on the windows, and the locks on the doors, and the big, high wall are to stop the children from running away and hurting themselves,' Marigold droned. 'Adult guests can come and go as they please.'

'You didn't seem confused,' Florence said. 'You seemed frightened. You were adamant we didn't tell Black Moss Manor where you were.'

'What's adamant?' Marigold's voice had taken on the sulky tones of a child who knows she's in trouble.

'Marigold, do you remember telling us that someone at Black Moss Manor wanted to kill your baby?' Florence pressed on.

'No, I didn't say that. I said, "take my baby". I was confused. I thought they were going to take my baby. For ad-ad . . .'

'Adoption?' I suggested, with an uneasy look at Florence.

'Yes, for adoption,' Marigold said. 'But only if I agreed. I got confused.'

'Is this what the Asters told you to say?' Florence asked.

Marigold stared back at her.

'What happened to Wendy?' Florence wasn't giving up easily.

Marigold's eyes were fixed on her son's head. 'Don't know any Wendy.'

'We'll let you get some rest now.' I stood up and nodded to Florence to do the same.

'Did she seem frightened to you?' Florence asked, as we walked back along the ward. 'Do you think the Asters put pressure on her?'

I said nothing.

'I went to Black Moss Manor this morning,' she went on. 'Something about it didn't feel right. Sally, did—'

'Florence.' I deliberately raised my voice, startling a dozing mother.

'What?'

'I can't get involved. I delivered her baby safely and I've checked up on her today. The hospital can take it from here. I've problems of my own to deal with and I'm not about to be dragged into yours.'

Florence blushed. 'Of course. I'm sorry.'

We neared the door of the ward.

'How long can she stay here?' Florence asked me.

'A few days. A week at most. Mothers of that age recover from the birth very quickly.'

'And then what?'

I sighed.

'No, you're right,' Florence said. 'I'll make the enquiries.'

We passed the nurses' station. As she pulled the door open for me, Florence said, 'I heard people talking at the station earlier. About what happened at your house last night.'

'Good to know it's being taken seriously,' I said.

'It isn't,' she replied in a low voice.

'What?'

'They're not going to follow it up. They're not even going to make an official report.'

I stopped walking. They were going to do nothing? I had two teenage daughters.

'What did he look like?' Florence asked.

'I couldn't tell. It was dark.'

'Tall?'

'Tallish. About Larry's height. And a similar build. To be honest, when I saw him, my first thought was that it was Larry, that he'd escaped somehow.'

'Larry's age?'

I shook my head. 'No, younger. He scarpered when he saw me.'

Florence said, 'We shouldn't be ignoring you. I can make a fuss when I get back. I'd have done it already, but I wanted to talk to you first.'

'I don't want you to get in trouble,' I said, although what I really meant was that of all the people at Sabden Police Station, Florence Lovelady was the last I wanted to feel obliged to.

'I think I'm expected to get in trouble,' Florence replied. 'It's what I'm becoming known for.'

# 41

## Florence

'No, Tom, listen,' I said. 'A young woman claims she's been held prisoner and threatened, that a friend of hers and her baby died. And then – big surprise – she changes her story when the two people she's most afraid of pay her a visit.'

Tom was making a show of tidying up his desk. Mainly, he was moving things around on it. 'She's a very unreliable witness, Floss,' he said. 'And the Asters are pillars of the community.'

We were in the CID room, the only two people left at the end of the day shift. I'd not been back long and I was tired, hot and hungry.

'Something isn't right at that place. I'm going to talk to Rushton about it.'

He moved a pencil sharpener from one side of the desk to the other. 'Wouldn't if I were you.'

'I spoke to five residents of Laurel Bank on the way back from the hospital,' I said. 'None of them could remember seeing the Black Moss children outside its grounds. Ever.'

'Proves nothing. Doesn't even suggest anything to me.'

'It feels wrong,' I insisted.

We were both silent for a second. I sensed we were both thinking back to the last time something had felt wrong to me.

'There are children and vulnerable young mothers involved,' I said. 'I can't do nothing.'

Tom shrugged his jacket onto his shoulders. 'I didn't say do nothing. I said don't talk to Rushton.'

'I'm not following. He's the superintendent.'

'Exactly, and you're on probation. If you keep running to the boss every time you don't like something, people are going to label you a grass. Talk to your sergeant. If he thinks it's worth following up, he'll pass it up the line for the right people to deal with.'

He was probably right. Except . . .

'What if he doesn't think it's worth following up?'

Tom pushed his chair back under his desk. 'Then it probably isn't.'

'Like the break-in at the Glassbrook house last night? If any other house in Sabden with three females living alone had reported a break-in, we'd have had cars round there straight away. Sally sees a man in her kitchen, pawing her elder daughter, and we don't even follow it up the next day?'

Tom took a deep breath and blew it out through pursed lips. 'I didn't know anything about that. No, don't look at me like that – I didn't.' He walked to the door and held it open for me.

'So, what are you going to do about it?'

He shook his head. 'I can't get involved with that family. Neither can you.'

I said, 'So the idiots are making all the decisions?'

Tom's face looked pained. 'Florence, you have to stop acting like you know better than everyone else.'

The night porter was already on duty when I got back to the nurses' hostel. He had a small, rather dirty, cream envelope in his hand.

'Came for you earlier,' he said. 'I wasn't here. I don't know who left it.'

I glanced down to see my name, misspelled, handwritten.

'Your man's upstairs,' the porter went on, as I tucked the note into my pocket. 'Been here a while.'

My man?

I climbed the stairs with some trepidation. As I turned the corner at the top, I saw the door to my room was open, and that a pair of workmen's boots were sticking out of it. I approached carefully. It was still light. I could hear other women on the floor, even the whistle of the kettle, but—

From inside the room came a clanging as something metal and

heavy was dropped. It was followed by a mumbled curse.

'Dwane?' I said, to the jeans-clad backside just inside my room.

Dwane Ogilvy, the town sexton and master carpenter, someone I considered to be one of my best friends in Sabden, was on his hands and knees. A toolkit lay on the floor and tools were scattered amid a layer of wood shavings.

He didn't look up. 'Hold this,' he snapped.

He meant the door that was hanging on its hinges. He wanted me to hold it in place. I did what I was told while Dwane wriggled out of sight.

'How are you, Dwane?' I managed. The door was heavy.

'Busy.'

I concentrated on keeping the door in place.

'You're reet,' he said, after a few minutes. 'Tha can let go now.'

I let go gingerly. The door stayed where it was.

'Good to see you, Dwane,' I said. 'What are you doing here?'

Dwane pushed himself off the floor and stood up to his full height of four foot five inches. His big, heavy face was glowing pink, and was damp in places. He glowered at me and I wondered if I'd ever seen him smile. I didn't think so.

'Fixing some extra locks on your door,' he said. 'No bugger's getting through that now. It was sticking a bit, so I shaved off t'bottom and rehung it. It's sound.'

I stepped further into the room. The simple, turn-a-key lock had become the sort of fixture you might see on a bank vault. Heavy-duty bolts lay at the top and bottom of the door. I wasn't surprised the door had started to stick. The extra weight would have been a major strain on the hinges.

'I've done window an' all,' Dwane told me.

'Dwane, what are you thinking of? Matron will have a fit.'

He sneered. 'It was her idea. She phoned me mam this morning. About your break-in.'

'There was no break-in.'

I'd said nothing about a break-in. I'd mentioned the writing on my mirror to the hostel's cleaner, in case she could think of how it had happened. She'd been as mystified as me. That was all. I hadn't wanted a fuss.

'I wasn't having you sleeping here without proper locks,' Dwane said. 'Not one more night.'

'Oh, you're back, Florence.'

I looked up to see that Jenny, one of the nurses, had appeared in the corridor. She was carrying a steaming mug in each hand. 'Kettle's just boiled if you want to make yourself a brew.'

'She can have mine,' Dwane said.

'Florence doesn't take sugar,' Jenny said. 'I've put three in yours.' She thrust it in Dwane's direction, forcing him to take it from her. 'You can drink it in my room,' she told him.

Jenny, I realised, was only about three inches taller than Dwane. She was so thin, though, as to look almost fragile beside him.

'Keep your door open,' I said. 'You know how strict Matron is about gentleman callers.'

I'd meant it as a joke, but Jenny's face darkened. 'Well, you'd know,' she said. 'Dwane, are you coming?'

'Got to get back,' he said. 'Mam'll have me tea ready.'

'Are you coming to the Black Dog later on?'

Dwane didn't look at her. 'Always do. What about you, Florence? Fancy a drink? It's ladies' darts match. I'll see you home safe after.'

I honestly didn't enjoy the look of dismay on Jenny's face.

'I said I'd go to Daphne and Avril's house for dinner,' I told him. 'I haven't seen them since I got back.'

'After, then. I'll be there till last orders.'

'I can't go to the Black Dog at the moment. It's where all the reporters will be staying. You and Jenny have a good time, though.'

'We can go somewhere else.'

'Are you done?' came a loud voice from the end of the corridor. We turned to see Matron striding towards us.

'Aye. You're reet,' Dwane told her, as he bent to gather his tools.

'Good. Well, we don't allow gentleman callers,' she told Dwane. 'Off you go, love.'

'See you later, Florence,' Dwane said, as he walked away.

# 42

## Sally

Roy Greenwood wanted to see me. Again. Honestly, what was with the bloke? God knows, he was the last man alive I wanted to spend time with, but for the moment, it didn't look like I had much choice.

He lived with his mother in a big terraced house not far from the funeral parlour. I was fifteen minutes late and would have been later but Mary had pushed me out the door with another of her 'Better get it over with's.

The girls had been playing up. I couldn't blame them, but I was starting to feel like I had no control over my own house. Luna had refused to eat tea, had declared she wasn't going back to school next term, and when Cassie had told her the consequences – a particularly dramatic version of interference by social services, being removed from the family home and sent into foster care – she'd announced it would be preferable to the misery she was suffering right now.

Watching my younger daughter sob, I'd made my decision. And that had given me another reason for answering Roy Greenwood's summons. The only reason. He didn't have any right to summon me and this would be the last time.

He answered the door so quickly he must have been hiding behind it and bent to kiss me on the cheek before I realised what he was up to. He put his hand on my waist as he guided me inside.

'The drawing room,' he said. 'On your right. Mother, Sally is here.' Roy followed me into the large, crowded, old-fashioned room that smelled of lily of the valley and spirits. 'Are there any finishing touches to the supper you need to attend to?'

His mother peered up at me from her armchair by the fire. 'No,' she said. 'Hello, Sally, dear. How are you coping?'

'Let me help you up.' Roy leaned over his mother and lifted her. She swayed as she came upright.

'Steady now,' he said, and a look of pain shot across her face. I realised he was holding her arms very tight, pinching into the flesh.

'Roy.'

His head snapped round as I called his name.

'I've no objection to your mother being here,' I told him. 'I've no secrets from Grace.'

Her eyes darted between us. She was as thin and frail as a dried blade of grass. He would snap her in an instant.

'Ah, but I have,' he said.

I caught another whiff of Grace's sickly perfume as Roy pushed her towards the door. He closed it behind her and turned back to me. A thin lock of hair had fallen over his forehead. He brushed it away and tried to smile at me, but the effort was beyond him. It came out as a sneer. 'Sit down, my dear,' he said.

'You wanted to see me, Roy.' I remained on my feet. 'I haven't got long. I have to get back to the girls.'

He stood not three feet away, staring into my eyes, but all expression had gone from his. They were like Cassie's eyes when she was sleepwalking, except that Cassie's eyes were always beautiful while Roy's eyes looked cold and dead. It went on for so long I half suspected him of having some sort of—

'Roy, are you all right?'

His eyes blinked back to life. 'Of course. I'm waiting for you to sit down.'

I lowered myself onto the very edge of an armchair. He smiled to himself as he took his own seat. 'I've been thinking about our last conversation,' he began.

'So have I,' I said. 'And I'm definitely leaving Sabden. The house can go on the market. I'll consult a solicitor about how much is mine and how much yours, but I can't afford to carry on paying you so much rent, and it's far too big for us anyway.'

'Not possible, I'm afraid, Sally,' he said.

'How is it not possible? I'm not a prisoner.'

'The house can only go on the market if I choose to sell it.'

'That's for a solicitor to decide. But whether we sell the house or not, you can't make us stay in it. I can get a midwifery job anywhere.'

'I've reconsidered the rent,' he said.

'What do you mean?'

'I'm prepared to put it on hold for the foreseeable future. I know things are difficult for you. And I'm going to pay you a dividend out of the business. Say, twenty pounds a week.'

It was less than Larry had earned, but it would be enough, just about, to keep us going. To pay the bills, feed and clothe us, even pay Mary for a few hours.

'Why would you do that?'

'Living here isn't good for my mother's lungs,' Roy said. 'She had a cough all last winter. I've been thinking about moving to somewhere on the edge of town.'

I wasn't sure where this was going, but I knew I didn't like the general direction.

'You have plenty of room now,' he went on. 'And after all, the house is mine.'

'That's not a good idea.'

'If you're worried about proprieties, don't. My mother will make a perfectly respectable chaperone. And in time, who knows?'

I stood up.

'Think about it,' he said. 'I'd have thought you'd be glad of some adult company. In the meantime, I'll bring your dividend round in person. Shall we say on Friday evenings, at seven o'clock?'

I walked to the door and pulled it open. There was a sudden noise down the hallway, but when I looked, there was no one there.

I paused on the doorstep. 'Did you never once suspect, Roy? All those months he was bringing children to the funeral parlour. How could it all go on under your nose?'

Roy stiffened. 'A lot of people might say the same about you, Sally. In fact, they are saying it. They're saying you provided the means to subdue the victims, that you made the effigies. There's talk at the station of charging you as an accomplice. Did you know that?'

He couldn't know that. He was lying.

'I'd be careful not to rock too many boats if I were you, my dear. It wouldn't do for the girls to lose both their parents, now would it?'

# 43

## Florence

It was Daylight Gate when I thanked Avril and Daphne for a lovely evening and said good night. I blew them both a kiss, climbed onto my bike and set off down the hill.

Daylight Gate meant the soft golden glow of a late-summer sunset was fading, the light growing colder and shadows lengthening. Temperatures dropped quickly on the moors and most people closed their doors and windows at Daylight Gate. Superstition was still rife in the place that had produced the Pendle witches and there were some older folk who weren't only shutting out the cold when twilight fell.

At the top of Laurel Bank I chained up my bike, and as the half-moon was rising in the south-eastern sky, took a footpath that led across the moors to the back of Black Moss Manor. I was curious to see the children's home when they didn't know they were being watched. Even without Marigold's wild accusations something about the place felt off.

By the time I'd reached the rear of the manor, it was coming up for nine o'clock in the evening. Sycamore trees, thin and spindly, their leaves spotted with fungus, grew just beyond the wall. After a few minutes, I found one that I could climb. I went up slowly – I hadn't got used to my mutilated left hand – until I was high enough to see over the wall.

Once again, the unnatural quietness of the place struck me. There were no toys at the back of Black Moss Manor. No swings, slides or football posts, no skipping ropes, skittles or balls.

The porch door swung open and children filed out of the building. The one who led the way seemed about twelve years old;

the smallest was little Robbie Brown. In all, I counted eighteen children, and then a woman – the one I'd started to think of as Sandra – followed. The door closed. Sandra blew on a whistle and led the children in a large circle round the rim of the garden. As they reached the rear wall, she raised her arms and began circling them backwards. The children copied her. She switched direction, circling forward instead and again, the children copied.

They were being exercised like zoo animals.

No sooner had the thought occurred to me than Robbie stumbled and fell. In a panic, he tried to push himself to his feet, but Sandra got to him first. I heard the whack of her hand on his bare legs. He started to cry. She raised her hand again. He stopped.

I found myself shaking. Of course, corporal punishment was a common way of disciplining the young. I could report seeing a child slapped and no one at the station would bat an eyelid. It happened. It was the soullessness of what I was witnessing here that bothered me; the robotic behaviour of children sucked dry of joy or fun.

That was what was wrong with the place. The children did not behave like children. They didn't run around, or shout, or fight. They didn't play.

The children walked round a few more times, and then Sandra lined them up along the back wall of the house and a man appeared. Not Frederick Aster.

Sandra and the children stood watching as the man carried a stack of cones past them and laid them on the ground in a straight line. I was reminded of the cycling proficiency test I'd done at school, when we'd had to ride our bikes in and out of cones to prove we'd mastered the art of steering. Except the gaps in this line weren't consistent. Some were over two yards, others less than one.

One child was called forward. The girl, around ten years old, stood staring directly ahead, and I found my heart rate climbing as Sandra tied a cloth round her eyes.

Sandra stepped away and blew her whistle. The girl began to walk forward. She was aiming directly for the first cone. She walked right up to it and stopped about a foot short. Then she sidestepped right and walked forward again. She came close to the next cone, paused, and took two steps left. She began to walk forward again.

The children all watched her intently. The adults didn't take their eyes off the watching children. And the blindfolded girl walked in and out of cones that she couldn't possibly see. When she successfully bypassed the third, I knew the chances of her having memorised the distances were slim. She sidestepped the fourth. This wasn't possible. She had to be able to see.

Her steps became hesitant. Her right foot tapped against the fifth cone. Sandra blew her whistle. The girl stopped, seemed to collect herself and set off again. She missed the sixth cone and was relieved of her blindfold.

Another child, a boy this time, took the girl's place and began the same strange game of negotiating a line of cones without vision. He managed six before knocking one over. A third child, a very young girl, managed only four.

I had no idea how they were doing it. The man was changing the distances with each new child. There simply wasn't time for them to memorise the positions of the cones, and besides, lack of vision is very disorientating. After the fourth child, the whistle blew again to signify the game was over and the children were escorted inside.

# 44

## Sally

I pulled open the shed door and found the crate with my jars and candles. I was shaking as I picked it up.

*It wouldn't do for the girls to lose both their parents.*

How dare Greenwood threaten me? And who would take him seriously anyway?

I stopped just short of the back door. Larry's three victims – Susan, Stephen and Patsy – were all given some sort of drug to knock them out. When they woke up again, they were in coffins, buried deep underground. An unthinkably cruel death.

Larry wasn't a herbalist. Larry didn't work in medicine, with access to all sorts of sedative drugs. It stood to reason the police would be asking themselves how he managed it.

I could have done it. Nothing in the world would have been simpler.

I pictured the detectives standing at my pantry door, looking at the shelves of bottles, jars, tubs and vials. Nettle-top tinctures for skin problems, horsetail tea for urinary tract difficulties, cleavers poultices for the mouth and throat, and dozens more.

'And are all these lotions and potions harmless, Mrs Glassbrook?' the sarcastic man called Sharples would say as he picked up a bottle of wolfsbane cordial. 'If I were to give this to your young lass now and say, "Drink it all down", would that be OK?'

A mouthful of wolfsbane cordial will kill a grown man. Plants can kill and cure, but how could I expect the police to understand that? To them, I would have a pantry full of poison.

I filled a bowl with salt and water that I could pour onto the ground in a wide circle round the house, leaving lit candles at intervals. Casting a protective circle is the first step in most spells. I lit the first candle and moved on.

My initial instinct, on arriving home, had been to run. If the girls had been awake, I'd have done exactly that, I'm sure, but they'd been in their rooms, according to Mary, who'd heard nothing from them for nearly an hour. Dragging them from sleep seemed mean, and besides, running would be like an admission of guilt, even I could see that. And where could we go?

Pouring the salt water as I went, I made my way round the house. As I lit each candle, I visualised the light going up, arching over the roof, meeting the salt trail at the other side. I was casting a protective dome over the house.

'Daughters of the night, hear my prayer.' I lit the last candle. 'Sisters of the moon, give me your blessing.' Inside the house, I would light more candles, draw a pentagram of salt and let my own blood drip onto a flame. Dark magic isn't something I've ever been drawn to, but I would curse anyone who tried to harm my children. Seconds before I left Greenwood's house, I'd reached up and brushed my hand over his shoulder.

'Dust,' I'd lied.

He'd looked pleased, even a little triumphant, thinking I was trying to appease him. He hadn't seen the greasy black hair I'd caught between my fingers.

Behind me, the gravel crunched. I spun round and caught Cassie about to slip into the bushes at one side of the drive. She saw me and stopped.

'What are you up to?' I demanded. 'Mary said you were in bed.'

Her face twisted into a pout. 'Mum, I can't stand being shut up all day. It's driving me mental.'

'You can't go out on your own.'

She came towards me slowly, sulkily. 'I wasn't on my own.'

'Who? Who was with you?'

Her eyes dropped, not before I caught the hint of a smile. 'It doesn't matter.'

'It does. Cassie, there are people who hate us.'

'Just school friends.' She looked past me at the candles. 'Are you doing a protection spell?'

I nodded.

'Can I help?'

Suddenly, I had no energy left to argue, and the spell would fail without energy.

'Go and wake your sister,' I said. 'This will need three of us.'

# 45

## Florence

I was almost back at my bike when I remembered the envelope I'd stuffed into my pocket earlier that evening. It contained a short note, on cheap lined paper, and a business card. The card looked as though it had been handled many times. A cascade of stars covered one third of it; on the rest, an address, the name *Hecate* and a single sentence: *I work during the darkling hours.* The accompanying note said, *I have information about the Larry Glassbrook case.*

The address was in a part of town I hardly knew. It was Four Beat, notorious for violence and prostitution, and there had never been any question of a young female officer being assigned to it. Especially at night.

*I work during the darkling hours.*

Even before I got close, I was becoming uneasy. The dense network of terraced houses that characterised so much of Sabden was thinning. There were houses with windows boarded up, and derelict premises. Dustbins overflowed and unwanted junk had been left to lie in the streets.

I could hear the river gurgling at the bottom of a gully nearby. On its opposite bank lay the town's reservoir, a great expanse of black water. The railway bridge spanned the water and built into the bank beneath it were three small cottages. The street was called Railway Bank, though the street sign had long since vanished.

I walked up to the door of number three and knocked. The door opened.

The woman on the doorstep looked around thirty years old. Her skirt reached all the way to her feet, and her cotton blouse left her shoulders bare. I didn't think I'd ever seen such long hair before. It hung down to the middle of her thighs and was a bright henna red.

'I'm WPC Lovelady,' I said.

'I know,' she told me. 'Blessings. Come this way.'

I followed the woman down a dark hallway to a small, square room at the back of the house, lit only by the fire and a weak lamp. Playing cards at the table was a girl of around fifteen, sufficiently like the woman for me to be sure they were mother and daughter. As I drew closer, I could see the cards had pictures on them: beautiful, colourful pictures of kings and maidens, swords and stars.

'This is Perdita,' her mother said.

'Hello, Perdita. I'm Florence.'

She'd arranged the cards in a circle; a group of three in the centre were hidden from view. Ignoring me, the girl turned one.

'She's scrying,' said her mother. 'The Fool. Interesting.'

'Is that supposed to be me?' I asked.

'The Fool represents new beginnings, optimism and trust in life,' she replied. 'So I'd say yes, you.'

'What was it—'

She held up a hand to hush me as we watched the girl turn the remaining cards. On the second, a skeleton rode a skeletal horse, a huge scythe in its hand. On the third and last, a tower falling down, flames shooting out of its windows.

'Death and the Tower,' Hecate said. 'You have a challenging time ahead.'

'Well, then I'd better get some sleep.' This woman was a time-waster and I'd been a fool to come here. 'Thank you for the entertainment.'

'I didn't ask you here to read the tarot,' she said.

'Why, then?'

She turned to a dresser on the wall. The room was so small that I could have touched anything in it without moving more than a step or two.

'This is you,' she told me, holding out a copy of the *Lancashire Morning Post*. The story was an update on Larry's arrest, and the accompanying photograph one of me, taken during the investigation.

'What about it?'

'Three times I left this paper front page up. Three times I came back into the room to find it open, at this page.'

I looked at the story again, and then at Perdita. 'Well, you don't live alone,' I said.

The woman said, 'Someone is trying to get through to you. From the other side.'

'I don't believe in all that, I'm afraid. And it's very late. Excuse me.'

I stepped towards the door; she remained in my way.

'It won't give up,' she said. 'It came to you, last night.'

Honestly, the nurses' hostel was leakier than a sieve.

'Do you have any idea of the energy needed for spirits to impact upon the physical environment? Making a candle flicker exhausts them. This spirit moved a paper three times and wrote on your mirror. You can't ignore it.'

Oh yes, I could. 'You said you had information about the Glassbrook case. Wasting police time is a chargeable offence.'

She held up the newspaper as though it were all the proof needed.

'You want me to consult the spirit world?' I said. 'I'll be laughed out of the station.'

'Then don't tell them. Ask your friends Avril Cunningham and Daphne Reece. They'll vouch for me.'

I thought about it. 'I'll give you ten minutes. Then I'm leaving.'

She led me back along the hall and, in the front room, switched on a dim lamp. The walls had been painted a deep purple. The curtains were heavy and dark, and the light so poor that the corner of the room sank away into nothing. There was no sofa, no armchairs, just a large circular table round which were six chairs.

'I'm a spiritualist.' Hecate steered me towards the empty hearth. Thick church candles sat in the grate, and above it hung a huge mirror that was covered in a gossamer-thin black veil.

'Look in the mirror,' she told me, as she bent to her knees and I heard the striking of matches.

Through the black gauze I saw my own face looking back at me. The softening effect of the fabric made me look older but was flattering at the same time. The candles that Hecate had lit in the grate sent a flickering light up around my face. It looked a little, only a little, as though I were burning.

'Look deep into the mirror,' she told me. 'Into it, not at it. Try to look beyond your face, to what lies on the other side.'

That made no sense, but I tried to look without focusing.

'Here on the blessed threshold, where spirit and flesh are as one, I call to you, the lost one. I ask that you join me and share your wisdom.'

She was pressing something into my hand.

'Drop the petals onto the flames,' she whispered in my ear. 'They're an offering. Send your energy with them. As much as you can spare.'

In for a penny. I let the petals fall, and as I heard the faint hisses as some of them reached the flames, I thought about the times I'd been at my best, winning a race at school, my graduation day, holding Marigold's newborn son, making love with Tom, and I thought about all those good and positive feelings floating down with the petals.

'I call to you across the black veil,' Hecate continued. 'Across the black mirror, accept our offerings. Come through and make your presence known.'

The flames in the mirror danced in response. For a split second, my reflected face took on an expression of terrible pain as the orange glow of the flames spread around it. Then Hecate began to speak.

'Oh, it hurts. No one said it would hurt like this.'

The voice coming out of her mouth could not have been more different to her own. Startled, I turned, but her eyes had left mine and were fixed upwards on the ceiling. 'Can't you do something? Please, it hurts too much.'

The voice was high and light, the voice of a much younger woman. Or a child.

I took a step away and felt the candle flames hot against my legs. I moved again, stepping round the table, half expecting her to stop me, but she seemed oblivious to me now. She started speaking again.

'I can't do it. It hurts too much. Please, just help me.'

*She's faking it*, I told myself. *She's an actress.*

A high-pitched wail came out of her mouth next. She was a good actress. The new voice sounded completely different.

'Who are you?' I said, hardly expecting an answer.

Hecate's head turned to me, and in the dim light, her eyes looked entirely black. 'You know who I am.' She laughed, and I was on the point of checking the window to see if I could escape that way. 'I'm Wendy.'

Oh, this was preposterous. Someone had told her about Marigold's traumatic delivery at the station, about her claims that someone called Wendy had died. Someone at the station, no doubt, one of my so-called colleagues. It wasn't the first time I'd been the subject of a twisted practical joke.

Hecate threw her head back and moaned again. 'I can't. Please help me. Please do something.'

A scream burst out of her, so loud, so desperate I lost my cool.

'Stop it,' I ordered. 'This is ridiculous.'

Her mouth opened again and I braced myself for another scream. What came out of her mouth was far, far worse. She made the high shrill sound of a newborn baby yelling.

'Stop it!' I was screaming at her. I couldn't help it. It was completely unnerving.

Hecate shuddered, as though waking from a deep sleep. 'What happened?' she asked.

As if she didn't know.

'Get out of my way now, or I'll arrest you for wasting police time.' I pushed past her and pulled open the door.

'Florence!'

I turned in the doorway, still furious.

'Don't leave in anger – you'll take the spirit with you.'

I left the house and cycled my way home. I cycled fast. I looked back often.

# 46

## Sally

The protection spell should have made me feel better. It didn't. Roy had terrified me. It was barely a month since Larry's arrest. The police would still be going over everything, asking themselves how he did it, why he did it. If there were questions he couldn't answer, they'd look to someone else. To me.

I thought of Cassie and Luna without me, of what would happen to them. My mum's sister lived in Scotland, but I hardly knew her. I couldn't rely on her to take them in. They would be orphans in all but name, and I'd seen enough young women brought up in care to know it would destroy my bright, sensitive, quirky daughters.

After the girls had gone to bed, I stood for a long time in my pantry, looking at the shelves stacked high with herbal remedies, wondering if I should destroy them. Pour everything down the sink and break each glass bottle into smithereens. It wouldn't work, though. Too many people knew about my pantry. Destroying its contents would make me look more guilty, not less.

# 47

## Florence

Wednesday, 6 August 1969

I cycled into work next morning, arriving an hour early for my shift and heading for the basement, where the station's archives were kept. Fortunately for me, the filing clerk, a woman called Kath, who would arrive at nine o'clock, was both efficient and organised. Her desk immediately inside the door had an index book and I quickly found the entry for Black Moss Manor.

There was only one file, all but empty. Two of the reports were single-sided sheets that I'd written myself, giving the briefest details of my handing over a young child to the home. One of them detailed three-year-old Robert Brown. There were several other reports written by my colleagues, all along the same lines.

I went back further and found a cutting from the local paper. It was a photograph story, dated 9 February 1958, showing a line of six men, one in uniform, facing the camera. The caption told me that he was Superintendent Harold Devine of Sabden Police Station, Rushton's predecessor. According to the copy, the proceeds of a police fundraising dinner were being donated to the Black Moss Manor Children's Home. The other men pictured were trustees of the home. On Devine's immediate left was Roy Greenwood, Larry's former partner in the funeral business; next to him was a man called Earnshaw, who was chairman of the town council, and then a W. H. D. Booth, a local solicitor. Next to Booth stood a man called Chadwick, wearing a chain of office, then a man called Frost, the owner and editor of the *Lancashire Morning Post*. Frederick Aster was last in line.

Hold on a second. Harold Devine? I looked more closely at

the tall, dark-haired man in his mid-forties. I looked at the shape of his head, the line of his jaw, the long, straight nose. I looked at what Tom would become in twenty years and thought, *Why didn't he tell me?*

'Florence Lovelady, as I live and breathe.'

I leaped in fright. I'd been so engrossed in my search I hadn't noticed the door opening.

'Glad I've found you.' Tom closed the door and locked it. 'I've come to listen to your apology.' He took the file from my hand and pulled me to him. 'You were in a dreadful mood last night.'

His hand went to the back of my head as he leaned down and kissed me. I didn't even try to stop him; Tom could make me melt with longing. He wasn't wearing his jacket and I loved the feel of his warm shirt beneath my hands. He smelled of Aramis, and his first cigarette of the day, and I couldn't get enough of him.

'Apology accepted.' He grinned as he broke away. I thought back to the photograph of his father and didn't know what to say.

'How did you know I was down here?' I said, instead.

'Desk sergeant told me. What're you up to?'

'I've been looking for stuff about Black Moss. It's a weird place, Tom.'

A weird place that he might know a lot more about than he'd let on. Watching him carefully, I told him about my stake-out of the night before.

He pulled a face. 'You were in a tree?'

Harold Devine wasn't a trustee of Black Moss though, just the man handing over a charitable donation. It might mean nothing. 'How do you think the kids did that thing with the cones?' I asked.

'Seriously, a tree?'

'Even before that, it was odd. Those children were like robots. They looked drugged.'

He frowned. 'Maybe they were tired.'

'No, it was more than that. I think I should say something.'

'So, you're going to go to your sergeant this morning and explain that you carried out an unofficial night-time stake-out of a respected local establishment and that it involved climbing trees? How's that going to go down?'

I knew exactly how it would go down.

'Why didn't you tell me your dad was the police superintendent here before Rushton?'

His surprise lasted only a second or two. 'You never asked.'

'Well, I wouldn't, would I? Pleased to meet you, Tom, and tell me, did you get your job on merit or through nepotism?'

'Oi! Dad retired years before I joined. I earned my place here, same as you.'

'Sorry. I was just surprised. Is he the reason you joined up?'

Tom smiled. 'Only thing I ever wanted to do.'

I smiled back. I couldn't help it. 'What should I do about Black Moss Manor?' I asked.

'Nothing.'

I opened my mouth. He held up a finger. 'For now. Let me think about it.'

# 48

## Sally

I left the girls in bed the next morning, the sound of their breathing reassuring me that both were still asleep. God knows I envied them another hour of avoiding reality. I wasn't nearly so lucky. I had a mother-and-baby clinic in St Joseph's Church Hall. Chaos from the moment the doors opened.

An hour later, the chaos was in full swing and I might as well not have been there for all the contribution I was making. Not a single mother had joined the queue for my weighing station. Lines waiting for the other midwives were over a dozen deep and still no one moved over to see me. After another half-hour, I was told to go into the back room and check the stock cupboards.

We were halfway through the morning when the impossible happened. Silence fell over the hall. Even some of the babies seemed to quieten down. I walked to the doorway and saw Roy Greenwood, in full funeral garb, walking down the centre of the hall towards me.

'Sally,' he said, as every single person in the room, even the bloody babies, I swear, watched us. 'Might I have a word?'

'I'm working.' The last thing I wanted was to leave the hall with Roy Greenwood. I had a feeling I wouldn't come back in. The police might be outside, waiting to arrest me, sending Roy in to make sure I came quietly.

The supervisor was in earshot. I waited for her to say that Sally couldn't be spared from her clinic duties, that he would have to come back later. She said nothing, just watched, a blank look on her face, as though I had nothing to do with her at all.

They all kept their silence as I followed Roy out of the hall, those women who I'd spent nearly twenty years helping. I'd held their hands and wiped their brows at the most painful, most frightening times of their lives and not one of them so much as gave me a friendly smile. Some of them even seemed to be enjoying the sight of me being led from the room.

In the daylight, Roy looked ill. He was pale even for him, and his skin had an odd, glassy look to it.

'What can I do for you, Roy?' I said.

'I was speaking to someone at the police station,' he said. 'They told me about your break-in.'

'Shouldn't that be confidential?'

When he leaned towards me, it was all I could do not to step back. 'Sally, I'm deeply concerned. Was anything taken? Did you get a look at him? Are there locks broken?'

'No to all three,' I said. 'And if you want to help, you can persuade your contacts at the station to take me seriously when I phone them in the middle of the night.'

The day wasn't warm, but beads of sweat had broken out on Roy's temples. 'That's why I'm here,' he said. 'I've spoken to my solicitor, Mr Booth of W. H. D. Booth and Partners. He's kindly agreed to represent you as a favour to me. He can have papers ready to sign this evening.'

'Thank you,' I said. 'Can I think about it?'

His dark eyebrows drew closer together. 'What is there to think about? You said yourself you were going to consult a solicitor about your situation.'

I had said that. I'd meant a solicitor who would take my side. Not one who was on Roy's.

'I'm making it easy for you,' Roy said.

'I need a few hours.'

He gave a heavy sigh of impatience and took a handkerchief from his pocket. 'I didn't want to mention this, I really didn't,' he said, as he mopped his brow, 'but I had a visit from the bailiff this morning.

In the parlour, of all places. I was in conference with the recently bereaved.'

'What has that to do with me?'

'It's not me who's in debt, Sally. It's Larry.'

'What?'

He shook his head. 'Ladies can be shockingly ignorant about what's going on under their noses.'

'How much?'

He held up a hand. 'A few hundred pounds. William – Mr Booth, I should say – will take care of it for now, but this proves what I've been saying, Sally. You need some proper advice.'

I wanted to tell him to go to hell. But he claimed to own my house. And he'd offered me money. In the short term, at least, I might need it. And there were debts, too? God, when would it end?

'I need to think about it,' I insisted. 'I'll call you tonight. I'll let you know then.'

He sighed. 'Very well, Sally, and I hope you'll do the sensible thing. But there is no substitute for some proper protection at home. I do think Mother and I should move in, just until the fuss dies down.'

He was lying. Once he moved in, I'd never get him out again.

'Remember what I told you last night, my dear? A respectable presence in the house will help to calm wagging tongues. I don't like some of the things I'm hearing around town, I really don't.'

Still lying. Please let him be lying.

'Well, I suppose I'd better let you get back,' he said. 'Have a good morning, my dear.'

# 49

## Florence

By my third day back, the only lingering reporters were from the local papers and I was cleared to go back on the beat. Together with PC Colin West, who'd never liked me and saw no reason to change his opinion that morning, I walked the various points on Two Beat, saw several groups of mothers and babies across zebra crossings and persuaded a lonely old lady that she couldn't spend her entire day in the doctor's surgery chatting to the patients because the men attending the urology clinic really weren't in the mood.

I looked for Tom during my refreshment break, but there was no sign of him. With fifteen minutes to spare before I was back on the beat, the station officer appeared in the canteen doorway and called me over.

'Woman in reception, Flossie,' he said. 'Says you left something round at hers last night.' Tight-lipped, he handed over a card and I glanced down to see *Hecate* and the cascade of stars.

'I don't want it,' the constable on the desk was saying, as I entered reception. 'Take it home with you.'

'Peace and blessings,' Hecate replied, trying to push something his way. She was dressed as she had been the previous night, if anything a little more crumpled.

'I'll have you for littering,' the constable threatened.

I picked up the bundle of dried plants from the desk. 'Come with me,' I said, as I made for the door. 'I'll walk you to the bus stop.'

The door slammed behind us. I didn't speak. I was too annoyed with her.

'They disturbed your sleep, didn't they?' She was struggling to keep up, her flimsy sandals no match for my sensible shoes.

I had slept badly, with weird dreams about childbirth and scary, zombie-like children, but I wasn't about to admit that to her.

'What do you want, Hecate?'

'They can reach us more easily when we sleep. The door between our world and theirs is open then.'

'I don't believe in contacting the dead,' I told her. 'And if you come to the station again without good reason, we'll charge you with wasting police time.'

'Perdita did another reading after you left.'

'Oh, for heaven's sake.'

She caught my shoulder. 'You have a gift, Florence. I've never known contact be made as easily as it was last night. This is important.'

I glared at her hand on my shoulder. She removed it. We both stopped walking.

'OK, tell me about the reading. What did the cards say this time?'

'She drew the Moon, Justice and the Page of Cups. A very significant combination.'

I looked at my watch.

'We think there are people – very young, vulnerable people – children probably, who need your help.'

I was on the point of turning to go back to the station. And yet . . .

'Where are these children?' I asked, because something had occurred to me. Police informants come in all shapes and sizes.

She shook her head. 'I thought perhaps you might know.'

It was too much of a coincidence, surely, that the morning after I'd started asking questions about Black Moss Manor, someone wanted to talk to me about children in danger.

I lowered my voice when I spoke next. 'If you want to talk to me, in confidence, I can make that happen. If you don't want to make a statement, I understand. But I need something more than vague messages about the spirit world.'

Hecate glanced around, increasing my suspicion that she wanted to tell me something and was afraid to voice it outright.

'Perdita had a thought,' she said. 'Something she thought the cards were trying to tell her.'

OK, if we were going to do it through the medium of tarot cards and seances. 'And what was that?' I honestly tried hard to keep the cynicism from my voice.

'Poison,' she whispered at me. 'She thinks they're being poisoned.'

'Right,' I said.

I had no idea whether I was falling for a nonsensical scam or being given a useful tip-off.

'They'll come again,' Hecate said. 'Now that they've found you.'

Maybe it was lack of sleep that made me see a shadow dart in the corner of my eye.

'I need to get back now,' I said. 'Thank you for your cooperation.'

'You know where to find me,' she replied, as I backed away. 'They won't leave you now.'

I turned.

'Look to the mirrors,' she called after me.

Damn it. I could not let that woman scare me.

# 50

## Sally

When we got back to the maternity home, I asked to use the phone. The supervisor wouldn't agree until I told her I needed to find a solicitor, and only then on condition I paid for the calls. Mainly, I think, she was hoping for more gossip.

I sat on the other side of her desk, under her watchful eye, because she refused to leave the room, and made seven calls to firms of solicitors. After the first two in Sabden turned me down, I moved on to firms in Burnley. It made no difference. Everyone in the North-West had heard of Larry Glassbrook; no one wanted to have anything to do with his wife. After the seventh refusal, I couldn't stand it any longer.

'Have another think about what I said to you on Monday, Sally,' my supervisor said, as I was on the point of leaving. 'A bit of time off might be in everybody's interests.'

I left the building and walked to the edge of the railway line. It was fenced off, and I couldn't climb the bank, but I could see the wild flowers that grew along it, reminding me that the whole world hadn't quite turned ugly yet.

I had a rule when I was feeling down – I looked up. Blue sky, white clouds, strong trees, can all lift the spirits. That morning, I could see the swaying purple columns of the sweet bay willowherb and smell the buddleia flowers on a nearby tree. The blossoms were already going brown, though, reminding me of how my life seemed to be turning rotten.

A month ago, I had value, and purpose. People welcomed me, relied upon me. Now, I couldn't move around town without being whispered about, shouted at or even spat at. I was jostled in crowds, more than one colleague had refused to work with me, and it was all done with an undisguised glee.

It was more than that, though.

In the last week alone, the number of women, children and elderly people appearing at the clinics with cuts and bruises had more than doubled. Each night saw trouble in the town centre, fights and vandalism. A tramp had died beneath the railway arches and his body had been left abandoned for days.

Something in the town had slipped. A veneer of civilisation had been rubbed away. It was as though with the unmasking of the killer – Larry – something dreadful had been unleashed.

I wasn't looking up anymore. Impossible with such thoughts. My eyes were on my feet and on the small yellow flowers I was crushing. Marigolds, like little yellow stars in a sky of emerald-green leaves. I felt a stab of guilt that I hadn't thought of Marigold in over a day. And yet, young and alone, with a baby to take care of and no means of earning a living, she was in a worse position than me.

No, I could not afford to feel sorry for Marigold. I needed all my energy, all my time to look after the girls and myself.

And yet who else was watching out for Marigold?

I would go and see her, I decided. On my way home from work. I could do that, at least. I'd try to get her to talk, to tell me about her family, and see if there was any chance of her making up with them.

Maybe, if I could help Marigold, I'd feel a bit better about myself.

# 51

## Florence

My shift ended and I was back in the basement, this time looking for cases of poisoning. Luckily for me, Kath, who'd left half an hour ago, had cross-referenced every file. Finding 'poisoning' on her index had given me several leads to follow.

I found the 1954 case of a young man who lived in the nearby village of Barley. Of limited intelligence and 'unpleasant personal habits', the boy was poisoned by his stepmother with arsenic. Another occurred in 1961, when a woman sent a pudding laced with hemlock leaves to her supposed friend but, in reality, love rival. The children delivering the pudding had tasted it, found it bitter and reported her to the police. Tests carried out on a dog saw the animal dead within hours.

Not all the cases I found were as dramatic, but every year, it seemed, people reported to the casualty unit with symptoms of poisoning. Most cases, after a brief investigation, turned out to be accidental. The berries of bittersweet and black bryony, for instance, looked a lot like redcurrants and had fooled more than one hungry child. The berries on St John's Wort were easily mistaken for bilberries. One old lady, who'd gathered mushrooms all her life, paid the price for identifying one incorrectly.

For a while, I assumed the last index entry was a mistake and I ignored it until I'd been through the other files. I'd found no mention of Black Moss Manor, of poisonings of children in local authority care, anything that might help me. I'd been at it an hour and was on the point of giving up when I looked at the last entry again.

*Godfrey's Cordial.*

Sighing, I found the file, but as I carried it back to the desk, I knew it hadn't been filed in error. Stapled to the front cover was a newspaper advertisement for a liquid remedy for sleeplessness in infants and newborns. The illustration showed a tall, stoppered glass bottle filled with a dark liquid. The copy promised hours of unbroken sleep for desperate parents.

I opened it, to find a medical report on the inside front cover listing the ingredients of Godfrey's Cordial. Mainly, it seemed to be a mixture of alcohol, caraway seeds, spices, treacle and opium.

The report went on to say that during the nineteenth century, one of the major causes of infant mortality was the widespread practice of giving children narcotics, especially opium, to send them to sleep. Laudanum, in particular, was cheap and its sale totally unprohibited. Godfrey's Cordial and similar remedies were widely available from chemists.

The sheer number of infant deaths attributed to Godfrey's Cordial, or similar, was shocking. Chemists in the last century were completely unregulated, so batches were often made too strong. Babies and young children overdosed. Or they starved to death, the drug making them disinclined to feed.

Godfrey's Cordial and all its imitators had been illegal for decades, but I figured it wouldn't be hard for someone with a bit of medical knowledge to knock up something similar. It would explain what I'd seen, without doubt. The listless, apathetic state of the children, the unusual silence in the home.

Hecate knew something. I was sure of that now. She'd tipped me off deliberately. She had a connection up at the children's home, and if I knew who that was, it might be my way in.

# 52

## Sally

After visiting Marigold, who seemed fine for the twenty minutes I sat with her, I got home not long after four thirty, to be greeted by the sound of the girls screaming at each other. Cassie was white, large-eyed and trembling. Luna's face, on the other hand, was red and swollen. Tears had streaked the make-up she wasn't supposed to wear, and her hair had come loose of its band and hung around her face like a mermaid's.

'What on earth is going on?'

Luna sank into a chair, let her head fall onto her arms on the tabletop and burst into loud, sobbing tears.

'Ridiculous fuss,' sneered Cassie.

'Luna,' I said. 'Talk to me.'

Luna sobbed harder.

'What's upsetting your sister?' With Luna refusing to be calm, I had no choice but to talk to Cassie. As I'd expected, Luna's sobs subsided a little to allow her to hear her sister's answer.

'John dumped her,' Cassie said. 'Although, they were never really going out in the first place. They were just friends. The rest was in Luna's imagination.'

Luna's sobs increased in volume.

'Well, you might have a bit more sympathy.' I put my hand on Luna's shoulder. 'Love, he probably just needs some time. People are saying very unpleasant things about us. He'll come round. I know he likes you.'

Cassie gave a snort. Then we were all three of us startled by the sound of the doorbell.

'I'll get it.' Cassie set off for the door.

'Stay where you are,' I told her. I was afraid it might be reporters or the police. I hadn't yet told either of the girls about our night-time intruder.

It was neither. As I opened the inner door, I saw two female figures on our doorstep. The older, fatter one was Daphne Reece, the town librarian, and the taller, younger one her lesbian partner, Avril Cunningham.

'Sally, hello.' Daphne spoke first. 'How are you, dear? We brought you a casserole.' She held a huge pot in her hands.

'We had Florence round for dinner last night,' Avril said. 'She told us about your intruder, and how the police aren't taking you seriously. We came to see if we can help.'

'And to make sure you and the girls are eating,' Daphne said.

I was on the point of telling them I didn't need help – none that they could give me, anyway – when I realised that Luna might rein in the dramatics if we had guests.

'Come in,' I said. 'It's very kind of you.'

They followed me into the kitchen to find the girls had gone. Daphne put the casserole on the worktop and sat down at the table.

'She likes to make herself at home,' Avril said. 'Be grateful she's not putting the kettle on. Sally, I want you to appoint me as your solicitor.'

Alarm shot through me as I remembered Roy's veiled threats. Was it happening, then? Was I going to be charged as Larry's accomplice?

Daphne said, 'You need someone to make those idiots at the police station take notice when you lodge a complaint.'

'I can also be Larry's solicitor,' Avril added. 'Strictly, I'm not a criminal lawyer, but I'd appoint a barrister to represent him in court. Larry may have broken the law, but he's still entitled to justice.'

'You need someone on your side,' Daphne said. 'And Avril won't charge you.'

'Why would you do that?' I asked. These women and I had never been friends. I barely knew them.

'Well, contrary to popular belief, some solicitors care more about justice than profit,' Avril said.

'Thank you,' I said. 'I accept.'

They looked surprised, as though they hadn't expected me to agree so quickly.

'Sally, are you still practising?' Daphne asked me, as I led them back to the front door.

'What do you mean?' I said, although I knew exactly what she meant.

'We want you to join us,' Avril said. 'It's not a condition. I'm your solicitor now whatever you decide, but we could use a woman of your skills.'

They wanted me to join their coven. These two ran one of the longest-established covens of witches in the county. They'd approached me before, but I'd known Larry would hate it, and I work better alone.

'Come by later in the week,' Avril said. 'I'll have the papers ready for you to sign. And do have a think about what we asked you. About joining us.'

'We don't just want you – we need you,' Daphne said. 'There are dark powers amassing in town and I don't mind telling you . . . we're scared.'

# 53

## Florence

I'd barely put the phone down on my father when it rang again.

'Sabden Nurses' Hostel.'

'Hiya, sexy,' said a voice I knew well. Tom.

'Hope you're not still at work,' I grumbled. *Or at home*, I thought. I hated to think of Tom at home, with his wife, a world I couldn't enter.

'Get your glad rags on. I'm coming to pick you up.'

Be still, beating heart. 'Not a good idea.'

'Not a date. I'm taking you to meet Dad.'

'You want me to meet your father?'

'Again, not a date, Floss. Do you want to find out more about Black Moss Manor or not?'

'I was going to see Marigold, actually.' I'd already made sure of visiting times. I wanted to check on her, of course, but I also wanted to have another go at getting her to talk. And I was bracing myself for a second visit to Hecate's house, see if I couldn't bully her into giving me some information I could use.

'Can't you do that tomorrow?' Tom pleaded.

Of course I could. I told him I'd be ten minutes and ran upstairs to comb my hair and put on my best dress. It was peach, one of the few warm colours that didn't scream at my hair, and with a white Peter Pan collar. Two minutes before I left my room, hating myself for being so gullible, I let the hot tap run in my sink. The mirror misted up. I thought perhaps I could see the faintest trace of the writing, but even in my agitated state, I knew it wasn't fresh.

*Look to the mirrors.* I could not let the woman get to me.

Tom wolf-whistled as I walked towards the car and I couldn't help feeling pleased that for once, he could see me at my best. I wore the police uniform proudly, but it was a long way from flattering.

'Not a date,' I reminded him. We drove out of town, and after a mile or so, left the main road to follow a single-track lane that climbed the moor.

'You want to stay away from that old prossie down at Railway Bank.' Tom dropped the car into second gear to climb the hill. 'She's a known troublemaker, and that's a rank part of town for a young woman on her own.'

'She's a spiritualist and a medium, not a prostitute.'

'She's a good medium, I'll give her that,' Tom replied. 'Mum uses her. But contacting spirits doesn't bring in enough to pay the rent. She makes it up in other ways.'

'What do you mean, your mum uses her?'

'Dad always drives her down and waits outside. No bugger'll mess with him.'

'I'm learning a lot about you today,' I said. 'I think she might be connected to Black Moss Manor. Maybe know one of the staff members.'

'Don't worry about the monkeys, Floss. I'm bringing you to the organ grinder.'

I wasn't sure how to respond to that, and didn't have much time anyway, because Tom had turned off the road into a private drive. At the end of it was a stone manor house that looked old, maybe even Elizabethan. It was modest in size, but beautifully elegant, the way houses of that period often are, with two wings to either side of a recessed main building and a large wrought-iron portico stretching from one wing to the other. We passed a sign saying *Beldam House*.

'Home sweet home?' I asked, thinking maybe Tom's parents rented a cottage on the estate.

'It's not much, but it suits us.' Tom had a smirk at the corner of his mouth as he slowed the car over the rough gravel. He wasn't kidding.

'You grew up here?'

He laughed. 'Nah. I grew up in a three-bedroomed police house up Earnsdale Road. Mum was left some money about five years ago. Dad had always wanted to farm, so they bought this place. It was the land he wanted, not the house, but I think he quite likes playing lord of the manor.'

We pulled up in front of the house beside two cars already parked: a Daimler and an Aston Martin.

'And you accuse me of being posh.'

'Having money doesn't make you posh, Floss.'

I couldn't argue with that. We got out of the car and went inside.

The house might once have belonged to landed gentry, but the Devines' more modest roots were obvious from the modern furniture in the interior. A huge old stone fireplace had been bricked up and replaced with an electric fire, a radiogram against the far wall was playing a Perry Como track, and in the corner was a shiny, gold-lacquered bar with drinks optics on the wall behind.

'We're in the lounge,' a deep voice called, and I followed Tom into a room where four people sat playing cards in front of a mullioned window. The three men stood up; the woman put a cigarette to her lips and looked me up and down. Tom and his father shook hands and then he introduced me.

Harry Devine was taller and broader than his son, and less handsome. Tom's looks came from his mother, Mary Devine, a thin, dark-haired woman in her forties who wore a floral-patterned dress and cherry-red lipstick. After shaking hands with me, Harry introduced me to Alderman Ernest Chadwick, a portly man in his early seventies. He clutched a glass of whisky in one large, purple hand and squeezed mine with the other.

'Pleasure, lass,' he said. 'Heard a lot about you.'

'And this is Albert Frost – Bertie to his mates – who runs the *Lancashire Morning Post*,' Harry said, as I shook hands with the fourth member of the party. Frost was very thin, with thick white hair and pale blue eyes.

I knew these two names. I'd seen their faces in an old newspaper story. Chadwick and Frost were trustees of Black Moss Manor.

'What'll you have to drink, Florence?' Harry said. 'Tom, sort her out, will you? Come and sit down, lass.'

We sat round another cold electric fire as Tom vanished.

'How you doing, love?' Harry asked me. 'How're you getting on?'

I followed his gaze to my bandaged left hand. Earlier that evening, Jenny had changed the bandage for me and it was spotless. I didn't like talking about my injury, about what I'd been through, but I wanted information from these people and sharing it myself might be a good start.

'I have phantom pain,' I said. 'It's the strangest thing, but I can still feel the missing finger. It throbs and stings and itches. I'm told it'll get better in time.'

'You hear that a lot about amputated limbs,' Alderman Chadwick said. 'Men I served with lost arms, legs, what have you. Still feel 'em hurting, years after.'

'Must we?' Mary's thin, arched brows drew closer together.

Tom was back carrying two drinks. 'I couldn't find the Babycham,' he said. 'Will gin do?'

I smiled at him, remembering the first – and last – time I'd drunk Babycham. The night Tom and I got together. When I looked away, I caught Mary watching me.

'Tom says you're worried about Black Moss Manor,' Harry said, with the air of a man who wouldn't tiptoe around a subject. 'So I asked these two up.'

'Can't they find you a nice job in an office somewhere?' Mary said. 'What about at Burnley or Blackburn? There must be roles more suitable for young women in the bigger stations. The superintendents all have secretaries, don't they?'

'I can't type, I'm afraid, Mrs Devine,' I said.

'Florence went to university, not secretarial school,' Tom added.

'What did you study?' Frost asked.

'Law,' I told him, wondering how I'd get the conversation back to Black Moss Manor.

'You could be a solicitor,' Mary said. 'You do hear about women doing that these days. And there's that Cunningham woman in town. Mind you, she is . . . well, you know.'

'Florence is going to be chief constable,' Tom said. 'If I don't get there first.'

They all smiled at that, apart from his mother.

'I am worried about Black Moss Manor,' I said. 'The children there—'

'Bet you were the only woman on the course,' Chadwick interrupted. 'I'm surprised you didn't land yourself a fella.'

Tom sucked an ice cube into his mouth and pushed it to one side of his cheek.

'Men don't want to come home to a bluestocking,' Mary said. 'Men want a bit of femininity.'

'Nice dress, Mum,' Tom said. 'Did I mention?'

She tapped the ash of her cigarette into a heavy crystal ashtray. 'No.'

'I've been doing school-crossing patrol just about every day since I joined the force,' I said. 'I know how young children behave. They're always chasing and play-fighting and squabbling and touching each other. They're brimming with energy and their skin glows like . . . I don't know, like apple skin. The children at Black Moss Manor couldn't be more different.'

'Very poetic,' Tom said.

'What?'

'Skin glowing like apple skin. Poetic. Just saying.'

'The children at Black Moss are listless and apathetic. They look drugged. But they're fearful as well. And the punishments seem unusually harsh.'

I thought back to what I'd found earlier about Godfrey's Cordial. Was that an accusation too far for the moment? Chadwick cleared his throat.

'They are problem kids,' he said. 'I'm not going to mince words. They probably need to be on some sort of medication. But Black Moss is a leading facility of its kind. Papers have been written about the work being done there.'

'And a lot of those children would face life in huge, faceless institutions if they didn't have the manor,' added Frost.

'True, I've always been very impressed with the place,' Harry said.

I told them about what I'd witnessed in the garden, the way blindfolded children had made their way round cones.

'I've seen that game.' Frost visibly relaxed. 'Not a game as such, a sort of test of spatial awareness. It's not the kid with the blindfold that's being tested, although it might look that way. It's one of the others watching. He or she will be giving instructions to the blind kid. It's a way of testing whether they know their left from their right, and how well they judge distances.'

'Could that be what you saw, Floss?' Tom said. 'You might not have heard the instructions. How far away were you?'

If he told them I'd been watching from a tree, I'd kill him.

'It's possible,' I said. 'It would explain it. But we also have a young woman in labour who ran away because she was terrified of what they were going to do to her and her baby.'

'Was that the retard girl?' Chadwick said.

I felt myself bristling, caught Tom's eye and knew I had to take it easy.

'Marigold is mentally handicapped,' I said. 'But that doesn't mean we have to disregard what she says. She talked about a friend of hers who'd died, who the Asters deny all knowledge of.'

'I tell you what,' Frost said. 'I'll have one of my reporters get in touch with the Asters. He can say he's doing a feature on children's homes in the North-West, especially those who specialise in handicapped kids. He can arrange to visit, have a good look around. I'll get young Whitehead on it. If there's anything going on, he'll spot it. Sometimes the press can go where the police can't. How does that sound, Florence?'

It sounded like a good idea. I said so and thanked Albert Frost.

Mary stood up. 'I'll make some sandwiches,' she said. 'Florence, would you give me a hand?'

*

'Your mum hates me,' I said, as Tom and I drove back down the hill.

'She hates all my girlfriends,' he replied.

'Really, because she was singing your wife's praises all the time we were in the kitchen. Eileen's a lovely girl, such a good cook, so house-proud.'

'Eileen *is* a lovely girl. Did you think I'd married a dog?'

God, that stung.

'Then maybe you need to concentrate on being married to your lovely wife and leave me alone.'

He whistled softly for a second. 'Where did that come from?'

It had come from his mother's hostility, from feeling like a fraud in his parents' house and from the sidelong glances Chadwick had been giving me when he thought Tom wasn't looking. 'I can't do this. I won't be your bit on the side.'

Tom pulled over. 'Listen to me.' He leaned across, caught my arm and turned me round to face him. 'Woodsmoke read me the riot act yesterday.'

It was so rare to see Tom entirely serious that it scared me a little. 'About me?' I asked.

He nodded. 'He made a good point, actually. When the Glassbrook case goes to trial, the defence will do everything they can to discredit the police investigation, and you and I are at the heart of the prosecution case. If they can throw some mud at us, it could undermine the whole case and Glassbrook could walk.'

'There won't be a trial. Larry's pleading guilty.'

'As far as we know, he is. What if he changes his mind? We can't risk it. You and I have to be good as gold until the case is over. Which is why I'm taking you straight back to the hostel with no funny business on the way home.'

I could feel tears pricking. 'I've just told you – I can't do it anymore. It's over.'

Tom took hold of both my hands. 'Oh no it's bloody not. When Glassbrook is safely behind bars for the rest of his life, I'm leaving Eileen.'

I stared at him. Had he actually just said what I—

He pulled a face. 'Don't make me go all mushy, Floss. I'll embarrass myself. You're all I can think about. I want to be with you. If you'll have me.'

Of course I would have him.

'The day after Larry goes away, you and I see Rushton and we tell him what's what,' Tom said. 'He'll arrange for me to be transferred.'

'You can't do that,' I said, thinking, *He'll do that? He'll do that for me?*

'I'm doing my sergeant's exams next year. I'd be moved anyway once I get a posting. You can stay in Sabden and finish your probation. We'll find a house somewhere in between.'

'That simple?'

He nodded and smiled at me. He looked completely, totally happy. 'Yeah,' he said. 'That simple.'

# 54

## Sally

Ever tried telling a teenage girl that the boy she likes isn't worth her time or attention? They never want to listen, and Luna didn't either. Neither did either of my daughters express any enthusiasm for the idea of visiting Larry on Saturday, instead showing a brief moment of unity when they declared they wouldn't set foot in prison and didn't care if they never saw or spoke to him again.

On the plus side, it was possible that the girls' friends might be drifting back. Tammy Taylor knocked on the back door shortly after Daphne and Avril left; she and Luna spent two hours in her bedroom. From what I could tell, as I stood outside the door, they were mainly bitching about John.

At Daylight Gate, I slipped outside and wandered through the orchard towards the hives. There were four along the boundary wall, where the bees had easy access to the clover and heather on the Hill. I kept a chair under the nearest apple tree and, after wiping it clear of leaves, sat down.

The forager bees were coming back. They'd been busy all day and would need to rest now. The younger, worker bees had less of a fixed routine and were still dancing about the hives' entrances. A late forager landed on my arm, light as thistledown. It happened a lot when I was sitting by the hives, still and quiet; they mistook me for home. I always took it as a compliment.

'I may have to leave you,' I said. 'I'm sorry.'

Without me taking care of them, the hives wouldn't survive for long. And yet I'd had them for nearly twenty years. Larry had built them for me as a wedding present.

The day darkened as my thoughts did. I'm not sure the sheer enormity of everything I'd lost struck me until I faced losing my bees, too.

*There are dark powers amassing in town and we're scared.*

I'd given Daphne's words so little thought earlier. My head had been full of Luna and Larry, of Roy and the threat to my job, but as the night gathered, so did darker thoughts. On the one hand, what Avril had said made no sense. Evil had visited our town, in the form of Larry, but he'd gone. It was over.

Except, it didn't feel that way. Instinctively, I knew exactly what Daphne meant.

The sky was a deep purple when I got up, stiff with cold, and walked back to the house. I was on the point of locking the back door when I heard the music.

A solitary guitar, a deep male voice. Somewhere close by, Elvis Presley was singing 'Are You Lonesome Tonight?' As he reached the end of the first verse, the backing singers began crooning along.

Larry's music. I had no idea which of the girls was playing her father's old records, but I couldn't bear it. I would break them all in pieces before I had to listen to those tunes again. Except, the music wasn't coming from the house. I switched off the lights and waited for my eyes to adjust.

The window in Larry's workshop was glowing. He'd kept a record player in there, for when the radio didn't play his favourite tunes frequently enough. For Larry, that always meant Elvis. His admiration of the singer had verged on obsession. Someone was in there now, playing his records.

The track ended. A few seconds went by and then another started up, 'Jailhouse Rock'.

I rushed through the hall and grabbed the telephone receiver.

'Sabden Police Station.'

'This is Sally Glassbrook. There's someone in my husband's workshop.'

'I see. And is that a problem, Mrs Glassbrook?'

I took a deep breath. 'Yes. The building should be locked. Someone has broken in.'

'Have you been out to have a look, Mrs Glassbrook?'

'No, because I'm scared. Can you send someone out here, please?'

'If you haven't been out there, how do you know someone has broken in?'

'There's a light inside, and they're playing my husband's records.'

'What tune?'

'I beg your pardon?'

'I mean, are you sure it's your husband's records? How do you know it's not a neighbour's music you can hear?'

'It's coming from his workshop.'

'All right, Mrs G, I'll make a report. Are you and your daughters safe inside?'

'We're in the house. Whether we're safe is a different matter.'

'I've got another call coming in. Bye for now, Mrs G.'

The line went dead. No one was coming.

As I walked back to the kitchen 'Jailhouse Rock' was building to its climax. I pulled open a drawer and took out a knife. I turned the key in the lock quietly and slipped outside, locking the door behind me.

The full moon lit up the night as I stepped across the grass towards the shed. At the door to the workshop, I stopped. The music started again. 'Love Me Tender'. We'd danced to this at our wedding.

The strangest thought occurred to me then. The man I'd seen in our house the other night, the one who'd been touching Cassie, had looked like Larry. Maybe this was Larry. Maybe he'd escaped and for some reason the authorities couldn't make the news public. The music was his way of signalling to me. With an odd sense of bravado, almost as though moving in a dream, I opened the door.

The workshop, a room of about twenty feet by eighteen, was dimly lit by a single candle. My eyes went to Larry's record player on the worktop opposite the door. Someone had stacked six seven-inch records, and the record player was playing each in turn.

Something heavy and solid fell, the clanging sound echoing in the silence.

Over on the far wall, the door to the woodshed was ajar. Beyond was a single, windowless room where Larry had kept his planks of beautiful solid hardwood. One of them had fallen over.

'Who's there?' I called.

Silence. Then the sound of a hinge creaking. Someone was opening the big garage doors that led out of the woodshed. I risked walking forward. Footsteps sounded, running across the gravel outside. Spotting a wrench on a worktop, I picked it up. Now I had two weapons.

The woodshed was in darkness. Without dropping the knife, I reached up and switched on the overhead light. The shed was empty, but the big garage doors, used to load up and transport the finished caskets, were wide open to the night. As I ran to them, I was sure I saw the figure of a man, dressed in black, vanishing down the drive.

Heart thumping, I closed and locked the doors.

The music was still playing as I stepped back into the main workshop. I'd barely switched it off when I heard the noise outside. Footsteps – slow and cautious, made by someone trying to be quiet but too heavy and clumsy to manage it. I stepped to one side of the door, the wrench in my hand held high.

A tall man stepped into the room. 'Sally?' he said.

I swung down. He sidestepped and I caught him on the shoulder. He grunted in pain and I brought up the knife. He grabbed my arm.

'Sally, for God's sake, what are you doing? It's me.'

I knew that voice.

'Put the knife down. Give it to me. Or drop it.'

I let the knife fall onto the worktop. That wasn't enough for PC Butterworth.

'Step away, Sally. Where I can see you. Where's the light switch?'

'Just to the left of the door.'

After he'd turned on the light, we looked at each other.

'I didn't know it was you,' I said. 'I was scared. Sorry.'

Randy took a look around the workshop. 'If you phone the police, you usually expect them to attend the scene,' he said.

'Not this scene,' I said. 'Not anymore.'

He didn't bother arguing that one. 'Well, fair play – I'm not sure they were planning to send anyone. I overheard mention of it at the station and thought I'd better have a look.'

'Mum, what's going on?'

It was Cassie, pale-faced and scared, at the back door of the house.

'Nothing,' I called back. 'Randy just called round to make sure we're all right.'

'You're not, though, are you?' Randy said in a low voice. 'You're really not.'

# 55

## Florence

Thursday, 7 August 1969

'Has it put your mind at rest?' Randy asked.

'A bit,' I said. 'They took me seriously, and a good journalist should be able to find out if anything's wrong. At least I don't have to talk to that daft spiritualist again.'

Randy and I were in the canteen. His eyebrows had bounced a bit when I told him about meeting Tom's parents, but he'd said nothing. He'd begun filling me in on the incident at the Glassbrook house when we heard a woman shouting. Everyone in the room looked up. One or two got to their feet.

'That's Sally,' I said.

Randy was already pushing back his chair. Together we ran out of the room and into the foyer. Sure enough, Sally was at the front desk, leaning across it.

'I have two teenage daughters!' she was yelling at the desk sergeant. 'What the hell is wrong with you?'

The foyer was crowded. Randy and I had to bypass several people in the queue to get to her.

'Come on, Sal.' Randy took hold of her arm. 'We'll make you a cup of tea.'

'State of it,' muttered a woman in the queue.

'Ruddy disgrace,' said another, who didn't bother to lower her voice.

Sally turned back and looked at both of them, daring them to challenge her openly. Neither did. I wouldn't have either. Her hair was loose and there was a wild look in her eyes.

'Sally, come with us,' I urged, and between us, Randy and I

persuaded her out of reception, along a corridor and into an interview room.

'What's happening about last night?' she demanded, before the door was even closed.

'Can I get you some tea?' I was hovering in the doorway. Sally in this mood made me nervous.

She faced us both. 'No, I don't want tea. I want to know what you people are doing about the threat to my daughters.'

'We need to get your locks changed,' I said. 'On both doors, on the shed, on Larry's workshop. I'll try and get someone round in the next day or so. Maybe Dwane will be free. That's the important thing.'

'No!' she yelled. 'The important thing is to find out who's breaking into my house.'

We all turned as we heard footsteps running our way. Then the door was pulled open.

'Emergency at Burnley General,' the constable managed, as he stood panting. 'They want us to take it because that young woman is causing it. You know' – his eyes went from Sally to me – 'the one who had the baby here.'

Sally and I looked at each other. Marigold.

# 56

## Sally

Florence and I ran along the hospital corridor with Randy close behind.

'This way,' I said, as we ran through the double doors, just missing a porter. In the maternity ward, I saw wide-eyed mothers clutching their babies.

'She's in here,' a nurse called, and we ran on, across the ward, stopping at the door to the bathroom. A small crowd of nurses, porters and orderlies had gathered. Randy bent double to get his breath back.

'How long has she been in there?' Florence asked.

'Thirty minutes,' the ward sister told us. 'She started making a fuss just after the doctor's afternoon round. We're frightened she might harm the baby.'

I pressed my head close to the door. 'Marigold, it's Sally,' I called. 'Florence is here too. How's Henry?'

From behind the door came the sound of soft sobbing, and a hiccup that I thought might be the baby.

Florence turned to the ward sister.

'What caused this?' she asked.

'She just went mental,' one of the nurses replied before the sister could open her mouth.

'Something frightened her.' Florence looked round at the faces in front of her. Some of them couldn't meet her eyes. 'Did someone mention Black Moss Manor?' she said. 'Have the Asters been back to see her?'

'She's due to leave us tomorrow,' the sister said. 'If her family won't come for her, she has no option but to go back to Black Moss Manor.'

'Someone told her this?' Florence asked. 'No wonder she's hysterical.'

Randy said, 'Can you all go about your business, please? Sister, maybe you should wait by the door of the ward. Let's see if WPC Lovelady and Mrs Glassbrook can't talk some sense into the young woman.'

Randy was the same rank as Florence, and not much older, but they took notice of him in the way I don't think they'd ever have obeyed her. The crowd wandered away until only the sister remained.

'Stand back if you would, please, Sister,' Randy said. 'On you go, Florence.'

Florence approached the door. 'Marigold,' she called. 'Everyone's gone. It's just me and Sally now. And PC Butterworth. He's here to look after you and Henry. Can you come out now?'

We heard Marigold quietly sobbing as I joined Florence.

'Marigold, please tell us what's wrong,' I said.

'I'm not going back. They'll kill us like they killed Wendy.'

Florence and I shared a look. Wendy again?

'Marigold, open the door and we can talk about it,' Florence said. 'You trust me and Sally, don't you?'

'They're coming for me. That nurse said they were coming for me tomorrow. I'm not going back.'

'Marigold, you don't have to,' I said. 'You don't have to go anywhere you don't want to.'

Florence frowned at me for making promises I couldn't keep. Our hands were tied if the local authority didn't step in to help Marigold. There was nothing I could do.

Except there was.

'Marigold, you can live at my house,' I said. 'You can stay with me until we sort something out.'

Randy's eyes opened wide as Florence took my arm and pulled

me away from the door. 'Sally, you can't offer that. You have enough to deal with.'

'Florence is right, Sal. It's not a good idea,' Randy said.

I looked from one to the other. 'Do either of you have a better suggestion?'

Surprise, surprise – neither of them did.

'She can have your old room,' I told Randy, before walking back to the bathroom door. 'Marigold, did you hear that? I have a room in my house that you and Henry can stay in. I have two teenage daughters, so there'll be five of us. How does that sound?'

'I don't have to go to Black Moss?'

'No.' A deep sigh seemed to force its way out of me. 'You can stay with me until we find you a proper home.'

The door opened. Marigold, tear-stained and red-faced, stood in the doorway. Baby Henry was fast asleep in her arms.

# 57

## Florence

Randy and I left the hospital first and waited in the Glassbrooks' driveway for Sally's car to appear.

'We're not supposed to be here,' Randy said. 'Rushton'll do his nut if he finds out.'

'And yet we're the only ones who seem to care,' I said.

Together we crossed the lawn towards the rear garden wall.

'You can't blame the guys,' Randy said. 'They just see Larry Glassbrook's family, the people who shielded a killer. We know them.'

We were silent for a moment as we looked around at our old home. With the blooming of the heather, Pendle Hill and surrounding moors had turned the richest shade of purple, and the colour almost seemed to be reflected in the clouds.

'I liked living here,' Randy said. 'I didn't see it. Larry, I mean.'

'Nor me,' I said. 'Not until . . .'

'Yeah.' He gave a heavy sigh. 'They were like my family.' The pain in his voice made me want to hug him.

We turned at the sound of an engine. Marigold sat in the passenger seat of Sally's car, baby Henry in her arms. We walked back across the grass to meet them.

'When did that happen?' Randy asked, when he saw the ugly scratch down the side of Sally's car.

'Sometime in the last couple of days,' Sally said. 'Someone ran their keys down it. I should be glad it's no worse.'

We went inside, and Luna wandered down to join us. She looked as though she'd been crying, but she brightened a little when she saw the baby.

'Would Cassie like to meet him too?' I asked as Luna rocked him in her arms.

'Where is she?' Sally asked.

'Out somewhere.' Luna sniffed. 'She wouldn't tell me where she was going. She borrowed your perfume, though.'

I made tea and settled Marigold in the old lodgers' parlour while Sally and Randy went to the attic to look for old baby clothes and equipment. When Henry was sucking contentedly, I said, 'Marigold, we really need to talk about Black Moss Manor.'

Her eyes dropped to the carpet.

'If they're harming young women like you, and their babies, we need to know about it. Others could be in danger.'

'I got confused,' Marigold said. 'They meant take my baby, but only if I agree.' She looked up. 'I don't agree. I'm keeping him.'

'Good for you. Did they ever give you anything funny to drink? Anything that tasted strange?'

A dull look came over her face. She shook her head.

'Did anyone hurt you while you were there?'

She mumbled something.

'What was that?' I prompted.

'They said I couldn't go out. I had to stay in my room. It was boring.'

As I watched, it was as though a light had suddenly switched on in Marigold's eyes. 'I sneaked out,' she said. 'I sneaked out to see—' She stopped. The light went out.

'Did you sneak out to see Wendy?' I asked.

She shook her head. I was sure she was lying.

'Did you ever see any of the children being hurt?' I asked.

Another shake of the head.

I decided to try a different tack. 'Tell me where you lived before Black Moss Manor. Where's your home?'

Again, that dull, closed look. This time, tears sprang into her eyes. Behind her, Sally appeared in the doorway.

'Did you live in Nelson, Marigold?' I asked.

'What's Nelson?'

Sally was frowning at me and I felt desperation taking hold. 'Marigold, what happened to Wendy?'

She frowned. 'We shouldn't talk about it. We're not allowed to talk about it. Ever.'

Sally stepped into the room. 'That's enough, Florence,' she said. 'Randy says you both have to get back now. He's waiting for you outside.'

I was getting nowhere with Marigold. Either she was terrified or genuinely confused. Possibly a bit of both. Nor could I interest anyone at the station in making further investigations into Black Moss Manor. The place was subject to regular local authority inspections, they told me, and any problems would have been picked up.

The incidents at the Glassbrook house were also being ignored.

'The Glassbrooks are being intimidated,' I argued. 'Their house has been broken into, Sally's car vandalised. They're seriously frightened and we're doing nothing.'

'They should leave town,' Woodsmoke said. 'They'll never be welcome here again. People will always say they must have known something.'

'You and young Randy need to watch yourselves, too,' Sharples added to me in a low voice. 'There's them as is asking how you lived in that house as long as you did without realising what was going on.'

'I did realise,' I said.

His eyebrows rose at my tone, but even Sharples knew which fights he could pick and which he had to walk away from. 'Aye, and you weren't there for long,' he said, 'but Butterworth lived there for two years. He'll be lucky ever to make sergeant after this.'

The implication was obvious. If Randy and I were to progress in the force, we couldn't champion the Glassbrooks. It might be too late for Randy even now.

# 58

## Sally

I had no choice but to leave Marigold and her baby with Luna and get back to work. It was early evening by the time I got home, and after checking on them quickly – all three were fine – I went upstairs to change. I pushed up the sash window to let air in and heard voices drifting up from below. There was a bench immediately beneath my window and Luna and Marigold were sitting on it, talking. A gentle gurgle told me that Henry was there too.

'Smiling at me,' Marigold was saying.

'Mum says it's not a smile at that age – it's wind,' Luna said.

'Wind comes out the other end.' Marigold made a sound like passing wind.

I'd turned away from the window when Marigold spoke again. 'Will my boyfriend come here, Luna?'

There was silence below.

'I didn't know you had a boyfriend, Marigold,' said Luna.

'How else did I get a baby, silly?'

There was no fear in Marigold's voice that I could hear. And yet, according to Florence, her baby was the result of incestuous rape.

'What's your boyfriend's name?' Luna asked. Good girl.

'Peter,' Marigold said. 'Peter Piper Picked a Peck of Pickled Pepper.'

'That's a long name.'

'That's not his name. That's a tongue-twister. Have you got a boyfriend?'

'No.' Luna's voice had turned cold.

'Has Cassie got a boyfriend?'

'I'm going in. I'll see you.'

I heard footsteps on the gravel as Luna walked away.

# 59

# Florence

Friday, 8 August 1969

On Friday, my fifth day back at work, I skipped lunch and caught a bus to the offices of the *Lancashire Morning Post*. It had an unimposing shopfront. The paint on the banner was peeling, and the photographs in the window didn't appear to have been updated since the late 1950s.

A bell rang as I entered. In the office immediately behind the counter, two men and a woman were working at desks, their backs to the door. No one looked up.

'Help you?' called the woman.

'May I speak to Mr Frost?' I asked.

'What about?' Still she didn't lift her head.

'Black Moss Manor Children's Home.'

One of the men looked up at that, the younger of the two, and I saw it wasn't a man at all but a tall young woman dressed in suit trousers, a shirt and tie. She was about my age, with a large plain face and very short, dark hair. Thick, black-rimmed spectacles suggested she was short-sighted.

'He's out,' the older woman said to her typewriter.

'When is he due back?'

'Tomorrow? Next week?' There was suppressed amusement in her voice.

'She's the police, Amy,' said the younger woman.

Finally, I had everyone's attention. The middle-aged woman even got to her feet and took a step towards the counter. 'Mr Frost doesn't usually work from here,' she said. 'We never know when he'll be in.'

'Can we help you with something?' asked the younger woman.

I looked at the man, who'd lost interest and resumed typing. 'Sir, is your name Whitehead?'

He shook his head. I shouldn't have been surprised. Frost had talked about 'young Whitehead'. This man was far from young. I looked at the woman.

'Miss Whitehead?'

'Abby Thorn,' she told me. 'Tim Whitehead left the paper four weeks ago. He went to work at the *Echo* in Liverpool.'

I was sure Frost had said Whitehead. 'Mr Frost said he'd ask him to look into a story at Black Moss Manor,' I said. 'Do you know if he asked someone else?'

Abby Thorn shook her head. 'There's only me and Alf here on editorial,' she said. 'Amy does the classifieds. He didn't ask you, did he, Alf?'

Alf raised both shoulders. I took it as a negative.

'Thank you,' I said. 'Sorry to disturb you.'

Outside on the pavement, I stopped to think. Frost's offer on Wednesday evening had brought all discussion about Black Moss Manor to an end. Even I'd agreed his suggestion was a good way forward. So, had it been a deliberate fobbing-off or a genuine mistake? I had no way of knowing.

'Florence?'

I turned back. The young woman, Abby Thorn, stood in the doorway.

'It is Florence, isn't it?' Not only was she unusually tall for a woman – at least five foot ten – but she also had very large hands and a thick neck. 'What's going on?'

I could not tell her. I could not be quoted in the paper commenting on a case that didn't officially exist and that I'd been told to stay well clear of.

'Sorry to bother you,' I said. 'I'm sure Mr Frost will fill you in when you see him.'

'You mentioned Black Moss. Is there a problem up there?'

Her voice was sweet, low and melodious. I had a feeling she'd be a wonderful singer.

I set off towards the bus stop. 'Must dash,' I called over my shoulder. 'I'm due back on the beat.'

# 60

## Sally

'A boyfriend?' Florence said, when she came to the phone.

'That's what she said.'

I was speaking quietly, keeping an eye out to make sure neither Luna nor Marigold came anywhere near. Cassie, of course, was out again. For a girl who had no friends anymore, she had quite a social life.

'Does that sound likely to you?' Florence asked.

'No,' I agreed. 'And neither did her story about people at Black Moss trying to kill her. About them killing someone called Wendy.'

'Whom nobody else has heard of,' Florence said. 'Maybe she does have a very powerful imagination.'

'Maybe.'

'You don't sound sure.'

I thought for a moment.

'She doesn't seem like a liar, does she?' Florence said.

'No, she doesn't.'

Florence made a sound of exasperation. 'Sally, I've no idea what to do. I've tried to get people at the station interested, but no one seems to care. I'm not allowed to visit her home in Nelson or to make any enquiries there.'

'It would help to speak to people who knew her before,' I agreed. 'Get an idea whether she makes things up or not.'

'Wouldn't it? But I can't do it. Even if I hadn't been told to leave well alone, they've got me so busy at the moment I barely have time to eat and breathe. I was late getting back from lunch after a complete waste of time, and if it happens again, I'll be on report.'

'I'll let you know if Marigold says anything else unusual.'

Florence thanked me, then said, 'Are you still going to see Larry tomorrow?'

'That's the plan.'

A short pause, then, 'Do you want me to come with you? I'm not supposed to, but it's my day off. No one would know. I won't see him, obviously – I'll wait for you outside.'

'I appreciate it, Flossie,' I said, using an old nickname without thinking, 'but I'll be fine.'

'Probably not appropriate anyway.'

'Not really.'

We wished each other good night and I put the phone down, hardly knowing what to think. My husband had attempted to kill Florence, in the cruellest possible way, and yet she kept trying to pretend she was on my side.

I went to find the girls. I'd pushed open the kitchen door when the strangest thought occurred to me.

Maybe she wasn't pretending.

# 61

## Florence

'Here will be fine, thank you, Sarge.'

'My pleasure, love. You have a good weekend off.'

I opened the door of Woodsmoke's car and climbed out. He leaned down so he could still see me. 'You'll be in demand every week, now we know you can keep score,' he said.

'No problem. Good night, Sarge.'

The station cricket team had had a friendly match against one of the Burnley stations that evening. It had lasted several hours and then we'd all gone to the Black Dog. Tom had been there, but so had his wife, Eileen, and CID had been conspiring to keep the two of us as far apart as possible. The chill of her gaze, though, had found me across a crowded room more than once.

I left the main road and began the short walk back to the hostel.

'Florence!' called a male voice and I turned to see two people walking towards me out of the fading light. I recognised the short, stocky figure of Dwane, and as they passed under a streetlamp, I knew the older woman with him too.

'You know me mam,' Dwane said.

'Hello, Lillian,' I said. 'Is everything all right?'

'No,' Dwane said. 'We need a word.'

The Ogilvys and I turned into the next street and followed a dimly lit row of terraced houses. Halfway, Dwane surprised me by banging on a door. It opened after a few seconds and Lillian led the way inside.

I counted five small wooden tables, round each of which sat a group of men, drinking, talking and playing cards or dominoes. The bare floorboards were covered in a layer of sawdust. Dwane eased himself ahead and climbed onto the brass footrest that ran round the lower edge of a bar.

'Port and lemon, Mam?' he asked. 'What'll you have, Florence?'

'Britvic Orange, please,' I said, looking around in some bemusement. The place looked as though someone had mocked up a pub in their front room.

We waited for our drinks, and then I followed Lillian into another room, this one with a patch of carpet and padded seats. There were women in here, who nodded to the Ogilvys and stared at me.

'What is this place?' I said. 'Is it legal?' I'd seen none of the usual notices about the licensee.

Lillian pointed at the wall and I looked to see a grimy oil painting that showed the street outside, maybe fifty years or so earlier. A pub sign outside the house we were currently in depicted a woman in a long skirt and hooded cloak standing in a doorway. I peered closer to see the writing on the sign. *The Wise Woman*.

We sat down at a corner table, but neither of the Ogilvys seemed to know how to begin. Dwane looked at his mother. She looked at her glass of port and lemon.

'Folk are saying as that young lass has to go back to Black Moss Manor,' Dwane said, after a few seconds. 'Is it true?'

'Well, she doesn't want to. But I'm not sure how long Sally can look after her. And at the moment, there isn't anywhere else.'

'She can't go back there. That place isn't right.' Lillian put her handbag on her lap and clasped her hands over it as though that settled the matter.

'What do you know about it?' I asked.

Another look between the two of them.

'They wanted me,' said Dwane. 'They wanted Mam to give them me.'

'What?'

'Little uns run in the family,' said Lillian. 'Dwane's dad's side. Some folk said I shouldn't marry him, because some of my kids would be wrong, but there ain't nothing wrong with our Dwane.'

'Absolutely not,' I said.

'Nor with the other two either. They're just not as big as other folks.'

'It takes all sorts,' I said, smiling at Dwane. He glared back.

'Hold on a second, when was this?' Dwane was older than me, in his late twenties at least.

'When he was a little lad. About five or six. Dwane was my first, and it was obvious from the start that he was going to be little. We weren't even sure he was going to live for a few weeks, but he was a tough little bugger.'

'Still is,' I ventured.

Dwane frowned at me to stop interrupting his mother.

'Was this the Asters?' I asked. I couldn't help myself.

'Aye,' Lillian said. 'They'd not been in town long then and the place had only just opened. Not long after the war, it was. Since then, it's always been the place where handicapped and crippled kids have been sent.'

'I'm not handicapped,' said Dwane. 'So, Mam didn't give them me. Nor our Lizzie or Michael either.'

I sat back in my chair to think. A facility that took in unwanted disabled children was one thing. One that aggressively persuaded families to give up such children was another entirely.

'They wanted you to give up your babies with dwarfism?' I asked. 'Dwane, Lizzie and Michael?'

'Gave me all the blarney about them being too difficult to manage, how they needed to be in an institution,' Lillian said. 'I wasn't having any of it. They threatened to get the local authority on the case, prove I wasn't a fit mother.'

'Uncle Stan got involved in the end,' Dwane said. 'He wasn't the superintendent back then, but he wasn't standing for any crap. They backed off. But they want that lass's baby and they won't give up easily.'

'They won't give up at all,' Lillian told me.

'Why?' I said. 'Why do they want handicapped babies so much?'

Neither of them had an answer to that one.

Dwane insisted on walking me back to the hostel. I watched him and his mother set off back towards the bus stop and then turned to go inside. A voice calling my name made me jump and I shot round to see Abby Thorn of the *Lancashire Morning Post* walking towards me, lit cigarette in her hand. She stopped a couple of feet from me and blew out a long stream of smoke. The gesture seemed almost aggressive.

'I remembered something about the children's home,' she said. 'After you left.'

I didn't reply. I could not talk to reporters.

'I thought you might be interested.'

'I'm listening.' I could let her talk to me, couldn't I?

'If you tell on me, I'll deny it,' she said.

'Me too.'

She gave me a grim smile. 'We listen in to police radios. It's how we get a lot of our stories. Just over three years ago – I checked back through my notebooks, so I'm sure about the date – I heard a report about a child missing from Black Moss. I drove up there, parking at the top of Laurel Bank and then walking up to the home. The man who runs the place – Aster, is he called?'

I inclined my head.

'He was at the front door talking to the driver of a panda car. He was saying there'd been a mistake. That the child had been found safe and sound, that the call to the police had been made in error, and he was sorry to cause a problem. I could hear all this as I got closer.'

'So what happened?'

'The police went away, and then other people arrived. More cars and vans, men on motorbikes. Quite a few of them had dogs. They all went up onto the moor. I could see their torches.'

'Where were you while this was happening?'

She gave a short, silent laugh. 'In the bushes. They had no idea I was there. They searched for the better part of two hours, and then the vehicles all left. Either they'd found the kid or they'd given up looking.'

'Did you follow it up?'

'Too right I did. I called the home the next day. They denied anything had happened. I called the police as well. All they could say was a call-out had been made in error. I got nowhere, and Frost told me to drop it.'

'It was good of you to tell me this. Thank you.'

Quite what I was going to do about it was another matter.

Albert Frost, one of the most important men in town, had fobbed off both me and Abby when we'd expressed concerns about Black Moss Manor. And what was this private army – men with vans, bikes and dogs – who'd been summoned to the place when the police had been dismissed?

'So, what are we going to do?' Abby said.

'I can't talk to you about ongoing investigations, Abby. You know that.'

She pulled a face, half turned away and then faced me again. 'Let's go up there,' she said. 'Let's go and have a look.'

'We can't drive up to a children's home at this time of night and knock on the door.'

'Who said anything about knocking? I just thought we'd have a look around.'

I shook my head.

'Well, I'm going.' At that, Abby Thorn turned and walked back towards her car, flicking her cigarette onto the gravel. I watched its light fade and die, and then hurried after her.

She parked at the top of Laurel Bank. 'We should walk from here,' she said. 'They'll hear a car.'

We set off up the dark, narrow track that led to the house. 'So, what happened to spark your interest in the place?' she said, when we were halfway up. Her voice had dropped and I realised she was nervous too.

I couldn't tell her about Marigold. I couldn't risk that poor girl being harassed by reporters. While I was still thinking how to respond, Abby spoke again. 'I get it,' she said. 'We have to learn to trust each other. Shush now.'

We turned the last bend to see the manor house. There was a soft light burning behind the ground-floor windows. The upper floor seemed dark.

'The Asters sleep at the front,' Abby told me. 'That's their car.'

Parked to one side of the front door was the large black Rover I'd noticed previously.

'Two of the staff members live in and don't drive,' she went on. 'Only a woman called Sandra Cartwright lives in town and comes in every day.'

'It looks quiet,' I said. 'I think they're all asleep.'

'Round the back.' Abby gestured towards a narrow path between the house and the laurel bushes.

Getting more uncomfortable by the minute – there would be hell to pay if anyone at the station found out what I was doing – I followed her. A little way along the side of the building, Abby stopped at a window. A second later, she was shining a torch into the room beyond.

'You came prepared,' I muttered.

'I'm the local Girl Guide leader,' she replied.

Unsure whether she was joking – she really didn't seem the type – I peered into the room. It was a nursery, for babies and very young children. The cots were all empty. We moved on. Through the next window we saw a small hospital ward, with four beds and assorted medical equipment.

'I asked for a tour the other day,' I whispered. 'I was only taken upstairs. I was shown none of this.'

Through the third and last window, we saw what looked like a doctor's consulting room.

'Seem a bit much to you?' Abby asked. 'For fewer than twenty kids?'

We moved on, following the line of the garden wall now, struggling to make our way in almost complete darkness.

'Abby.' I was growing increasingly nervous. 'We won't see anything else. There's only one way in at the back and I'm sure they keep it locked.'

She ignored me. We were practically on the moor now; I could see the copse of sycamore trees, even the one I'd climbed on Tuesday night. Abby marched right up to the garden door and pushed at it. Locked, of course.

'Give me a leg-up,' she said.

She couldn't be serious. 'Are you mad? You can't climb it.'

'How high is it? Seven feet at most.'

'How will you get back?'

'I'm not going over – I'm just going to look.'

'Oh, for God's sake. I can only hold you for a few seconds.'

I clasped my hands together; she put a foot onto them and leaped. I thought I couldn't hold her – she was even heavier than she looked – but she grabbed the top of the wall and transferred her weight until she was sitting on it.

'Abby.' She was way above my head. 'I think you should get down. If we're seen . . .'

In response, she swung both legs over and disappeared. I heard a thud as she landed on the other side.

'What the . . . ? Abby, what are you doing?'

I was going to lose my job because of this idiot. I tried the door again. Still locked. And then I heard the sliding back of bolts and it opened from the inside. Abby stood in the doorway.

'No locks, just bolts,' she said. 'One high enough to stop the kids getting out. I'm going to see if the back door's open.'

'No.' I caught hold of her. 'You absolutely can't break in. It's against the law.'

'I won't break anything.' Her smile faded. 'Look, Florence, if I'm seen, I'll say I came alone. As long as you promise not to report me or arrest me. Deal?'

No, it was not a deal. I still had hold of her arm.

She tugged gently to get free. 'If anyone comes, hoot like an owl.'

*Hoot like a . . . ?*

'Abby, you can't go in there.'

'Relax – it will probably be locked. And it's a kids' home. What can happen?'

She set off at a slow jog, heading for the back door.

*Please let it be locked. Please let it be locked.* This was a seriously bad idea.

It wasn't locked. Abby pulled open the porch door, turned to give me a wave and then went inside.

I should just go, leave her to it, deny ever having met her tonight. I was grateful she shared my concerns about the place, but it was not worth losing my job over.

A sudden sound made me look up. On the upper floor, someone had opened a window and was looking out. I couldn't make out who it was – the room beyond was dim – but if he or she had been a few seconds earlier, Abby would have been seen.

This could not get any worse.

Then it got worse.

I heard a car coming up the track towards the manor. Visitors meant someone would still be up. It might even be a police car. Someone could have spotted us and called the police.

Hoot like an owl, she'd said. I'd never hooted like an owl in my life. And how would she hear me inside the building? Leaving the garden, I pulled the door closed and ran. On the corner of the house, I took stock, trying to get my breath back, thanking my lucky stars I was wearing dark clothes. A second car, a black Daimler, was parked next to the Asters' Rover. I heard the front door opening and a voice that I thought was Fred Aster's.

I had to get Abby out of there. I ran to the front and hammered on the door. Heart pounding, I stepped back and pulled out my warrant card. After several seconds, the door opened and Frederick Aster stood in the doorway. He was still dressed, in a shirt, tie and jacket.

'What are you doing here?'

'Good evening, sir.' I tried not to let the nerves show in my voice and knew I was probably failing. 'I wouldn't have disturbed you, but I saw lights on and cars parked outside. I assumed you were probably up, as I see you are.'

'What do you want?'

'I've come for Marigold's things.'

'Her things?'

'Yes, the things she left behind on Monday. Not much, I admit, but important to her. A nightdress, some clothes, a hairbrush, I think.'

'It's nearly midnight.'

'Just gone eleven, sir. And, as I say, I wouldn't have disturbed you but I noticed cars parked. I hope there's not a problem? None of the children ill? If we can be of any assistance, I'll be only too happy to call the station.'

He was looking at me as if I were mad. In fairness, I couldn't blame him.

'Come inside,' he said.

Oh no. I didn't want to go inside. He stepped back, though, and I had little choice but to follow. The hall was dimly lit. And empty.

'What on earth?' Judith Aster was at the top of the stairs.

'The constable has come for Marigold's personal possessions,' Frederick told her.

'I've just finished work,' I lied. 'I was passing.'

'As you are upstairs, perhaps you can oblige?' Frederick said to his wife.

Judith stood at the top of the stairs for a second, glaring at her husband, before walking away.

'Can I offer you a drink, Miss Lovelady?' Frederick said to me.

'No, thank you. I'll get out of your way as soon as I can.'

'You are not on duty. I understand you drink gin. Occasionally Babycham.'

I edged closer to the door; I was drinking nothing in this place. He sidestepped, effectively blocking my way out.

'You are causing quite the stir around town, Constable,' he said. 'My wife and I are flattered by your interest.'

From upstairs came a hoarse, inhuman cry.

'What was that?' Instinctively, I stepped towards the stairs. My first thought, I admit, was that Abby had been found.

His hand fell on my shoulder. 'The children have nightmares,' he said. 'My wife will deal with it, once she has attended to your request.'

A door opened behind us. I spun around, but the door in question – one that led towards the medical wing – was only an inch or two ajar. I had the feeling – no, I was certain – that someone was listening behind it. Abby? Or the mysterious visitor?

Judith appeared again at the top of the stairs, an old shopping bag in her hand. When she reached the bottom, she held it out to me.

'Thank you so much,' I said. 'She'll be most grateful.'

Neither of them spoke as I walked to the front door. 'Are you sure I can't help you with anything?' I said, when I'd opened it and was feeling a little safer.

'Good night, Miss Lovelady.' The door was firmly closed behind me.

As I stepped outside, I heard an owl hooting. I turned to the side of the house and saw a dark figure peering at me.

'Who visits a children's home at night?' Abby asked, when we were back in her car. She hadn't turned on the engine. When she lit a cigarette, she did it with shaking hands.

'Did you see anything inside?' I asked.

'Kitchen, pantry, back corridor. I heard someone at the front door and lost my nerve. Damn, I should have stayed.'

'No, you shouldn't.' I angled Abby's rear-view mirror so I could see back up the lane. 'I heard a scream,' I said.

'Shit, really?'

'More like a muffled cry,' I said in a low voice. 'The sound people make when they're gagged.'

I knew only too well what that sounded like. Thanks to Larry, I'd heard a lot of muffled cries from behind a gag. My own.

Abby seemed to guess I was talking from experience. The look on her face had become one of sympathy. She even reached out a hand, as though to pat mine, only to change her mind before she touched me.

'What's going on up there?' I said. 'Visitors arriving at a children's home in the middle of the night. I don't like it.'

'Are you thinking what I'm thinking?' she said.

I didn't want to put into words what I was thinking.

'Are you familiar with the Westfield case?'

I shook my head.

'Westfield Children's Home in Liverpool,' she said. 'A few years ago – 1965, I think – a housemaster was convicted of buggery and indecent assault. He served four years. There was a case in Leicestershire the same year. And there have been a few complaints about the Christian Brothers' schools.'

'Drive me to a police box, please,' I said.

'Why?'

'I'm calling this in.'

'Are you nuts? On what grounds?'

'OK, I'll walk.' I tried to get out of the car.

She stopped me. 'Florence, you cannot make an official report. Where's your evidence?'

'I'll do it anonymously. I'll claim to be a concerned resident.'

'And when the police arrive, Fred Aster will tell them about your surprise visit. No one will be fooled. Florence, be sensible. We can't do anything tonight.'

She was right. Whatever was going on in the building behind us, for now at least, we had to let it happen.

# 62

## Sally

Saturday, 9 August 1969

The visitors' hall in HMP Manchester was huge, and six massive skylights let in a dull, dust-filled light that reached every corner. It felt like a room in which nothing went unseen.

Eyes were everywhere. The prison guards stood, backs to walls, scanning everyone who came in with a ruthless, robotic efficiency, and in my nervy, keyed-up state, it looked like every prisoner was watching me. Only when I was about halfway across the room did I realise they were all just curious about Larry Glassbrook's wife. The attention was for him, as usual.

As I approached Larry's table, a cloud moved and a beam of dirty yellow light shone through one of the skylights, making his hair gleam the purple-black of a crow's wing. He stood and held his arms wide as though to hug me. I hadn't touched Larry since the night he was taken from us and I didn't want to now. I stopped short of his table and tried to think of something to say.

His hands dropped to his sides. 'You look beautiful,' he told me.

He didn't. His hair needed washing. He hadn't shaved in thirty-six hours – I could time his beard to the hour – and there was a graze on his face. Not beautiful, and yet . . . I'd expected him to be diminished somehow, by prison. He hadn't been.

'It's good to see you,' he said.

I had nothing to say. I couldn't even look at him any longer. I let my eyes drop to the cheap metal and plastic table between us. Would I be allowed to leave early? If I ran to the door now, would someone stop me? Was I a prisoner too, until the time came for my release? Already, my sense of the world outside was fading.

'You should sit down, love. How was your journey?'

As though to set an example, he pulled out his own chair and sat. I did too.

'How are the girls?' he asked.

Common ground. We could talk about the girls for a minute or two. 'They're OK,' I said. 'They're coping. They send their love.'

He smiled and ran his fingers through his hair, Elvis-style. The gesture actually hurt me. It genuinely physically hurt me to see him do it. 'You always were a terrible liar,' he said. 'How are they really?'

I tried again. 'Having trouble with their friends. Fighting with each other. Cassie has been sleepwalking.' I almost told him about the man I'd seen in the kitchen with her and decided against it. For now. 'And Luna has been having her night terrors. But they're getting up in the morning and—' I stopped.

'You're taking each day at a time?' he said.

I nodded, and we were quiet for a while.

'Avril Cunningham's coming to see me next week,' Larry said. 'There's not a lot she can do for me, to be honest, but she says you and the girls need help.'

'Roy says he owns our house,' I said. 'Is it true?'

He flinched at the look on my face. 'Sal, when Roy took me on, I didn't have a bean. Neither did Mam and Dad. He bought that house for us. Gave me a partnership in the business. We'd have been nothing without Roy.'

*We'd have been free*, I thought.

'So, me and the girls, we've got nothing?'

Larry shook his head. 'No, that's not right. There was a contract, a sort of apprenticeship agreement. He was going to hand over the business to me when he retired at sixty-five. That's only ten years away. At the same time, as long as we kept up with the rent, the house would be made over to us. If anything happens to him, the house is left to us in his will.'

'But none of that can apply now?'

'That's what we need Avril to sort out. I'll suggest that I give up all interest in the business, in return for you and the girls being allowed to live in the house and inherit it when he dies. If she can do that, you'll be safe.'

'He wants to move in. He says he'll give me money every week if I let him and his mother come and live with us. He says we need protecting.'

'What from?'

'From people in the town. From the press. From troublemakers.'

'He might have a point at that.' Larry was nodding. 'It might not be a bad idea, Sal. In the short term. It's a big house. I don't like the idea of you and the girls living there on your own.'

I'd expected Larry to object to the idea of the Greenwoods moving in. Not to see the sense in it.

'He's a decent bloke, Sal. He works hard. And he's listened to in the town. The council, the police. He's a sound bloke to have in your corner.'

He didn't want to be in my corner, he wanted to be in my bed. It was the first time I'd admitted it to myself.

'I want to sell the house,' I said. 'I want to move. Somewhere different. Far away, where no one knows us.'

Larry said nothing. He held my eyes and I thought he'd stopped blinking.

'What do the girls say to that?' he asked, after a few seconds.

'Cassie doesn't want to,' I admitted. 'But I think she'll come round.'

'And Luna?' His voice had hardened for some reason.

'Luna's keen to move,' I said. 'She doesn't want to stay.'

Larry didn't reply.

'She's had boyfriend trouble. That John Donnelly, he's dumped her.'

For a second, the look in Larry's eyes frightened me. 'Good. I don't want the girls anywhere near that lad,' he said. 'Either of them.'

'Well, you should have thought of that before, because controlling them now might be beyond me.'

'Love, I'm sorry. But he's not a good influence.'

I didn't understand Larry's sudden dislike of John Donnelly, but I was prepared to take advantage of it. 'So we should move?'

He shook his head. 'You can't.'

'Why not?'

Nothing.

'Larry, why can't we move?'

He sat upright. 'How's Florence? I liked old Flossie. Did she ever come back?'

I wasn't sure I could hate him more than I did at that moment.

'Why?' I said. 'Why did you do it? Why the torture? Why the effigies? You're not a witch, Larry – you can't stand all that stuff.'

His eyes left mine.

'Tell me why,' I said, 'or I'm never coming here again. You'll hear nothing from me or the girls again, unless you tell me why.'

At that moment, a bell rang, startling us, and the officer in charge called out, 'Time, ladies and gentlemen. Say your goodbyes, please.'

'Tell me why,' I repeated.

'Out of love,' he replied. 'God's truth. I did it out of love.'

# 63

## Florence

I walked the short distance from the bus stop to Nelson Police Station. We were part of the same Lancashire force, and my visit here would be reported back, I knew, possibly before I left the building. On the other hand, I was as entitled to make enquiries as any other member of the public.

My visit to Black Moss Manor last night had strengthened my resolve. If the horrible suspicions Abby had voiced were true, I was closing that place down. But while we were effectively blocked from investigating officially, finding out more about Marigold and what had taken her there seemed the only way forward.

'We haven't had a WPC here,' the station officer said when I'd showed him my ID and explained that I was here unofficially. 'How's it working out?'

'Very well,' I told him. 'I'm sure more will follow me.'

Something changed on his face. 'Oh aye. You're that one.'

I inclined my head. 'I'm that one. Can I ask you about a family called McGowan? There are seven families in town, according to the electoral roll. I'm trying to track down a particular one.'

He frowned. 'What's this about?'

I explained what had happened, leaving out Marigold's fears about Black Moss Manor and my own distrust of the place.

'I like the girl,' I added. 'I'd like to reunite her with her family if I can. Seven families is a lot to check up on. Can you help me narrow it down?'

The station officer looked at my list and, after a second, stabbed his index finger at one of the entries.

'Couple in their seventies,' he said. 'No kids in the house for years. I don't know the others, I'm afraid.'

'Have you come across a Down's syndrome girl at all?' I asked. 'Anyone reported missing?'

He disappeared to check the logbook and came back a few minutes later.

'Nothing,' he said. 'She's not on our list of missing persons either.'

It had been worth a try, and at least I'd crossed one family off my list. I had a map, several hours ahead of me and was wearing decent walking shoes. I thanked the station officer for his time and got to work.

By the time I got back to Sabden, it was early evening and the Glassbrook family were in the garden. Luna and Marigold lay on the grass, tickling baby Henry with daisies. Someone – Luna, I guessed – had fastened daisy chains round his neck, wrists and ankles. Sally was in a garden chair, pulling the flowers off dried lavender heads. Cassie sat next to her, a Polaroid camera on her lap.

'Cinzano?' Sally offered, and I saw that she had a drink in front of her.

It wasn't my favourite drink, but it sounded like a good idea. As she went into the kitchen to get it, I turned to Cassie.

'Did Dwane come round?' I asked.

She nodded. 'He changed all the locks and put new bolts on the front and back doors. And bolts on our bedrooms too. He said we'd sleep better with them. He's nice, isn't he? Not creepy at all.'

'No, not creepy at all,' I agreed.

Sally came back with my drink. She'd used a lot of ice and garnished it with fresh thyme.

'Mum, why can't I go out?' Cassie said.

Sally sighed.

'Florence will keep you company,' Cassie went on. 'Just for an hour.'

'Not tonight.'

'Cassie wants to go out,' Marigold said to the baby. 'Do you want to go out?'

The baby gurgled.

'He's sticking his tongue out,' Marigold squealed. 'Put it away, cheeky.'

'How did you get on?' Sally asked me in a low voice.

'Not well. No McGowan family in Nelson is claiming Marigold,' I said. 'I checked on them all. I'm not sure she's from there at all.'

'She's not,' Cassie said.

Sally and I both looked at her.

'Has she said something?' I asked.

Cassie had a small, rather annoying smile on her face. 'She's said a lot of things. Her accent is different to ours. She's not from anywhere round here.'

'I haven't noticed,' I said.

'Well, you wouldn't,' Sally said. 'No offence but all Northerners probably sound the same to you.'

To be fair, they did.

'What have you picked up?' Sally asked her daughter.

'Her vowels are different,' Cassie said. 'She doesn't say "about" – she says "aboot". And when she uses the long 'a' sound, she stretches it out. You know, "awaaay". She did it just now.'

'This is a bit subtle,' I said.

'No, it's not,' Sally said. 'I can tell the difference between a Burnley accent and a Blackburn one. I hadn't noticed with Marigold, to be honest, but now you mention it, Cass.' Sally turned to me. 'Cassie has perfect pitch. You can trust what she says.'

'Where, then?' I asked Cassie.

Sally answered. '"Aboot" instead of "about" suggests further north to me.'

'She's not Geordie, though,' Cassie said.

'No, you're right,' Sally agreed. 'Further north but still west.'

'Lancaster?' I suggested. 'Carlisle?'

'Marigold,' Cassie called over to her, 'where did you live before Black Moss Manor?'

Marigold's face closed up. 'Not going back there.'

'No, we know you're not,' Sally said. 'We just want to know where you lived before that.'

'Another place.'

'What sort of other place?' Cassie asked.

'Big house.'

Sally and I were silent. I gave Cassie a nod, telling her to go on.

'What else can you remember?' she asked.

'Water,' Marigold told her.

'A river?'

'No. Big water. A lake.'

'A big house by a lake?' Cassie clarified.

'And mountains.'

'Well, I'll be,' said Sally. 'She's from the Lake District.'

# 64

## Sally

The morning after my visit to Larry, I was in the back kitchen, chopping mallow leaves, when I heard Marigold sing her way into the bigger room beyond. She put Henry into a lined wooden box on the kitchen table – one we'd already established was splinter-free – and began to load his dirty nappies into the twin tub.

'Poo, poo, stinky poo.' She had a way of singing out her thoughts that was childlike but quite endearing. I remembered the girls doing the same thing when they were very young.

'Blimey, Marigold, they're a bit ripe.' Cassie had followed her in. 'What are you feeding him?'

I let my knife slow down. Cassie was acting under my instructions. I didn't want to turn round, but through the outer window I could see the two girls reflected. Cassie leaned back against one of the cupboards.

'Luna says you've got a boyfriend, Marigold.'

Marigold gave a sly glance at Cassie. 'Have you?'

Cassie gave me an equally sly glance. 'Not yet,' she said. 'But when I do, he'll be very handsome.'

'Mine's called Peter. He's very handsome.'

Marigold turned on the tap and I didn't catch what was said next.

'What does he look like?' Cassie said, when both taps had been turned off.

No answer. Cassie caught my eye in the window reflection.

'Is he blond like me? Or ginger like you and Florence? Or dark like PC Butterworth?'

Marigold closed the machine lid. 'Dark. But not PC Butterworth. It's not him. He is a policeman, though.'

Again, Cassie looked at me. I made a little gesture with my hand. *Keep going.*

'How do you know?' Cassie asked. 'Does he wear a uniform?'

'No. I saw his badge.' Marigold giggled and looked down. 'When he took his clothes off.'

'Where did you meet him?' Cassie asked.

'At Black Moss Manor.'

I almost turned round at that. Marigold had met her boyfriend in the place that terrified her? It made no sense. According to what the Asters had told Florence, Marigold had gone to Black Moss Manor two weeks prior to going into labour. Mind you, they'd also told Florence she came from Nelson.

'Marigold,' Cassie said, 'does it hurt, when you make a baby?'

'A bit.'

'Did you make the baby at Black Moss Manor?'

'Yes. In my bedroom.'

'But you don't want to go back there?'

'No.' There was fear in Marigold's voice again. 'It's better here. They don't make me do any of the bad things. And it smells nice.'

'Except when Henry fills a nappy,' Cassie said.

Marigold giggled.

At that point, the phone began to ring and Luna appeared to tell me Roy Greenwood wanted to speak to me.

# 65

## Florence

Cassie was sitting beneath an apple tree when I arrived at the Glass-brook house on Sunday evening. I left my bike leaning against the wall and joined her in the orchard.

Behind her, the heather had deepened in colour, and a darker variety had bloomed over the last couple of days, giving the Hill the illusion of undulating dips and crevices. Once out of the wind, the evening was warm, and the humming of the bees around us seemed unnaturally loud.

'Have you been to church?' Cassie's silver-grey eyes roamed over my dress.

I nodded. 'Evensong. There isn't a lot to do in the nurses' hostel at weekends.'

Cassie looked down at the grass for a second. 'Flossie, can I ask you something?' she said.

'Of course.'

'If you liked someone and everyone you knew didn't want you to be with him, what would you do?'

I watched her face carefully, wondering if this were about Tom. Cassie was a smart girl. She was sly too and could be spiteful.

'I think I'd ask myself why they didn't want me to be with him, and whether or not they had a point,' I said.

In my case, they definitely had a point.

'They think he belongs to someone else,' Cassie said. 'They think I'm stealing him.'

No guile that I could see, but I was not about to be judged by a teenage girl.

'I don't believe people belong to anyone other than themselves,' I said. 'People aren't possessions.'

'That's what I think,' she said, eagerly.

'But people make commitments,' I said. 'Those promises shouldn't be broken lightly. Maybe not at all.'

So when was I going to take my own advice?

'Greenwood's here.'

Without either of us noticing, Luna had approached. I was shocked to see her. She'd always been a thin child, but she seemed to have lost weight. Her skin was almost transparent over the bones of her face, and her eyes looked both enormous and very red and blotchy. 'That's his car,' she went on.

Cassie and I turned to see a dark green Riley being driven towards the house. The engine switched off and Roy Greenwood emerged. I heard a soft swish of fabric as Luna dropped to the ground beside us.

'He wants to move in with us,' Cassie whispered.

Luna's head shot round in horror. 'I don't believe you. How do you know?'

'I heard him talking to Mum. He wants to move in so he can look after us.'

Both their faces looked identical at that moment.

'He can't,' said Luna. 'Mum told him that, didn't she?'

'She tried. I tell you, Luna, I'm leaving if he moves in. I wouldn't be able to sleep at night.'

'We should go in,' Luna said, getting up. 'We can't leave her on her own with him.'

Cassie got to her feet. 'He'll send us away. He did last time.'

I stood too. 'He won't send me away,' I said.


Sally, holding Marigold's baby against her shoulder, had just opened the door to Roy Greenwood when Luna, Cassie and I entered the house through the kitchen.

Greenwood looked our way. 'Girls, can one of you take the baby? And some tea would be nice. In the drawing room.'

As he vanished from sight, Sally looked towards us helplessly. I walked over and took the baby.

'He's got colic,' she said. 'He needs to be kept upright or he'll scream.'

'Where's Marigold?' I asked.

'Asleep upstairs. She's exhausted.'

I handed the baby to Cassie. 'Don't worry about the tea,' I said in a low voice. 'Keep Henry quiet for ten minutes and then bring him back and say you can't do anything with him. I'll stay with your mum.'

Giving me a look that might have been gratitude but, equally, could have been resentment at my interference, Cassie took Henry. She and Luna went back to the kitchen and the door closed behind them. As I entered the Glassbrooks' sitting room, Greenwood turned from his position at the window and his expression dropped.

'What are you doing here?' he said. 'I understood you were to have no contact with the Glassbrook family.'

Close up, Greenwood was looking less smart than he usually did. There was a stain on the sleeve of his jacket, and he'd shaved badly. I could see a spot of blood on the collar of his shirt.

'And yet events keep overtaking us.' I turned to Sally. 'Sorry to barge in. I know you must want a quiet day after seeing Larry yesterday, but I thought I might take Marigold and Henry to the park. Give you and the girls a break.'

My real reason, of course, was to get Marigold to talk, to find out whether she really did come from the Lake District, and whether she felt confident to tell us anything more about what had been going on at the children's home.

'That young woman is part of the reason I'm here,' Greenwood said. 'Sally, are you out of your mind to be taking her in? You have far too much on your plate as it is. And I thought we agreed you wouldn't visit Larry.'

Sally moved closer to me. 'I have spare bedrooms,' she said. 'And I know about babies. Who better?'

Greenwood took a step towards us. 'Sally, may I speak to you alone?'

'No,' I said. 'Sorry to be rude, Sally, but I need to ask Mr Greenwood some questions.'

Sally took a chair and looked interested.

'I can't imagine what about,' Greenwood said.

'About Black Moss Manor,' I countered. 'I understand you're a trustee, sir.'

Greenwood frowned down at me. 'What if I am?'

'How often is it inspected by the local authority?' I asked.

'It isn't a local authority facility,' Greenwood said. 'If you did your homework, you'd know that.'

'I do know that. I also know that the local authority has ultimate responsibility for all children's homes. So inspections must happen. How often?'

'You would need to ask the Asters.'

'What's the complaints procedure?' I said. 'If someone is concerned about the home, who do they complain to?'

He gave a little snigger. 'To the Asters, of course.'

'And then what? Suppose the Asters ignore the complaint, which they would, if they're responsible for the discrepancy?'

'I really have no idea.'

'Where does the money come from? Is it all raised by charity, and are the accounts filed publicly? Where can I see them?'

'Is this an authorised police inquiry?' Finally, the man was fighting back. I was a bit surprised it had taken him this long. But while his attention was focused on me, it wasn't on Sally.

'Call me a concerned citizen,' I said, just as a loud knocking at the front door made us all jump.

'That will be the Asters,' Greenwood said. 'I thought it best to nip this nonsense in the bud before it gets out of hand.'

'Roy?' Sally looked aghast. 'What have you done?'

Ignoring her, Greenwood stepped forward, as though to leave the room. I beat him to it, closing the door on both him and Sally. Sure enough, both doctors and PC Colin West were at the front door.

When I opened it, West stepped forward as though to enter the house. I stood my ground.

'Good evening,' I said. 'What can I do for you?'

Judith Aster was wearing a dark tweed coat with a grey scarf and a pale cream dress. She made me feel like a schoolgirl in her best dress.

'We've come for Marigold and her baby,' she said.

'And why do you need police for that?' I asked. 'If Marigold is willing to go with you, police officers are hardly necessary. If she isn't, there's no law I'm aware of that can force her.'

'We're taking her into our care for her own safety and that of the baby,' Frederick Aster said. 'Is she here?'

Both looked on the verge of pushing past me.

'Can I see the paperwork, please, PC West?' I said.

I was racking my brains trying to imagine what paperwork they might have. And whether I could get Avril up here in time to counter it.

'What's going on?' I heard Sally's voice behind me.

'Sally, would you step aside?' said Greenwood, from further back in the hall.

'Mrs Glassbrook, we've come to relieve you of Marigold and the baby,' Judith Aster said. 'They're coming back with us now. Can you gather her things, please?'

'I'm going to insist on that paperwork,' I said.

'A word, love,' West said to me. 'Step outside, please.'

I had a feeling that once I left my post, the Asters would quickly gain admittance to the house.

'Excuse us a second?' I said. 'I need to speak to Sally.'

Closing the front door on the Asters and PC West, I turned the key to activate the internal lock and slipped it into my pocket. At the other end of the hallway, the kitchen door opened and the girls appeared. Luna was holding the baby now.

'What's happening?' she said.

'Cassie, lock the back door,' I said. 'Do it now. Keep hold of the key.'

Cassie vanished.

'I need to talk to Sally and the girls in the kitchen,' I said to Greenwood. 'Excuse us.'

'Sally, it's up to you,' I said, when the kitchen door closed on Roy Greenwood. 'Actually, it's up to the three of you. If you can't manage Marigold and Henry, no one will blame you. They aren't your responsibility.'

In the hallway, we could hear angry banging on the vestibule door.

'Can they take her?' Sally asked me.

'Child protection isn't my strong point,' I said, 'but I'm pretty certain they'd need a court order to forcibly remove her from your house if she wants to stay here and you're happy to keep her.'

We could hear Greenwood talking to the Asters through the front door.

'What if they have one?' Cassie asked.

'If they have, there's nothing we can do. But I doubt it, because they'd have shown us already.'

'So why are the police here?' Sally said.

'I imagine the Asters requested a police presence in case Marigold caused them trouble. After what happened in the maternity ward, I can see the duty sergeant agreeing to send a car out here.'

Right on cue, PC West appeared at the door of the back kitchen and peered through the glass. I gave him a cheeky wave.

'It's up to you, Sally,' I said. 'And Marigold, of course, but I doubt they'll be able to take her if we stand firm.'

'I need to think about the girls,' Sally said. She looked at her daughters. 'It's a lot to ask, having a young baby in the house. And Marigold isn't easy.'

West rapped on the back door.

'Baby Hen's all right.' Luna hugged him a little closer. 'Besides, he's a witch baby with six fingers. He belongs with us.'

'I agree,' said Cassie. 'They should stay here.'

Sally and I shared a look. West rapped louder.

'Entirely up to you, Sally,' I repeated. 'No one will blame you.'

Sally had opened her mouth to speak when screaming sounded from upstairs.

'Marigold!' Sally rushed back into the hallway, followed by the girls.

'Luna, be careful with the baby!' I called, as I let PC West in.

'What the hell are you playing at?' he spat at me. 'You'll find yourself on report for this.'

In the hall, raised voices were competing with Marigold's screaming. I held up a hand in front of West to stop him pushing past me.

'Do you have any legal authority to remove Marigold McGowan from this house?' I asked him. 'A court order? Anything?'

'No,' he admitted. 'I'm here to make sure there's no trouble. Good job causing so much.'

'If Marigold wants to stay, and Sally is happy to keep her, it's not a police matter, is it?'

He frowned. 'Guess not.'

I hurried back to the hallway. The Asters were still peering through the glass of the front door.

'Where's the key?' West demanded, from behind me.

'Couldn't say,' I replied.

Marigold was halfway down the stairs, on her bottom, clinging to the banister, wailing. Behind her, Roy Greenwood was trying to pull her up. Marigold's dress was damp at the breasts where milk had leaked, and there was a small puddle on the wooden staircase. She was terrified. Cassie was lower down the stairs, yelling at Roy, 'Leave her alone! Take your filthy hands off her, you pervert,' while Sally was pleading with the two of them to stop shouting and calm down. Luna, sensibly, had remained at the bottom of the stairs, out of the way, but baby Henry was wailing along with the rest of them.

I reached out, took the whistle from PC West's pocket and blew it. Silence fell.

'Out of my way, please, Sally. You too, Cassie.' I pushed past them on the stairs. Marigold stared up at me with a frightened, pleading face. Several steps higher, seeming to tower over me, stood a sweating, red-faced Roy Greenwood. The exertion had taken a lot out of him, and he looked as though he needed to sit down. Well, he could. In a cell.

'Roy Greenwood, I am arresting you on suspicion of assault and actual bodily harm. You do not have to say anything, but anything you do say may be taken down in evidence and used against you.'

Greenwood looked as though he couldn't believe his ears. I held his stare for a second, then glanced back over my shoulder.

'Constable West, cuff this man, please.'

And then I held my breath. Colin West was no friend of mine, but to ignore a fellow officer's arrest was a serious breach of police etiquette. There were a few seconds of stalemate and then Greenwood himself came to my aid. He sneered down at West. 'Don't you dare,' he said.

Few police officers will take that. West pushed past me, turned Greenwood roughly round and slipped cuffs on him.

'I hope you're sure about this,' he muttered, as he led Greenwood from the house.

# 66

## Sally

On Monday mornings, the Family Planning Association ran a clinic in one of the church halls in Sabden, which the local authority midwives took it in turns to staff. I arrived at the same time as Jenny Renfield, one of the trainees, and we spent the first hour getting ready.

'Sally, can I have a word, please?'

I looked round to see my supervisor in the doorway.

'We open in ten minutes,' I told her. 'Doctor will be here anytime.'

'We'll use his office,' she said.

I followed her through and she turned to face me the minute the door was closed. 'Sally, I'm putting you on suspension. I need you to collect your things and go home until we sort things out.'

How quickly fear takes hold of you, leaping like a hungry dog on an abandoned bone.

'Sort what out?' I said.

She looked down at the empty desk. 'There've been complaints. More than one.'

'About my husband?' I was pretty sure they couldn't sack me for what Larry had done.

She found a stray paper clip and began twisting it. 'No, about Marigold McGowan. People say you're exerting an unhealthy influence over a vulnerable young woman. She belongs in care, and you're getting in the way of that.'

She made it sound like I was exploiting Marigold.

'I've been trying to help a girl who's frightened and desperate.'

'Not your place, Sally. Of course, if you agree that the girl can move back into care, we might be able to sort this out faster.'

The fear grew. This was no longer between the two of us. I could see shadowy, powerful figures lurking in the background.

'I throw her out and I get to keep my job – is that it?'

The supervisor got to her feet. 'Oh, don't be so dramatic. Black Moss Manor is a perfectly respectable establishment.'

'So why is she terrified?'

'She's backward. You can't judge her by the standards of normal people. So, what is it to be? I can phone Black Moss, have her collected today and this could all be over with.'

I was tempted, I can't deny it. Marigold was nothing to me. I was putting my girls at risk to help a stranger.

'I have a solicitor now,' I told her. 'I expect you'll be hearing from her.'

# 67

## Florence

The phone call from Sally could have come at a better time. Patsy Wood, Larry's last teenage victim, was due to be buried that afternoon and every officer who could be spared was expected to attend the funeral. We were to leave within the next few minutes. What Sally had to say, though, pushed all thoughts of the coming ordeal to the back of my mind.

'A policeman?' I cupped my hand round the phone. 'Are you sure that's what she said? Her boyfriend is a policeman?'

I couldn't help the glance around. No one in earshot.

'That's right,' Sally replied. 'I heard her myself. I meant to tell you yesterday, but . . .'

'Events got ahead of us.' I had a sudden flashback to the chaos at the Glassbrook house. Not how I'd planned my Sunday evening. 'And she said she made the baby at Black Moss Manor?'

'Yep.'

I gave myself a moment to think. Or maybe a moment to tell myself that things weren't spiralling out of control.

'Are you at work?' I asked Sally.

She didn't reply for a moment. Then, 'I've been suspended,' she said. 'For taking in Marigold. I'm at home right now.'

This was getting worse.

'You need to talk to Avril,' I told her.

'I'm seeing her later.'

Well, that was something, at least.

'Did you hear Greenwood was released without charge last night?'

Sally was silent for a moment and then said, 'Are you in trouble?'

'No more than usual.'

I was trying to sound light-hearted, but I was still smarting from the meeting I'd just had with Rushton and Sharples. 'Privately, I think most people here are on my side, but nobody wants to rock the boat and tip a local bigwig overboard.'

'What are you going to do?' Sally asked. 'About what Marigold said?'

'I've got no idea,' I said truthfully. 'This is serious.'

'I could sit outside the station with her, watching who comes out, but if she gets excited and starts calling out to this Peter, whoever he is, it might get . . .'

'Awkward,' I said, and then jumped as one of the constables opened the door.

'Flossie,' the PC said. 'The boss wants you. Upstairs.'

Actually, not awkward, dangerous. I couldn't let Sally do that.

'Sally, I've got to go. Don't do anything. I'll get back to you.'

They say eavesdroppers rarely hear good of themselves and so it proved that day. The door to the CID room was ajar, propped open with a fire extinguisher, and I made no sound as I stepped inside. The untidy, paper-filled room was divided down the middle by a line of tall cabinets and the voices I could hear were coming from the other side.

'Sorry to say I told you so, boss, but . . .' Sharples sighed. 'She's a bright lass, I'll give you that, but more trouble than she's worth. This Greenwood business—'

'That git was out of order,' Tom said.

'She does cause trouble,' Woodsmoke said.

'Even Tom's not arguing with that,' Sharples said.

I'd stopped walking. I made myself start again.

'And she's got a right bee in her bonnet about Black Moss Manor,' said Sharples. 'The Asters are that close to making an official complaint. Boss, I'm telling you – she's emotional, unstable and prone to hysterics. She's a frigging liability.'

I held my breath while I waited for the argument. It didn't come.

I reached the end of the cabinets and saw the group of men gathered round Sharples's desk. Rushton and my line sergeant were the only ones in uniform. Sharples, Woodsmoke and Tom were in unusually smart suits. All three wore black ties.

Sharples saw me first and scowled. 'Speak of the devil,' he said.

I ignored him. 'You sent for me, sir,' I said to Rushton.

'Aye, Florence,' Rushton said, as the others dropped their eyes and moved away. Even Tom.

'We've just been talking about this afternoon,' Rushton went on. 'And we're all agreed it's better you don't go.'

They were talking about Patsy's funeral. I'd found her. I'd pulled her out of a premature grave, setting in motion the events that led to Larry's arrest. And I wasn't to be allowed to stand at her real grave and mourn.

# 68

## Sally

'I'll write to the health authority requesting your immediate re-instatement,' Avril said. 'They'll argue, of course, and string it out for as long as they can, but they won't win. They can't sack you for helping a young handicapped girl.'

Well, that was something. 'How long will it take?'

'Weeks at the very least. More likely months, I'm afraid. Especially if they want to make things difficult for you.'

It was exactly what they wanted. Months. In which I'd have no income, other than what Roy gave me. Meanwhile, Avril had slipped a pair of reading glasses onto her nose and was reaching for an overstuffed box file.

'I've had a look through these papers you gave me. And the situation is a little clearer.' Avril opened the box and I saw that the previous shambolic mess had been organised into discrete stacks, each colour-coded with a header sheet.

'There are a few debts' – she gave me a reassuring smile – 'but nothing major and we're some way off final demands. I can try to organise staged payments for you. The important thing to sort out, for now, is the house, wouldn't you agree?'

I agreed.

—'First of all, it looks as though Roy was telling the truth when he said he owns your house,' she began. 'He bought it in 1952. I've found a rental agreement between him and your husband, so on the face of it, Larry was, as Roy has suggested, a tenant.'

I was clinging to the very faint hope in her words: on the face of it.

'Where the situation does become a little more complex,' she said, 'is in a letter of wishes that Roy and Larry both signed at the time the house was bought, when Larry had completed his apprenticeship.'

She handed over a sheet of paper.

'That's a copy,' she said. 'In it, Roy declares his intention of retiring in 1979, at age sixty-five, and at that time making Larry a full partner in the business. Larry would then be eligible for fifty per cent of the profits and would inherit a half-share upon Roy's death. There's even a copy of Roy's will attached that confirms exactly that.'

She took off her glasses. 'The letter of wishes also states that at the time of Roy's retirement, the house would become wholly owned by Larry. To all intents and purposes, that would mean by you too.'

'But not anymore,' I said.

'It also makes provision for Larry, his heirs and successors to inherit the house and the business should Roy die before he reaches retirement age. As he's only in his mid-fifties that doesn't feel like something we can rely upon, I'm afraid.'

She smiled, to suggest that she was joking.

'I didn't know any of this,' I told her.

'Quite so.' She put her glasses down and placed her hands together in a prayer gesture. 'Now, the question is, Sally, what do you want to do?'

'I want to leave Sabden,' I told her. 'But if the house isn't ours, I'll have nothing.'

She nodded. 'I know. Well, we can approach Roy informally and ask if he would be willing to sell the house and give you some of the equity on the basis that Larry has been paying rent and working for him for many years. He may feel he has a moral obligation to honour the time that Larry has already invested.'

'And if he doesn't?'

'We can take him to court and sue him for a share. I'd be inclined to ask for a third, but be prepared to take a quarter.'

'Would that work?'

She threw up her hands in a 'who knows?' gesture. 'Impossible to tell with courts, to be honest. Has Roy given you any indication of his plans?'

'He wants to move in with us. He's offered to pay me an allowance out of the business if I agree.'

Avril leaned back in her chair. 'Well, I wasn't expecting that, I'll admit. On the surface, it's a generous offer. And you are used to living with lodgers.'

'He wouldn't be a lodger, though. And the girls hate him.'

Avril said, 'I see. Well, only you can decide, Sally, and I'll do whatever you want. But his offer will be taken into account by a court. It will be harder for us to demonstrate that he's acting unreasonably.'

'He knew that, didn't he?'

Avril said nothing.

'Do you know Florence arrested him yesterday? He was terrifying Marigold, trying to drag her down the stairs and hand her over to the Asters.'

'My goodness, no, I didn't.'

Quickly, I filled her in. By the time I'd finished, a deep frown line had appeared between her brows.

'Well, it might throw a new light on things if he's exhibiting violent behaviour. I must say that is worrying.' She shook her head. 'Sally, you have enough on your plate at the moment. It's admirable you want to help that young woman, but—' She stopped and got out of her chair, clearly agitated. 'And as for Florence,' she went on, 'Daphne and I are very fond of her, but she's young and idealistic, and she doesn't have two daughters to look out for. Making an enemy of Roy Greenwood is not a good idea. Not a good idea at all.'

I was reminded of Avril's warning when I got home to find his car on the drive and him sitting in the driver's seat, waiting for me.

'We need to talk,' he said, as he climbed from his car. 'I've had a letter from Larry.'

# 69

## Florence

While everyone else went to Patsy's funeral, I was given a stint on the front desk. It wasn't a job I minded, normally. You see every aspect of police work at the front desk, but this afternoon, for some reason, it was unnaturally quiet, giving me far too much time with only my own thoughts for company.

I'd known, when I joined the Lancashire force, that lots of my new colleagues didn't believe women should be police officers, and I'd been determined to prove them wrong. As far as they were concerned, though, I'd done the opposite. Even Tom was starting to doubt me.

'All right, young Florence.'

I turned to see Randy had come in through the back office, and that he'd actually made me a cup of tea.

'Upsetting things, funerals,' he said. 'Especially when it's kids.'

I took the mug from him gratefully. 'I don't think anyone here's made me tea before.'

'Don't bloody tell anyone. I'll never live it down.' He sat down by my side. 'How you doing?' he said. 'Generally speaking?'

I gave him a look. 'Is everyone worried about me?'

'Only those who care.'

I had to laugh, I suppose. So I tried. I honestly did.

'Do you think I'm emotional, unstable and prone to hysterics?' I asked him.

No response.

'A snappy "no" was the answer I was hoping for.'

Randy seemed to think for a second, then, 'I think you have a good brain, a good heart and good instincts.'

'Thank you.'

He got up. 'Anything I can do?' he asked me.

'Yes,' I said.

He began backing away. 'Me and my big mouth.'

'Get me some info on the staff who work at Black Moss Manor,' I said, before he could run from the room. 'I think there are three, as well as the Asters. One of them's called Cartwright, or something similar. Find out their names and whether they have any connections in town. In particular, I want to know if one of them is called Peter.'

He pulled a face. 'Blimey, anything else?'

'You've lived here all your life,' I said. 'And you're a man. People will talk to you.'

'I'm promising nowt,' he said as he scarpered.

# 70

## Sally

Roy followed me inside. I led the way into the lodgers' sitting room – of all the rooms in the house, it felt the least like our home – and took Larry's letter to the window. My hands were shaking as I pulled the single sheet of paper from the envelope.

'I think he makes his wishes perfectly clear.' I could hear from Roy's voice that he was drawing closer.

*Dear Roy,*

*I know you're keeping an eye on Sally and the girls and helping them out with money. Thanks, mate. I appreciate it, I really do. The girls need a dad, someone to keep them straight, make sure they don't step out of line. The same with Sal. She'll face a lot of flak in town – she needs someone to watch out for her. It's a lot to ask, I know, but Sal says you've offered that you and Grace will move in with them. It would mean a lot to me if you could do that.*

*Anything I can do to make things easier, just let me know. I can't be there for my girls anymore. It's good to know you can.*

*Thanks, mate.*

*Yours,*

*Larry*

It didn't matter how many times I read it, it wasn't going to say anything different.

'Shall we say tomorrow?' Roy said.

'Where are you going to sleep?' I asked, regretting it immediately. I knew exactly where Roy wanted to sleep.

'I'll take Ron Pickles's old room for now,' Roy said. 'I suggest Cassandra share Elanor's room and Mother takes Cassandra's. Once we've made arrangements for that young woman, another good-sized room will be free. There's the room at the top of the stairs, of course, but that's quite small and we may prefer to keep it for guests. Not that guests are a good idea in the short term, and I don't approve of school friends spending the night.'

'The girls won't share a room,' I said. 'They're not getting on well at the moment.'

'The girls will do as they're told.' He took a step closer.

I sidestepped to put some distance between us. 'And what about Marigold? You were arrested for assaulting her yesterday. You can't expect her to share a house with you, and I'm not throwing her out.'

'That was all a terrible misunderstanding, made far worse by that impulsive and hysterical policewoman,' Roy said. 'You weren't in the hallway, Sally – you didn't see.'

'See what?'

Roy took a handkerchief out of his pocket and ran it over his forehead. 'The young woman came out of her room and saw the Asters in the vestibule,' he said. 'She went into hysterics and I ran up the stairs to calm her down. The policewoman jumped to entirely the wrong conclusion. I explained that to the officers at the station and they fully understood.' He put his handkerchief away but sweat was breaking out on his temples again. 'This is just between the two of us, but I'm not sure she's going to be in a job for much longer.'

'I don't believe you.'

'She's upset too many people. She's arrogant and she doesn't follow the rules. She's very unlikely to pass her probation. The superintendent is fond of her, which is why she's lasted as long as she has, but there are questions about his future, too. And her morals leave a lot to be desired. It's well known she's playing fast and loose with a married man.'

That, at least, was true.

Roy sidled closer. 'She isn't stable, Sally, and I don't think she's a good influence on the girls.'

Already he was talking about my daughters as though he had an interest in them.

'As for the young – Marigold, is she called? Well, whatever you think best, my dear. Maybe she and Mother will be company for each other when you and the girls are out.' He looked at his watch. 'Well, I have a busy week ahead of me if I'm moving house. Not to mention running the business single-handed. But someone has to put food on the table.'

I saw his hand come towards me and felt the soft movement as he touched my hair. His finger brushed the side of my neck. 'A new chapter for us both.' He leaned a little closer. 'How very exciting.'

# 71

## Florence

During my teatime break, I met Abby in the Wise Woman. It seemed appropriate, somehow, and one of the few pubs in town where I could be reasonably certain of not bumping into anyone from the station.

'Frost won't let me investigate Black Moss,' she said, as we put our drinks down. Britvic Orange for me, a pint of cider for her. 'I phoned him today.'

'He promised,' I said.

'Spun me some line about there being a local authority review taking place and it not being a good time for them.' She downed two inches of her pint. 'Told me we could think about it again towards the end of the year.'

Frost had played me for a fool. They all had.

'On the positive side,' she went on, 'I found Robert Brown's grandparents.'

'Well done. Where?'

She named an old folks' home in town. 'They haven't seen him since you took him away. They've been up twice and not even been allowed in. Told that visits are upsetting for the youngsters.'

'Did they take it any further?'

'Florence, they're in their seventies. I doubt either of them can read or write much. What can they do?'

I was beginning to wonder what any of us could do.

'The car we saw up there on Friday night belongs to Ernest Chadwick,' I said.

'Alderman Chadwick?'

'The very same. I thought I recognised it and looked up his registration number. He's one of the trustees.'

Along with Albert Frost, Abby's boss, Roy Greenwood, Councillor Earnshaw and a local solicitor called Booth. Black Moss Manor was protected by some very important men. Which in itself felt odd.

'I can look into his background,' Abby said. 'See if he's got any history of kiddie-fiddling. Ask around a bit. People do love a gossip, especially about their town councillors.'

We both fell silent. I imagined the look on her face was also on mine.

'Child abuse scandals are exposed when the children speak out,' she said. 'We have to find people who spent time at Black Moss when they were kids.'

'There's Marigold,' I said. 'But she won't talk.'

'She can't be the only one. That place has been open for years. Dozens of kids must have left. There must be some of them in town.'

'The local authority will have files on all current and former residents,' I said. 'But I can't approach them unofficially.'

'I could try,' Abby suggested. 'Although I doubt they'd give confidential information to a journalist.'

'The really frustrating thing is I'm sure there are other people who know something bad's going on up there,' I said. I told her about the apparently ghostly message on my mirror, about Hecate Collins insisting that the dead wanted to talk to me. 'No one dares speak out,' I finished. 'Which means it must be really bad.'

'Or they daren't go up against the people behind it,' Abby replied. 'Is there no one at the station who would back you up?'

I thought for a moment. 'Rushton might.'

'The superintendent?'

'He's a good officer. And I think he likes me.'

I looked at my watch. 'I've got to get back,' I said. 'Abby, be careful. If we are right, I dread to think what these men will do to protect themselves.'

# 72

## Sally

He could not force me to live with him. I closed the front door, harder than I needed to, and locked it. He might be able to move in, install his mother in my sitting room and force the girls out of their bedrooms, but he could not make us stay. Neither could Larry. School had finished for the summer and there was nothing to stop us moving to another town and starting again. I would tell the girls now. They would never agree to living with Roy. I was almost at the kitchen door when I wondered how easy it would be to find another job while I was suspended.

In the kitchen, Mary and Luna were at the sink. Cassie sat at the table, watching them, that odd faraway look on her face. Marigold was on her feet, gently rocking Henry against her shoulder.

What was I going to do about Marigold and Henry? I couldn't support five of us.

'Has he gone?' Mary didn't bother looking round.

'He has,' I told her. *For now*, I added silently.

'Pretty.' Marigold was peering over Luna's shoulder. 'Pretty flowers.'

Mary had gathered foxgloves from the garden and she and Luna were pulling off the purple, bell-shaped flowers. A pan of water was already boiling on the hob.

'Make sure you wash your hands, Luna,' I said.

I watched Marigold stretch out her hand towards a flower on the very edge of the sink. She couldn't quite reach it without stepping forward.

'I know.' Luna gave an impatient sigh.

The tall column of purple flowers leaped into Marigold's hand and she caught it by the stalk. I looked at the others, but Luna and Mary were intent on their task, and Cassie had momentarily turned away. The window was open, but that had been quite some draught.

'Oh no, Marigold, you can't have that.'

Marigold had been gazing at the flower, holding it close to Henry. As Luna snatched it back, her face crumpled.

'They're dangerous,' I said. 'Foxglove is a poisonous plant. If you got some of the juice on your fingers and baby Hen sucked them, he could get very ill.'

'Luna doing it,' Marigold complained.

'Luna and Mary will wash their hands carefully and clean the sink area when they've finished. A tiny bit probably wouldn't hurt them, or you, but it would be dangerous for the baby.'

Marigold hugged Henry tighter and glared at the flowers. I leaned forward and closed the window. It could have been a freak draught. It could have been.

'How's Alfie doing?' I asked Mary. In controlled doses, foxglove is a beneficial treatment for heart disease. Mary had been treating her husband, Alfie, for some time with a syrup made from foxglove flowers.

'Well enough,' she said, as Luna dropped the flowers into the pan of boiling water and added sugar.

I didn't tell them about the Greenwoods moving in. I couldn't face it. I helped Mary and Luna clear up, then cooked supper. Baby Henry was colicky, but I gave him a teaspoon of my own baby cordial of sodium bicarbonate, ginger, fennel and honey, and he was soon a lot happier.

When the girls were settled for the evening watching television, I left the house. The sun had gone by this time, and as I drove out of town, I caught sight of the moon above Pendle Hill. It was in its last phase and would disappear altogether in a day or so. A sense of foreboding stole over me, even as I drove faster.

On Well Head Road, at the point where a track led up the Hill, I parked by five other cars and glanced up to see the low flames of a bonfire. Light was leaving the sky and the shadows were deepening as I started to climb. After a hundred yards, I could hear drums.

I was heading for a flat area of land about halfway up Pendle Hill. No one was sure whether it was naturally formed in the limestone beds or hollowed out at some point to allow building. No one knows what once stood there. The remains of walls and even primitive plumbing are inconclusive. It's assumed, though, by many in town, that this is the site of Malkin Tower, home of the Southern family and Mother Demdike, the most notorious of the Pendle witches.

When I could hear voices as well as drums and the crackling hiss of the fire, I walked slowly round the last bend. You choose your moment to interrupt a gathering of witches. Barge in at the wrong time and energy they've been working on could go all over the place, causing serious damage.

The witches, thirteen of them, were all women. There was no doubt on that score: they were all naked. Covens often work without clothes – sky-clad, as they call it – believing that clothing creates a barrier between them and the natural energies they are trying to harness. It was another reason why I'd always been reluctant to join the moon coven. Dancing about naked with a lot of middle-aged women had struck me as rather ludicrous.

There was nothing comical about what I saw that night. Maybe it was the cold starlight, maybe the warm, flickering glow of the fire on their skin, but the women looked timeless, even beautiful. Twelve held hands, forming a large circle as they sidestepped and twisted in a choreographed movement that was impossible to follow. Their hair flowed in the wind, and the fire showered them with sparks. The thirteenth followed the circle round, more slowly and alone, because her job was to keep the drumbeat going.

The women were chanting. I couldn't hear what they were saying, but their voices were low-pitched and musical under the wind. The drumbeat increased in tempo and volume. The singing did, too, and the dance got faster. A sense of excitement began to build inside me, and even on the outskirts, I felt a part of something powerful.

Their steps became smaller, less regular; the beauty of the dance faded but was replaced with a wild and frantic energy.

I held my breath. The drumbeat grew to a crescendo; the dancers stopped and released hands. They held their arms skyward and shouted something to the moon. Then silence fell.

'So mote it be,' said a solitary voice, the drummer, and the coven relaxed.

The circle broke apart. Several of the women bent to seek firewood; others went to find clothes. The drummer turned and took a few steps towards me.

'Sally,' said Daphne Reece. 'We're so glad you could come.'

# 73

## Florence

The evening shift had another hour to go. A little earlier, we'd had a rush of calls, and now the sergeant and I were the only ones left in the building. As things quietened down, he sent me to make tea. I was on my way back with the tray when I heard him shouting.

'Flossie? Where are you?'

I put the tray on the floor and ran back to the front desk. He was on the point of putting down the phone.

'Can you drive?' he said.

*Give me strength.* 'Yes, Sarge, I can drive. What's happened?'

'I've just had the keeper from the reservoir at Railway Bank on the line. Someone's messing around near the water. Kids, he thinks, but he's not sure. He's worried they might go in. They've been playing knock-and-run on his front door as well. Making a right bloody nuisance of themselves.'

I looked around for my hat. 'You want me to drive up there?'

'No, I bloody don't. The boss will do his nut if he hears I've sent you out after dark.'

'I'll go and retrieve the tea, then, before someone falls over it.' I turned away before he saw the smile on my face.

'I've no bloody choice, have I?'

None at all. It was send me or do nothing.

'Drive up there,' he grumbled. 'Have a word with Mick – that's the res keeper – and wait for someone else to arrive.'

I crossed to the cupboard and found the keys to the panda car.

'I mean it, Flossie. You make him a cup of tea and make polite conversation until back-up gets there.'

'Absolutely, Sarge. Tea and sympathy. Wait for the professionals. Your tea's in the corridor, by the way. On the floor.'

The reservoir keeper's cottage was in a grim spot. Some distance from the nearest homes, untouched by streetlights, in a strange no-man's-land between the edge of town and the open moor. An unkempt, unlit single-track road led up to it. As I got closer, I could make out lights from the three cottages on Railway Bank, but they were five hundred yards away across the water.

The keeper's cottage, a single-storey wattle-and-daub building with a threadbare thatched roof, was in darkness. No one came to the door when I pulled up, blue lights flashing.

'I'm here, Sarge,' I said over the radio. 'All seems quiet.'

'Aye, well, stay where you are. Colin will be with you in ten minutes.'

'I'm supposed to be putting the kettle on. I'll give him a knock.'

I found a torch in the glove compartment, picked up my truncheon and got out of the car. The night was cool, a light wind brushing down from the moors; the reservoir stank of rotting weed. I took my time, having a good look around, keeping alert for hiding kids, who might get an extra thrill from the arrival of the police.

This was no place to play, especially in the dark. The reservoir was a huge, brick-lined tank, with sloping sides but no surrounding wall. Only a narrow, cobbled strip-way lay between the front door of the cottage and the water, and nothing but a short stretch of iron railing stopped people from falling in. A lifebuoy, soiled with age and fungus, was clipped to the railing.

Not too far away, a wolf howled.

What I mean is, someone or something howled like a wolf. It could have been a dog from one of the nearby farms, roaming the moor at night, but far more likely to be the kids the keeper had complained about. I shone my torch in what I thought was the right direction and heard a rustling in the undergrowth.

'Police!' I called. 'Come out now.'

Nobody did; I hadn't really expected they would. I knocked on the front door of the cottage and listened for sounds inside. Nothing.

The bushes moved again.

'This is private property. Show yourselves now.'

Still nothing.

From inside the cottage, I thought I heard something. I took my eyes away from the reservoir bank for a second, and as I did so, something sizeable fell, or jumped, into the water.

Stopping only to grab the lifebuoy from the railing, I ran towards the sound. The black water shone like an oil slick and was almost as motionless. I couldn't even see a ripple.

Then the howl again, from further round the reservoir. On the opposite bank, a light appeared. I shone my torch across. A beam shone directly back. They were playing with me. I was about to turn, to go back to the car, when something struck me on the side of the head and I fell into the water.

# 74

## Sally

The women dressed, served warm, spiced wine from flasks and we sat round the fire. I recognised Lillian Ogilvy, Dwane's mother, Marlene Labaddee from the flower shop in town, the spiritualist from Railway Bank who called herself Hecate, and my own housekeeper, Mary. I knew she'd been asked some time ago to join the coven but hadn't imagined she would accept. She nodded at me, unsmiling.

'Why on earth do you want me to join you?' I said. 'I've caused so much misery.'

'We're afraid,' said Daphne. 'We expect you are too. When women are afraid, they're stronger together.'

'What are you afraid of?'

'Darkness,' said Daphne, after a moment. 'Things we don't understand but know to fear.'

'Power and corruption,' said Marlene in her rich, rhythmic West Indian voice. 'Spreading like a cancer around us.'

'Wolves,' said Avril. 'Circling the flock with blood on their muzzles.'

Silence fell. They were all looking at me.

'I've no idea what you mean,' I said.

Still silence. They knew I was lying. I knew, as they did, that something was very wrong in Sabden. I'd assumed it sprang from Larry, that what he'd done had unleashed something unspeakable. Now I wasn't so sure. Maybe Larry hadn't spawned the rottenness in the town, maybe it had been the other way around.

'Is this about Black Moss Manor?' I tried. 'Isn't that a matter for the police?'

'Aye, and how's that working out for Florence?' Lillian said.

'Florence is getting nowhere,' Avril said. 'She's being blocked at every turn.'

'She has no idea what she's dealing with,' Daphne said. 'She's putting herself in harm's way.'

'She can't mess with them,' added Mary. 'Few folk can. I'm not even sure we can.'

'Who?' I said. 'Who are you talking about?'

Hecate leaned over and whispered something in my ear.

'They're not real.' I tried to laugh and failed. 'They're bogeymen. A fairy story, told to frighten children.'

I looked round at the pale, serious faces staring back at me. *They believe it*, I thought. *They believe the Craftsmen are real.*

Something washed over me then. For a second, it felt as though every ounce of strength had fled my body, leaving me weak as a kitten. This was real fear, I realised. Numbing, crippling fear.

The Craftsmen – if they were real, and I still wasn't sure I believed it – were something we learned about in nervous whispers, behind closed doors, when we were sure no one was listening.

They were – supposedly – witches, like us, but not like us; dark witches, who used the ancient power for dreadful ends, and so much stronger than us, because their power was temporal as well as spiritual. Men, of course, because only men enjoy power like that; only men see their evil go unpunished and unchecked.

These women thought they could take them on. And they wanted me to join them.

'I can't,' I said. 'I need too much help myself right now.'

'Then let us help you,' Avril said. 'And when you are stronger, you can help us.'

# 75

## Florence


Cold, black water rushed over my head. Its bitter oiliness poured into my mouth. My legs were tangled in something. I was sinking.

No, this was not going to happen.

I kicked, again and again. Everything was black. Was I swimming up or down? Neither. I was sinking again. The thick wool of my uniform was sodden. My shoes felt like lead weights.

My head broke the surface. Paddling frantically, I tried to get my bearings before I went under again. The stillness of the water's surface had broken into a thousand choppy waves.

There! The brick-lined bank was that way. I pushed towards it and a wave broke over my head. Something struck me, but it was only the lifebuoy that had fallen in the water with me. I grabbed hold of it and felt a surge of hope. I spat. Drew in breath. Spat again. The ring kept me afloat. I kicked out towards the shore.

A torch beam shone on me. 'Who's there?' a man's voice called. 'Hold on.'

Someone was coming for me. Whoever had pushed me in was coming to finish the job. I could hear him pulling off his jacket, shoes landing on the bank. He dived, and another wave washed over my head. I tried to kick away, towards the middle of the water. A hand grabbed my hair.

Someone was holding me, tightly, round my neck.

'Hold still,' he grunted.

He pulled me through the water. The sky was dull and black, and all the stars seemed to have fled. Then I was being lifted up, dragged and then dropped on the hard brick of the reservoir bank. Kneeling by my side was a man in shirtsleeves, coughing and spitting. He turned and we made eye contact.

'You have got to be kidding me,' spat Colin West. 'You stupid fucking reckless bitch.'

# 76

## Sally

It was late when I got home, and the wine I'd drunk was making me sleepy, but I was calmer than I could remember. The women had taken me under their protection. All their energy in the coming weeks, they'd promised me, would be focused on safeguarding me and the girls.

Avril would work towards getting me reinstated at work and establishing my legal position with regard to the house. While she did so, I was not to worry about Roy.

'Let us deal with Roy,' Avril said.

'His mother's a decent woman,' Daphne said. 'He'll moderate his behaviour while she's in the house.'

'And his being there will give you some protection in the short term,' Avril added.

'It safeguards Marigold, too,' Marlene said. 'With two more respectable adults in the house, who can argue she isn't safe?'

For the first time in weeks, I didn't feel alone.

Then, as I made my way through the dark garden, a man ran from the house.

I'd drunk wine. I'd been absorbing the courage of the other women for over an hour, and so I found the nerve to do something I'd never normally dare. I ran after him.

Any other time, I'd never have caught him, but he missed his footing. He went down hard on the grass, grunting in pain. I caught up, picked up one of the stone garden ornaments and held it high above his head.

'Don't move,' I told him, 'or I'll knock your brains out.'

I was going to do it anyway. How dare he invade my home and threaten my daughters? I swung my weapon high.

'Mum, no!'

I gave a startled half-look back. Cassie was racing across the lawn in her dressing gown. Behind her, I saw Luna appear in the kitchen. She too set off towards us.

The man on the ground appeared to have given in. 'I'm sorry,' he said. 'Don't, please.'

'Mum, don't.' Cassie caught hold of my arm. 'Don't hurt him.'

'You bitch!' Luna threw herself on her sister. 'You lying, cheating, whoring bitch.'

I dropped the ornament and tried to pull them apart. Luna's attack was vicious. The man – John Donnelly, I could see now – leaped to his feet and took hold of Cassie round the waist. It took nearly a minute to pull them apart, and by the time we did, Cassie was crying too. Luna had run her nails down her sister's face and actually held several strands of Cassie's hair. John, red-faced and unhappy, held onto Cassie and looked at me nervously.

I looked from one to the other to the third. 'What am I missing?'

'John dumped Luna for me,' Cassie said, as Luna snivelled. 'He's going out with me now.' She smiled up at him through her tears.

'Tell her she can't, Mum. Tell her he's mine.'

John still had his arms round Cassie's waist. I wanted to scream at him to let go of her, but one of us had to stay calm.

'Is this true?' I asked him. 'Do you want to go out with Cassie now?'

He looked me full in the face. 'Yes,' he said.

'John's younger than you,' I said to Cassie. 'Why would you want to go out with someone from the class below you?'

'Not much,' Cassie said. 'Only a few months. He knows what he wants. He's always wanted me. He only hung out with Luna so that he could get closer to me.'

'Liar!' Luna yelled.

I took a deep breath. 'Go into the house,' I said. 'Both of you. I want to talk to John.'

The girls never disobey me when they can see I mean it. I waited until the back door had closed before turning back to John.

'I didn't mean any harm,' he said. 'I haven't done any harm.'

'Was it you before?' I asked. 'In the kitchen, with Cassie, that night I came down?'

He nodded, rubbing at his left knee. 'She let me in. We didn't mean to wake you up.'

'And in Larry's workshop?'

'Sorry. We were only talking. And playing records.'

'You have no right to sneak into my house at night.'

'I'm sorry. I couldn't come any other time. Luna's been going mental.'

'You used Luna and you hurt her badly.'

His big, dark eyes were pleading with me. 'Luna and I were mates. That's all. I didn't know she felt that way about me. It was always Cassie I liked.'

'Cassie is only sixteen. You are fifteen. What if you get her pregnant?'

'I won't.'

'John, I'm a midwife. How many young girls' lives do you think I've seen ruined by teenage pregnancies?'

'If she gets pregnant, I'll marry her. I love her. I think about her every second of every day. I'll never hurt her.'

I wasn't myself, because there was something about this handsome boy in the darkness that I was warming to. At the same time, I was hugely relieved to learn that it had been he, not some malevolent stranger, that had been in the house with Cassie. Even so.

'Cassie cannot have a boyfriend right now,' I said, feeling a wave of misery that Larry wasn't here to send the youngster packing with his tail between his legs. 'When you're older, when you've both finished school, if you still feel the same, we'll see.'

'I'll feel the same. I always will.'

A cloud moved at that moment, allowing a soft wave of moonlight to wash over us.

'Good God,' I said. 'Did I do that?'

John's hand went to his face and he dropped his eyes. 'Must have been when I fell,' he said. 'Not your fault.'

'Let me see.'

He stepped away, but I held his shoulder. 'That's not a fresh wound,' I said, looking at the grazed skin, the congealed blood, the beginnings of a bruise. 'That was done earlier today, at a guess.'

'I fell.' Still he couldn't meet my eyes. 'The pub's full of uneven floors.'

'Is everything all right at home?'

'Course it is. Me and Mum look after each other.'

I sighed. So much wrong with the world.

'Go home, John. Take care of yourself. I'll be phoning your mother. I don't expect to see you here again.'

'But—'

'Go!'

He set off, limping, down the drive.

# 77

## Florence

Tuesday, 12 August 1969

'Frontstroke, backstroke, fancy diving too,' one of the detectives sang, tunelessly, as I walked towards the back door of the station the next day. 'Don't you wish you never had anything else to do?'

They'd been waiting for me to arrive. I never normally saw groups of officers hanging around in the car park after their shift was over. And it seemed every member of CID who smoked was outside; that meant pretty much all of them. Even Tom was there, although he kept his eyes on the ground.

'That you, Flossie?'

I heard Rushton's voice as I entered the building. He was leaning over the stairs, looking down at me from the first floor. 'Get yourself up here, lass.'

I climbed the stairs and followed Rushton into his office.

'You OK?' he asked me.

I stood to attention in front of his desk. 'Yes, thank you, sir.'

'PC West's official report is that you fell into the water and he dived in to pull you out.'

'I was watching someone on the far bank when I was struck from behind, sir. The blow to the head made me lose balance and fall. PC West is quite right to say he pulled me out, and I'm grateful to him.'

He frowned at me. 'How's your head now?'

'Sore. I had one of the nurses look at it this morning. There's no skin broken.'

'The call from the reservoir keeper was a hoax,' Rushton said. 'He's denying all knowledge of it.'

I hadn't known that. It didn't surprise me, though.

'It's black as bloody Hades out that way,' Rushton said. 'So it's possible West didn't see whoever hit you.'

'Yes, that's possible,' I agreed.

He sighed. 'Flossie, I can see kids playing knock-and-run, hanging around the res at night. I can even see them making a hoax call to the police. But physically assaulting an officer? Committing what could be construed as attempted murder? Does that sound likely to you?'

'Not really, sir.'

Rushton leaned back in his chair. 'So the alternative is that someone knew you were on duty and lured you out there specifically to do you harm.'

'Sounds even less likely, doesn't it, sir?' I said.

He gave a heavy sigh and got to his feet. I watched him walk to the window and look out, although his view was of a brick wall, seven feet away across an alley.

'Is there anything you want to tell me, love?' he asked.

This was my opportunity.

'I'm waiting,' he said.

'Black Moss Manor,' I said, and watched him take in a deep breath. He seemed to droop as he stood at the window. It was a long time before he turned back and nodded at me to go on.

Rushton listened while I told him about the odd, listless state I'd found the children in, the cold, even cruel way of exercising them, the harsh corporal punishment and the strange games. He raised his eyebrows high when I told him I'd watched from the moor but didn't comment. I told him about Marigold's horror of the place, of the Asters' bullying tactics to try to get her to return, even using our own officers to back them up. I told him about my drink with the Ogilvys, about the home's unusual interest in handicapped children. I was just getting to Marigold's worrying claim that a policeman boyfriend had fathered her child when the door opened and DI Sharples poked his head inside.

'They've arrived, boss. I've stuck them in the meeting room.'

'Thanks, Jack. I'll be right there.'

Sharples left, leaving the door wide open.

'Flossie, there's something I need doing urgently.' Rushton got to his feet. 'I want you to have a look at the incidence of violence in pubs and see how it relates to late opening hours.'

'Sir, I've already—'

'You might have to do a few visits around town – in or out of uniform, your choice. I'll see you get access to a car and I'll ask your sergeant to spare you for five days. Will that be enough?'

The report into pub violence had taken hours; I'd given it to Rushton days ago.

'Sir, I—'

He fixed me with a hard stare. 'Florence, it needs doing properly. If there are any warrants needed, any arrests made, any charges brought, I'm going to need facts and evidence. And I can't spare anyone else to help. You're on your own. Do I make myself clear?'

We held eye contact. His eyebrows had practically disappeared into his hair. 'Have I been overestimating your intelligence, Florence?' he said, in a voice that only I would hear.

'No, sir,' I said. 'I understand. Thank you, sir.'

'Daylight hours only, mind you. No more solitary night-time jaunts. I need your word on that.'

Back at my desk, I heard Rushton giving the orders that would effectively second me to CID again and clear me to investigate Black Moss Manor for the next five days. Only I was to do it alone, and without telling anyone. Rushton had also told me something even more significant than that he shared my concern: he didn't trust everyone in the station.

Almost immediately, the phone rang. It was Abby.

'I've actually got some leads.' She was speaking quietly, as though not wanting to be overheard. 'I think I'll be buying a lot of drinks tonight. Wish me luck.'

'Be careful,' I whispered back. 'I'm on duty till ten or I'd come with you.'

'Relax,' she said. 'I'm good at this. Gotta go.'

She put down the phone. I spent a few minutes pretending to make notes, when I was really wondering who it was, specifically, that Rushton didn't trust. Then, without telling anyone in CID where I was going, I left the station before cycling a few hundred yards to the local offices of Lancashire County Council.

Mrs Finley, the manager who came to find me after ten minutes, was a woman in early middle age, a little on the plump side, with an open, pretty face and kind brown eyes. I found myself warming to her as she offered coffee and took me into an office with fresh garden flowers on her desk.

'How are you, Miss Lovelady?' she asked me, once I'd taken a seat. 'How are you really?'

I hadn't given my name at reception.

'It's good to be back at work.' As I smiled at Mrs Finley, I saw her eyes drift to my bandaged left hand. Right on cue, it started to hurt.

'What can I help you with today?' she asked me.

'Black Moss Manor Children's Home,' I said. 'I understand it's privately run but that the council has ultimate responsibility.'

'Inspections take place twice yearly,' Mrs Finley said. 'We've always found everything in order.'

The door opened behind us and a woman in a blue overall carried in a tray with two china coffee cups and a plate of fig rolls.

'Why are the children educated in the building rather than attending local schools?'

I had to wait several minutes for an answer while the coffee lady left the room and Mrs Finley enquired about milk, sugar and would I like a fig roll? I sipped my coffee. It was hot and fresh.

'Are you an expert in child psychology, Miss Lovelady?' she said at last.

'No, but—'

'Then you're not in a position to comment on decisions taken in the best interests of problem children, are you?'

I put my cup down and took out my pocketbook and pencil.

'How many children are there at Black Moss?'

'I believe the capacity is twenty, but the number will fluctuate as children arrive and leave. Are you sure you won't have a fig roll?'

'No, thank you. Where do they go, when they leave?'

'To adoptive families. Is your coffee warm enough?'

'Can I see details of adoptions? Say, over the last five years?'

Mrs Finley sat back in her chair, using the third finger of her left hand to brush away imaginary crumbs from the corner of her mouth. She wore a wide gold wedding band and an engagement ring of diamonds and rubies. 'I'm afraid not,' she said. 'Those details are confidential.'

'Do you have a register? A list of all children currently in the home?'

'I do.' She smiled again at me.

'And may I see that?'

'Confidential, I'm afraid.'

I sat forward in my chair. 'Mrs Finley, we've received a very serious complaint about Black Moss Manor, and I've witnessed behaviour there that has concerned me. You are doing nothing to put my mind at ease.'

From the expression on her face, I was a mildly amusing curiosity. 'I'll tell you what I can, Miss Lovelady,' she said, 'but you must appreciate that there are rules. Is there someone more senior at the station who I can call? Your supervisor, maybe?'

'Are all the children at Black Moss Manor handicapped?'

She began fiddling with the rings on the third finger of her left hand, twisting and stroking them. 'Not all of them,' she said. 'But Black Moss Manor has the facilities and expertise to deal with difficult children. It's possible someone inexperienced like yourself might have seen normal behaviour of retarded youngsters and assumed a problem where none exists.'

'I took a child there myself earlier this year. A Robert Brown, who did not seem in any way retarded, as you put it. What can you tell me about him?'

'Nothing.'

She smiled again, and I wondered how I could ever have thought this woman pleasant. By this time, she was reminding me of a mean old cat my grandmother had when I was small. It had purred and rubbed itself against me before unfurling its claws and drawing blood.

'Mrs Finley, do you understand that I'm carrying out a police investigation?'

Her smile vanished. 'No, young lady, do you understand that my sole concern here is for the well-being of the children in local authority care? Protecting their interests, and their privacy, is paramount for me, even if it isn't for you.'

I got up and thanked her for her time. The door was open, and I was halfway through it when she called me back. 'Miss Lovelady?'

I turned, even then hopeful she might have changed her mind about cooperating. Her eyes dropped to my left hand, but not before I saw them gleaming.

'Did it hurt?' she asked me.

Back at the station, it was coming up for five o'clock. The civilian staff and most of CID who weren't working priority cases were going home for the night. I waited until the duty detective had left the station on a job and went to find the telephone directory for Cumbria. I looked up *Orphanages*, *Children's Homes* and *Homes for the Handicapped*, and found only one place that seemed to fit the bill. The Thirlmere Home for Handicapped Children.

'Marigold?' said the blunt, Northern voice that answered the phone. 'Of course I remember Marigold. How is she?'

Even I could tell that this woman's accent was similar to Marigold's. Cassie had been right.

'She's well,' I said, excitement and nerves fighting to get the better of me. 'She's living with a friend of mine – a nurse and her two teenage daughters. She seems happy.'

'Well, that's nice.' The woman seemed uncertain. 'But I rather thought she'd stay at Black Moss. They certainly seemed very keen to have her, and they've always been very particular about who they take.'

'Do you mind telling me why a transfer was necessary? Was it because of the pregnancy?'

The woman was silent for several seconds, then, 'What pregnancy?'

'I'm sorry. Maybe you didn't know. Marigold was pregnant when she arrived at Black Moss Manor. She had a baby boy.'

'Good Lord. No, I think there must be some mistake. We'd have been told. There would have been an investigation. Our boys and girls aren't allowed to ... to fraternise. We have very strict procedures in place.'

A suspicion was growing in my head.

'Marigold gave birth last Monday. Can I ask when she left you?'

'Well, that would explain it.' The relief in the woman's voice was apparent down the phone line. 'Marigold moved to Black Moss Manor in March 1967. Over two years ago.'

# 78

## Sally

Roy moved in with us late on Tuesday afternoon, escorting his mother over the threshold like a visiting queen. Within ten minutes of their arrival, the girls, including Marigold and the baby, had fled to Luna's room and locked the door.

Within an hour, Roy had sacked Mary. 'Sally isn't working anymore,' he announced. 'There are five women in this house perfectly capable of housework, and I'm not one to encourage idleness.'

Mary went without a word, but if she'd looked at me the way she did at him, I'm not sure I'd have slept that night.

Two hours after the Greenwood invasion, as I was starting to think of it, unfamiliar smells had stolen their way around the house, the mothballs that Grace used to preserve her ancient clothes, and the heavily spiced oil Roy put on his hair. Almost worse than both was the sticky-sweet scent of lily of the valley, the perfume that Grace used.

The girls only came down for dinner when I told them I wouldn't be serving food in their bedrooms, so it was come down and eat together or starve. Marigold believed me; the other two couldn't deal with her sobs. After a mostly silent meal, during which Marigold sat, trembling, as far from Roy as she could, he took me to one side.

'That was a little early for me to eat,' he said, as his hand settled in the small of my back. 'From tomorrow, Mother and the young people can eat at six. You and I will dine together an hour later. Preparing two meals shouldn't be a problem, as you won't be working.'

That evening, the girls and I huddled in the lodgers' sitting room round the tiny black-and-white television while the Greenwoods sat in our room. After an hour, Roy interrupted to announce that I was making his mother feel unwelcome and should join them in the bigger parlour. When I suggested she might not enjoy the same television programmes as the girls, he agreed.

'We can move the colour television into the smaller room for the girls,' he said. 'Mother and I prefer the radio. And we need to clear room for her piano. It'll be arriving next week.'

At nine o'clock, he sent his mother and the girls to their rooms and insisted on pouring me a glass of the sweet sherry he'd decided I liked.

'Alone at last,' he said, as he chinked glasses with me. 'How nice.'

He pulled a face as he sipped his Tío Pepe. 'I think this has turned,' he said. 'Ah well, waste not, want not.' He drank the whole glass down and went to pour himself another.

# 79

## Florence

I was on the point of getting into bed when the night porter rapped on my door. 'Phone, Florence. Police station for you.'

'Florence, we're sending a car to pick you up,' the desk sergeant told me, after I'd run downstairs in my nightdress. 'Can you be ready in five minutes? Uniform preferably, but don't worry if not.'

'What's happened?'

'Woman's been attacked on Market Street. Bloke broke into her bedroom. Badly beaten up by all accounts. And we could be looking at a rape.'

'I'll be ready, Sarge.'

'Flossie, I don't need to tell you this, but we need to get this one right. The victim's a reporter.'

It was as though a cold wind had blown through the hostel. 'Who?' I asked.

'Woman called Abby Thorn. Works at the *Post*. Right, car's on its way. You've got three minutes.'

Abby lived above a greengrocer's shop on Market Street. There were already two panda cars parked outside and a waiting ambulance.

'Ambulancemen are inside with her,' one of the attending constables told us, before shaking his head. 'Nasty one.'

There was one advantage to being a female constable that night, I learned. None of the men wanted to deal with a badly injured rape victim. They let me in and I ran through the shop, past the scared-looking shopkeeper and his wife and up a flight of stairs at the back. The door was open and I walked through into the living room of Abby's flat.

The furniture was cheap and old-fashioned, and I knew immediately it wasn't hers. The huge black-and-white photographs on the walls were though, and I almost smiled to see the clever images of Times Square in New York and London's Fleet Street. So were the framed front pages of national newspapers featuring big news stories. She'd hung them to inspire her. I knew this room. I could have lived in one just like it.

I could hear male voices from behind a door and so I knocked and pushed it open. Abby, wearing men's pyjama bottoms and a T-shirt, lay on a single bed, an oxygen mask to her face. The shirt, and the pillow beneath her head, were stained with blood. The mask hid much of her face, but I could make out the swelling beneath her right eye. Her worst injuries, though, seemed to be to her neck. A thick choker of red weals and bruises encircled it. Someone had tried to strangle her.

'She's stable,' one of the ambulancemen said to me. 'We're going to bring a stretcher up. You OK to stay with her?'

I was, of course. I kneeled by her side, and when she stretched out a hand, I took it. Her grip tightened and it was that gesture, so totally uncharacteristic of the brusque, brave woman I was getting to know, that frightened me more than anything. Then her other hand reached up and pulled off the mask.

'He was waiting for me.' Her voice was low and rasping, as though forcing itself through broken glass. 'He was in the wardrobe.'

I turned in horror. The big double wardrobe was immediately behind me.

'He came out when I was in bed.' Her voice broke as she began to cry.

'Shush.' I picked up the mask and guided it back towards her face. 'You have to keep this on. I'll take your statement later.'

She started to argue, but a coughing fit claimed her and she let me fasten the mask round her head. Then the ambulancemen returned and she was carried out.

# 80

## Sally

Wednesday, 13 August 1969

At a quarter past six in the morning, the dark moon rose. The children, Larry's victims, had all disappeared during the dark phase of the moon.

The sky was clear, and as I stood at my bedroom window in the pale, rosy-grey light, I could see the faint outline of a circle in the south-east sky. And I found myself hoping – longing – that a child would vanish, that the predator was still out there, that he'd been biding his time and would strike again today. I looked out at the dawn, praying with all my heart that another child would suffer a horrible, torturous death and knowing I'd be glad of it, because it would mean Larry would come home and save us.

I should have known better. I should have known that spells cast in anger can backfire, and mine did that day. A few hours later, Luna went missing.

# 81

## Florence

I stayed by Abby's bed until well into the early hours of Wednesday morning, until a nurse whispered in my ear that I was probably keeping her awake.

I slept for a few hours before returning to the hospital. Wood-smoke and Tom were there when I arrived, but both agreed that I should be the one to take Abby's statement. I led the way into her room and sat on the single chair beside her bed. Woodsmoke and Tom stood either side of the door, as though on guard.

Abby was breathing unaided, and that had to be a good thing, but the injuries she'd sustained were far more apparent. Her right eye was hardly visible, and the swelling had obscured all the clean, strong lines of her face. Her pale skin was red, purple, even black in places, and there was a nasty cut below her lip that had been stitched.

'You OK to do this, Florence?' Woodsmoke asked.

Abby's eyes met mine and I knew exactly what she was trying to tell me. If she could do it, so could I. And vice versa.

'What time did you get home last night, Abby?' I began.

Woodsmoke took notes and Abby struggled to make damaged vocal cords do her bidding. As I talked her through the previous night, we learned that she'd arrived home shortly before eleven o'clock, after spending the evening interviewing people in town for a story she was working on. She declined to say what the story was about. 'Confidential,' she said, with a pointed look at me. She had been aware of no one watching her that evening, or recently. She'd had no cause to be alarmed.

At one point, her voice gave up completely. Tom shot forward, helped her to a sitting position and then stood by her side, holding a glass of water to her lips every few seconds.

When she'd recovered, she went on to say that she'd used her key to get into the shop through the back door and had gone straight upstairs to her flat. The door had been locked, as usual, and she'd had no reason to suspect anything was wrong.

Tom spoke. 'Sorry to interrupt, but the theory is that the intruder sneaked through to the back while the shop was busy. He was lucky to find the spare key Miss Thorn keeps above the door frame.'

Abby hadn't noticed anything amiss in the flat and had gone straight to bed. When she told us about the creaking of the wardrobe door, about the dark shadow that had emerged, leaping upon her before she even drew breath to scream, I heard Woodsmoke swear under his breath.

'He hit me,' she said. 'He held my hair and he hit me.'

She hadn't needed to tell us that; her battered face spoke volumes.

'How many times?' I asked.

She shook her head. She couldn't remember.

'Then he got on top of me, and his hands went round my throat. I couldn't breathe.'

Tears filled her eyes. Tom held the glass to her lips.

'Next thing I remember is the ambulancemen arriving,' she said.

'The shop owners next door heard something that didn't sound right,' Woodsmoke added. 'They went to investigate and saw Miss Thorn halfway down the steps. They called the police and the ambulance.'

Silence fell. Tom was watching me. Woodsmoke cleared his throat.

'Abby, I have to ask you this,' I said. 'Did he rape you?'

She shook her head.

'No?'

'I thought he was going to. He laid on top of me. He had an erection. I could feel it. But he didn't.'

'Did something happen to disturb him?' I asked.

No answer.

'Can we leave it at that for now?' she said. 'My throat . . .'

I turned to check with the sergeant. 'Course we can, love,' he said. 'You've done very well. We'll leave you in peace now.'

I got up to go.

'Florence?'

I turned back to Abby.

'Can I talk to you? Alone?'

After a moment, Woodsmoke nodded to Tom and they both left the room. I sat down again by Abby's side.

'He said something to me,' she said. 'He spoke to me.'

I waited.

'Just before he went. He took his hands off my throat and he said, "Next time, I won't stop".'

# 82

## Sally

Grace insisted on accompanying me into town on Wednesday morning and a visit that should have needed less than an hour ended up taking over two. When we got back, I put the kettle on and began putting away the shopping. The vials of foxglove syrup that Mary and Luna had made were on a shelf in the pantry, and worried that Marigold might be tempted by the pretty colours, I moved them higher up, out of reach. Grace had obviously been tidying in here too, and I tried not to let my annoyance show as I moved things back to where they should be.

'Where's Luna?' I asked Cassie, who'd wandered down to join us. I could hear baby Henry fretting in the other room and Marigold trying to sing him into submission.

Cassie shrugged.

'Tell her I want to see her, please,' I said.

'What for?'

'I just do.' And that was the truth. I was never comfortable during the dark moon and this one was bothering me more than usual. I wanted to see both my girls. I wanted to touch their hair, smell their skin and hear their voices, even if what they had to say would be troublesome and mean.

Cassie left the room and didn't return. For several minutes I suffered Grace's complaints about the winds so far out of town and then something occurred to me. I went back into the pantry and counted the small glass bottles labelled *Foxglove Syrup*. Ten. I counted again and looked around to see if any had been put in the wrong place. They hadn't. Only ten. And that was all wrong.

I have a process when I'm making something potentially dangerous. I fill twelve bottles, and each is labelled with the date and a batch number. Mary and the girls know the rules. I found the logbook on a lower shelf. Sure enough, twelve bottles. Mary would have taken one. That meant someone other than Mary had taken a vial of foxglove syrup.

There was still no sign of Cassie, or Luna, so I went looking. I found Cassie in the room she now shared with her sister.

'Where is she?' I said.

Cassie looked up. 'I couldn't find her.'

The missing vial slipped to the back of my mind. I searched the entire house, including the attic, before admitting to myself that Luna had gone, and that I'd been a fool. I'd prayed that morning that a child would disappear. The energy created during magic spells is powerful, especially if not properly managed and targeted. It can backfire and cause untold harm to the creator. If Luna got hurt today, it would be my fault.

# 83

## Florence

Woodsmoke and Tom were waiting for me outside. Ignoring them I climbed into the panda car and pulled out of the hospital car park. The gravel screamed beneath the tyres as I pressed hard on the accelerator. The first set of traffic lights I came to were red. I turned on the blue lights and siren and went racing through.

I was breaking several police protocols and was about to smash several more. I didn't care. I was going to look those bastards in the eye and tell them they didn't scare me. For the first time in my life, I think, I'd truly lost my temper.

I was going to confront Frederick and Judith Aster, look the two of them in the face and say, '*I see you*. I know that what you are doing here is unspeakable and I will bring it to an end.'

And I would do it alone.

I drew more than one startled housewife to her door as I sped up Laurel Bank. I didn't even drop my speed when I reached the narrow track up to the manor house. Only when I pulled up outside did I switch off the siren.

I was going to be on report, even for driving here in such a manner. What I was about to do would probably get me suspended, and if I stopped to think about that, I might not be able to go on. I jumped out and hammered on the door, only then registering that the Asters' car was not parked out front.

Some of the wind slipped out of my sails.

I knocked again. Without the Asters, there was a chance I might get inside and have a proper look around.

Nothing. No one was coming to answer the door.

Remembering the way Abby had accessed the house the other night, I set off. I'd reached the corner when I heard the high-pitched scream of a young child. Knowing it gave me the excuse I needed to enter the building, I ran to try the rear door. Not only was it unlocked, it was open, caught upon a tuft of grass. The mud held traces of footprints going away from the property.

I released the truncheon from my belt as I neared the building. The porch door opened to my touch and I stepped inside a small, cramped cloakroom. Paint had peeled off the walls, and there were patches of mould in the corners. Smears of dried mud criss-crossed the tiled floor. Children's coats and outdoor boots lined one wall. The room smelled of feet and unwashed clothes.

I heard running footsteps and then a high-pitched laugh. Behind me, the back door slammed shut. I jumped round, but there was no one there. Just the wind. A second door led into the building itself, and heart racing, I pushed it carefully, closing it behind me. As I stepped into the kitchen, I looked up: at the shelves, the stained wooden worktops, the door beyond that led further into the building, the hooks on which hung saucepans and colanders and kitchen utensils. I wasn't looking at the floor.

But blood has a way of drawing attention to itself, and something pulled my gaze down to the red pool, gleaming as though still warm, creeping its way along the cracked and dirty tiles of the kitchen floor.

# 84

## Sally

Cassie tried to hide it, but I could tell she was as scared as me when she learned Luna was missing. Even Grace was worried.

'Call Roy,' she told me. 'The police won't ignore him.'

She was right. Nothing mattered more than finding Luna. All three of us gathered round the phone. Roy kept me hanging for several minutes.

'She'll be with friends,' he said, and I could tell from his hushed tone that he was with other people.

'She doesn't have any,' I told him. 'Not anymore. And I've already phoned the ones who used to be her friends. No one has seen her. And none of them offered to help me look.'

I was still smarting from the phone calls I'd had with Luna's supposed friends. Tammy Taylor's mother had put the phone down on me.

'Well, you can't blame them for that.' I heard Roy's footsteps on the polished floor of the funeral parlour. 'I'm with clients. Can I call you in an hour?'

My free hand clenched into a fist. 'The whole point of you and your mother moving in was so you would help us. If you can't, I'll pack your bags and have them waiting on the doorstep.'

I heard a sharp intake of breath down the phone as I made eye contact with a very unhappy-looking Grace.

'I'll call the superintendent.' Roy's voice had ice in it. 'And I'll look forward to your apology when this turns out to be a fuss over nothing.'

'Grace, I'm sorry,' I said, when I put the phone down. 'I didn't mean it. I'm just—'

'I know,' she said. 'You're right to be.'

'Mum, she might be at the Black Dog,' Cassie said. 'She might have gone to talk to John.'

'I phoned Beryl. She hasn't seen her.'

'Beryl doesn't know what day it is half the time. Let me go. John will help me look for her.'

I didn't want Cassie to leave, but I was running out of options. I nodded, and she pulled on shoes and ran out of the house.

'What can I do?' asked Grace.

'Stay here in case she comes back,' I said. 'And keep an eye on Marigold.'

'Sally.' Grace took hold of both my hands. 'It didn't leave with Larry, you know. It's still here.'

'What didn't?'

'The evil. You have to find her.'

# 85

## Florence

I couldn't go any further without stepping in blood. I heard the sickening squelch beneath my shoes, caught hold of the counter so that I wouldn't slip and stepped properly into the kitchen.

It was a large room, and whatever had happened here had been in the middle of clearing away after the midday meal. A stack of dirty plates and cutlery lay on the draining board by the sink. One drawer had been upturned, and assorted kitchen knives lay scattered in the blood. A pan of water on the cooker was hissing and spitting. I leaned over to turn off the gas and heard a low moan.

'Help us.'

The woman slumped in the corner was conscious but with that dull look in her eyes that said she might not be for long. Blood was pumping from a wound on her left thigh. I grabbed a towel from the sink and bent low so that I could press it onto her leg.

'I'll get help,' I said. 'What happened here?'

The towel turned red in seconds. I got up to look for another; every step I took spread the blood further around the room. 'Press hard,' I said, giving her the second towel. 'Who did this?'

She could barely speak. 'Kids,' she croaked, as the blood still flowed. 'Danger.'

I pulled off my belt. 'I need to put a tourniquet on you,' I told her. 'You're losing too much blood.'

'Kids,' she said again.

'I'll find them.' I had no choice but to kneel in the blood. Her skin felt far too cold as I wrapped my belt round her thigh and pulled it tight. When I looked back down at her wound, the blood flow had slowed.

'That's better. You should be OK now if you lie still. I'll call an ambulance.'

She was panting now, and her whole body was shaking. 'Kids,' she repeated.

'I know. I'll find them. Don't move.'

I picked up my truncheon, now slick with the woman's blood. The kitchen door opened into the main entrance hall, and in the pale light from the barred windows, I saw tiny red footprints becoming fainter as they ran towards the stairs. I followed them into the room and stopped dead.

Where the candle chandelier had hung on my last visit swayed a human figure. Made of sacking, it had a torso, arms, legs and a head, even a crudely painted face. From the solid regularity of its shape and the tiny piles beneath it on the wooden floor, I could see that it was stuffed with sand.

I stepped closer, scared but fascinated, to see that it was full of small wounds. Something had cut into the sacking, creating inch-long tears. They were knife cuts. I knew that because of several knives lying on the floor around it, and because of the one that remained stuck directly where the figure's heart would be.

Something moved behind me and I spun round. My eyes travelled up to see several small faces watching me from the landing above my head.

'I'm a police officer,' I called up to them, shocked at how unsteady my voice sounded. 'You're quite safe now. You can come down.'

The children sprang to their feet and ran out of sight.

Screaming rang out again from somewhere on the ground floor and I had a frozen moment of not knowing what to do.

Panic threatening to get the better of me, I turned back towards Judith Aster's office. Somewhere in the building, a door slammed shut.

I half expected to find Judith Aster slumped over her office desk in a pool of blood, but there was no sign of her. I got straight through to the station officer.

'Bloody Norah,' he said, when I'd filled him in. 'How do you do it, love? Right, go back to the injured woman and stay with her until help arrives. Barricade yourself into the kitchen if you can. Randy's five minutes away. Do you hear me?'

'Sarge, the kids—'

'That's an order, Flossie.'

'Yes, Sarge.' I put down the phone.

I stood trembling in Judith Aster's office, and as I always did when I was afraid or miserable, I thought of my mother. There was a day when I was only a child, when we'd been out, just the two of us, looking across some fields to the village of Bletchley, not far from where we lived.

'One day, Florence,' she'd said to me, 'you'll hear your name being called. When that happens, you can't hide away and pretend you didn't hear it.'

Somewhere in this building, right here and now, my name was being called, and I knew I'd never live with myself if I cowered behind a locked door while children were being attacked.

Telling myself it was standard procedure to check the ground floor first, knowing all the while I didn't want to get trapped upstairs, I crossed the corridor and pushed open a door.

I'd found more children. Eight of them, sitting at small wooden desks, facing an empty teacher's station.

'You're all safe now,' I said. 'I'm a police officer. Everyone's safe.'

Not one of them looked my way. Most stared straight ahead at an empty blackboard. One had his head on his desk. I reached back and banged on the door to get their attention. Not one of them batted an eyelid.

'Where's your teacher?' I said. 'Who can tell me what happened here?'

Nothing. I stepped closer to the nearest child, a girl of around ten years old. Her eyes didn't move. She showed no sign of even knowing I was there. I touched her shoulder and her head dropped onto the desk.

Was she dead? I felt her neck – warm – and her wrist. There was a pulse, but the hand I lifted fell back limply when I let it go.

'Hello!' I went from one child to the next, touching their shoulders, their foreheads, trying to get them to acknowledge me. They were like little zombies. It was one of the creepiest things I'd ever seen.

Giving up – they were all alive at least – I was about to step out into the corridor when I heard a scuffling noise behind. I turned quickly. The children hadn't moved. And yet I'd definitely heard something. I waited.

Only seven children. I'd counted eight a moment ago.

'Who moved?'

No response.

Completely unnerved, I left the room. Back in the entrance hall, I ran to the front door, pulled back the bolts and made sure it would open. Upstairs, I heard running footsteps.

With every step up towards the upper floor, I thought of my colleagues, who would be charging up these steps now, not creeping, who would be calling out instructions, reassuring the scared, not praying for help to arrive. I checked the leather strap on my truncheon, tightened my grip on the carved handle, felt its reassuring weight.

At the top of the stairs, on a wide, well-lit landing, I had no way of knowing where to go first. To the front of the building was the Asters' suite of rooms. Their door opened on to a sitting room, comfortably furnished, with floor-to-ceiling bookcases. It was empty of occupants, as were the bedroom and bathroom. Back across the landing, the first three mother-and-baby rooms were all empty too. The fourth and last was empty, but seeing it made me pause.

At first, I thought I was looking at an old-fashioned commode. It was a chair, with a large circle cut away in the seat. It wasn't a commode, though: there was nowhere the bowl could fit. And besides, why would a commode need restraints? On the arms and on the splayed footrests were leather straps and buckles. It was a birthing chair. With restraints.

The room stank of fresh paint, and the walls were white and clean. They'd been painted over recently. Harder to deal with, though, was the staining on the wooden floorboards. Blood had spread across this room. It had been cleaned away, but the stain remained. It was hard to avoid the conclusion that someone had died in here.

Only the two wings to search.

I went left, pushed open the first door I came to and found a dormitory. From the clothes hanging on wall-mounted hooks, I could see it was where the boys slept. It was a long, narrow, low-ceilinged room with twelve beds. All were empty but one. In the furthest bed from the door, I caught sight of a tuft of red hair and half ran towards it.

'Robbie?' He didn't stir when I touched his head. There was vomit on the pillow.

'Robbie?' His little face was a deathly shade of greenish-white. His lips were cracked, his tongue caked in fur. His eyes lolled open and then closed again without focusing. I picked him up, gathering his blanket around him, and heard movement.

'It's safe,' I called. 'I'm a police officer. Come out.'

Nothing. I set off, Robbie in my arms.

A giggle.

'I'm taking Robbie downstairs. I'll come back. You're safe now.'

No reply. I made it to the door and down the stairs.

Someone had closed the front door and I knew it hadn't been the wind. The wind could not fasten two bolts, one at the top and one at the bottom. Someone had locked me in.

The sacking figure swung as though someone had pushed it seconds before.

Footsteps sounded, fast and light, running towards me. I spun round a second too late. Pain stabbed at my left leg, just behind the knee. Had it not been for Robbie's blanket, I think the wound would have felled me, but the knife got tangled and the attacker's aim went astray. I found my balance, gasped in pain and stared in disbelief.

My attacker was a child.

# 86

## Sally

I was running out of options. I'd driven to the houses of all Luna's ex-friends. I'd phoned home to learn that no one, not even Cassie, had been in touch. I had no choice but to appeal to Roy again.

As I passed the public library on the way to the funeral parlour, it occurred to me that the coven might be the only people in town who would actually want to help me. Annoyed that I hadn't thought of it before, I parked and hurried into the library. Daphne was at the front desk. She put the phone down when she saw me.

'Sally, darling, Luna's here,' she said. 'I thought you might be getting anxious.'

For a second, I couldn't speak. Energy I'd been gathering for nearly an hour seemed to drain away. 'She's fine,' Daphne continued. 'I found her in the reference library a few minutes ago.'

I leaned against the front desk, relief washing through me. I could cope with anything as long as my girls were safe. I glanced over towards the reference library. Sure enough, Luna's freshly dyed, bright red hair was visible through the glass.

'I'm sorry,' Daphne went on. 'I should have called immediately.'

'No, I'm overreacting. I just . . .'

'I know.' Daphne gave a heavy sigh. 'Now, the thing is, Sally, I was wondering if I could keep her a bit longer.'

'Keep her?'

'She seems a bit down.' Daphne leaned towards me over the counter. 'Hardly surprising given what she's been through, but I just felt . . . I don't want to step on your toes, dear, but sometimes the closest of families need a break from each other.'

If I knew my daughter, she'd been sobbing hysterically and declaring she couldn't bear to go home.

'I thought I'd give her supper at our house,' Daphne said. 'Make a bit of a fuss of her, and then she can stay over in Florence's old room.'

Florence had lived with Avril and Daphne for less than a week.

'Would it be too much of a liberty, dear? Avril can run her home in the morning.'

'It's very kind of you,' I said. 'It will do her good to have a night away. Thank you.'

It would do me good, too, knowing that one of us had escaped, even temporarily, the prison our house had become.

# 87

## Florence

A boy, not much more than seven years old, with fair hair cut close to his scalp, stood just out of reach. He held a kitchen knife in his right hand. I heard a giggle behind and risked a quick look back. Two more children had appeared, both with knives, and I had no way of defending myself. Not with an unconscious Robbie in my arms.

*Kids*, the woman bleeding in the kitchen had said. I'd thought she was worried about the children. She'd been trying to tell me the kids had attacked her.

Barely had I processed the improbable horror when more children appeared. I had five of them, then seven approaching me. The stupor that had held them earlier, if it had been real and not faked, had gone and they were alert and quick-witted. Even so, something in their eyes was missing.

Finally, the shrill of a siren approaching from the road outside.

'The police are here. Put the knives down and go and sit in the classroom. Now!'

I thought one or two looked hesitant, even scared, but the boy who'd attacked me darted forward again. I had to leap out of his way, nearly tangling my feet in Robbie's blanket.

A banging at the front door made some of the kids jump, but not the blond boy. His eyes weren't leaving mine and I had the feeling that if I looked away for a second, that knife would find its way into my flesh again.

'Florence!' yelled Randy, banging again.

'I'm in here!' I called back. 'Come round the back. Quick as you can, and watch yourself.'

'Florence, let me in!'

'Negative. Officer in peril. Proceed with haste.'

I heard his footsteps running away from the door. It would be three, maybe four minutes before he reached me. In the distance, I could hear more sirens.

'Do you hear that?' I said, my head twisting this way and that as I tried to make sure no one sprang me. 'More police. They will arrest you all and they will put you in prison. If you think this place is bad, wait till you see what prison is like. This is your last chance. Put your knives down and sit on the floor.' I thought for a moment. 'Hands on heads.' Nothing. 'Now!' I yelled.

The door to the kitchen crashed open and Randy stood in the doorway. From his pallor, I judged he'd seen the injured woman. He took a moment, then strode in, blowing his whistle.

'You lot, put your weapons down and get on the floor.'

His eyes met mine. It was ridiculous. And yet I could see he was as scared as me.

The blond boy dropped his knife and ran. After a split second, the others followed.

# 88

## Sally

I'd expected Roy to be pleased that Luna was out of the house for the evening – she was the least able to hide her dislike of him – but he glared at her empty chair.

'I'm surprised at you, Sally,' he said, when I'd explained. 'Do you really think those two are a good influence on a young girl?'

Cassie said, 'Lesbianism isn't catching,' before shrinking a little into her seat at the look he gave her.

Roy turned to me. 'How can you possibly know the impact that bohemian behaviour can have on a young mind? I'd better drive over and collect her.'

'She's staying the night.' Out of the corner of my eye, I could see Cassie, Grace and even Marigold watching us nervously.

Roy said, 'Did you think to consult me?'

'No,' I said.

His eyes flashed dark and his mouth tightened. 'That attention-seeking little bitch caused me to miss a meeting and wasted valuable police time today. To say nothing of the worry she gave you and Mother. She is not being rewarded with unhealthy attention from those two queers.'

'Call my sister a bitch again and you'll be sorry,' snapped Cassie, getting to her feet.

Roy swung round to face her; Cassie held her ground. He took a deep breath, and another, and I saw his hands clenching into fists. He said, 'Call them. Tell them I'm on my way.'

'Roy, she's staying where she—'

He pushed me out of the way and made for the kitchen door.

He missed it, walking instead into the wall-mounted cupboard just inside the room. Marigold gave a nervous giggle as Grace pushed herself to her feet.

'Sit down, Roy,' she told him. 'I'm not sure you're well.'

I wasn't sure either. His eyes had lost focus. I pulled out a chair and between the two of us Grace and I guided him into it.

'You're running a temperature,' Grace said. 'Do you have a thermometer, Sally?'

I went to get it. His temperature was 101.

'Not dangerous,' I said, 'but you're probably coming down with something. Best go straight to bed. I can bring you up some soup?'

'I'm not hungry.' He got to his feet and swayed. I didn't think I'd ever disliked anyone more, but I was a nurse. I gave him my arm and led him up the stairs. At the door to his room, he declared that he could manage, and I breathed a massive sigh of relief.

# 89

## Florence

It was several hours before we were able to vacate Black Moss Manor, and much of that time we spent arguing. A team from social services arrived and tried to make us leave. They would deal with the children, they said, our presence was only upsetting them. Woodsmoke, the officer in charge, was having none of it. He had two stab wounds to process and that made it a police matter.

The only staff member on the premises, the woman I'd found bleeding in the kitchen, was rushed to hospital. A second ambulance came for Robbie.

More officers arrived and began a search of the building. As one of them remarked, it was like a creepy game of hide-and-seek. The children didn't want to be found, and they knew this building a whole lot better than we did. Several of my colleagues suffered minor injuries from having missiles hurled at them by unseen assailants.

As soon as I could, I slipped out and dressed my own wound with a first-aid kit from the panda car. I knew Woodsmoke would try to send me to hospital too if he could.

It took an hour to round up all the children, and the team from social services continued to countermand every order the sergeant gave. Before the second hour was done, I was sure he was about to start arresting them. As ambulances became free, the children were taken to nearby hospitals for observation and any necessary treatment. By the time the sun was setting, the building was empty apart from echoes and bad memories. I can't honestly say it felt any different.

'Were you right? Was it Godfrey's Cordial?'

I turned to see Tom in the doorway. He'd been on another case all day and this was the first I'd seen of him.

'Either that or something like it,' I said. 'We found various weird and wonderful potions in the kitchen. They're all being taken away to be analysed.'

We were a long way from knowing all the facts, but it was hard to avoid the conclusion that the children had been habitually drugged to keep them manageable, and that withdrawal symptoms, possibly because supplies had run low, had led to the violent, irrational behaviour we'd witnessed that day.

Tom took a step into the room and whistled as he looked round.

'It's pretty impressive,' I agreed.

We were in the basement, in a space I'd have expected to be dark and dingy, the creepiest part of an unpleasant building, but which actually seemed brighter, and more modern, than any hospital facility I'd been in. There were no windows, but the electric bulbs were powerful. White tiles covered the walls and floor, and gleaming counters ringed the room. Other smaller rooms leading off this one held medical supplies and equipment.

'You and Sally delivered a baby in a cell,' Tom said. 'What did they need all this for?'

'This is nothing,' I said. 'Come through.'

I led Tom into the next room, a large school gymnasium, with a highly polished floor, full of climbing, swinging and jumping equipment.

'What the hell's that?' Tom asked, as a high-pitched screeching rang out.

'That would be the monkey. He's very excitable.'

We moved on, through another door, to find cages stacked on either side of the last basement room. From a central cage, the thin monkey screamed at us.

'Five rabbits, three guinea pigs, two hamsters, and the white mice won't stay still long enough for me to count them,' I said. 'The gerbils are staying in their tunnels. I think there's one black rat, but I can't be sure.'

'They loved their pets,' Tom said, wrinkling his nose.

'Do these look loved to you?' I'd also found a sixth rabbit, dead in its cage. 'Come and look at this.' I led the way to a large upright freezer and opened the door. Several dead animals lay on the shelves.

'Christ, are they planning to eat them?' Tom said. 'Have we phoned the RSPCA?'

'They can't move them all today. They've asked that we make sure they have food and water. They'll collect them tomorrow.'

We set off back upstairs. Neither of us wanted to stay in the room with the animals.

'We found the Asters in town,' Tom said as we crossed the gymnasium. 'They'd gone to visit a Sandra Cartwright, who also works here, so we got three of them in one go. They're all at the station. The injured one's under arrest in hospital. That leaves one more still on the run.'

We heard footsteps and then Randy appeared in the doorway. 'I'm driving you to the hospital,' he said. 'Woodsmoke's orders.'

'I live with thirty nurses,' I said. 'I don't need a hospital.'

Randy looked uncertain, his eyes going from Tom to me.

'It stopped bleeding hours ago,' I said. 'If anyone at the hostel's worried, I can go in the morning.'

Randy said, 'He said you might say that. In which case, I'm to drive you home and make sure you stay there.'

'I'll drive Florence home,' Tom said.

'I've got a car outside,' I said. 'I'll drive myself.'

'That reminds me, Tom – Woodsmoke wants you,' Randy said. 'I think he needs you to take charge of searching the Asters' rooms.'

For a second, I thought Tom was going to argue, but he shrugged and set off for the door. 'I'll see you later, Floss,' he said, before he vanished.

'The sergeant did that himself earlier,' I said when Tom's footsteps had faded.

Randy nodded. 'I know. I need to tell you something. I went to see Sandra Cartwright myself first thing this morning. Before I started work.'

'The woman we've just arrested? The one the Asters were visiting?'

'She and my mum were at school together. She told me some stuff. We don't know the half of it, Florence.'

'Randy!' We heard Woodsmoke a second before we saw him in the doorway.

'I'll come and find you later,' Randy muttered in my ear. 'Ten o'clock. Meet me in the hostel car park.'

# 90

## Sally

After we'd cleared away the dishes, Cassie went to her room and the rest of us to watch television. I turned up the volume so that Grace could hear, and then she, Marigold and I watched *Coronation Street*, *The Avengers* and then the news. I think we'd all fallen into a sort of TV stupor when we heard yelling from upstairs. I could make out Roy and Cassie. And then a third voice.

No one else should be in the house.

'Dirty little whore!' Roy was yelling as I reached the stairs.

'Get off him, you maniac!' shouted back Cassie.

Before I was halfway up the stairs, there was a scuffle and then someone was thrown over the banister from the landing. I heard Cassie scream, just as the figure hurtling towards me shot out a hand and stopped himself from falling further. He lay on the stairs, panting. It was John Donnelly, with no shoes on his feet, his shirt unbuttoned, his nose bleeding.

Cassie yelped again as Roy appeared at the top of the stairs. He was in a dressing gown, which swung open. His face was deathly pale, and I could see sweat gleaming on his chest. As John scrambled to his feet, Roy thundered down the stairs towards him.

'He hit me. Mum, he hit me.' Cassie's pale face peered over the banister. She too was in her dressing gown.

John pulled himself to his feet a second before Roy sprang at him. The two of them fell into me and I had to grip the banister tightly to stop all three of us from tumbling down.

'Stop it, both of you.'

They ignored me, locked in a tussle. John was younger and fitter, but Roy had weight and gravity on his side. One of them – I'm not sure which – caught me under the chin and I almost fell. I bit back the pain and opened my mouth. 'Grace, call the police!'

Through the banister, I could see Grace in the sitting room doorway, pale and shocked. She didn't move. Behind her, Marigold trembled with Henry in her arms. Roy had his hands round John's throat by this time and was choking him. I pulled myself up and clutched at Roy's hands as Cassie ran down to join me. Between us, we managed to pull them apart.

'Leave,' I hissed at John.

He stood his ground.

'We're fine,' I said, feeling Roy's weight pressing into me and knowing he would spring again any second. 'Go.'

John backed down the last few steps, seemed about to say something to Cassie but then turned and ran, barefoot and half dressed, through the front door. Roy turned back to Cassie.

'Don't you dare.' I placed myself directly in his path.

Cassie fled, scrambling back up the stairs and into her room. I heard the lock being pulled and breathed a sigh of relief, even as Roy pushed me out of the way and followed her up. I thought about following but ran down the steps instead.

Upstairs, Roy was banging on Cassie's door. 'Open this door, you little tart,' he yelled.

I picked up the phone and dialled 999. 'Police,' I said. 'My daughter is being attacked.'

Roy, faster than I'd have believed he could move, was coming down the stairs towards me. I held eye contact with him as I gave the address to the police and asked for immediate assistance. Roy reached the bottom of the stairs.

'Put the phone down,' he said in a low voice.

I held out my left arm, hand splayed, to ward him off. He paused.

'You have to come now,' I said into the phone. 'My family and I are in danger.' Only when the operator assured me someone would be with me shortly did I put down the phone.

'You leave tonight,' I told Greenwood. 'Your mother can stay until it's convenient for her to go home. You will never come in here again.'

He took a step towards me.

'I call upon the powers of the night to curse this man.' I yelled the words, holding both arms above my head. 'I summon the power of the dark moon to strike him down.' I was bluffing, of course. No witch can summon up powers in that fashion, but a good percentage of witchcraft is the ability to make people believe. And, sometimes, to scare them witless.

'What the hell do you think you're doing?' Roy had stopped moving, not nearly as sure of himself as he had been. His breathing had quickened, too. I began muttering under my breath and let every ounce of hatred I felt towards him show in my eyes.

'Stop that,' he complained.

'Don't touch her!' Cassie, dressed now, had appeared at the top of the stairs.

Roy turned to face Cassie. 'Filthy little slag,' he snarled, and then he staggered back against the wall.

'Roy, you're ill.' Finally, his mother ventured out of the sitting room doorway. 'This isn't you talking. Let's get you back upstairs. I'll bring you something to drink.'

Cassie was creeping down the steps. I shook my head at her, trying to tell her to stay out of the way, but she kept coming. She reached the bottom a second before the Greenwoods got there.

'She was rutting with that publican's boy.' Roy tried to pull away from his mother to reach for Cassie.

'I'm warning you, Roy, that's enough,' I said. 'Grace, take him into the sitting room. I'm calling a taxi.'

Her face took on a pleading look. 'He's not well.'

'He's violent and unstable. I want him out of my house.'

'Like mother, like daughters. Slags, the lot of you.' Greenwood pushed his mother away and stood upright. His hands went to the waistline of his pyjama bottoms and tugged at the cord that held them up. 'Is this what you want, you pair of slags?'

Cassie yelped in horror and ran for the front door. She pulled it open and fled out into the night.

# 91

## Florence

Randy was late. Ten o'clock came and went. I waited in the car park for fifteen minutes before I checked with the night porter to see if anyone had left a message. No one had.

I hung around another ten minutes and thought about cycling into town, but if Randy wasn't at the station, what would I do? All around me, it seemed, people were lying, obfuscating, concealing.

The porter wandered outside for a cigarette in the evening air. 'You waiting for your young man?' he asked.

'A colleague,' I said. 'I think he's forgotten.'

'Happen busy,' the porter said. 'There were a lot of sirens about an hour ago. Something's happened up on the Burnley Road, I reckon.'

A cold, hard feeling, one I couldn't quite identify, began to grow in my stomach.

'Here he is,' the porter said. 'His wife know you two have a thing going, does she?'

The car wasn't a panda but a gold Ford Cortina, and it was Tom, not Randy, who was pulling into the car park. The heavy mass inside me grew bigger. Tom switched off the engine and got out. The porter moved away and I walked towards Tom. I knew the feeling inside me now. It was called dread.

'What's happened?' The last time I'd seen that look on Tom's face had been the night we arrested Larry Glassbrook.

Tom pulled open the passenger door. 'Get in,' he told me, but his voice was gentle, and it trembled a little.

'I can't go anywhere. I'm waiting for Randy.'

Tom said nothing. I got in the car. When he'd climbed back into the driver's seat, he didn't start the engine.

'Sharples sent me,' he said. 'It's bad, Floss.'

I was thinking, *At least it's not you. Nothing's happened to you, so it can't be that bad, can it?*

Tom ran the back of his hand over his eyes. 'Randy's panda car was involved in an accident up on the Burnley Road. Hit-and-run. He was driven into a ditch.'

'Is he OK?' I asked, knowing he couldn't be. Tom wasn't here to give me good news.

'They took him to Burnley General. I'm sorry, Floss. I know you two were mates. He was dead on arrival.'

# 92

## Sally

I followed Cassie from the house, but by the time I'd manoeuvred my car round Roy's, she'd vanished. I figured she could only be going to the Black Dog. It took just minutes to reach the town centre, and as I pulled into the empty car park, sure enough, I saw Cassie vanishing through the staff entrance.

Close behind, I made my way along the back corridor towards the kitchen, hearing voices before I reached it. Cassie crying. Beryl complaining. John pleading.

'She can't go back there, Mum – he's a nutter.'

'You told me you'd stay away from her.'

'I love her.'

I pushed open the door to find the three of them grouped round the central work table, which was piled high with dirty crockery from the evening meal. Cassie was bright pink from running. John's face was streaked with blood, but it wasn't flowing. They both looked OK. Beryl opened her mouth to protest my arrival and thought better of it.

I turned to her son first. 'John, are you all right? Did he hurt you?'

'He ran home barefoot,' Beryl snapped at me. 'His feet are cut to ribbons.'

John's feet were dirty, but there was no blood that I could see.

'Is there anything you need me to take a look at?' I said. 'My bag's in the car.'

He shook his head. 'I'm OK. I shouldn't have left you with him.'

I gave him a half-smile. I didn't object to John, not really. 'Good. Cassie, come with me.'

She stepped away from me. 'I'm not going back there.'

'You don't have to. I'm taking you to join Luna.'

'She can stay here,' John said.

'No, she can't,' Beryl and I said, together.

'Why not?' Cassie snapped back. 'We've slept together before. Better that than be raped by that creep Greenwood.'

'I'm sure he—'

'He wants all three of us, Mum. You, me and Luna. Probably Marigold as well, he's that sick. I'm staying with John. You can't stop me.'

'I can,' said Beryl.

John moved to Cassie's side and put his arm round her. She leaned against him as though her body had been carved to fit exactly into his, and I thought, *They're made for each other. The timing is wrong, but these two are a pair. They are meant to be.*

'Mum, we mean it,' John said. 'We're getting married. I'll be old enough in a few months. You can't stop us.'

'Neither of you can get married without your parents' permission.' I tried to make my voice gentle. 'Not until you're eighteen. If you both still want to in two years, well, I'm sure it won't be a problem.'

I was playing for time. A lot can happen in two years.

'Yes, it will,' said Beryl, her voice verging on shrill. 'You can't get married. Not ever.'

'Why not?' For the first time, I thought I saw doubt in Cassie's eyes.

Beryl started looking around for something – her cigarettes, a drink – and in that moment, I knew what she was about to tell us. I backed away until I found a wall I could lean against. My poor girl. My poor, poor girl.

'Why not?' John repeated. 'Mum, why can't I marry Cassie?'

Whatever Beryl had been looking for, she didn't find it. She gave up. 'Because you're brother and sister,' she said.

A moment of silence that I wished could last for ever. Then—

'Liar,' Cassie spat.

John had turned pale.

Beryl spoke to Cassie. 'I'm not lying. I was seeing Larry before he started going with your mum.'

Cassie's head shot round to face me, her eyes angry, as though I was to blame. Was I? I knew Larry had been seeing Beryl before he and I got together. Was this my fault?

'So?' Cassie said. 'John's younger than me. You'd have to have kept seeing him even after my mum and dad got married.' Her words were defiant, but I could see from her face she was starting to believe it.

'I never stopped seeing Larry.' Beryl couldn't look at any of us as she made her confession. 'Not for more than a few months. When I found out I was pregnant with John, I talked Ted into marrying me.'

I thought perhaps I'd always known that Larry's betrayal went far, far deeper than I'd been prepared to admit.

John was shaking his head, mouthing the word 'no'. I could see from his face he wasn't taking it in.

'It's not right, what you've been doing,' Beryl said. 'I blame myself. I should have told you before, but I never thought—'

'I don't believe it,' Cassie shrieked. 'I bet you were shagging half of Sabden. John could be anyone's.'

'Cass—' John began.

'Cassie, it's true,' I said. 'Look at him. He looks like your dad.' I couldn't believe I hadn't seen it before. John looked like Larry had when I met him. They were the same build, had the same colouring. Their eyes were practically identical. Larry had a son, and he— Oh God.

Cassie pulled away from John and her face crumpled. I was about to go to her when the inner door burst open and we saw Ted Donnelly, Beryl's husband, in the doorway.

He was in shirtsleeves, the braces of his trousers frayed and grubby. He was overweight, losing his hair and looked years older than his actual age, which I guessed was around forty-five. His face was heavy and lined, his features indistinct, and his ears were covered with thick hairs. He had a brown beer bottle in one hand.

'Ted.' Beryl looked wary. 'How long have you been there?'

'Long enough.' He looked at John. 'Knew you weren't mine,' he said. 'Waste of fucking space like you.'

'Cassie, we have to go,' I said.

She shook her head.

'The lot of you can piss off.' Ted swayed in the doorway and I realised he was even more drunk than usual. 'Out! Go on, get out.'

'We're going nowhere,' Beryl said. 'John is going to bed. Sally, take your lass and leave.'

There was nothing I'd rather do, but Ted was looking at the boy he'd just learned wasn't his son. 'Little bastard,' he sneered. 'Little bastard of a lying whore.'

John snapped. He yelled something I couldn't catch and flung himself at his father. Ted had had a lot to drink and was taken off guard. He staggered back and the two of them fell from the room. Beryl rushed after them, Cassie a second later. I was the last to arrive in the doorway, and as I did so, I heard a sickening crash and a moan of pain from John. Ted had struck him over the head with the bottle. Glass fell around John's shoulders, and blood sprang out of a cut on his forehead. He slumped against the wall, dazed.

His anger far from satisfied, Ted was trying to get to the boy, Beryl holding him back. Cassie ran to John. Ted flung Beryl away from him and staggered back to get his balance, just as John sprang at him again. They both fell against the cellar door. It burst open, revealing the black hole of the steps. John grasped the door frame and steadied himself. Ted stumbled; his arms flailed; he missed his footing and vanished from our sight.

We stared at the dark doorway in horror.

I counted six thuds as various body parts hit the stairs and then finally the stone floor. For long seconds, none of us moved. Then John pulled away from Cassie and made for the cellar steps.

'Let me,' I said, holding him back. 'I'll go.'

I found the light switch. I could see Ted, but not what state he was in. 'Wait here,' I told the others.

Before I got to the bottom of the steps, I was sure Ted would be badly injured. He'd landed on his head, and the rest of his body had crumpled around him. I thought his neck might be broken. I reached him and kneeled by his side.

I didn't stay in the cellar long.

When I reached the top of the stairs again, I pulled my sleeve over my hand, wiped my fingerprint off the light switch, closed the door behind me and faced the other three. 'Who else is in the pub?' I asked.

'Is he all right?' John asked.

'He's dead. Who else is in the pub?' I said.

'No one,' Beryl told me, as John turned away and leaned his head against the wall. 'The staff left after last orders. I cash up on Wednesdays.'

Cassie wrapped her arms round John.

'Any customers?' I asked. 'Anyone staying upstairs?'

Beryl shook her head.

'I'm taking Cassie home,' I said. 'Beryl, you and John go upstairs to bed. In the morning, you look for Ted and you find him at the bottom of the cellar steps.'

'But—' she began.

'It was an accident,' I said. 'And that's what the police will be told. They don't need to know anyone else was involved.'

'We can't—'

'Ted is known to be a drinker. People in the bar tonight will have seen that he had a lot, maybe more than usual. He tripped at the top of the steps and fell. It was a terrible accident. And you knew nothing about it until the next morning.'

Beryl shook her head.

'The alternative is that John is arrested and charged with manslaughter,' I said. 'Possibly even murder. What good would that do anyone?'

This time, no one argued with me. I took Cassie's hand, pulled her away from John, and the two of us left the pub.

# 93

## Florence

'Sure you're OK to do this?' Tom asked me, for the third time, as he braked to a sharp stop in front of a parked car.

'This' was to attend a call-out to the Glassbrook house. Sally had dialled 999 again. I brushed a fresh crop of tears away. 'I'm OK.'

'Guess it's what we signed up for,' he said, as he got out of the car.

Tom was right. Randy's death just had to be worked through, filed away until I had the time to face it properly. I followed Tom as we hurried round Roy Greenwood's car and knocked on the front door. Nothing happened. The house had an empty feel about it. By unspoken agreement, we set off for the back of the house.

'How long since the call came in?' I asked.

'Best part of an hour,' Tom replied.

I looked at my watch. It was gone eleven, an hour since Sally had phoned claiming she and her family were being attacked.

Tom saw my face and held up both hands. 'No one available. We were either up at Black Moss Manor or out on the Burnley Road. And Sally's been crying wolf a bit too often of late.'

We'd reached the back of the house. 'Christ knows, though,' Tom said, 'we don't need any more bad news today.'

The door was unlocked.

'Sally?' I called in a low voice.

No reply.

'I don't like this,' I said, unnecessarily.

We checked the pantry, the room where Sally did her laundry and both sitting rooms. On one sofa, I found baby Henry's blanket.

At the foot of the stairs, Tom banged hard on the wall. 'Police. Can you all leave your rooms?'

Nothing.

Pulling away from Tom, I ran up. He caught up with me at the top of the steps. 'You know who sleeps where?' he asked.

'I used to.' I looked at the door directly in front of me. 'That was Randy's room.'

'Focus. Where's Sally's?'

Sally's room was empty, as was the one next to it, which the two girls now shared.

'Jesus!' Tom snapped as he stepped back into the corridor. I looked over his shoulder to see Grace Greenwood in a long white nightdress. Her hair was loose and stuck out around her face like white straw as she stood outside the room that used to be Cassie's.

'Is Sally back?' she asked. 'She ran out after Cassie.'

'Ran where?' Tom said.

Grace shook her head.

'Where's Marigold?' I asked.

'In her room, I expect.' Grace indicated the room that Randy used to sleep in. 'Have you seen Roy?'

'I'll go,' I told Tom, and pushed open the door gently, afraid to startle Marigold and wake Henry. I let the light from the hall seep into the room and felt a cold weight in my heart. That room, too, was empty. Worse, there were signs of a struggle. Henry's cot had been roughly pushed against the wardrobe, as though someone had fallen against it, and the bedclothes had been pulled up and off the bed. A bedside lamp had tumbled over.

'Florence!' Tom called. I ran back along the landing and into the room that used to belong to Ron Pickles. The whole room stank. Switching on the light, I saw Tom kneeling on the floor beside Roy Greenwood, who seemed to have collapsed while trying to get into bed.

'Get an ambulance!' Tom had pulled open Greenwood's dressing gown and was using both fists to pump at his heart. 'I think he might have had a heart attack.'

I didn't wait to be told twice. I ran out of the room, past the scared-looking Grace and down the stairs. I did what I was told, but I knew Tom was wrong. I'd seen heart attacks before. Greenwood's room stank of vomit and diarrhoea. His skin had been a greenish-white, except where it was scarred with red weals. Blood had pooled in his eye sockets, running down his face like tears. This was no heart attack.

# 94

## Sally

My house had been taken over by police. They'd been ignoring me for weeks and now they were everywhere, looking for Marigold and Henry. A constable poked his head into the kitchen. 'Nothing,' he said. 'She's not on the premises.'

He vanished, as the clock in the hallway struck one.

'What about the park?' I said to Florence, who was taking my statement. 'She likes the swings.'

I was clutching at straws. Marigold was nervous in the dark; she'd never go to the park by herself at night.

'We're checking everywhere close by,' Florence said. 'Carry on, please, Sally. You said Roy frightened Cassie and she ran out.'

'I followed Cassie out of the house,' I said. 'I found her at the bottom of Wraithe Road and drove her to Avril and Daphne's. We didn't go in straight away, though. Cassie wanted to talk, so I pulled over for a while. Avril and Daphne agreed to let her stay, and I came back here. The ambulance was pulling away as I turned into the road, and there was no sign of Marigold anywhere. Have you heard how Roy is?'

Florence finished writing and looked up. 'So, you last saw Marigold here?'

There was something Florence wasn't telling me. Her eyes were filling with tears and she kept wiping them away when she thought I wasn't looking.

'What's wrong?' I asked. 'What's happened?'

She shook her head. 'Busy day,' she said. 'And it's late. When did you last see Marigold and the baby?'

'They were here when I left. Have you checked the garden? It's not that cold out. She may have found keys to the shed, to Larry's workshop.'

'We've checked,' Florence said. 'And the entire house. Even the attic. There's no sign of them. And Henry's pram is missing.'

'She would have been scared,' I said. 'Roy was out of his mind. I shouldn't have left her.'

Florence put a hand on my shoulder. 'We'll pick her up soon,' she said. 'She can't have gone far.'

'What does Grace say?' I hadn't seen Roy's mother since I'd got back.

'Mrs Greenwood says Roy told her and Marigold to go to bed after you and Cassie left the house. They both did and she fell asleep. She doesn't know what happened after that until Tom and I arrived.'

The kitchen door opened then and a thin man who I remembered from the night of Larry's arrest appeared. Sharples, his name was. He was followed by another plain-clothed police officer and, finally, by Tom Devine. Florence got to her feet. The thin man locked eyes with me.

*He knows*, I thought. He knows what I did tonight. He knows that Ted Donnelly wasn't dead when I found him at the bottom of the cellar steps. He will be, by morning, if no one finds him: the bleeding from his head wound was too severe for him to survive more than a few hours, but he wasn't dead when I left him.

I made a call in that cellar. I could try and save a man so that he could carry on beating up his wife and child, maybe even have his son charged and convicted of a serious offence. I could see the boy my daughter loved serving time in a juvenile prison, or I could let nature take its course.

'Lovelady, go with DC Devine, please,' Sharples said. 'You're needed up at Black Moss Manor.'

'What's happened?' Florence asked.

Sharples glared at her, but Devine answered in a low voice. 'It's on fire,' he said. 'We might need to evacuate the nearby streets.' He walked to the back door and held it open for her. I had the impression he was hurrying her out. Florence turned back to me. 'I'll see you tomorrow,' she said. 'Don't worry about Marigold – we'll find her.'

'That will do, Lovelady,' Sharples said, and took another step towards me. 'Sally Glassbrook?'

'That's me,' I said, thinking, *He knows who I am. Everyone in town knows who I am.* At the door, Devine was trying to pull Florence from the house. She was resisting him.

'What's going on?' she said. 'Sir, what aren't you telling me?'

'Get her out of here, Tom,' Sharples snapped. And then he turned back to me.

'Sally Glassbrook,' he said, 'I'm arresting you on suspicion of the murder of Roy Greenwood.'

Roy was dead? That wasn't possible. I think I was on the point of opening my mouth to say, *No, you mean Ted Donnelly. I may have killed one man tonight. I didn't kill two,* when I was turned around and my hands clasped behind my back.

'You do not have to say anything,' Sharples droned. 'Anything you do say may be given in evidence.'

Roy could not be dead. I'd made sure of it.

I was pushed from my house and into the waiting police car and all I could think was, *How? How did she do it?*

# PART THREE

### 1999
### *Twenty-four hours after*
### *Larry Glassbrook's funeral*

Lancashire Morning Post
Wednesday 11 August 1999
By Abby Thorn, guest editor

**Police Superintendent Missing After Met Chief's Son's Kidnap**

Police Superintendent Tom Devine is believed missing this morning, following twenty-four hours that evoked bitter memories of Sabden's darkest days. Devine's parents, Harold and Mary, have expressed grave concerns for their son's safety; Lancashire constabulary are declining to comment at this time.

They say a week is a long time in politics; well, it seems a day can be even longer in the county-home of the Pendle witches, the Moors Murderers and convicted murderer Larry Glassbrook.

Yesterday morning, the funeral service for Sabden's most notorious former resident took place amid a heavy police presence and watched by crowds of angry townsfolk. In the late 1960s Glassbrook abducted and murdered three local teenagers; his modus operandi, to bury his victims alive, making these some of the most notorious and heinous crimes in England's history.

To the surprise of many, the funeral was attended by Florence Lovelady, currently the most senior serving female police officer in Britain, who was responsible for catching Glassbrook thirty years ago.

Simultaneously, causing more than one Sabden resident to question the timing, the remains of the four children found at the former Black Moss Manor Children's Home were cremated in a brief service at the town's crematorium. Which event, people are asking today, was intended to deflect attention from the other?

More was to come: hours later, in an astonishing twist, Ben Brown, Lovelady's fifteen-year-old son, was abducted from his hotel room in a manner identical to Glassbrook's method of kidnapping his young victims. Brown was missing for several hours before being found alive and unharmed. He is expected to return to his home in London with his father today.

Superintendent Devine, a former colleague and old friend of Assistant Commissioner Lovelady, led the hunt for the missing teenager, before losing contact with his colleagues in the early hours. Privately, several of these same colleagues have admitted they fear the worst.

Lovelady was unavailable for comment this morning.

The apparent coincidence of a teenage boy being abducted on the very day that the notorious Glassbrook was laid to rest, especially a child who, through his mother, is so close to the original investigation, hasn't escaped the notice of several town residents. Some are even questioning whether justice was really served all those years ago. And so we ask ourselves this morning: where is Tom Devine? What really happened to Florence Lovelady's son last night? And, most importantly:

What secrets has Larry Glassbrook taken to his grave?

# 95

## Florence

What secrets will I take to my grave?

I get up from the bench where I've been reading Abby's leader piece in this morning's *Post*. It's still early, but I'm wearing full dress uniform and am already drawing attention. I have no hope of anonymity today.

I leave the paper behind on the wooden seat, front page up, so that the photograph of Larry's coffin being lowered into the ground stares up at the world, and I think Abby is right. A day is a very long time in Sabden.

Because Larry, I've learned, was innocent after all. Larry, a victim like so many others, took the blame for murders he didn't commit. Larry was the bravest, kindest, most noble man I have ever met and a part of me, I realise, has known this all along. I want to scream it aloud, not to rest until everyone hears what I discovered in the last twenty-four hours, and yet I know that's impossible. Larry went to his grave a monster, and a monster he must remain.

It is only a short walk back to the hospital where my son lies sleeping, guarded by his father, red-eyed and crumpled after an early flight from Paris. I nearly lost Ben last night. The few hours he was missing were, and will remain, the worst of my life. There cannot possibly be pain equal to what I felt during that time. I have stared into the abyss . . .

Tom's disappearance is already the focus of police attention this morning. In the short time I've been out, I've seen more patrol cars than I'd expect, even allowing for the events of last night. It's possible some of his colleagues suspect what I know: that Tom betrayed me, that he was involved in Ben's abduction. If so, they'll believe him to have left the area, and will put their best resources into looking for him. They won't find him. I hid his body far too well for that.

The hospital is in sight and I must pull on the mask of normality once more, so that those closest to me don't suspect how much I've changed. I crossed a line last night. I became the very thing I hunt: a monster.

Oh, well.

# 96

## The Poisoner

The poisoner is clever.

As so many of her sisters have left behind the ways of the old craft, the poisoner has learned to adapt with the times. The poisoner knows her enemies, and that her enemies have grown wiser. Their skills, in many ways, outstrip hers. There are few traps she can set that they are unable to spring.

The ancient skills – the gathering of plants and fungi, the boiling of syrups and the distilling of tinctures – will not avail her now because she knows that every contact leaves a trace. The men who find the dead are trained to be suspicious. The men who cut open the dead will find the atropine, the aconitine and the digitalis, and track them back to their source.

The foxglove is no longer her dear friend. The paralysis of bittersweet has turned entirely bitter because the toxicology tests will find it. The autumn crocus, one of her favourites for the painful death it brings, will still cause organ failure in her victims – and her own imprisonment. The poisons that served her grandmothers and great-grandmothers are no use to her now.

Carbon monoxide, though? Now, that has some possibilities.

The poisoner is clever. She has learned to adapt with the times. And she has a plan.

# 97

## Cassie

The day after we put Larry in the ground, Avril and Daphne are strong-arming me again. They're bloody tenacious for a couple of old dears, and frankly, I've had it up to here with them. They get me as far as the church gate.

'Why?' I plant my feet like a toddler. 'Why the hell are we doing this again?'

'We're doing nothing again.' Avril's bony hand lands on my shoulder. 'What happened here yesterday had nothing to do with us.'

My own dad's funeral had nothing to do with me? These two are loco.

'So much hate,' Daphne adds. 'It's still here. I can see it.'

'You're looking at litter,' I grumble, adding, 'you daft old bat,' but only in my head. Fair play, though – there's crap everywhere: fag packets, sweet wrappers, even beer cans. Clearly entertainment wasn't enough for the great, unwashed mob of yesterday; they also brought refreshments.

'A short, private memorial service,' says Avril. 'Respectful and loving, for those who knew Larry best.'

'Whatever,' I say.

It's two whole days since Avril and Daphne pitched up at the Black Dog and found Tammy, Beryl, Mary and me screaming at each other like fishwives. I went along willingly enough as they frogmarched me out of the building and into their spare room. The tension in the pub was beginning to wear me down and I was sure that John would be with me in hours.

He didn't come. All day long, as I bit my nails and tried not to snap at Avril and Daphne, I told myself he needed time, that he'd spend the day packing his things, making arrangements for the pub, telling his children. When the light faded, I sneaked out. His van wasn't in the pub's car park. It didn't matter, I told myself. We had the rest of our lives. I could give him a day.

I'd been sure, so sure that he'd come to the funeral yesterday, that he wouldn't leave me to face it alone. Bastard didn't show. I sat in the gallery, looking down on Luna playing chief mourner, on Florence trying, and failing, to be inconspicuous and knew he wasn't in church. Afterwards, I stood at the back of the crowd, recognised by no one, watching people spitting on my father's grave – on his father's grave too – and finally, I knew it was over.

John doesn't want me. All my plans have come to nothing. And now I know what despair feels like.

God, that bunch of weeds Daphne is carrying stinks. Her arms are full of garden roses, daisies and buddleia. There were no flowers for Larry at his official funeral yesterday – on my instructions, I admit – and Daphne seems determined to make up for that now. She was in the garden at dawn. She's a sweet old thing, I suppose. Daft as a brush but kind.

'What are they doing here?' At the far end of the churchyard, beside the mound of earth that covers Larry, stand my mother and sister. 'I thought Luna went back to London.'

'Not yet,' Daphne replies.

Sally is wearing a dress I remember. At this distance, she almost looks young again. Her hair looks better, too. Luna has done this.

'I don't want to speak to them,' I say.

Behind my mother and sister, I can see Dwane, dressed as he used to when he took care of the churchyards. He meant it, then. He dug my father's grave himself.

Idiots. They're all idiots.

Avril hands me a handkerchief. 'Cassie, I know you're in pain, but we have to stay together,' she says. 'What we're facing is too important.'

'What?' A fresh unease creeps over me. 'What are we facing?'

They speak together.

'Soon,' Avril says.

'Tonight,' Daphne says.

I start to say that I'm leaving once this carnival is over, but I'm distracted by new arrivals. Through the church gate comes Marlene Labaddee, followed by Hecate, the spiritualist. Her daughter, Perdita Collins, was in my year at school. Perdita would hold seances in the school library when the teachers weren't around, using an upturned glass and letters cut from an exercise book. Petrifying Perdita we called her. The woman walking by Hecate's side is obviously Perdita, but Perdita grown up looks different. Her hair is dark and well cut. She wears a smart suit, unlike her mother, who still favours crushed velvet and cheesecloth.

I see Jenny Ogilvy, Dwane's wife, and Mary, our old housekeeper. They are all witches. Larry would have pissed himself laughing.

The witches have brought wild flowers. I see mugwort, meadowsweet, guelder rose and mallow, flowers that take away heartache, ease pain, soothe a troubled soul. I hope they work for Larry. I doubt they would for me right now.

Beryl Donnelly walks through the gate carrying a single red rose. If she's wise, she'll stay well clear of my mother. I swear if Tammy is here, I will rip her throat out. Then a tall man in a dark suit appears and something about him suggests police officer. Behind him comes Florence Lovelady, in uniform this time, and from a side door, the vicar appears.

I have nothing to fear from Florence anymore, I realise. Nothing she can do to me can compare to losing John. It no longer matters what Larry did or didn't tell her. Let her do her worst.

'Who knew my dad was so popular,' I say as I set off again, because I might as well get this farce over with so that I can leave this godforsaken town for good.

# 98

## Florence

I hate this town.

Watching the hire car with my husband at the wheel turn the corner and disappear on the road south feels like the hardest thing I've ever done. For a second, the urge to leap into my own car and chase his down the road is close to irresistible. I resist, of course. I'm not done here yet.

I will always hate this town. The worst period of my life was spent here and I've carried its legacy on my back ever since. Sabden came close to destroying me, and the twenty-four hours I've been back have been harder than I could have imagined. Once again, it almost robbed me of everything I hold dear.

I still can't leave.

Thirty years ago, I failed. I played a part in closing down Black Moss Manor, but I didn't dig deep enough. Distracted by grief, by demands that came at me from every side, I gave up too quickly. I accepted part-truths as answers and turned a blind eye to the questions that really mattered.

It was more than child neglect, and it didn't end in 1969.

For thirty years I've been telling myself that the darkness I always sensed here was down to Larry and that in arresting him, I drove it away. I could not have been more wrong. The evil in this town never left. In less than a day, so much has happened, and I've been forced to confront truths I should have acknowledged years ago. I know about the Craftsmen now, and if I don't face them, then who will?

All is silent in the churchyard behind me. The short, private service for Larry's close family and friends has finished, and the others have left. I am alone. I turn on the spot to make sure, checking the shadows that dart around the headstones as the clouds move overhead. Yes, quite alone. The ghosts have gone, for now.

The town cemetery is bigger than I remember. At the western edge, not far from the crematorium, I spot a tall man in the uniform of a police superintendent. At the sight of him, I feel the tension of the last few days slipping away and notice, with a stab of guilt, that my longing to be elsewhere is lessening.

Thirty years after I fell in love with him, Tom Devine is still one of the handsomest men I have ever known. There are lines on his face, of course, and silver in his hair. His jawline isn't as tight as it once was, and he no longer has the slender wiriness of youth. But his eyes are the same deep blue, and his face has kept its strong, clean lines. He is better-looking now, I think, than he was in his twenties, or perhaps that thought simply reflects how much I have changed.

Or maybe I haven't changed at all. Maybe I'm still the green young girl in love for the first time. As I walk towards him, as his face breaks into that familiar smile, I see the creases in his skin fade and know that the passing of time means nothing.

Even his death means nothing. His death, at my hands, binds him to me forever.

'Thought I might find you here,' I say, when I'm close enough to see that he is standing by a line of simple metal urns. The label on the one closest to him reads, *Awaiting collection by the Lancashire Constabulary. Four unknown infants.* We sit on the low wall surrounding the crematorium and look at them.

'Thirty years on and Black Moss Manor is still giving us grief,' I say.

Ghost Tom sighs in my ear. 'Old bones, reduced to ashes. Let it go, Floss.'

'That's exactly what they want us to do.'

His head flicks round to look at me. 'They? Who is they?'

Very good question. 'I checked up on the Asters before I came here,' I say. 'My PA phoned me this morning. Frederick and Judith's medical licences were revoked when they went to prison. The GMC has no idea where they are now.'

'I'd put money on them going abroad,' Tom says. 'Finding somewhere that doesn't have a GMC.'

I'm still looking at the urn containing the children's ashes. 'If these are old bones, why didn't we find them in 1969?' I ask.

'The children were accounted for,' Tom says. 'The place had records. There was no reason to dig up the back garden.'

'Except they weren't accounted for. Not properly. Lots of documents were destroyed in the fire. And we didn't follow up the adoptions. We didn't check that the children really were where they were supposed to be. I meant to, but—'

'You had a lot on your plate,' Tom says. 'It was a hard time for all of us. Losing Randy felt like the last straw.'

I wonder if Tom's mention of Randy is deliberate, and tell myself that Tom, even in death, will be cunning. I remember Randy's death hitting me like a body blow, how in the days that followed it became almost impossible to think straight.

'He's here somewhere, isn't he? Where is he?'

'Think back. The whole force was here. It poured down. You lost a shoe in the mud.'

I remember. I set off down the path and cross the grass. Randy has a headstone now. *Randall Trevor Butterworth, 1943–1969. A much-loved son.*

'Was it an accident?' I ask.

Tom has followed me. 'According to the coroner.'

'He was due to meet me the night he died. He'd been to see Sandra Cartwright that morning. She told him something.'

'And he didn't say what?' Tom asks. 'He didn't give you any clue?'

'We were interrupted.'

'Lot going on that day. From what I can remember, though, Sandra Cartwright's testimony in court matched that of the Asters and the other staff members.'

Tom's right. Or rather, this imaginary conversation is dredging up useful buried memories.

'They all claimed to have no knowledge of the children being drugged, each blaming the others. None of them admitted any wrongdoing.'

'Hard to see what she could have told Randy,' Tom says.

I think for a moment. 'The Asters were arrested at Cartwright's house, weren't they?' I say. 'What if they'd got wind of her talking to Randy? She could have been threatened into toeing the party line.'

'Why would she lie if she knew she'd be sent to prison for it?'

'Faced with spending a couple of years in prison or ending up like Randy, which would you choose?'

My phone rings before Tom can respond. I pull it from my bag and walk away down the path.

'Ma'am, this is Brian Rushton,' the familiar voice tells me. 'I hate to ask, but we have a bit of a situation here. Any chance of you stopping by the station?'

Brian Rushton is a detective inspector in town, someone I met in the hours after Larry's funeral yesterday. He is also the son of my old boss, Stanley Rushton. He evades my questions but gives me enough information to convince me I probably should go. Besides, I have a favour to ask. I tell him I'll be right over and put away my phone.

When I turn back to tell Tom, he's vanished. Ghosts tend to do that.

# 99

## Cassie

I can hear a melody in my head. A dark one. It's winding its way in and out of my thoughts like a torn black ribbon. The breeze from the moor brings snatches of it. I hear it in the whispering of the grass, and the birds call out lyrics. It will be a song of lost love, of shattered dreams, of a future filled with despair. I close my eyes and try to bring the melody into some sort of discernible pattern. It's years since I've had a hit record, but this one might do it. Or be rejected by the entire industry as too fucking grim to sell.

'If I'd known you had a drink problem, I might have tried to keep the pub.'

The wine glass flies from my hand as I start upright in my chair. John is less than six feet away across the grass.

I stand and I'm not too steady on my feet: I can't remember when I last ate anything, and I've drunk at least half the bottle. I'm thinking, *Why is he here?* I do not need him to tell me it's over. I worked that out for myself. When he is only two feet away, when he's close enough for me to see that he's shaved within the last couple of hours, he glances around and looks at me, a question in his eyes.

'Is there somewhere we can go?' he asks.

'What for?'

'Last time I tried to make love to you, we were interrupted.' His eyes repeat their side-to-side sweep of Daphne and Avril's garden. 'Neighbours,' he says.

The bed I've been sleeping in is narrow, but we don't care. Our clothes vanish like clouds in the wind and our bodies cling together.

My limbs wrap round his, he lifts and holds me, and we seem like pieces of a puzzle, complex and difficult, but finally in the hands of a master who will make us complete.

My hair wraps round his neck and I see it as silver coils, binding him to me. We are not remotely alike, John and I. He looks like Larry, and I am a carbon copy of my mother when she was young, but when I look into his eyes, I feel that I'm staring at my twin, that we are two halves that have finally found each other.

He kisses me and the world goes away. We fly together through the darkness, we bathe in the golden light of the moon, and the stars catch fire around us.

We take our time. We are not teenagers, and while the urgency is there, so too is a nervousness we never knew before. He lies beneath me on the narrow bed and I'm glad because I know I can make it last longer this way. I move against him slowly even as he keeps his eyes tight shut.

He grips me hard, his fingers squeezing so that I have to bite my lip not to cry out, but I'm glad of that too, because it shows how much he needs me. Beneath me, he begins to moan. I move faster and for a while, I forget to plan, I even forget to think. All I can do is feel. And rejoice. I am home. I am whole again.

When it's over, hours or minutes later – I've no sense of time – my skin burns as though we've flown through fire.

'I don't care,' I tell him. 'I don't care if you're my brother.'

A heavy sigh. 'I suppose I don't either,' he says.

And with those five simple words everything has changed. We've acknowledged the truth, and know that it makes no difference.

'Genetic sexual attraction is actually quite common,' I tell him.

He thinks about this for a second. 'Good to know. Still illegal.'

'Do you care?' I ask.

'No,' he tells me.

I kiss him, and for a while we don't speak. Were we still teenagers, we'd make love again, but we're content now to hold each other close. I feel his fingers tracing a pattern round my left shoulder.

'How did it go, earlier?' he asks. 'At the church.'

'Bit more dignified than the day before.' I suppress a shudder. I'm not sure I'll ever forget the sight of people spitting on my father's coffin.

'It was always going to be a circus,' John says. 'I hear Luna came back.'

'She's still here. She took Mum home earlier.'

I wonder, as I say this, whether Mum has been talking to Luna and I wait for the stab of jealousy.

Yesterday, in the hours after Larry's funeral, desperate to escape my own thoughts, I went up to Mum's nursing home again. Still she wouldn't speak to me. Even after all pretence between us must surely have been ripped away, she wouldn't talk.

'I looked for you,' John says. 'Yesterday, I mean, when it was over. You'd vanished.'

I thought I'd seen everyone from my hidey-hole in the church gallery; I'd missed the only one I really cared about.

The stab has missed its mark. I don't mind, I realise, if Mum has been talking to Luna. I may even be glad of it.

'Things went nuts in the evening,' John says. 'There was no way I could get away.'

'I heard.'

I hold him a bit tighter. Daphne and Avril have told me nothing about the events of yesterday in the hours after Larry's funeral. I overheard them talking, though, when they came back to the house at dawn, when they thought I was fast asleep in my room. A teenager missing. A senior police officer believed to be involved. A major police operation. And Florence Lovelady at the centre of it as usual.

'Bloody mental.' John shudders in my arms.

Talking of others has brought the world back. It's time to face it again.

'Where does Tammy think you are?' I ask.

'She knows I'm here.'

My heart stops beating.

'I told her last night,' he says. 'When the police finally let us go.'

Suddenly, lying naked in his arms feels entirely wrong. I sit up. 'Told her what?'

'That I'm leaving her. That I need to be with you.'

I'll kill him if he's joking. I'll take one of Daphne's knives and this room will be spattered with the scarlet red of his blood before the hour is up.

'She's threatening to go to the police,' he says. 'Thanks to your tantrum on Monday, she knows I killed my dad.'

Ted Donnelly was not his dad, but I let that go. 'It was self-defence. And an accident,' I say. 'In any case, it doesn't matter. Mum won't change her story now, and I sure as hell won't.'

'What about my mum?'

'She won't risk you going to prison.'

'She might, if it will keep me away from you. And Tammy is claiming you killed Roy Greenwood.'

I sigh. 'Still on about that, is she?'

Christ, with Tammy's accusation and Larry's letter to Florence, I could be in big trouble.

'It's bollocks, obviously, but she can make it difficult for you,' John says. 'Even if no charges are brought, she'll make sure my kids know everything. I'll probably never see them again.'

He's weakening. He could face the risk of police action, or the possibility of losing his family. Not both. I think back to my plan, hatched over long nights in my Salford flat, finalised on my visit to John and Tammy's home. I think back to my plan to deal with Florence, after I learned that Larry had betrayed me with his last, damning letter. I can do it. I know I can.

Except . . .

'Go back to the pub,' I tell him. 'Get your passport and what money you have and pack a bag. I'll pick you up in an hour.'

He doesn't move. 'What?'

Suddenly, it's all so clear. 'We can be at the airport an hour after that. We get on the first plane that has seats.'

He half laughs. 'We can't just run.'

'Who said anything about running? We're going on holiday. You think the police will chase us for two deaths they couldn't prove were anything other than accidental thirty years ago? They have better things to do.'

I can't believe I didn't think of this before.

He shakes his head. 'Are you serious?'

'Yes. Come on, get your pants on. Where do you fancy? India? Thailand? Brazil?'

He stares at me, and then a smile breaks over his face. We finish dressing and run downstairs as a wave of pure joy sweeps over me.

'You can't pack everything,' I tell him. 'An hour. Be ready.'

He pulls open the front door and turns back to kiss me, only stopping when he sees the look on my face. Over his shoulder, I've seen what he can't. The police patrol car and the uniformed officers heading towards us.

'Cassandra Glassbrook?' A woman in a dark business suit is holding out a police warrant card. 'I need you to come with me, please. You're wanted for questioning in relation to the death of Roy Greenwood.'

This woman is Perdita Collins. Petrifying Perdita is a police detective.

I say nothing. John says too much. He tells me not to worry, that it's ridiculous, that everyone knows I couldn't possibly have done it, that it will all be sorted out soon.

I'm not so sure. After all, the dark moon is rising again. And no secret stays buried for ever.

# 100

## Florence

The station is busy when I arrive. People are upset and distracted after the events of last night, especially the disappearance of their boss, but after I've announced myself, I'm taken straight through to Brian Rushton's office on the first floor. His room is next to the station superintendent's, but when I steal a glance inside, there is no sign of Tom.

Detective Inspector Brian Rushton, whom I have known for a little over a day, looks and feels very familiar. He is in his early forties, with his father's dark hair, heavy eyebrows and narrow, slate-coloured eyes. Unlike his father, he doesn't smoke heavily.

'Appreciate this, ma'am,' he says. 'You'll be wanting to get off, I know.' He closes his office door. 'Tammy Donnelly came by a short while ago to accuse Cassandra Glassbrook of poisoning Roy Greenwood.'

If I'd had to guess, it wouldn't have been that.

'That was thirty years ago,' I say.

'And he was cremated and his ashes scattered. So, no chance of forensic evidence, even if I could get enough of a case together to justify digging the poor bastard up. The thing is, I know you were there when it happened. Do you want to sit down?'

I sit and think back. That terrible night: the fire at the children's home, Randy's death, Marigold's disappearance, finding Roy in a pool of sweat and his own vomit.

'Tom called the ambulance,' I say. 'Roy died shortly after he arrived at hospital. We took Sally in for questioning.'

'That's right. I've read Dad's old file. She certainly had a motive.

According to Greenwood's will, and to a letter of wishes that he and Larry Glassbrook drew up, the Glassbrook family inherited the business and the house if Roy died before retirement. It was all a bit irregular and everyone expected his mother to contest the will, but she didn't.'

'The post-mortem report indicated poisoning, but it was impossible to pin down what substance had been used,' I say. 'Sally had recently made a herbal treatment of some sort that was known to be dangerous in the wrong doses, but it was all accounted for.'

'Foxglove syrup,' Brian confirms. 'Twelve small bottles, eleven of which were in the house, the twelfth with their housekeeper. According to Tammy, who is the niece of the housekeeper, Cassie showed a particular interest in the foxglove syrup and a bottle disappeared for a short period of time.'

'Thirty years ago,' I say. 'This is supposition and hearsay.'

'And according to the pathologist at the time, Roy's symptoms weren't completely compatible with the known symptoms of foxglove poisoning. Some similarities, but not enough for certainty. And his mother, Grace, said he'd been ill for some time, before the two of them moved in with the Glassbrooks. According to Dad's file, the information was sent to the prosecution service, but they decided not to proceed. A lot of people thought Sally Glassbrook got away with murder. Now, it looks as though it might have been Cassie who did.'

'If Sally had a motive, Cassie did too,' I say. 'She was easily smart enough to have found out about the will. And she hated Roy. Mind you, we all did.'

Rushton says nothing.

'If there wasn't enough evidence thirty years ago, there'll be even less now,' I say. 'Tammy's opinion won't be enough.'

'Put that to one side for a moment. You knew the family back then. You lived with them. Were any of the Glassbrook women capable of murder?'

When I speak, I'm weighing my words carefully. 'In most circumstances, I'd say Sally was not, but to protect her children, possibly.

Roy was a dangerous man who was fixated on the family.' I think some more. 'As for the girls, yes, I'd say they were capable. But that counts for nothing. You need at least a reliable witness. Or a confession.'

'We're talking to the housekeeper, Mary,' Brian says. 'You're right that Tammy Donnelly alone won't be enough. Is there any possibility of a confession?'

'From Cassie Glassbrook?' I can't help but laugh. 'When hell freezes over.'

'That's what I thought.' Brian sighs. 'I have to go through the motions, though. We're bringing her in now.'

'Good luck with that.'

Brian looks at his watch, clearly wanting to be elsewhere. 'You said there was a quid pro quo.'

I explain about my interest in the children's remains found at Black Moss Manor and ask to see the post-mortem report.

'Can't see why not,' Brian says. 'It's not something I've been involved with, but I'll see if I can dig it out. You know they were cremated yesterday?'

I tell him I do, but I'd like to see the report all the same. He leaves and comes back ten minutes later with a file.

'I'll have to leave you to it,' he says. 'Cassie's arrived.'

When Brian has gone, I sit at his desk and open the file. Starting at the back, I find the call-out report; the photographs taken during the operation to retrieve the bodies; the statement from the water company workers; the statement from the manager of Black Moss Manor Residential Retreat, a Mr Lee. Towards the front, I come to the post-mortem report. It goes into substantially more detail but is basically what Perdita told me over the phone. Four children, in similar stages of decay, believed to have died during the early part of the twentieth century.

There are photographs, taken in the mortuary, and I lay them out side by side on Brian's desk. The first is of a child believed to be between six and eight years old, of indeterminate sex. These bones have been pieced together on the mortuary gurney like a jigsaw puzzle. Nothing holds them together. The bones are almost brown with age and have lost structure at their extremities.

The second photograph shows a much more intact skeleton, with pieces of connective tissue. A child of around ten, according to the notes, with an overly large head. The third child is the smallest, aged between three and five. He or she has a twisted foot, but again the bones have been pieced together and are darker in colour. The fourth child has hair and skin. This last is thought to be around fourteen or fifteen. It's impossible to be sure, but the face has a feminine look about it to me. Could this be Marigold? She was small for her age.

I'm no pathologist, but I'm sure the photographs tell a different story to the report. I think back to what Tricksy told me over that ridiculously expensive lunch and conclude that these bones have been in the ground for between five and twenty years. Significantly, though, they are in very different stages of decay. These children didn't die together.

# 101

## Cassie

Just my luck, I bump into Florence Lovelady on the way out of the station. She doesn't even have the grace to look surprised.

'Can I drop you somewhere, Cassie?' she says.

She has got to be kidding. I've spent three hours being grilled by a succession of detectives, even Brian Rushton, Tom Devine's immediate deputy. I'm hardly going to crack now over a lift home and a girly chat.

'I'm OK, thanks,' I say, although I've no clue how I'll get back to Daphne and Avril's. I left their house in a hurry, without my bag.

'I'm driving your way,' Florence says. 'It's no problem.'

On the other hand, Florence remains a problem to be dealt with. I still have no idea what Larry said to her in his letter. Maybe it is time she and I had a chat.

As we set off towards her car, I test the theory that attack is the best form of defence. 'Why did you lie about Marigold?' I say.

Her footsteps slow. 'Who says I did?'

'You told me you'd found her family in the Lake District, that they'd agreed to take her back. You said she was happy to go. You and Mum both told me that. Was it true?'

Florence stops walking. We stand and stare at each other across the pavement.

'No,' she says. 'It wasn't true.'

'What the fuck?' For a second, I'm so mad I forget to be wary.

She sighs. 'It was wrong, I admit. But your mum argued that you and Luna had been through enough. That it would be the last straw for you to know some harm might have come to Marigold.

She asked me to tell what she called a "little white lie" and I agreed. We both hoped Marigold would be found before you found out the truth. We shouldn't have done it, Cassie, but we had your best interests at heart.'

'So, what did happen to her?' I ask.

There are actually tears in Florence's eyes. 'I don't know,' she says. 'She vanished the night Greenwood died. We looked for her, I promise we did, but there was no trace, either of her or the baby. I left town not long after that.'

'Does Luna know? The truth, I mean?' I ask.

Florence shakes her head. 'Not to my knowledge. There wasn't much in the papers. Your mum could have kept it from her too.'

I've got her on the wrong foot, so I take a big risk. 'Did my dad write to you before he died?'

Florence looks surprised. 'Yes,' she says. 'He did.'

'What did he say?'

'You can read it if you like. It's very short. In fact, you can have it. It's at my hotel. I can't go back yet, but we could meet up later.'

'Cass, over here!'

We both turn to see John on the other side of the road.

'Looks like you're sorted,' Florence says. 'I'll see you later.' She leaves me as John spots a break in the traffic and runs across.

# 102

## Florence

The uniform I'm wearing, and my Met warrant card, get me access to the pathology department at Burnley General Hospital, but once I'm in it, the main corridor is deserted. There is no one at the small reception desk, and all the doors I pass are locked. I'm on the point of giving up when a technician strolls in and asks if he can help me.

'I remember that case,' he says, as he and I walk towards the examination rooms, cadaver stores and offices. 'What is it you need?'

'One of the children could have had Down's syndrome,' I tell him. 'I need to know if there was any sign of that on the report.'

He steers me into an office. 'Let's have a look.' He proceeds to open a filing cabinet at the back of the room. He must be breaking all sorts of protocols, but I say nothing. I will ride my luck as long as I can.

'Here we go.' He pulls a file from the cabinet. When it's open, I see the same photographs I looked at in Brian Rushton's office.

'This one,' I say, as I point to the largest of the four corpses. 'I'm wondering if this subject had Down's.'

The technician shakes his head. 'Don't remember the doc saying anything about that. He dictates onto a tape machine and has one of the girls type it up. I remember something about dwarfism but not Down's. Hang on, the report's here.'

He turns the pages of the file. I'm not really following as he starts to mutter under his breath. I'm thinking, *Dwarfism?*

'Aye, here we go,' he says. 'Subject three, a child aged between nine and eleven years, has a pronounced brow and relatively short arms and legs, indicative of achondroplasia, or disproportionate short stature. Death is estimated to have occurred between four and six years ago.'

I read none of this in the report in Brian Rushton's office. I step round the desk until the technician and I are standing side by side and I can read over his shoulder.

*Subject one, a child aged between six and eight, of indeterminate sex, in an advanced state of decomposition. Believed to have died in the early to mid-1980s. Subject two, a child of around three or four, with a twisted foot, who died probably in the late 1980s. Subject three, a male child of around ten, with congenital dwarfism, who died in or around 1995. And subject four, a girl in her mid-teens, who has been in the ground only two to four years.*

Who is probably not Marigold, because there is no suggestion of Down's syndrome in the report, but whose death, all the same, cries out for vengeance.

I mean justice, I think, but I am incandescent with rage. Because the report prepared by the pathologist who examined the four skeletons and the one in Brian Rushton's office are completely different.

# 103

## Cassie

'I thought you were never coming out,' John says. 'I've been here three hours.'

He takes my arm and steers me along the road. 'Are they done?' he says in a low voice.

They are not done.

'They've told me not to leave town. If I try to leave Sabden, even to go back to Salford, I'll be arrested.'

He sighs. 'I guess that means India's off.'

We reach his van and climb inside.

'I think we need to talk,' he says.

'Go the pub,' I tell him. 'I need to see Florence's room. I'll go in the front way and help myself to her key.'

'What?'

'I have to check something. It won't take long. We'll talk after. I promise.'

'Er, excuse me. You've just spent three hours in the nick. Are you that keen to get back?'

'Florence isn't going back to her room just yet. She told me. Tammy is more of a problem. Will she be there?'

'She's gone to her mother's. To break the bad news about her lying, cheating pervert of a husband. It's still not a good idea, Cass.'

'It's important. You don't need to have anything to do with it. Go in through the kitchen, find something to do and make sure Tammy doesn't come back.'

'Or Florence Lovelady, I assume.'

'Yes, that too.'

We separate when we get to the pub. John, clearly unhappy, goes in through the kitchen entrance. I use the front door. There is no key hanging in the space for number seven. I shouldn't be surprised, I suppose. Florence was ridiculously fussy about her privacy when she lived with us.

I slip behind the counter and find the strongbox beneath it where the spare keys were always kept. It's locked too, of course, but the key that opens it was always kept in the top desk drawer and it still is. A minute later, I'm running up the stairs to room seven.

Florence's room is the largest in the pub, a big double overlooking the moor. From the neatly made bed, I know that the cleaners have already been in, so I'm less likely to be disturbed. Beneath the window there is a large, old-fashioned desk but there is nothing on it other than hotel literature and the local paper. I cross to the wardrobe and pull open the door. Her suitcase is inside. It too is locked, but the zip-up compartment on the side isn't, and sure enough, I find a file inside and carry it to the desk.

On the front cover, someone has written: *August 1969*.

My heart beating fast, I flick through. It's a very old file, the papers yellow with age, mainly containing newspaper cuttings of the closure of Black Moss Manor. Larry's letter isn't inside. I'm about to check the rest of the room when something occurs to me and I slip my hand back into the side compartment of the suitcase. Bingo.

My dad's writing on a long, slim envelope, postmarked the day before he died. This is it.

I take it to the window and pull out the single sheet of paper.

*I've kept them safe for thirty years. Over to you.*

Is this it?

The door behind me opens. I nearly wet myself, but it's only John.

'What's going on?' he says, not without a glance back down the corridor.

'Larry wrote to Florence. I need to know what he said. It could be important.'

He looks down at the letter in my hand.

'Is that it?' he says.

'I don't know. Maybe.'

He takes it from me. 'We have to get out of here,' he says. 'And you've got some explaining to do.'

I don't argue. We put Florence's room to rights and head out. This time, he drives out of town. After a mile or so, he turns left onto the moor and I know where we're heading.

'I didn't bring towels,' I say, as we near the Black Tarn.

''Thank Christ for that.' We get out and walk, hand in hand, to the lake. John says nothing, and I know he is waiting for me to talk.

'I did it,' I say, as we stand at the water's edge, watching the lapping of the water against the shore. 'I killed Roy Greenwood.'

'I know,' says John.

# 104

## Florence

Dwane's new home, a stone-built, detached house on the edge of town, is a far cry from the cottage that used to house his entire family. This house has huge picture windows and a large garage. The oak front door is a splendid creation with a great cathedral-style arch of stained glass. A recurring motif runs through all of the coloured panes: a tiger lily. I remember Dwane once trying to give me some carved tiger lilies, telling me they were the colour of my hair.

His wife, Jenny, answers my knock. My smile fades quickly at the look on her face.

'I'd like to speak to Dwane, please,' I say, when Jenny has stood on the doorstep for several seconds, saying nothing.

'Workshop.' She steps back inside the house. 'Round side. Mind the dog. He bites.'

I follow the path round to the side of the house and unlatch the garden gate. A tiny Yorkshire terrier comes hurtling towards me, barking furiously. He comes close and yaps up at me. I bend and pat him. His barking stops. His tail wags hard. I've lost count of the number of times Ben has nagged us to get a dog. Ben! I have to take a moment, take some deep breaths and count to ten. Dealing with all this is so much harder when he isn't with me.

At the bottom of Dwane's garden is a one-storey building the size of a small house. Followed by the dog, I make my way across the lawn. I knock on the doors and, receiving no answer, push one of them open.

Inside, I see coffins and caskets in various stages of completion, but it is the vast table close to the door that catches my attention first.

Dwane's model town. Thirty years since I first saw it, and it still takes my breath away. The whole of Sabden, reproduced in miniature.

'You still like small things?' he says to me, and I look up to see him in the far doorway.

'You've made it bigger.'

I see the Victorian municipal buildings of the town centre: the library, the town hall, the masonic lodge, the old secondary school, but most of the mills I remember from 1969 have disappeared from Dwane's model as they have from the town. Thirty years ago, huge brick chimneys dominated the skyline of this small town, and factories stood every few streets. Not anymore.

'Town got bigger,' he tells me. 'New estates all over the place.'

'And changed,' I say. 'I didn't realise how much until I saw it like this.'

I prowl round the outskirts of Sabden in miniature, finding Daphne and Avril's house, the Glassbrook house, the flower shop on the main road, Glassbrook & Greenwood. I see the Perseverance Mill and stop.

'I'll knock it down,' Dwane says. 'Just say the word.'

'No.' I force myself to look away. 'That wouldn't be true.'

'Thought you had to get off,' Dwane says.

'I'm staying another night. I'm not done here yet.'

His lips purse, a frown crumples his face and he picks up a wood file.

'You never told me how you came to run Glassbrook & Greenwood,' I say.

Dwane starts to file a decorative trim and sawdust flies up in a golden cloud around him.

'Larry asked me to work for him,' he says. 'After Roy Greenwood died, he inherited the business. He couldn't run it from prison, so Sally ran it and I made the caskets. When she got worse, I took over and Jenny stepped in.'

As Dwane is speaking, I'm looking round the room and I spot something else against the far wall. A potter's wheel. The shelves above it are full of clay and porcelain figures in various stages of completion. I wander over and, behind me, sense that Dwane has stopped working.

'What happens now?' I ask. 'Now that Larry's dead?'

I spot a small male figure. About six inches high, the boy has an oversized head and rather short arms and legs. His hair is thick and curly. I reach out and lift it off the shelf.

'They made me a full partner years ago. Sally's a . . . what do you call it? A sleeping partner? Careful with that.'

I put the figure back. 'I'm glad, Dwane. You deserve it. You're one of the cleverest people I know.'

'Good with me hands is all.' I hear the sound of filing again.

'Is this you?' I'm still looking at the figure.

'No.'

I turn and watch the back of his head for a few seconds.

'Larry asked me to look into the children's remains found at Black Moss Manor,' I say. 'The ones that were cremated yesterday.'

'Oh aye.' He doesn't look up.

'I saw the post-mortem report a short while ago. I blagged my way into the pathology department at Burnley General.'

'Sounds like you.'

'One of the dead children had dwarfism,' I say. 'And he didn't die decades ago, like we've been led to believe. He died around five years ago. So, I was wondering if there are any other families you can put me in touch with who had dwarfism in the genes. Maybe offshoots of your own family. You had lots of brothers and sisters.'

Dwane has fallen very still.

'Dwane?' I say. 'Is this about the Craftsmen? Are they behind Black Moss Manor? Is that what you're all frightened of?'

He turns to face me and seems angry. 'Go home, Florence. And drive carefully till you're well away from this place.'

'You know I won't do that.'

'Then I can't help you.'

He turns back and starts filing again, so furiously I think he's going to break the trim.

\*

I'm almost at my car when he catches up with me, the little Yorkshire terrier running at his side. In his right hand, he's holding the statue of the boy. The one that looks a little, only a little, like Dwane.

'I never wanted kids.' He's out of breath. 'I didn't want a kid to be like me. Our Raymond was an accident and we were lucky with him, but Jenny got pregnant again when we thought she was too old.'

He looks down at the figure in his hands.

'He was born at home, on a Friday night,' Dwane says. 'I got called away. I've sometimes wondered if that were deliberate. I was away and Jenny was on her own with Raymond and a midwife.'

'What happened?'

'Stillborn. A little lad. Dwarf, like me. Big head, short arms and legs.'

'I'm sorry.'

'Broke Jenny's heart, it did. She always wanted a big family. So I make her a figure every year on his birthday. To show her how he'd look, if he were still with us. This was last year's.'

He holds out the figure again and I take it. Now that he's told me, I think I can see something of Jenny in the face of Dwane's son.

'That's lovely,' I say. 'What's his name?'

'David. He'd be fifteen now,' Dwane says. 'Same age as . . .'

'As Ben,' I finish for him.

Dwane takes my hand. 'You all right?' he says after a moment.

I nod and see from Dwane's face that he has more to tell me.

'They told us he was stillborn,' Dwane says. 'The midwife was gone before I got home. She'd taken the body with her. "Rules," she said. I never saw him.'

'That must have been hard.'

'Aye. Thing is, Jenny's never believed it. Just before the midwife took him away, she swears she heard him cry.'

I take my time. Slowly, I close the car door and lock it. I'm going nowhere in a hurry. I think Dwane knows, from the look on my face, what is coming. 'Oh, Dwane,' I say. 'Oh, Dwane.'

Nothing will stop my tears falling. After a while, Dwane starts to cry too.

# 105

## Cassie

The waves fan out like lace on the pebble shore. All warmth seems to have gone from the day and I'm shivering with cold.

'How?' I ask John. 'How can you possibly know?'

John won't look at me. 'The police didn't keep you three hours for nothing. And I know you.'

I wait a moment before asking, 'Does it make a difference?'

'To me? No.'

He bends and picks up a stone, hurling it out across the water. It skims three times before sinking with a greedy plop.

'Greenwood was an evil bastard,' he says. 'I was there that night, remember? I'm not proud of running away like I did, leaving you and your mum to deal with him.'

'You were fifteen,' I remind him.

'How did you do it?' John's voice has tightened, and I know it's bothering him more than he'll admit.

'Poison,' I tell him, thinking, *What else? I am a poisoner.*

'The police thought it was Sally, didn't they?'

'They suspected her, but there was no proof. They couldn't pin down what had poisoned him. Forensic science wasn't what it is now.'

'Would you have let her go to prison?'

'No,' I say, although the truth is, I'm not sure. Yet another of the questions that have haunted me over the years.

'Do you mind?' I ask him again.

'Let's just say I'm going to insist on doing the cooking.' He wraps an arm round my shoulders and I lean against him, giddy with relief.

'They can't charge me,' I say. 'I thought Larry might have told Florence. He and Mum knew. That's why I needed to find his letter, but if that's all he said to her, she has nothing. And Tammy wasn't even around at the time. They won't charge me based on what her aunt Mary told her thirty years ago.'

'Tammy won't let me go,' John says. 'If she can't get you in trouble with the police, she'll come after me. And thanks to you, she knows I killed Ted.'

'I was an idiot.'

He doesn't argue.

'We could get rid of Tammy, problem solved.'

My tone suggests I'm kidding. I'm not. I always knew it might come to this.

'Don't even joke about it.'

I think back to the kitchen in the Donnellys' flat, to the position of the old boiler. 'If Tammy lives, you lose your kids and your grandkids. Even if the police can't charge either of us, she'll make sure your family know everything.'

'Nothing we can do about that.'

I think about the position of the flue on the outside wall. If I block that up, carbon monoxide will build up in the flat. It's invisible and odourless. Old boilers leak all the time. All I have to do is make sure John isn't there that night.

'But if Tammy's taken off the scene, the kids don't need to know anything.'

'I can't believe I'm hearing this.'

'I've done it once. So have you. Second time should be a lot easier.'

He turns to me and I see that he's angry. And, also, a bit scared. 'Cassie, will you pack it in? It's not happening.'

He's scared of me.

'So we let her win?'

He walks a little way down the beach before turning back and shaking his head. He means it. He won't let me kill Tammy. I should be angry with him and yet, for some reason, I'm not.

'And while we're on the subject, what's with that voodoo doll they were wittering on about?' he says. 'Why've you made a voo-doo doll of me?'

I don't want to kill her, I realise. I'm glad he won't let me.

'It wasn't a voodoo doll. It was a clay picture. For a love spell.'

His head drops to one side. 'Oh, and how does that work?'

'I make one of myself as well. Then as the moon starts to wax, I bind them together with silk and blessings, I burn herbs I've been gathering for days now, and then you love me for ever.'

'You fucking idiot.' He comes back and puts his arms round me again. 'I'm going to do that anyway.'

# 106

## Florence

The Wise Woman hasn't changed in thirty years. The houses around it have, of course. Some have been pebble-dashed; most have satellite dishes; tubs of geraniums and busy Lizzies brighten up window ledges. Some doorsteps have more smeared glass milk bottles than bowling alleys have pins, which was something you never saw in the old days. Number 13 is the same though. I push open the front door and make my way through the dim saloon to the bar.

'I got you a Britvic Orange!'

Abby Thorn is a little stouter, and her short hair is completely grey now, but I'd have known her anywhere.

'I can't believe this place still exists,' I say as I join her.

'Someone bought the building years ago,' she tells me. 'Runs it as a cooperative. The regulars take turns behind the bar.'

'Who'd do such a daft, impractical thing?'

'Me.'

She laughs at the look on my face. 'I live in the flat upstairs,' she says. 'When I'm in town, that is.'

I sit and chink glasses, surprised at how pleased I am to see her.

'I've been trying to talk to Tom Devine all morning,' she says. 'No one knows where he is. You seen him?'

I taste my drink and decide that one sip is enough. Some things are best left in the past. 'No,' I say. 'Not today.'

She waits.

I look up. 'So, what have you got?'

'Black Moss Manor is owned by a trust and run as a retreat,' she says.

I nod. I know this already.

'Because it's privately owned, and doesn't have charitable status, it doesn't have to file details of trustees or owners,' she goes on. 'But I've got a mate who works at the Inland Revenue, and he owes me a favour. Strictly off the record, he found out tax returns are filed every year by W. H. D. Booth and Partners on behalf of a Mr and Mrs Frank Taylor.'

W. H. D. Booth rings a bell. He was a trustee of the home back in 1969, as were Roy Greenwood, Councillors Earnshaw and Chadwick, Albert Frost, the newspaperman and Harold Devine, Tom's dad, who brought us all together one night to find out what I knew, to palm me off.

'Abby,' I say. 'Have you heard of the Craftsmen?'

She shakes her head, but a wary look steals over her face.

'I learned about them last night. A sort of brotherhood, completely hush-hush, only very influential, important men allowed, fingers in lots of pies, none of them wholesome.'

She gives a half-sneer. 'Sure you're not thinking of the freemasons?'

'There could be some overlap.' I'm holding back the biggest revelation, that the Craftsmen practise dark magic; I don't want to be written off as a loon. 'I think Black Moss Manor could have been one of their projects.'

'Never heard of them,' she repeats, 'but the secret brotherhood stuff, rich men conspiring to make each other richer and shaft the rest of us? Yeah, that sounds very Sabden.'

I've probably taken this as far as I can, and I remember Abby has just given me two new names.

'And this Mr and Mrs Taylor, do you know anything about them?'

'I can't find anyone who's ever met them,' Abby says.

'Could they be the Asters?' I ask.

She shrugs. 'They went somewhere when they got out of jail.'

In return, I tell Abby what I've learned. That the children found buried behind Black Moss Manor almost certainly died within the last twenty years.

'Hang on,' she says. 'The *Post* ran a story saying they were old remains. Pathologists read papers, don't they? He'd have said something.'

'Not necessarily. The post-mortem report is dated 16 July,' I say. 'That's a whole week after the story ran in the *Post*. The story was speculation, which the police never bothered to correct. The pathologist's job was to report to the police, not to brief the press.'

'So how did a completely different report end up at the police station?'

'Very good question,' I say.

She's still frowning. 'I can't believe there was no follow-up.'

'The children were cremated yesterday. The same day we buried Larry Glassbrook. Someone knew all the press and public attention would be on the other side of town.'

'Jeez.'

'Yep.'

Abby drinks and thinks. After a few moments, she says, 'So kids died there after the home closed down?'

'Yep.'

'How is that possible?' she asks me. 'It would never have got a licence to run as a children's home again.'

I've been thinking about this. 'Unofficial fostering would be my best guess. The trustees of the old home were very influential men. I'm guessing they pulled strings, persuaded people to turn a blind eye. Some of the kids who used to live there went back. Others joined over the years. The scale was reduced – maybe a handful of kids, compared to twenty or so in the old days – but whatever was going on there continued.'

'If only we knew what that was.' Abby gives me that smug grin I remember so well.

'What?' I say.

'I found Sandra Cartwright,' she says. 'Want to pay her a visit?'

Sandra Cartwright is the woman who worked at Black Moss Manor in the 1960s, who Randy Butterworth went to meet the day he died.

'She went to prison,' I remind Abby. 'Her story was exactly the same as the Asters'. Why would she change it now?'

'Maybe she won't,' Abby says. 'But it's worth a try. Seeing as how she's dying.'

Sandra Cartwright is spending her last days in a hospice attached to Blackburn Royal Infirmary. She is shrunken, yellow with age and illness, and when Abby and I enter her room, I don't expect her to be conscious, let alone have anything useful to say. We sit either side of her bed, and her eyes flutter open. They widen in alarm as she takes in my uniform.

Abby and I have spent some time discussing how to play this. We know we will only get one shot.

'Matron tells me that Father Peter came to see you two days ago,' I begin. 'Did you make a full confession?'

Cartwright's eyes narrow, then flit from me to Abby.

'I'm a Catholic,' I say, stretching the truth a little. I haven't practised in years. 'What about you, Abby?'

'Very devout,' she says. 'Never miss Mass.'

'So, we know that a confession to a priest counts for nothing if the sin is continuing,' I say.

'Nothing at all,' Abby says mournfully.

'You need to confess to us now,' I say. 'Then you can go to Christ in peace. You need to tell us the truth about Black Moss Manor.'

Cartwright's eyes, a dirty blue in a pool of yellow, fill up with tears and her mouth trembles. I remind myself that while she might be frail, and dying, and afraid, she is also as evil as they come and deserves no pity.

'I know you were threatened by the Asters, and the trustees of Black Moss,' I say. 'I know you were going to tell Randy Butterworth the truth. I know they had him killed, and I understand that you were scared. But they can't harm you anymore.'

'It's time to consider your immortal soul,' Abby says.

'Four children were buried in the grounds behind the manor,' I say. 'I need you to tell us who they were and what happened to them.'

I honestly didn't expect it to be easy, but I guess imminent death has more of an impact than I could know. Sandra Cartwright begins to talk.

An hour later, Abby and I climb into my car. My hands are shaking, and she's been uncharacteristically silent since we left the hospice.

'Did you get all that?' I ask.

Abby pulls the tape recorder out of her pocket and checks it. 'Yep,' she says, after a second. 'I took notes too. Do you believe it?'

I take my time.

'I mean, it was pretty out there,' Abby says.

*Out there* doesn't begin to describe what we've just heard.

'I believe she believed it,' I say.

'I can do some digging,' Abby offers. 'Find out if there's anything to back up what she claimed.'

'That would be helpful,' I agree.

'Is it enough?' Abby asks. 'Have we got enough?'

I shake my head. 'Not on its own. If we could get her into the witness stand possibly, but that's not going to happen. I doubt she'll be with us this time tomorrow. And a good defence lawyer will tear that tape to bits. She had no legal adviser. She could have some sort of dementia. She could have been coerced.'

'So, we've achieved nothing?'

I refuse to believe this. 'Give me those names again,' I tell her.

Abby opens her notebook. 'Wendy Howarth and her infant son—' she says.

'No,' I interrupt. 'Wendy isn't one of the four. If we believe what Marigold told us, Wendy died in or before 1969. Her body and that of her baby would have decomposed completely. Go on.'

'Ian Wilson,' Abby says. 'Seven years old. An undiagnosed haemophiliac who bled to death. Then Nigel Yates, three years old, found dead in his room one morning. Believed to have been killed by one of the other children.'

'Subject three was David Ogilvy,' I say. 'Dwane and Jenny's son, who died of exposure on the moors trying to escape.'

'And Beverly Robinson, who hanged herself in her room, because she couldn't bear it any longer. Bitch remembered all their names. Did you notice that?'

'I don't believe in hell,' I say. 'But if I did . . .'

Abby says, 'Me too.'

'She's beyond our reach,' I say. 'It's the Asters we need to find.'

We sit for a few seconds longer, thinking. Then Abby says, 'So where do we go from here?'

'You go home, sit in front of your Amstrad, write all this up and send it to someone you trust,' I say. 'And do that research you just promised.'

She opens her mouth to protest.

'Abby, they won't take this lying down. They came for us both before, and you're an easier target than I am. I want you keeping your head down. Go home, lock your doors and don't open them again until I come for you.'

'Florence, I'm not—'

'Someone other than the two of us has to know what Cartwright just told us. You'll do that better than me.'

She must see the sense in this because she doesn't argue.

'So what are you going to do?' she says.

I smile at her. 'I'm going to force their hand.'

# 107

## Cassie

'Hungry?' John asks me, as we drive down off the moor.

'Starving.' I'm fiddling with the radio dial, in the mood for happy, inspiring music. I can't remember when I last ate. I'll make up for it now. I'll start with a big, fat English breakfast, then a ploughman's lunch washed down with cider. A short nap with John, and then a long, lazy dinner.

'Get something in town?' John suggests.

Town will do. A Big Mac will do. Whatever. I find Radio One as a song by Creedence Clearwater Revival gets under way. 'Bad Moon Rising'. I hear the opening lyrics and my appetite fades.

'John, let's just go. Let's grab our things and stay at my place tonight.'

He swings onto the main road. 'You've been told not to leave. And running won't look good for me if Tammy goes to the police about Ted.'

He's right, but . . . I can't listen to this song right now. I don't need reminding that the black moon will rise again tonight. I turn the dial and find BBC Radio Lancashire.

'Police in Lancashire are still refusing to confirm the rumoured disappearance of Sabden police superintendent Tom Devine,' says the newsreader. 'Devine was instrumental in bringing notorious serial killer Larry Glassbrook to justice back in 1969, and his alleged disappearance so soon after Glassbrook's funeral could, it's believed, be linked to that event. Here's our reporter Abby Thorn talking earlier to Detective Inspector Brian Rushton.'

'The superintendent is not on duty today,' Rushton's voice comes over the radio. 'I've no further comment to make for the time being.'

'Detective Inspector, can you confirm that a police search for him is under way?' asks the female reporter. 'Do you believe he may have come to harm?'

The question is left hanging and the presenter takes up the story.

'Tom Devine's parents, Harold and Mary, have declined to comment. In other news, plans for a Burnley bypass have been put on hold—'

I switch off the radio. John looks as surprised as me. 'Tom Devine missing?' I say. 'What the hell's going on?'

# 108

## Florence

Thirty years after we last did exactly this, Tom and I are walking together up the laurel-lined path towards Black Moss Manor. Thirty years ago, he held my hand. He doesn't today. He's annoyed with me.

'Bad idea, Floss,' he says, as I approach the front door.

'No one asked you.'

The stone walls have been sandblasted clean. The drainpipes and the slate roof have been repaired, and the drive at the front re-gravelled. A narrow border of herbaceous plants runs along the front of the building, and the new door is painted a glossy deep blue. Black Moss Manor looks very different, feels exactly the same.

'Where are the cars?' I say.

'Come again?'

'This place is supposed to be a retreat now, for professional people suffering work-related stress,' I say. 'Where are the residents' cars?'

'Maybe they arrive on foot, hiking over the moors in the manner of a pilgrimage.'

I hear a noise from inside the building. 'Someone's coming.'

'I can't get involved with this.'

I agree. His presence will be a distraction I can do without. 'So go for a walk.'

As Tom's footsteps fade, others draw near. The door opens and a man stands before me. He is youngish, around thirty, and has light brown hair. His eyes are narrow and deep-set, a bright, clear blue, and there is a dimple in the middle of his chin. I can't help feeling that I've met him before.

'Can I help you?' He sounds nervous. His voice, too, is familiar.

I hold up my warrant card. I have no real authority in Lancashire, but most people won't realise that. 'Assistant Commissioner Florence Lovelady of the Metropolitan Police,' I tell him. 'May I speak to the person in charge?'

His puzzled expression relaxes. 'About the children's remains? We've been expecting you. Come in.'

I follow the young man into the hallway. A large oak table stands in it now, highly polished, with a huge copper bowl of fruit. There are flowers in the empty hearth. The light is soft and clear, very different now that the bars have been removed from the windows.

'I'm Bracken Lee,' the man introduces himself. 'I've got the files ready.'

This is going better than I could have hoped. He is expecting a police visit, has assumed that I am it. I follow him past the stairs and into the room I remember being Judith Aster's office.

'Please.' Lee indicates that I should sit. I do, glancing out through the window to see that the land at the back now has the semblance of a garden. There is no one in it.

'No residents out taking the air?' I ask.

'It gets chilly on the moor, WPC Lovelady,' he says. 'You must remember that.' He passes a file across the desk. 'This is the record of every child who died here since 1925. Summary on the inside front cover. The file itself is mostly made up of death certificates, details of burial, letters sent to close family.'

'Very thorough,' I say. 'But surely these records were destroyed by the fire?'

Lee is still on his feet, standing almost to attention on the other side of his desk. 'They must have been in a part of the building that wasn't so badly damaged. They would have been returned by the police after the investigation was completed.'

I have no memory of this file being given to the police.

'Did you ever meet the Asters?' I watch him carefully. 'The two doctors who ran this place when the fire occurred.'

He makes an apologetic shrug. 'Before my time. I've only been in charge for five years. I'll save you some time, if you like. Every child that died here since 1925 was buried in town. You'll find the undertakers' invoices, if you look.'

I break eye contact to flick through the file. Sure enough, there are invoices from Glassbrook & Greenwood. I recognise Larry's handwriting.

'Are Mr and Mrs Taylor available?' I ask.

'Not here, I'm afraid,' Lee says.

'When will they be back?'

'Next week sometime. I'm not sure. But I can help with any questions.'

'Were they ever known as Aster?'

His stare hardens. 'I think I just told you I never met the Asters.'

'No, you didn't. You told me it was before your time when they ran the place.'

Lee says nothing, but his jaw has tightened.

I look at the file again. Eight funerals between 1946 and 1969, including three babies. Exactly as Larry told me.

'So, the four children found outside predate all known records,' Lee says. 'We suspected they were old remains when they were found.'

'Or deaths that weren't officially recorded,' I say. 'Bodies that needed to disappear.'

'Children in local authority care didn't disappear,' Lee says. 'Not even back in the Dark Ages.'

'When did children last live here?'

He frowns. '1969. I'm surprised you need to ask.'

'There have been none here since?'

'The children's home was closed down.'

'Are there any children here now?' I ask.

He shakes his head. 'Why would there be?'

'Earlier today,' I say, 'I read the post-mortem report on the four children found outside. Someone down at the station owed me a favour. And I saw photographs of their remains.'

He holds my gaze steadily, but I've been interviewing suspects for a long time. I can see the shift behind the eyes. 'And what did you learn?' he asks.

'I can't tell you that, I'm afraid.'

His face darkens before he gives a small, sly smile. 'The children's remains were cremated yesterday. I saw it happen.'

I allow him his moment of triumph, but I make sure it's short. 'There are some remarkable advances being made in forensic science,' I tell him. 'Especially in the field of DNA. It's in its early stages, but tests are being carried out into identifying DNA in cremated remains.'

Lee shakes his head. 'That's not possible.'

'It's not easy. And possibly not admissible in court yet. But if there are traces of bones or teeth in the ashes, the results can be very encouraging.'

He stares at me, unsure whether or not I'm bluffing.

'I have the ashes.' I drop my voice almost to a whisper. 'I was at the crematorium earlier. I took the urn.'

His stare hardens; then he picks up the phone and dials a number.

'Rob, it's me. Where are you, mate? . . . Right, can you get in here? Now.'

Lee puts the phone down, and I decide I have no desire to meet Rob. I stand up. 'Are you from Lancashire, Mr Lee? You don't have an accent.'

'I was adopted as a baby. I don't know where I came from originally.'

I fish my keys from my bag and grip them tightly in my hand. 'I think I've seen enough. Thank you.'

I leave the office first, striding ahead along the corridor. As we cross the hall, I can feel the tremor of suppressed energy in the man at my side, but he is small, a little on the podgy side, and I'm not sure he would be much of a threat alone. Even so, I make sure to keep an arm's length from him.

On the doorstep, I relax a little and hold out my right hand to shake. 'How did you know I lived here before?' I ask. 'I told you I'm with the Met. And why did you call me WPC Lovelady? I haven't been known as that for years.'

He extends his own hand. 'Oh, everyone knows you, Florence.'

Ordinarily, I'd respond to that, but I'm looking down at his hand. A perfectly normal young man's hand, except for a minor deformity that, for some reason, he never bothered to have corrected. My hunch for the last few minutes has been that this familiar-looking young man is the son of Frederick and Judith Aster. He isn't. I feel the extra finger of his right hand pressing against mine.

He knows exactly what I'm thinking.

'I was born with it,' he says. He still has my hand, is standing uncomfortably close to me.

'I know,' I say. 'I was there.'

His eyebrows rise as I pull my hand free. I don't look back as I stride to my car, and I'm some way down the drive before I look in my rear-view mirror. Watching me drive away is the man who was born Henry McGowan, Marigold's son.

# 109

## Cassie

John drops me off at Daphne and Avril's house but won't come in, and I realise that he'll never readily acknowledge me as his partner among people who know us. The stigma of incest is too strong. On the plus side, he's told me to pack. He'll find a room in town, he says, and will pick me up in two hours.

'Darling,' Daphne says, when she sees me. 'We've been worried – well, goodness, don't you look different? Something's cheered you up.'

I cross the kitchen and put my arms round her. They reach, just about. 'Sorry I've been a bitch,' I tell her.

She gives a little squeak of surprise.

'Where's Avril?' I ask. I should probably apologise to her too. I might not hug her, though. All those bones.

'On the phone.' Daphne glances towards the study door. 'Talking to Dwane, I think. We're a bit worried about Florence.'

I wait for her to tell me why. She doesn't.

'What's going on with my mum?' I ask. 'I know she hates me, and she's probably got reason to, but why is she pretending to have dementia?'

Daphne gives herself a second. 'We all have our coping mechanisms,' she says. 'I think Sally got to the point where she couldn't handle life anymore. So, she took herself out of it. And she doesn't hate you. What nonsense. Cup of tea, dear?'

'And that was down to me?' I ask. 'Mum giving up on life?'

Daphne stops moving for a second. 'What on earth makes you think that?'

I can't tell her. And then I wonder if she already knows.

Daphne has fallen silent, and still. She's looking out of the kitchen window, up into the sky. I open my mouth to ask her if she's OK and then I realise what she's doing. She's looking for the black moon.

'I'm going to find a room in town,' I say. 'I won't disturb you any longer. I'll go and pack.'

'You can't leave yet.' Daphne pulls herself together and takes china from the cupboard. 'There's a meet tonight.'

'What meet?'

'The coven.' Daphne seems unable to find the tea, moving everything around in the cupboard. 'We're gathering at Daylight Gate, on the site of Malkin Tower.'

'It's the dark moon,' I point out, although she obviously knows this herself. 'And the caddy's right in front of you.'

'Even so,' Daphne says. 'Ah yes. Thank you, dear.'

The moon coven never meet when the moon is black. Even I know that. At that moment, Avril appears in the doorway.

'Was that Dwane?' Daphne asks.

'Marlene.' Avril's face is grim, even by her standards. 'Florence was last seen heading up towards Black Moss Manor.'

'Oh Lord.' Daphne puts down the teapot. 'She's thrown down the gauntlet, hasn't she?'

Avril says nothing. Her face says a lot. If only I could read it. It doesn't look like a huggable face, though. I'll definitely skip the hug.

'They'll do something,' Daphne says. 'Now the children are cremated, they'll think they're untouchable.'

'What's going on?' I ask. 'Who are "they"?'

*The Craftsmen*. The words spring, unbidden, into my head. They're talking about the Craftsmen.

'I need to get her on the phone.' Avril heads for the door again.

I've been so self-absorbed since I've been back, I've failed to see what's been going on around me. I know in my heart that it's important, that it dwarfs, by far, my own problems, but it scares me.

'You've got a lot on your minds,' I try. 'You really don't need me getting in the way. I'll just nip upstairs and pack.'

'Cassie, you're staying with us,' Daphne says, and I don't think I've ever heard her voice sound so commanding. 'You're coming to the coven.'

When I turn back, the sweet, fat old lady I've known since I was an infant looks very different. I remind myself of something I should never forget. You don't mess with a witch.

'Daphne's right,' Avril says. 'We wanted to talk to you. It's time. But Florence has set events in motion and I really—' She breaks off. I wonder if she might be about to cry.

'Get her on the phone,' Daphne tells her partner. 'Find out where she is.'

Avril hurries from the room. Daphne steps towards me.

'After tonight, you're free to do whatever you want, with whoever you want. But first, there will be a reckoning.'

'Why can't you—'

She holds up a hand, but it's the glitter in her eyes, more than the gesture, that shuts me up. 'You're lost, Cassie. You have been for years. We can help you find your way home, if you trust us.'

'But—'

'And we need help too. There's more going on than you know about, but you're involved whether you like it or not. We need you.'

'I don't—'

She bangs her hand down, hard, on the kitchen table. 'Cassandra, you're a witch,' she says. 'Your place is with us.'

# 110

## Florence

I might have overplayed my hand. Worse, I might have underestimated the people I'm up against. I've spent much of the day provoking them – stealing the urn with the children's remains, persuading Brian Rushton to show me the post-mortem evidence, taunting Bracken Lee. I can't expect that they won't fight back.

They'll come for me.

I can't go back to my room at the Black Dog; it's the first place they'll look. I can't go to Avril's offices, or to the house she shares with Daphne. They will look for me there next. Dwane will be on their radar screen too. Meanwhile, the day is drawing to a close. The sun is low on the horizon, and the moon, when it rises, will be black.

Once I'm safely away from Black Moss Manor, I pull over, phone Scotland Yard and wait to be put through to the commissioner. His swearing, as I explain my situation, exceeds even my expectations and I've seen him up against it more than once. When I finish, he's uncharacteristically silent.

'Is it enough?' I prompt.

'Tell me again what you've got,' he says.

'A post-mortem report that does not match the one at Sabden Police Station.'

'Neither of them in your possession,' he reminds me.

'Cremated ashes that could contain DNA linking one of the dead children with Dwane and Jenny Ogilvy.'

'Equally it might not. And that's unproven technology.'

'A taped and witnessed interview with Sandra Cartwright going into quite some detail about what was going on at Black Moss Manor.'

'A good defence lawyer will tear that to pieces.'

'The expert opinion of anthropologist Caroline Trickster that the remains found could not date back to when the children's home was operational.'

He grunts down the line. 'That will be useful. But only if we have the dodgy report.'

'And a man calling himself Bracken Lee, who I believe to be the child of a woman who vanished back in 1969. If I'm right, he'll have fake adoption papers that won't hold up under scrutiny.'

'Florence,' he says, 'I'm honestly not certain what we do with that one.'

'Is it enough?' I repeat.

'To set events in motion, probably. To stand a chance in court, though . . .'

He's right. 'I need to flush them out,' I admit. 'Can you get a team up here? Today?'

My boss sucks air in over his teeth. 'It's a big ask, Florence.'

'Four dead kids, sir. At least four.'

'Even if you prove foul play, you don't actually have a suspect.'

'That's why I need to force their hand.'

He sighs again. 'And how do you plan to do that?'

I tell him. He swears some more.

'Florence, it will be several hours, at least, until I can get officers up there. And these people sound dangerous.'

'I'll stay out of their way. I've got friends here.'

He swears again and hangs up; I have to hope he'll come through. In the meantime, all I can do is put my own plans in place. I drive to the Glassbrook house on the edge of town. The housekeeper, Mary, lent me her keys yesterday immediately after Larry's funeral and I keep forgetting to give them back. I park and get out. When I open my car boot to find the urn, I'm surprised by the sight of Ben's leather jacket. I pick it up and it smells of him. It feels like Ben is with me again, and with Ben by my side, there is nothing I can't do.

I close the boot and carry the urn over to Sally's old beehives. They'll be as good a hiding place as any.

The kitchen looks as I left it hours earlier. The hallway is a little different, though. The hallway is occupied. By a tall, dark-haired man who, in the dim light, looks exactly as he did thirty years ago.

'I thought I'd find you here,' says Tom.

# 111

## Cassie

God knows the last thing I want to do this evening is dance round an open fire on Pendle Hill with a load of daft old women. My bags are packed. John and I have a room booked above a pub some way from the Black Dog. I want to start the life I've been dreaming of for thirty years. But Avril and Daphne have been kind to me and neither was taking no for an answer.

A burst of gold sparks shoots into the air. Across the bonfire, Avril's face looks like a skull in the light from the flames. By her side stands my mother and then Luna.

'We are few,' Avril says. 'But we stand together.' She steps forward and throws a handful of herbs. The flames change colour and a bright flicker of sapphire blooms in the fire's heart.

There are seventeen of us. Talk about overkill. The maximum number for a coven is thirteen and they've all showed up. We three Glassbrook women and Florence Lovelady are the bolt-on extras.

'We are weak,' says Marlene Labaddee, casting more herbs. 'But we are cunning.' She is standing next to her daughter, a little to my right. On my other side are Jenny Ogilvy, Dwane's wife, and a woman I think is his sister. I'm surprised to see Mary, our old housekeeper, and bloody astonished that Petrifying Perdita is here with her mother.

'We are old,' says Daphne. 'But we have wisdom.'

'They fear us,' says Avril, as Daphne throws her herbs.

'They fear us,' Marlene repeats.

It becomes a chant that even Luna joins in with, after an amused look at me.

'They fear us. They fear us.'

Daphne, who has led the moon coven since I was a child and still does, it seems, in spite of her advanced years, holds up her hands for silence.

'Be seated, sisters,' she says. 'Florence has the voice.'

As the rest of us sit, Florence remains on her feet. The firelight softens the lines of her face, making her look younger, almost the woman I remember from years ago. She's changed out of her uniform and is wearing a simple pair of jeans, a sweater and a leather jacket.

Most of the other women have gone full metal coven, with flowing skirts, lanterns and cloaks. Somehow Florence, in her ordinary dress, is that one who would make my superstitious hackles rise. Were I to be afraid of witches, she's the one.

'We've known for years,' she begins, 'that there is something very wrong in this town.'

No one argues.

'I knew it thirty years ago,' she continues. 'Sabden is run by people – by men – who are rotten and corrupt.'

The fire burns, the sky darkens and the wind around us picks up. The women are silent.

'Larry knew it,' Florence says. 'That's why he sent me back. But he shouldn't have had to. I should have stayed, thirty years ago, and fought them then.'

'You were little more than a child,' Daphne interrupts. 'You couldn't possibly have challenged the Craftsmen back then.'

The Craftsmen? That name again. Am I actually going to find out what it means?

'We were glad when you left,' Daphne goes on. 'We didn't want you to come back.'

'The Craftsmen went after my son,' Florence says. 'And I will hunt them down.'

'You've already made them pay,' Avril tells her.

Florence's face tightens as her head darts around to confront her old friend. 'Not nearly enough.'

Avril and Daphne look troubled. I have no idea what they are talking about, but it seems far more happened last night than I was aware of.

'I'm sorry to interrupt.' Luna's voice cuts through the night like a bell. 'But I don't know who the Craftsmen are.'

It is typical of my sister to make this gathering about her.

'They're witches, like us. But not like us. A group of men in town who practise the ancient craft, but for dark ends,' Daphne tells her.

'Who are they?' Luna asks, and I half expect her to pull out a notebook and take names.

'Important businessmen, leaders of the town council, lawyers, police officers, the Worshipful Master of the Lodge,' says Avril. 'All of them, perhaps. Maybe none of them.'

'The truth is, we don't know,' Daphne says. 'No one does. We might suspect. We might even be sure in some cases, but this is not something that can be proven.'

'And you think they're involved with Black Moss Manor?' Perdita asks.

Florence nods her head. 'The trustees of that place have always been among the most powerful men in town. They wouldn't have been so invested in a home for handicapped children unless it served some purpose for them. Yes, I think Black Moss Manor was a Craftsmen project. One of several.'

We wait for her to go on.

'Thirty years ago, we closed the home because the children in it were being neglected,' she says. 'We found evidence of an illegal soporific medicine and we left it at that. We should have realised – I should have realised – that we were only scratching the surface.'

I'm about to ask what she means. Luna jumps in first.

'A lot of the children there were handicapped,' Florence tells her. 'But they didn't take handicapped children because they had the expertise to look after them – they actively sought out children who were different.'

Florence glances towards Jenny Ogilvy. 'They were interested in children with dwarfism. Dwane's mother was pressured to give up her smaller children for adoption.'

She looks from Mum and Luna to me now. 'They were keen on Down's syndrome too. Remember how eager they were to keep hold of Marigold McGowan and her baby? There was a fifty per cent chance he'd have Down's syndrome and they wanted him.'

'Why?' I ask.

Florence says, 'They thought disabled people might have special abilities. I met a woman called Sandra Cartwright today who worked there in the 1960s. She told me that the day we closed the place down, an experiment went wrong. The children were supposed to be throwing knives at a sort of dummy, suspended from the ceiling, but some of them started hurling them at the two staff members instead. One of them was badly injured. The other fled.'

'The children were being trained to throw knives?' Luna sounds incredulous. 'What the hell were they? Circus performers?'

'They weren't throwing them with their hands,' Florence says. 'According to Sandra Cartwright, that is.'

A shiver runs through me, even though I'm close to the fire. 'What, then?' I ask.

'With their minds,' Florence replies. 'Cartwright claims they were throwing knives with their minds.'

A reaction shudders around the group, but I can't tell whether it's prompted by disbelief or fear.

Luna's brows form one continuous line. 'Are you talking about telekinesis? There's no evidence that's even a thing.'

'We all know what it means, don't we?' Avril says. 'Moving objects by will alone.' She, too, looks doubtful. 'Florence, I think Luna may be right.'

'No evidence that's commonly known about,' Florence says. 'But a journalist friend of mine, a woman called Abby Thorn, spent some time digging this afternoon. There have been rumours for years about governments funding research into psychic abilities. Anyone who managed it stood to make an absolute fortune.'

'Marigold could do it,' my mother says. 'Marigold was a . . . what's the word? Telekinetic.'

My head turns sharply to Luna. Hearing our mother talk still comes as a shock, but Luna seems only mildly puzzled by what she's saying.

'I saw her.' Sally insists. 'Twice. The first time was while she was in labour. She made my bag fly off a chair. I'm not sure she even knew what she'd done.'

'I remember that,' Florence says. 'I thought it was a wobbly chair.'

'Then after she moved in with us, I saw a flower leap into her hand.'

'A foxglove?' The words come out of my mouth before I stop to think.

My mother turns to me. 'You were in the room. Did you see it too?'

I wait for a second. I'm actually talking to my mother. 'I thought it was a draught,' I say. 'The window was open.'

'Why are governments interested in psychic research?' Luna asks.

'I'm not sure they are anymore,' Florence says. 'But Abby found out today that in the decades after the war, interest was huge. The Americans had something called the Stargate Project to investigate the potential for psychic phenomena in military intelligence. It was only terminated four years ago. And they believed that other national governments, most significantly the Russians, were doing it too.'

'A psychic arms race?' Luna is smiling, possibly sneering; it's still hard to tell.

'What sort of experiments?' I ask.

'Mainly remote viewing. And precognition – you know, being able to see events in the future. There was also a project at Stanford in California. One of the psychics involved was Uri Geller. Remember him?'

Heads are nodding. The man who bent spoons.

'They studied mind control,' Florence says. 'Telepathy. There was even talk of psychics who could kill with their minds. They practised on animals. And there were a lot of animals at Black Moss.'

'According to Sandra Cartwright, the experiments with animals weren't the worst of it,' Florence says. 'Because they'd discovered something.'

She gives an uneasy glance at Jenny Ogilvy.

'Cartwright told us they learned that pain increases psychic ability,' Florence goes on. 'They had a young woman called Wendy who gave birth at the manor. They took measures to extend her ordeal, increase her pain. She and the baby died. Marigold got wind of this somehow and it terrified her. That's why she ran.'

Around me, faces are hardening, turning from curious to angry. More than one woman makes the traditional sign to ward off evil.

'Even if this is true, it was thirty years ago,' Perdita says. 'It stopped. You and your colleagues closed the place down.'

'We didn't,' Florence says. 'Or only temporarily. It's still going on.'

'Are you sure?' Avril asks her.

'I am,' Florence says. 'For three reasons. The first is Larry.'

'What's he got to do with this?' I ask, and see that Luna, too, has stiffened at the mention of his name.

'Larry saw the news story about the four corpses found at Black Moss and he didn't buy the line that they were ancient remains. He said the conditions here would not allow small, soft bones to survive for more than a couple of decades.'

'If Dad said that, it must be right,' Luna says, with a glance at me.

'He *was* right,' Florence says. 'An anthropologist I know confirmed it. And I saw the post-mortem report today at Blackburn Royal Infirmary. Very different to the one on file at Sabden Police Station.'

'That's impossible,' Perdita says.

'It should be,' agrees Florence.

For a moment, the two women stare at each other.

'That means someone at the station is definitely connected to the Craftsmen,' Perdita says, when she breaks eye contact with Florence. 'What have I been telling you?'

'They always were,' Avril replies. 'The Craftsmen would never have been able to operate the way they have without police protection.'

'You still have no idea who?' Daphne asks.

Perdita shakes her head.

Mary gets to her feet, grimacing. I remember that she must be in her seventies, and that climbing Pendle Hill and sitting on the cold ground won't be easy for her.

'The second reason is that Sandra Cartwright gave me names today,' Florence says. 'She named the four dead children. None of them were even born in 1969 when we closed down the home.'

Another uneasy glance at Jenny.

'I think one of them was Dwane and Jenny's son, David,' Florence says. 'I took the ashes today. DNA tests may prove it.'

'Where are the ashes now?' asks Perdita.

'In a very safe place,' replies Florence.

Another moment of stalemate between the two police officers. Perdita is finding it hard to accept the alleged corruption among her colleagues.

'And the third reason?' I prompt.

'Marigold McGowan's son is still alive,' Florence says. 'He's known as Bracken Lee now and he runs Black Moss. That suggests to me the Craftsmen took him as a baby and brought him up.'

'How can you be sure it's him?' asks Perdita.

'Right age. He looked familiar. He admitted he was adopted as a baby. And he has a sixth finger on his right hand.'

'That's not proof, Florence,' says Avril.

'I looked into his eyes,' Florence says. 'We knew each other.'

Mary walks away from the bonfire, rubbing a hand against the small of her back.

'What do we do?' Daphne looks like nothing more than a scared old woman. 'What can we possibly do?'

'Ladies, you do nothing,' Florence says. 'These men are ruthless. Thirty years ago, they tried to drown me, and they beat up a journalist I was working with. They murdered Randall Butterworth and they tried to kill me too. The police will handle it from here.'

'Florence, we can't trust the police,' Daphne says. 'Sorry, Perdita dear, but it needs to be said. Especially after last night.'

A shadow falls over Florence's face. Marlene stretches out a hand and covers hers. I turn to see Luna looking at me, a question on her face. I shrug.

'It won't be the Lancashire Constabulary who carry out the investigation – it will be the Met,' Florence says. 'My own officers. They should be here in a couple more hours.'

'I agree you have a case, but it's flimsy,' Perdita says. 'By the time the Met arrive at Sabden station, that fake report will have vanished. Your interview with Sandra Cartwright sounds completely far-fetched and is full of holes. And even if the ashes reveal some DNA, I doubt it will be admissible.'

'I know,' Florence agrees. 'That's why I need to flush out the people who are behind Black Moss.'

'How?' Perdita asks.

'They'll be looking for me already,' Florence says. 'They know I took the children's ashes, and that I've seen both post-mortem reports. They probably know I've spoken to Sandra Cartwright. Bracken Lee's adoption will be on record. If his papers were faked somehow, or if they don't exist, I'll find that out. The people at Black Moss know I can expose them.'

'Does anyone else really not like the sound of this?' says Daphne.

Florence glances at her watch. 'I'm going to be spending the rest of the evening at the Glassbrook house. The Craftsmen know I have keys. Sooner or later, they'll come for me there, and when they do, I'll be wired up and my colleagues will be waiting. When they spring me, we'll know they have something to hide.'

'It's risky, Florence,' Avril says.

She smiles. 'Yes. For them.'

Mary, who has been standing for some minutes now, who I think we've all forgotten about, calls out to get our attention. 'Car at the bottom of the Hill,' she says. 'We've got company.'

# 112

## Florence

The women are on their feet. I approach the edge and look down. Sure enough, the headlights of a vehicle can be seen approaching the spot where we all parked. It could be just another hiker. Somehow, I know it's not. The Craftsmen have found me.

'We have to go,' I say. 'Now.'

These men are dangerous. No one knows that better than I do, and I can't risk the women getting caught up in whatever they have planned.

'What's up?' asks Luna, as she joins me. 'Who is it? Do they want us?'

'There's another way off the Hill,' Jenny says. 'We have to get to the summit and then head towards Wiswell. I can ring Dwane and have him meet us.'

I wonder if they can see me, lit by the backdrop of the fire. Taking Luna by the hand, I step back from the edge.

'What's the problem?' Cassie complains. 'We're not doing anything wrong.'

'Exactly,' Luna says. 'We haven't even slaughtered the chickens yet.'

Fleeing across the countryside in darkness? It hardly seems wise, and yet it will take the people below a while to reach this spot. We have time to get away.

'We should go,' I say. 'Jenny, you lead the way. I'll bring up the rear. Leave the fire. It will burn itself out.'

'Flossie,' Luna says, 'aren't you overreacting?'

I face her directly. 'You have no idea what these men are capable of!'

Daphne folds her arms across her bosom. 'I agree with Luna. I can't possibly run across the countryside pursued by marauders,' she says. 'I'm nearly eighty.'

'It's pushing it for me too.' Avril sits again. 'Marlene, you're carrying more weight than you used to. And Mary doesn't look as though she's been hiking much of late. I'd sit yourselves back down, ladies.'

As I stare at them, open-mouthed, some of the women obey Avril and sit. Others look uncertain. 'What the hell are you doing?' I say to Avril. 'They'll be here in minutes.'

'At least thirty,' Daphne says. 'More if they're not familiar with the way up.'

Avril tosses more wood onto the fire.

'Exactly,' I say. 'We've got time to get away.'

'You go,' Avril says. 'Take Jenny to make sure you don't get lost. We'll stay here.'

'We'll hold the fort.' Daphne's eyes are gleaming. 'Lay down some covering fire.'

I can't believe what I'm hearing. 'Is this a joke to you? Do you remember what they did last night?'

'Florence, we have to get moving.' Jenny takes hold of my arm. I catch Perdita's eye and know my concern is shared.

'I should stay here,' she says to me. 'They won't mess with a local police officer.'

'I think you'll be surprised who these people will mess with,' Avril tells her. 'But they're not interested in us. It's Florence who needs watching. Go with her.'

'My car is at the bottom of the Hill,' I say. 'They'll know I'm here.'

'I drove it,' says Daphne. 'Might have scraped the left wing, dear. I'm sorry. My eyes aren't what they used to be.'

'You really should go,' Avril tells me, and I see that she, too, is getting anxious. On my behalf.

'They're on their way up,' Mary says. 'Three of them, I think. Bugger me, they've got flaming torches.'

'How very medieval,' Luna says. 'What about pitchforks?'

'I'm not leaving you all,' I say.

'They won't hurt us.' Daphne is rummaging in her bag now. 'A bunch of barmy old women. Damn it, I forgot the wine.'

'Not to mention two lawyers.' Luna pulls out her phone. 'One of whom is about to text the senior partner in her firm to tell him she was last seen on Pendle Hill if anything happens to her.'

'That's a good idea.' Avril pulls out her own phone.

Perdita does the same. 'I'm calling this in. The entire constabulary can't be bent.' She steps away from the group a little.

'And an internationally recognised songwriter,' says Luna. 'My sister can't disappear. She's working on a new musical with Andrew Lloyd Webber.'

'How do you know that?' Cassie asks.

'Hello – internet?'

They're right. No one will mess with this lot. I give in to the tugging on my sleeve and Jenny and I start climbing the last stretch towards the summit. Perdita finishes her call and follows us.

# 113

## Cassie

After Florence and the other two leave, more wood is thrown onto the dying fire. 'Are we just going to wait for whoever's coming up the Hill?' I say, trying not to sound nervous.

'No,' says Daphne.

'We've twenty minutes at a push,' Mary says. 'They know their way up.'

'Twenty minutes should do it,' Avril says.

'Do what?' Luna asks.

'We're not done here,' Daphne says. 'Cassandra has the voice.'

Everyone falls silent. Everyone, apart from Mary, looks at me. No one is smiling. I turn to look up the Hill, but Florence and the others have already vanished.

Suddenly, I feel alone. No one around me seems at all concerned by the approaching threat. It's almost as though they expected this to happen. It occurs to me then that Florence's departure was slickly managed.

Still, they look at me. This feels like a court, like I'm on trial. And yet I have the voice.

'Are you waiting for me to confess to something?' I try to put the sneer into my voice, but the mood of the group has changed in the last few minutes. It has become something else. I remember, maybe too late, that this is not a gaggle of middle-aged and elderly eccentric women. This is a gathering of witches.

Witches who confess to their crimes are hanged, or drowned, or burned in purifying fire. The fire in our midst is burning brighter and higher since Florence and the others left. As soon as the men below us were spotted, the women began stoking it. My heart is hammering. I tell myself that Florence is a senior policewoman. She would not condone a crime as hideous as burning someone to death.

Florence has gone; Perdita has gone.

Avril clears her throat. 'It will be easier if you do,' she says.

Of course it will – for them. If I confess my sins – murder, planning another murder, incest – they can do what they want to me with an easy conscience.

'Cassandra, you've been carrying a burden too long,' says Daphne. 'It's time to throw it off.'

'We can't help you if you don't trust us,' my mother says.

My mother hasn't spoken directly to me in years. I thought I'd never hear her do it again. She's deceived me all this time and now she's asking me—

'Why the hell would I trust you?' I ask her.

Her eyes fall as she hears the hate in my voice.

'Trust me,' says Luna.

For the first time in decades, I look properly at my little sister. She is as tall as I am now. The hair she used to hate, used to dye ridiculous colours because it wasn't a pale ash blonde, is a dark gold now. She's still dyeing it, but finally she's found the shade that's right for her. She dresses well too.

'You hate me,' I tell her.

'I got over him.' Then she grins. 'I hear you didn't.'

'Tell us what you did,' Avril says. 'You'll feel better.'

She's right. I've been carrying this secret for too long.

'I killed Roy Greenwood,' I say.

No one seems surprised. 'Why?' asks Daphne.

'I found his will,' I say. 'The day before he and his mother moved in with us.'

Avril inclines her head. 'I gave a copy to Sally,' she says. 'We weren't a hundred per cent sure it would stand, in the changed circumstances.'

My mother says, 'But you realised that if Roy died without

changing it, there was a good chance we'd inherit the business and the house. We'd be safe.'

'Exactly,' I say, remembering the sense of dreadful possibility I'd felt as I'd read the terms of Greenwood's will.

'You always were a bit too fond of snooping,' Mary says.

'And sneaking around,' Luna adds.

I glare at her and she sticks her tongue out. For a second, we're teenagers again.

'It wasn't really about money, though,' I say, truthfully. It had been the sheer, crippling fear of the man. In less than a day, he'd taken over our house and I knew he had his sights set on Mum. To my shame, I might have gone along with that, but I knew he wouldn't stop with her. I saw the way he looked at me, and at Luna, even at Marigold. None of us would have been safe.

'You were terrified of him,' Luna says. 'We all were. He was unstable. And dangerous.'

'How?' asks Avril. 'How did you kill him?'

Again, I have a feeling she already knows.

'Foxglove syrup.' I glance across the fire to where our old housekeeper is keeping watch. 'Mary and Luna made a batch. I sneaked one of the vials and poured some into the dry sherry. He was the only one who drank it. I wasn't sure it was working, but then he got ill. I added a bit more and he collapsed. He died a few hours later.'

'Definitely three of them,' Mary calls back to us.

'This was the night I stayed with Daphne and Avril?' Luna says to me. 'The night Marigold vanished? Honestly, I miss all the fun.'

My mother shoots her a dark look.

'I'm glad,' Luna says. 'Greenwood was a monster. I'd have done it myself if I'd known about the will. I wish you'd told me, Cass. I'd have . . .'

'What?' I say.

She shrugs. 'Held him down. Shared the burden. Whatever. The point is, I'm glad you killed him.' She reaches out, as though to take my hand.

'She didn't,' says my mother.

Luna freezes. Everyone else turns to my mother, apart from Avril and Daphne, who continue to watch me.

'Yes, she did,' Mary interrupts. 'Some of that foxglove syrup went missing. She took it and she killed him. I'm not saying he wasn't a wrong 'un, but—'

'I did take the syrup,' I say, because I'm not about to have Mary speak for me. 'I poured it into the sherry. He drank it. I killed him.'

'I found the vial.' My mother gives a long, deep sigh. 'I saw there was one missing from the store cupboard and I searched the house until I found it. I looked in your room first.'

She holds my stare.

'I replaced the vial you took with one containing a solution of rosehip and sugar,' she says. 'That's what you put in the sherry. It would have made it a bit sweeter, that's all.'

I shake my head. I remember Greenwood breaking into a sweat, his rising temperature, his loss of balance. I remember my excitement at realising it was working, and at the same time, my abject horror at what I'd become.

'I put the foxglove vial back in the cupboard,' my mother says. 'By the time the police looked, it was all in order.'

'Greenwood was poisoned,' I say.

'Yes,' my mother agrees. 'But not by you.'

I'm not taking this in. For thirty years, I've been a murderer. It was another of the ties that bound me to John. We'd both killed, on the same night. Thirty years on, I'd been prepared to kill his wife, his mother, even his dog, because I believed myself already a killer.

'Strictly speaking, you still planned to,' says Daphne. 'You're probably guilty of something, albeit a lesser offence. This is not something we should tell Florence.'

'Or Perdita,' Hecate adds.

A murmur of agreement ripples through the group.

'Halfway up,' Mary calls back. 'We've about ten minutes.'

A couple of the women exchange nervous glances, but I no longer have any interest in the men coming up the Hill.

'Who, then? If I didn't kill him, who did?' I'm suddenly overwhelmed with fear that my mother did, that she took upon herself the burden of ridding us of the man.

'Not me.' Luna holds up her hands in a 'don't shoot' gesture.

I turn to my mother. 'Did you do it?' She takes my hand, the first time she has touched me in years, and shakes her head. 'No,' she says.

I believe her. My mother is not a killer.

I look across at Mary. There was no one else in the house. She shakes her head. My mother squeezes my hand to get my attention back. 'Grace killed him,' she says.

Grace Greenwood? Roy's mother?

'It couldn't have been Marigold,' Luna says. 'There was no one else. Did Grace use the foxglove syrup? She was always snooping around in your cupboards.'

'Roy's symptoms weren't compatible with foxglove poisoning,' my mother says. 'There was nothing else in the house that was deadly enough.'

'I remember there being some similarities, but not enough that the police could charge you with any confidence of a conviction,' Avril says. 'And also, Grace was prepared to testify that he'd been ill for some time.'

'Because she'd been poisoning him for weeks,' my mother says. 'He'd been abusing her for years. She was afraid of what he might do to us.'

'Did she tell you this?' I ask.

Sally nods. 'The morning I was released. She promised to confess if I was charged. She wouldn't let me go to prison.'

'So you kept quiet and hoped for the best?' Luna says.

'Why didn't you tell the police?' I ask. 'What did we owe the Greenwoods?'

My mother gives me a look I remember well. She is saying, *Think about it. Use your brain before you open your mouth.*

'She agreed not to contest the will if you kept quiet,' I suggest. 'She let us have the house and the business.'

'All she wanted was to go home and live out her days in peace,' my mother says. 'I saw her a few times before she died. She never regretted what she'd done.'

'What did she use?' asks Marlene.

'Lily of the valley water.' My mother looks from Luna to me. 'Do you remember that perfume she used to wear?'

'God, yes,' Luna says. 'It stank.'

'She made it herself. She grew the flowers – in the garden, in hanging baskets, in tubs, indoors and out.'

Marlene looks impressed. 'A very deadly poison,' she says. 'Blurred vision, disorientation, vomiting and nausea, increased blood pressure. Ultimately, cardiac arrest.'

I've pulled away from my mother; I no longer want her touching me.

'Why?' I ask her. 'Why did you let me think I'd done it?'

'She didn't know what you'd done,' Luna says. 'It was a misunderstanding.'

'She knew. She found the vial in my room. And she threatened me.'

'What do you mean?' Luna is looking bewildered. 'When?'

'A couple of days later.' I'm remembering my panic-stricken search of my room, turning round to see Mum in the doorway, the vial in her hand.

'This what you're looking for?' she'd said.

'You told me you'd never mention it again,' I say to her. 'That no one would ever know it had gone missing, as long as I behaved myself.'

My mother's eyes are full of pain, but she can't look away from me.

'I behaved myself. I stayed away from John because I was terrified of going to prison. You told Dad, didn't you? I got a letter from him just after he'd been sentenced, telling me he knew what I'd done, and that I had to have nothing more to do with John, that I had to leave Sabden and never come back.'

'He was your brother,' my mother says.

'Still is, come to that,' says Luna.

'Beryl did the same thing, didn't she? She told John you and she would keep quiet about the accident at the pub if he left me alone.'

'What accident?' Luna asks.

'Maybe we don't need to confess everything tonight,' Daphne says.

'You blackmailed us into separating,' I say.

'We did it for your own good,' my mother says. 'Me, Beryl, your father. We thought the two of you would get it out of your system in a couple of years.'

How can she not get it? I could sooner have ripped my heart out.

'You'd never have been able to get married.' She almost seems to be pleading with me now. 'You couldn't have had children. You'd have been outcasts. You might have been sent to prison.'

'She's too old for children now,' says Luna. 'So that's one problem solved.'

'I would have had a lifetime with the man I love,' I say. 'We could have moved abroad. I could have been happy.'

'We were acting for the best.'

'You paved the road to my hell,' I tell her.

'Well, it's not too late,' says Luna. 'You're still young. Ish. You still look good. You could do with a haircut. And that ageing rock chick look? Let's be honest, now, it's a bit tired.'

'Luna, please.' My mother holds up her hand to stop my sister talking.

'It's not right,' Mary says. 'He's married to our Tammy.'

'I used to be married,' says Marlene. 'It doesn't last for ever.'

'Me too,' says someone else. 'Left me for a woman who works down the paint factory. I got over it.'

'But were you married to close relatives?' asks Luna.

'Luna, will you shut up?' my mother and I yell at the same time.

'They've stopped,' Mary says. 'They're about five minutes away, but they're not climbing anymore. They're talking.'

'Luna's right,' says Avril. 'Take children out of the mix and we're talking about societal norms. If you and John leave Sabden, no one need be any the wiser.'

Round the fire, heads are nodding. Are they actually giving me their blessing?

'Well, I'm glad we sorted that out.' Daphne gets to her feet. 'What's happening, Mary?'

'They've turned round,' Mary answers her. 'They're going back down. They're running. That's not wise. Not on that slope.'

For a moment, there is silence.

'We have to go,' Avril says. 'Sisters, as fast as you can. Get your things.'

The women jump to their feet. Luna and I exchange puzzled glances.

'What's happening?' Luna asks. 'If they're going, what's the problem?'

Avril pulls out her phone and presses a number. 'If they're not coming up here anymore, it means they know Florence has left us.' She presses the phone to her ear. 'Damn, it's not ringing.'

Daphne has walked to the cliff edge. 'Those are men moving with purpose,' she says. 'I think they know where Florence is.'

# 114

## Florence

Perdita and I are breathing heavily when we make the summit, and we wait for Jenny to catch up. When she reaches us, we huddle together against the wind.

'He'll meet us by the old tithe barn,' Jenny shouts. 'He's leaving right away.'

Perdita goes ahead this time and I walk with Jenny. We follow what is little more than an indentation in the ground and the wind pushes us along.

'What do you think they did to him?' Jenny says, when the wind drops enough to make conversation possible. 'My baby, I mean.'

'If they thought he had special abilities, they'd have looked after him,' I tell her.

'Until they killed him.'

I can think of nothing to say to her.

'Do you believe in that stuff?' she asks me. 'That psychic stuff?'

'I want to say no, but . . .'

I think back to the night long ago when I watched blindfolded children make their way round obstacles and then to Albert Frost telling me it was a game to test spatial skills. There is always another explanation for what we find hard to accept. The mirror writing that unnerved me so much could have been the work of human hands, or it could have been 'that psychic stuff'. The knife that stabbed my leg the day we raided Black Moss Manor could have been thrown by a strong, small hand or moved by the power of a young mind.

We reach the edge of the summit and descend as quickly as we dare. Jenny falls and rolls several yards down the slope. Perdita gets stuck in mud. Below us, I can see a church steeple, and a cluster of roofs. At the bottom of the Hill, we climb a wall to cross a field. A pair of horses watch us curiously. Another field and I think I can see telegraph wires.

'Which way's the barn?' I ask, as we climb over the last wall onto the road.

Jenny points west and we set off. She pulls out her phone and dials a number. 'He's not answering,' she says, after a minute.

'Signal's bad out here,' Perdita tells her. 'The Hill blocks it.'

'How far?' I ask.

'Quarter of a mile,' Jenny tells me.

We walk on and hear nothing but the wind, an occasional barking dog and the startled bleating of sheep.

'Try him again,' I say.

'Nothing,' Jenny says after a moment.

I try. Dwane's number rings; he doesn't answer. I try to swallow down my unease, but my mouth remains dry. The barn is in sight now, a low-roofed building close to the church.

'There's Dwane's car.' Jenny's pace picks up and I, too, can see the large silver vehicle.

'Jenny, hold on.' I catch hold of her shoulder. 'Ring him again.'

She points to the silver car. 'He's there. I can shout.'

There is a solitary light in the car park of the tithe barn and the outline of Dwane's head and shoulders is visible in the driver's seat. He is staring straight ahead.

'Ring him,' I insist.

Dwane would not be sitting in his car. He'd be striding up and down the road, telling us to get a bloody move on, he hasn't got all night.

We hear the phone ringing in the car.

I stop, catching hold of the other two. 'Go back,' I tell them. 'Get over the wall and hide. Perdita, take her. Do it now.'

Perdita and I turn, dragging a reluctant Jenny with us.

We can go no further. Our way is blocked by three tall men.

# 115

## Cassie

Luna drops me off at Daphne and Avril's house a little after eleven.

'Stay by the phone,' she says. She drives away with our mother in the back seat before I've properly closed the door. I find my borrowed key and climb the front steps.

The witches hatched their plan while we were hurrying back down Pendle Hill, after they failed to contact any of the three women who'd left us. We were to separate and go to the places where Florence and the others were most likely to take refuge. Avril and Daphne should already be at the Glassbrook house. Hecate has gone to Dwane's house, Mary to the Black Dog, and my mother will wait at the nursing home. Marlene and her daughter are heading to Black Moss Manor. Once Luna has dropped our mother off, she'll head back to Sabden Police Station to report our concerns about Florence, Perdita and Jenny. With her London legal connections, she is the one most likely to be taken seriously.

I can't help noticing that John's van isn't outside Daphne and Avril's house. I tell myself not to worry, that I trust him, but I open the front door with a heavy heart. The dark house feels horribly empty.

I've been told to stay by the phone, so I do. They say a phone that is stared at will never ring, but this one proves me wrong, trilling out its call to action after only five minutes. I half jump out of my skin, but a phone call so soon can only be good news about Florence. Or John. I pick it up. Whoever is calling remains silent.

'Hello,' I repeat, wary now.

'Is he there?' Tammy says.

'No,' I say, because I can't think of anything else.

'He went to tell the kids,' she says. 'I expect he's on his way.'

It's happening, then. How odd that I should get confirmation from his wife.

'He left something behind.' Her voice is flat and heavy, as though she's been crying. It will have cost her to make this phone call.

'I'll tell him,' I say. 'Thank you.'

'I don't want to see him again. If you want it, come now. I'll give you ten minutes.'

I'm going nowhere near the Black Dog tonight. 'It's not important. I'll give him your message.'

I'm ready to put the phone down when her next words almost stop my heart.

'It's that effigy you made of him. Ten minutes. Then I'm smashing it to a pulp.'

# 116

## Florence

'Ma'am, can you hear me? Ma'am? Florence, wake up.'

I open my eyes to find I'm in a shed, of sorts. The stone walls are crumbling in places. There is straw on the ground, and it smells of livestock. Directly opposite me, sitting on the ground as I am, with her legs outstretched, her wrists and ankles tied like mine, is Perdita. Her hair has come loose from its ponytail, and there is a smear of mud across her face.

'Are you OK, ma'am?' she says. 'Can you tell me your name?'

I force myself to speak. 'I'm Florence Lovelady, it's 1999, and Tony Blair is the prime minister. Where are the others?'

Perdita's eyes close. 'I think they may have shot Dwane,' she says. 'I couldn't really tell. I heard gunshots and Jenny screaming.'

I can't get my breath.

'I don't know about the rest,' Perdita says. 'Daphne, Avril, all of them. Those men took my phone. Yours too.'

'You made a call, didn't you? You phoned the station to say we were being pursued.'

'Before we left the others,' Perdita reminds me. 'Someone will look for us. I've no idea where we are, though. Did you see anything before they grabbed us?'

I bring my hands to my head. There is a stickiness close to the crown. 'The last thing I can remember clearly is seeing Dwane in his car,' I say. 'Then those men.'

'I don't think we're far out of town,' Perdita says. 'I think we're somewhere on the moors.'

'Doesn't narrow it down much.'

She doesn't respond to this, and so I look around again. I see a dull lantern, a low ceiling strewn with cobwebs, wooden beams.

'Ma'am, what have you told your colleagues at the Met? Have you told them enough to find us?'

Perdita can't keep the panic from her voice. Many officers spend their entire careers without ever once fearing for their lives. Which is exactly how it should be.

'I expected them about ten o'clock,' I say. 'A tactical team, from special operations. They'll have gone to the Glassbrook house and let themselves in. They'll know by now that something has gone wrong. What about you? Your mother will know you're missing. Is there anyone else? A husband? Boyfriend?'

'I live with a police officer, but he won't be expecting me back. What do the Met know?'

'What do you mean?'

'I mean, will they be able to work out what's been going on here? Without you? Will they be able to find the urn with the children's remains?'

'I told them I suspected corruption at Sabden Police Station and couldn't trust the local force. I gave them Bracken Lee's name. They'll have started running the checks on him.'

Perdita says, 'Did you name anyone at the station?'

'I hardly know them. I knew Brian Rushton's father well, and Brian himself seems like a dedicated, trustworthy officer, but who knows?'

'You know Tom Devine,' Perdita says.

I register that she has not said 'the superintendent'. 'I used to know him,' I acknowledge.

When she speaks again, the tone of her voice has changed. 'People say you knew him well.'

'It was a long time ago.'

'Some feelings never go away,' says Dwane.

My head spins. Dwane and Jenny Ogilvy are sitting in the corner of the shed, leaning back against the wall as Perdita and I are doing.

Dwane has a tiny, perfect hole in his forehead. I hope he doesn't turn round. The damage at the back will be horrible.

'Never,' echoes Jenny. She and Dwane are holding hands.

'I'm so sorry,' I say to them.

'Florence, what is it? What can you see?'

Perdita is already afraid, and I'm not cruel enough to make it worse if I can help it. I close my eyes and count to ten.

'Florence, this is freaking me out. What's going on?'

When I finish counting, when my breathing has settled again, I open my eyes. Dwane and Jenny have gone.

'I'm OK,' I say. 'Just a bad headache. Tell me what took you into the police. When you and I met, you were reading tarot cards.'

She makes an attempt at a smile. 'I remember.'

'Not the usual upbringing for a police officer.' I'm not just making conversation. I need Perdita to be at her best, to feel calm and strong. Reminding her of why she became an officer of the law in the first place is the best way to do that. 'I thought you had a very different future ahead of you,' I say.

'Does it matter?' she says.

'Was it a rebellion against your mother's unconventional lifestyle? We're more influenced by our mothers than we realise.'

'My mother isn't a charlatan. She really does make freaky things happen.' Perdita's tone has changed completely.

'If you say so.'

'The difference is, she believes in the supernatural and I don't.' Perdita sounds angry now. 'When I was a kid, I wanted to know how she did it. How she made the planchette move on the Ouija board, how the right cards appeared in the tarot. I wanted to know why things kept moving around our house by themselves. She said it was a poltergeist. I knew it was the two of us doing it somehow.'

'Interesting,' I say, keeping my voice light, although my heart is starting to beat very fast.

'I did a psychology degree, specialising in unconscious phenomena. I came up with a theory of my own that human beings have an invisible magnetic force around them that can be used to manipulate the physical world. It always works best with people who aren't very bright, or who are distracted by something else.'

'People who are handicapped in some way? I'll bet handicapped children are the best subjects, aren't they?'

She says nothing.

'You're a very smart woman, Perdita, and yet in your mid-forties, you're still a detective sergeant. Do you ever feel frustrated by your lack of progress?'

She scowls. 'Not everyone wants to head up the Met.'

'No. And you had a reason for staying in Sabden. Tell me something. When did you take your theory to the Craftsmen?'

# 117

## Cassie

How could I have forgotten that effigy? It contains John's essence. Tammy cannot destroy it without harming John.

It will take me less than ten minutes to get into town. I can be back in twenty. I don't want to see Tammy, but it can't be helped. As I jump into my car, I wonder if she'll damage the effigy anyway out of spite. She may not believe, as I do, in its inherent power to harm. I drive as quickly as I dare and pull into the car park at the rear of the pub. John's van is here, in its usual place by the back door. Next to it is a little red Renault that I know belongs to Tammy. Other than that, the car park is deserted.

I make no sound on the gravel. There is something puzzling to one side of the back door. A large van tyre, with a plastic dustbin lid duct-taped directly over its inner ring. I step closer and see that a small hole, about an inch and a half in diameter, has been cut into the plastic of the dustbin lid. I'm unsettled by this odd contraption, but I can make no sense of it and time is ticking on.

The kitchen is empty. Mary is supposed to be here, but there's no sign of her. Just a suitcase and two gym bags by the central table.

'Hello?'

No one answers. On the table, I spot a mobile phone and John's old black leather wallet. He's in the building somewhere.

'John?'

Nothing.

This is wrong. I've never thought Tammy someone to fear, but there is an energy in this building that is fierce and angry. From a knife block by the sink, I pull out the biggest.

I move to the kitchen door and open it. 'John!'

'Down here!' calls Tammy, and through the open cellar door I can see a dim light shining. Keeping the knife behind my back, I look down. The once-white paint is stained and peeling. Against one wall is a line of gleaming silver barrels, and the smell of stale beer seeps up towards me.

'What's going on?' I call. 'Where's John?'

Tammy answers back. 'He's down here.'

I take a step down and my foot skids. I catch hold of the rail and the knife clatters to the flagged floor beneath me. When I look down, I see something damp gleaming on the steps. Tammy has greased them. She wants me to fall.

I picture John slipping on the steps as I've just done, not catching himself. If she's harmed him, I will rip her heart out with my bare hands.

I dart down the steps, holding tight to the rail and, at the bottom see a brick archway that will take me deeper into the cellar. The next room is piled high with cardboard boxes of crisps and crates of soft drinks. There is another room beyond this. I grab the knife and I'm halfway to the doorway when the lights go out.

# 118

## Florence

Perdita, wide-eyed, says, 'I don't know what you mean.'

'How long did they give you? An hour? When are they coming back? Or are they outside, listening?'

'Florence, what are you talking about?'

'You were supposed to make me talk, weren't you? I'm bloody annoyed that I did. It doesn't change anything, though. There are decent police officers in town right now – they'll find out what's been going on in that hellhole on Laurel Bank. The people behind it will go to prison. And so will you.'

Her face changes completely then, all uncertainty leaving it. 'You really are uncommonly ignorant, you know that? The work at Black Moss Manor has huge validity.'

I laugh. 'No one has ever proven that psychic ability exists, let alone that it can be harnessed.'

She shakes her head as though she pities me. 'That's what you're supposed to think.'

'Telekinesis isn't real.' I'm provoking her. For all I know, it could well be real.

'It's entirely real. So is remote viewing. So is telepathy.'

'Bullshit. There's no evidence. There's never been any evidence.'

Her voice rises. 'There's loads. But whenever it seeps into the public domain, it's dismissed as a magic trick. By us. That's what people said about Uri Geller and his bending spoons – just a magic trick. We do it deliberately. Most magic tricks are infinitely more spectacular than anything telekinesis can do, so people believe us.

But in among all the fake magic is the real thing, and we're getting better all the time.'

'Have you actually seen this for yourself?'

Her face takes on a defensive look. 'I trust what I'm told. And they gave me an hour, to answer your earlier question. It will be better for you if you talk to me.'

'I've nothing else to tell you. My disappearance will be enough to get my officers a warrant to search Black Moss Manor. Your games here are over.'

'Where's Tom Devine?'

And now we're getting to it. The real reason I'm here. 'The superintendent? How should I know?'

'He was last seen on his way to meet you. In the early hours of yesterday morning. He never came back.'

I pull a puzzled face. 'That's interesting. I saw him several times today. At the cemetery, outside Black Moss Manor, in the Glassbrook house. Mind you, I often see people who aren't really there, so that probably doesn't help you much. You seem real enough, for what it's worth. More's the pity.'

She takes a second or two to process this, and her eyes grow wary. She says, 'So did you see him or not?'

I pretend to think about it. 'Probably not,' I say. 'It was probably all in my head. He seemed real, though. He was looking good.'

She cannot move any further away from me, but she seems to press against the wall. 'Are you actually mad?'

I look her straight in the eyes and smile. 'Almost certainly.'

She seems to brace herself to ask her next question. 'Is he dead?'

'I do see dead people,' I tell her. 'But I'm not going to apologise for that. If I'm mad, your maniac friends made me that way.' I raise my voice and shout, 'Hey, Dr Frankenstein, come and say hi to your monster!'

'Stop it.'

I've freaked this woman out. The people she works for won't be so easy. I wonder when they'll make an appearance. I am almost certain, now, that they are listening outside.

'What have you done to Tom?' she asks again.

There is genuine fear in her voice. I remember that she told me she lives with a police officer and feel a stab of jealousy.

'Did you kill him?' she says in a small voice.

'Tom was the love of my life,' I tell her. 'Why would I kill him?'

'Tom is the love of mine,' she snaps back. 'That's why I'm going to kill you.'

I laugh. 'Oh, my dear, I think you'll have to join the queue.'

Right on time, the door opens.

# 119

## Cassie

I'm plunged into a blackness that feels complete and endless.

'Fuse box.' Tammy's voice comes from all around me. 'Don't bother looking for it. It's two feet above your head and I've just moved the stool I stood on.'

I've no chance of finding John in the dark. I have to get back upstairs and call for help. I reach out, hoping to feel the soft cardboard of one of the boxes. There is nothing there. I take a step. Still nothing and I've already lost my sense of direction. I make myself walk forward. Sooner or later, I'll hit one of the cardboard box-lined walls and then I can make my way round it. I can move silently.

I've never had to move in complete darkness before.

Light appears. A torch beam shines directly on my face. I run towards it, knife in front of me, but the light goes out. I hear her footsteps scuttle away and I hit the wall.

'Steady,' Tammy giggles.

I get my breath.

'I'm here,' Tammy taunts, and the torch is switched on again. This time, she shines it on herself, directly upwards, so that her face looks like a grotesque mask. Then the angle of the beam shifts and I see the effigy of John in her left hand.

The beam drops and moves along the flagged floor. She's leading me deeper into the cellar and I'm stupid to go along with it. On the other hand, that torch is my best way of getting out of here and finding John. I'm armed. I don't think she is. I head in the direction of the torch beam, but she's switched it off again and already that brief flicker of light is a deceptive memory. I walk into something large and heavy.

As I get my breath again, I realise the smell has changed; stale beer has been replaced with rotting vegetation and damp. I suspect I'm getting close to the river.

The torch beam appears again, long enough for me to see wooden barrels that look decades old. Some are upright; others lie flat as though ready to be rolled away. Tammy is standing beside a low, stone-lined archway.

She stumbles away, through the archway. I'm afraid of her, but I'm also afraid to lose the light, and so I move too and duck inside the arched tunnel just in time to see her climbing a set of narrow steps at the end. Her legs vanish, and I've just a gleam of light to guide me.

The steps are crumbling and slick with damp. I have to bend low to climb up. I expect the torch to switch off again, but I follow the beam and, in its light, see John at last, lying face down on the stone floor. The torch is on the ground now, angled so that I can see his face and the stone effigy by his right hand. No sooner do I see this than I'm stepping towards him, thinking, *Where is Tammy?*

A heavy door slams shut. Too late, I turn back to see that John and I are trapped.

# 120

## Florence

Bracken Lee is first through the doorway. The two men who follow him in have removed their balaclavas and this gives me an odd feeling of hope. They intend to kill me, of course, but they were masked when they ambushed us earlier. Dwane and Jenny may not be dead after all.

Lee pulls me to my feet. I cannot walk with my ankles bound and so he and another man carry me outside to where more people are waiting. As I'm thrown to the rough ground, I recognise the Asters. They are older, of course, smaller and thinner, but I'd know them anywhere. I don't look at them, though. Instead, I make eye contact with the tall, grey-haired man who in his late seventies is still handsome, still has the bearing of a senior police officer.

'Where's my son?' Harry Devine asks me. Mary Devine at his side says nothing, but I know given the chance she will rip my throat out. She aims a kick, catching me on the thigh before Harry holds her back.

I struggle to a kneeling position so that I can see around me. We are high on the moors, but still in the shadow of Pendle Hill. Surrounding us is a circle of evergreen trees and just a few yards away the edge of a deep freshwater lake. Locals call it the Black Tarn. Tom and I swam in it many years ago and then made love on the banks. I am not surprised that they have brought me here.

'Hold her under,' Mary says. 'She'll soon talk.'

'We don't have the time,' Fred Aster says. 'The town is crawling with her people.'

Tom and I made love under a full moon. There is no moon

tonight, nor was there one when I was last here. There are nights when the deeds are too dark for even the moon to witness.

'Mr and Mrs Taylor, I presume?' I say, twisting on the ground so that I can see the Asters. 'You're going down for murder this time.'

I kneel in the mud as they glare down at me.

'And don't expect an easy ride in prison,' I say. 'Even hardened criminals don't take kindly to child killers. A couple of doctors who torture handicapped kids? I can't see either of you lasting a year.' Deliberately, I focus on Judith. 'And the women always get it worse.'

I note with a grim satisfaction her shudder of fear.

'Where are the ashes?' Fred Aster asks me.

'Want my advice?' I say. 'Give up the names of every other lowlife behind the Black Moss project, living or dead, let's get all the filth out into the open. And every other unspeakable project you people are involved with. Bring the Craftsmen down. Wipe them off the face of the earth and you might stand a chance of living beyond the next few months.'

Perdita has been set free of the plastic ties that held her wrists and ankles and comes to join us. I ignore her, but she grabs hold of me and starts to drag me towards the lake.

'Give it here, Perdy,' a voice says, and I am lifted, carried a few yards and then thrown down into the water's edge. Immediately someone – Perdita, I guess – leans on my shoulders and my head goes under.

# 121

## Cassie

I rip open John's shirt and put my hands on his bare chest. Warm. It takes a few seconds to be sure, but I can tell his heartbeat from my own. Two hearts. Still beating.

'John?'

I use the torch Tammy left behind – presumably so that I can see how dire my situation is – and shine it along the length of his body. There is no wound that I can see, no trace of blood. I pull off my jacket and fold it beneath his head.

'John, talk to me.'

I can't rouse him, but he's alive. I get to my feet and look around. I'm in the medieval cell that I have heard of but never seen before, because John's family always kept it boarded up. Centuries ago, prisoners were kept here on their way to Lancaster Gaol.

It's small, maybe ten feet by eight, and not quite big enough to stand upright. Directly above us is an iron grate.

The stone walls have crumbled away in places to reveal the earth behind. Close to the ground are the remains of manacles and iron rings. The door – panelled wood held together with heavy iron nails – could be hundreds of years old but is solidly built and fits perfectly into the stone archway. There is no handle on this side. There is a grille, though: five vertical bars in a foot-square gap.

I step close and shine the torch through. Tammy is standing there.

'They kept witches in here in the old days,' she says. 'Beryl told me.'

'Where is she?'

'Passed out as usual. I'll break the news to her in the morning.'

I will not ask her what news. I won't play her game. She tells me anyway.

'That you and John have run away together. That I've no idea where you are. That she'll probably never hear from him again.'

'My car's outside, you daft cow,' I snap, even as I'm thinking that I left my keys upstairs. She can drive it away, abandon it, and no one will ever know. The police won't look for me in Sabden, not if my bags have gone from Daphne and Avril's house. Not if John's bags have gone too. They'll assume we've run away together.

'I'll sort something out,' she says. 'I've got the rest of the night.'

'You'll never get away with it,' I say. 'People will hear us shouting. I've got one of your kitchen knives here. I'll dig my way out.'

'You'll be dead by morning,' she tells me.

I look around. The cell is grim, but there is nothing in here that will kill us.

'Must get on,' she says, and the shutter on the grille comes down. A second later, the sound of banging rings. I try to lift the shutter, but there is no leverage on this side.

'What are you doing?'

'Making you airtight.'

She means to suffocate us. Has she not seen the grate above us? We have a source of fresh air.

'I've made a cover for that grate,' she says, as though reading my mind. 'A plastic dustbin lid on an old tyre from John's van.'

I remember the hole in the dustbin lid. It would fit a pipe. Suddenly I understand her plan. She's going to gas us.

I spin round and look for something I can use to block the grille. 'He's your children's father,' I say. 'I thought you loved him.'

'I do. But I'll have him dead before I see him rutting like a farm animal with you. I'll probably use your car. Is your tank full?'

It is. It is full.

'There are worse deaths than carbon monoxide poisoning,' Tammy says, as she carries on banging. 'You'll feel dizzy, a bit sick. You might get a bad headache, but then you fall asleep and don't wake up. Witches had it worse, in the old days.'

# 122

## Florence

When I reach the point where drowning feels inevitable, when I have no choice but to let water flood into my lungs, they pull me up. One of them performs some rudimentary first aid, pumping my arms until the water pours out and I can breathe again. I'm struggling to see but I sense someone crouching beside me at the lake edge.

'Last chance,' Bracken Lee says. 'Tell me where the ashes are.'

'Your mother was a sweet girl,' I gasp. 'She'd be ashamed.'

I twist around to look him in the face. 'They murdered her, you know, these friends of yours. A terrified seventeen-year-old girl and they killed her in cold blood.'

I'm pulled to a sitting position and Judith pushes Bracken out of the way.

'If you tell us, we can let you go,' she says. 'Without the ashes, and the post-mortem reports, which we can take care of, you have nothing. Tell us and this will all be over.'

She's lying; they won't risk a loose end.

'She loved you,' I call to Bracken. 'She'd have given her life to protect you. Maybe she did.'

'Sandra Cartwright died an hour ago,' Judith says. 'You have nothing.'

Harry Devine's face appears in front of mine. 'Last chance,' he says. 'Tell me where my son is.'

'Let me talk to his mother,' I say.

Mary is ushered forward.

'What would you do,' I say to her, 'to someone who harmed your son?'

'I'd send them to hell where they belong,' she spits at me.

I laugh. 'So why were you people stupid enough to harm mine?'

'We're out of time.' Frederick steps forward. 'The police officers from London will have met up with her friends. Sooner or later, they'll come here. We have to finish this now.' He turns to the younger men. 'Can you deal with it?'

'We've got it,' Lee says.

The Asters, the Devines and Perdita walk away, and I see that at the edge of the water, a rowing boat is waiting. They are going to drown the witch.

# 123

## Cassie

I've dragged John to the door in the hope that some air will reach him through the gap at the bottom. I'm using the knife handle to bang at the shutter, but Tammy's nails are holding.

I don't like to look back at the grate. I've woven my jacket into its iron mesh, but I know the carbon monoxide is getting through. My head has been aching for some time now, I'm feeling sick, and I have to stop what I'm doing every few seconds to regain my balance.

Tammy left us at midnight. I heard the engine of my car start up at ten minutes past. It's now nearly one in the morning. John and I have been breathing in carbon monoxide for almost an hour.

Of course, I tried to pull the grate out of its base, but it wasn't moving four hundred years ago and it isn't moving now. When the tyre landed on top of it, I tried to push my hands through the bars so that I could block the pipe, but the squares are too small. Tammy's vile contraption is working. Long before my car runs out of petrol, John and I will be dead.

The cramped, claustrophobic room seems to be closing in on me. I can't stand up any longer, so I stop trying. I lie beside John and wrap my arms round him. He hasn't stirred and I'm glad. He will simply slip away and die in my arms. I let my head fall onto his shoulder and close my eyes.

'Cassie!'

'Cassie!'

I'm at the bottom of a deep well, one that stretches endlessly above me, and my sister's voice, impossibly far away, is echoing down.

'Cassie, are you down there? Shit, I can't move this thing. Cassie, say something.'

'Step aside, miss. There's some sort of fabric in the way. I'll see if I can push it out.'

I know that voice. He's a police officer. He spoke to me today.

'Cassie! Hold on. The police are here. They know where you are. Hold on, Cassie.'

From a long way away, I hear footsteps.

The pub car park is packed. I sit on the steps of the ambulance, a blanket round my shoulders, an oxygen mask over my face, and watch Tammy being led to a waiting police car. She does not look at me, or at John, who lies behind me in the ambulance. The car drives away and she is gone from our lives.

'It was sheer chance I saw your car.' Luna sits next to me, unusually close, but I don't ask her to move away. 'If the lights had been green, I'd have driven straight past. I was coming to tear you off a strip for leaving Avril and Daphne's house, and then I saw that pipe. Jesus, Cass.' She squeezes my arm and then quickly takes her hand away, as though embarrassed.

'You ready, love?' The paramedic behind me has been attending to John, who is still out cold. 'Two minutes and we'll be off.'

I lift the mask from my face. 'What's happening about the others?'

'Put that back on,' Luna snaps. 'Dwane and Jenny are fine. They were tied up in Dwane's car at the tithe barn. Perdita was found a couple of minutes ago, wandering down the Nelson Road. She says she and Florence were driven away from the barn by masked men and then she was dumped on the roadside.'

'Florence?' I ask.

Luna shakes her head.

# 124

## Florence

I'm carried to the boat. Bracken and another man push it into the water; a third man stands on the shore and watches. The others walk to their waiting car.

The wind picks up as we leave the shore behind. The man I don't know rows, and Bracken sits opposite him. I crouch on the wet floor. The boat is small, only really big enough for two. Beneath the oarsman's seat are two very large stones. Rope is knotted round both. Before I leave this boat, those stones will be tied to me. The plastic ties round my wrists are tight enough to cut into my skin. When I go overboard, I won't have use of my legs or arms.

In the old days, when witches were openly persecuted, drowning was used not as a means of execution but as a trial. The woman accused was thrown into a body of water. If she sank, she was innocent. Floating, though, could only be achieved by supernatural means and proved she was in league with the devil. She'd be dragged out of the water and hanged.

I am a witch. I have to float.

We travel on and the only sound is the splashing of oars. The night is very dark and the edges of the lake have vanished in the gloom.

''Bout here, do you think?' The oars pause. I hear the dripping of water and then a sound like that of other oars.

I have been to this lake before, but never noticed an echo.

Bracken looks around. 'Bit further,' he says.

A second before the oars strike the water again, we hear something. 'What was that?' the oarsman asks.

'Fox,' I say, quickly, because I too have heard it. 'They hunt during the dark moon.'

'Shut it,' Bracken says.

We are not alone on this dark lake; whether that will help me or not is anyone's guess.

We glide on, over the still, black water. The Black Tarn is glacial, formed by ice millions of years ago and believed to be very deep. Not that it really matters. Six feet of water is enough to drown me. I take a deep breath and remember my son telling his dad and me about sub-aqua diving.

*You pant for a few seconds, to expand your lungs. Then you take one God Almighty breath and hold it.*

I start to pant, visualising my lungs getting bigger and fuller. The men think I'm panicking and grin at each other.

'This'll do,' Bracken says. His accomplice stops rowing and pulls in the oars.

I keep going, taking massive breaths and pushing out the air. The oarsman rolls one of the stones out from under his seat.

I have to do it now. I suck in air until my lungs feel as though they will burst, and then, before either man can react, I stand and throw myself over the side.

I hit the water and cold wraps me in its grip, but I've swum in this lake before. It is summer. The cold will not kill me. My body weight takes me down and I force myself not to fight it. I can't spare the energy and I can't come back to the surface too soon. Above me, the boat will be rocking, the two men struggling to balance it. They may not have seen exactly where I hit the water. If I'm really lucky, their torches will have gone overboard too.

I can see nothing in the blackness around me. Only the cold stinging my eyes suggests they're open. I hear a ringing in my ears, but it isn't an unpleasant sound.

My sinking slows and stops altogether. I lie motionless, as though cushioned by the water. The temptation to move, to struggle against my bindings is close to overwhelming, but I know I have to be perfectly still.

*The air in your lungs acts like the air in a life jacket. Just taking in a deep breath will make you rise in the water.*

I've been in the water for maybe ten seconds. I have a minute, at least, before my breath gives out.

The human body is naturally buoyant, women's bodies more so than men's because of their greater fat content. I'm a woman in middle age, and however hard I might try to keep the extra pounds off, they have found their way onto my midriff and hips. I've floated on the surface of calm water many times.

It's working. I'm moving upwards. I can't see the surface – the sky is too black, and there is no trail of moonlight to guide my way – but I'm trusting to the laws of physics. Twenty seconds, I think, since I hit the water.

The cold ceases to hurt and a creeping numbness is claiming my limbs. Blood will be racing from my extremities to keep my vital organs pumping, but soon, they'll start to slow down. I tell myself that that is a good thing. The cold will slow down my oxygen consumption, buying me extra time. I continue rising, more slowly than I would like, but I tell myself that too is a good thing. The men in the boat will not row back to shore immediately. They will wait to make sure I stay down.

Without thinking, I pull on the tie round my wrists. The movement proves to be a mistake. I start to sink again. Panic rises.

*I am a witch*, I tell myself. *I will float.*

Thirty seconds. Holding my breath is no longer easy. My chest is growing tight, but I am moving upwards again. I see movement, the surface of the water. My face breaks through and I release air slowly. I take two deep breaths and listen for the sound of shouting, for a torch beam to hit my face.

I drift down and panic rears again. When I've floated on water in the past, I've had two free arms to use as balance, two hands to waft gently. My arms are tied together at the wrists. I force myself to be still, but despair is beginning to grab hold. I cannot bob up and down at the surface for ever. I can't even do it for many minutes. I risk a huge kick with both feet and shoot upwards, breaking the surface once more, but barely have I seen rippling black water before I go down again, this time faster. This time, I sink deeper, and this time I'm not alone. Tom is in the water with me, not feet away, strangely luminous in the black depths. He is drowning, as I am, gulping for breath, as I will be any second now.

I kick again, go up again, breathe and sink. When I break the surface once more, I know it may be for the last time. I am gasping when a hand grabs hold of my hair. I'm pulled backwards through the water and come up against something hard. The boat. I wait for the hand to push me under.

Another hand reaches into my armpit.

'Don't make a sound,' a voice whispers in my ear. 'Hush it. They're not far.'

I don't make a sound.

For long minutes, I'm held against the boat, clinging to the last minutes of life, which seem infinitely precious now. I hear a voice in the distance, and perhaps the splashing of oars.

'Right, I'll risk it. Stay quiet.'

Two hands have me now and I'm pulled upwards. I hear the water falling away and the drops hitting the surface seem torturously loud. I want to kick my way up but don't quite dare. Then I'm pulled over something hard and painful, and land in the bottom of a boat. I feel hands, warm against my own, the cold of metal, and the tie round my wrists breaks apart. Then my legs are free and I struggle to sit up.

I am in another small rowing boat, surrounded by rods, nets, other fishing equipment. I have been rescued by a night fisherman.

The man in the boat has a blanket, which he wraps round me. He puts a finger to his lips and then quietly picks up an oar and pushes us through the water towards the edge. I watch a pinprick of light that I think must be the other boat. Only when car headlights switch on, sweep across the water and drive away does my rescuer speak to me.

'They're not going to believe this down the anglers' club.'

# 125

## Cassie

The keys are where Avril told me they'd be. I'm ten minutes early, but I need a moment by myself. It's many years since I've been in our old house, and on the day I left, I thought I was a killer. It will take me some time, I think, to get used to the woman I am not.

The hospital discharged me an hour ago. I'd wanted to spend the day with John but he'd insisted otherwise. 'You've stuff to sort out with your mum and Luna,' he'd said, and he'd been right.

The two of them had been at my bedside for much of the night. We'd talked, but there was still so much I didn't understand.

The kitchen smells of dried herbs and lemons, as it always did. Also of dust, and old fabric, which it never used to.

The vials of foxglove syrup were emptied long ago, and there's no reminder in the old pantry of what I once meant to do. I walk through to the sitting room and find the bottle of Tío Pepe that I can't believe my mother kept. I'm on the point of pouring a glass, to see if I can taste the extra sweetness of rosehip syrup, when I hear a car pulling up outside. I make my way back to the kitchen and wait for Florence.

'How's John?' she says, the second she appears.

'They're keeping him in for another day,' I reply. 'Tammy gave him some weird sedative. She won't say what it was and they want to keep an eye on him.'

'And you?'

'Worst hangover ever. They told me to get lots of rest, ideally in the fresh air. Are you OK?'

'I'm a whole lot better knowing that certain people are behind bars.' Florence puts her bag down on the kitchen table, pulls out her phone and glances at it. 'Brian Rushton and my officers picked up the Asters early this morning – did you hear? They've been charged. Perdita Collins and the Devines are under arrest too.'

'Good,' I say. 'Not about Perdita, though. Avril and Daphne are gutted. And her mother will take it badly.'

Florence looks at the screen of her phone again. 'No sign of Bracken Lee. And we've found nothing conclusive at Black Moss Manor. These people are good at covering their tracks.'

'I'm glad you're OK,' I say, and realise I mean it. I feel different today, as though all the spite, the envy, the unhappiness that has been eating me up for so long has been stripped away.

I don't even want Tammy to go to prison. How can I blame her for loving John a little too much?

Talking to Mum again has helped a lot. She's agreed to leave her nursing home and move back here. She hasn't agreed to selling up yet, but just getting her back into the world feels like huge progress.

I also had a chance earlier to ask Avril and Daphne about why she faked dementia for so long. They both know, I'm sure of it, but insist Sally will tell me when she's ready. They both seem sure, though, that it was nothing to do with me, or my attempts to poison Roy.

'What will you and John do?' Florence asks me.

'We haven't really thought about it,' I say. 'There's been no time. Go abroad, I suppose. We won't be able to help the scandal, not when Tammy's trial takes place.'

I wonder if John and I can refuse to press charges, whether that's even a possibility when it comes to attempted murder. I can ask Luna.

Florence has fallen silent.

'You disapprove?' I ask.

She shakes her head. 'Oh, Cassie, in the greater scheme of things . . .'

Music starts to play above our heads. Elvis Presley's 'Always On My Mind'. When I look at Florence, her face has gone white.

'What the hell?' I say.

She lets go the breath she's been holding. 'It's Luna. She did it the other night. Scared me half to death.'

We climb the steps to the first floor, past Florence's old room and mine, and sure enough, the narrow door to the attic is unlocked. I go ahead. As I reach the top, the music stops and I step into the attic to see Luna and my mother at Larry's old record player.

'Do you mind if I have these, Cass?' Luna says. 'We can split them, if you like.'

'I thought you were in hospital.' My mother gets awkwardly to her feet, brushes a fine black dust off her skirt and takes a step towards me.

I assure her that I'm fine, and that John is too, and then Florence has to answer several questions about her own health. While my mother is quizzing her, I wander around the attic. It's large, stretching the length and breadth of the house, and full of accumulated junk. It must be years, decades, since I've been up here. There are packing crates stacked high, shelves of old books, a great leather trunk, suitcases by the score.

A fine black dust has covered the floorboards and most of the flat surfaces. I can see footprints made by Luna and my mother, and as I walk, I feel a faint crunching beneath my feet, as though I'm walking on fine cinders.

'I'm fine too, if anyone cares,' Luna says. 'Who fancies a drink? What time does the Black Dog open, Cass?'

I ignore this. I'm distracted by our old doll's house, a miniature replica of the house we're standing in. I open the hinged front to see my old room, just as it used to be. 'Dad made this, didn't he?' I ask.

It too is covered in dust, in which something is glinting. I peer closer. Insect wings.

'Of course he did,' my mother says. 'He'd have done anything for you two. Do you remember your cribs?'

Her arm round my waist, she steers me over to an elaborately carved crib that seems to glow, even through the dull sheen of dust. The head and foot both depict a woodland scene on a winter's night. Larry carved stars for me and a bright full moon.

'You were born in February,' my mother says, as though I might have forgotten. 'So he carved you a frost moon. This is apple wood. He cut an old tree down in the garden.'

'Where's mine?' says Luna. 'Or did I just have Cassie's hand-me-down?'

My mother gives Luna a look I remember well. 'Yours was made from plum wood. A summer night, and the buck moon.'

'Where is it?'

A cloud seems to pass over my mother's face. 'It's downstairs. Randy carried it down for baby Henry.'

'It's still down there?' Florence has wandered over to the narrow window and is staring down at the window ledge.

'We never used that room again,' says my mother.

'Do you think we'll ever find out what happened to Marigold?' Luna asks.

For a moment, no one answers. I have the feeling we only have half of Florence's attention. She is looking around the attic curiously.

My mother says, 'They took her that night. Her and little Henry. They took advantage of me being out of the house and came for them both. It was my fault.'

Florence says, 'They didn't take her to Black Moss. It was on fire.'

'I'm not sure that makes sense,' says Luna. 'Grace would have heard if there'd been a disturbance. I don't remember her being deaf.'

'And Marigold wouldn't have gone quietly,' I add. 'She'd have screamed the place down.'

Florence and my mother share a look.

'She had a good pair of lungs on her,' my mother agrees. 'Remember the night she gave birth?'

Florence smiles. 'And when she locked herself in the toilets in the maternity ward?'

'You're right, love,' my mother says to me. 'She wouldn't have gone without a fight.'

'So they killed her here,' Florence says. 'Or maybe Roy did it alone.'

'He was ill.' My mother shakes her head. 'He could barely walk.'

'Really?' I say. 'Because I remember him being perfectly capable of beating up John.'

'He was still alive when Tom and I got here at eleven o'clock.' Florence frowns.

'He was on his feet and moving around when I ran out of the house,' I say. 'That was just before ten.'

'What could he do in an hour?' Florence says.

'Anything at all to Marigold,' my mother says. 'I should never have left her.'

'Can we please stop blaming ourselves for what the monsters in this town do to us and others?' Luna says. 'I mean, seriously, can we?'

'I think it probably was Roy.' Florence almost seems to be talking to herself. 'He had an hour. He killed Marigold. Then he contacted the Craftsmen and told them to come and collect the body and the baby. They did, and then he went back to bed because he really wasn't feeling well.'

'It must have been that way,' I say.

Florence is looking doubtful again, though. 'I can see them spiriting away a baby,' she says. 'They're very portable. The body of a full-grown woman, though? That's not so easy. Not at short notice.'

We're silent while we think about this.

'Sally, when was the last time you had a clean-out up here?' Florence says.

My mother's mouth tightens.

'I'm not being rude,' Florence says. 'If Luna's cot is still downstairs after thirty years, that suggests you didn't come up here much.'

'I haven't been up in years,' I say. 'Mind you, I haven't lived here for years.'

'After that night,' Florence says, 'how thoroughly did the police search the house? Did they come up here?'

We all stare at her.

'I wasn't involved,' Florence goes on. 'The superintendent reinforced his rule about my having nothing to do with Larry's family.'

'I was in a cell for two days,' my mother says. 'The girls stayed with Avril and Daphne.'

'Mary said nothing about it when we came back,' Luna says. 'Are you sure there was a police search?'

'Yes,' Florence says. 'I remember talk of it. I remember people saying the house and garden had been thoroughly searched and no trace of Marigold or her son found.'

'You searched the night she vanished,' my mother says. 'I helped with that. We looked everywhere. Even up here.'

'We were looking for a woman in hiding, not a dead body,' Florence replies. 'And it was a quick, surface search. We didn't search forensically. Not that night.'

We all fall silent once more.

'Has anyone else noticed that there seems to have been an unusual amount of insect activity in here?' Florence asks.

I look down at the floor, at the crispy black dust that we've been walking on. I look at my mother and sister and know that we are all thinking the same thing.

'It's not possible,' Luna says. 'We'd have smelled it. Her.'

My eyes go to the large packing trunk against the far wall.

'The last time I saw your father, he told me he knew a thing or two about dead bodies,' Florence says. 'About how they break down and decompose in various circumstances. Roy did too.'

Florence is looking where I am. At the large leather trunk.

'Roy didn't know he was going to die that night,' she says. 'What if he was told to hide the body, just for a day or so, until someone could come along and dispose of it properly. Where in the house would he put it?'

'What's in that trunk, Mum?' says Luna.

'Curtains,' my mother replies. 'Sheets. A few old bedspreads.'

'Marigold vanished in summer,' Florence says. 'This room is far from airtight, so there'd have been a lot of insect activity.'

Florence is fishing in the pocket of her jacket. When she pulls out her hand, she's holding a pair of purple disposable gloves.

'We'd have noticed the smell,' Luna repeats.

'We did,' says my mother. 'I had to call someone out to look at the drains. It was just after Randy's funeral. Do you remember how hard it rained?'

'The smell would have lasted a few weeks, a couple of months at most.' Florence is pulling the gloves over her hands. 'And if she was in an enclosed space, it would have been contained. Curtains would soak up the fluid leakage.'

Luna looks over at me. 'Cass, why don't you take Mum downstairs?'

My mother shakes her head, but she comes to stand beside me all the same, as Florence walks to the trunk. She slips the catches open and then lifts the lid. It falls back against the wall. Luna walks slowly to join her as Florence lifts a sheet from the trunk.

'Oh,' says Luna.

My mother takes my hand and we join the others. Looking troubled, Luna steps to one side so that we can see.

Lying in the trunk, curled in a half-foetal position, recognisable only by her long, strawberry-blonde hair and her pale pink dress with white daisies, is Marigold.

# 126

## Florence

Friday, 13 August 1999

We meet at Daylight Gate. The day has been overcast, and heavy cloud has gathered as night draws near. The twilight will not last long.

Daphne and Avril arrive first. Daphne's arms are full of garden flowers, and lots of them are bright orange and yellow clustered blooms. Marlene and her daughter come next, with more flowers, then Mary and the Ogilvy family. We haven't told Hecate, Perdita's mother, that we're meeting. She is no longer someone the women can trust. Sally will take her place in the coven.

For half an hour, maybe longer, we talk and drink wine. One or two of the women admire the jewelled velvet pouch that is hanging from a ribbon round my neck. I tell them it's a gift from Sally.

Many of them are curious about the police investigation. I tell them that while the fake post-mortem report has disappeared from the police station, the real one, still in Blackburn Royal Infirmary, will confirm that children died and were buried illegally at Black Moss Manor in the last twenty years. There are charges to answer, and the Asters, who have indeed been masquerading as the Taylors, will be tried for murder. Whether the charges stick is anyone's guess.

'The judge will probably be a Craftsman,' says Mary.

The women exchange nervous glances, as though it is still unlucky to say the name out loud.

'Even they can't flaunt the law entirely,' I say. 'We'll get them. Slowly but steadily. Have courage, ladies.'

Marlene asks, 'Any sign of Bracken Lee?'

I shake my head.

The sky is darkening and so we light the circle of candles round the bonfire that the Glassbrook women and I spent all day building. The garden isn't overlooked, but we're close to other houses. What we are doing must be done quickly.

Behind us, the kitchen door opens and Dwane comes out to join us. We have wrapped Marigold's remains in a linen sheet of Sally's. Thirty years after her death, there is little of her left and Dwane carries her easily. With a face that is grim even by his standards, he walks to the bonfire and places his linen parcel in the centre of it.

We've soaked the wood in petrol. There is kindling and lots of fire-lighters at its heart. This must happen quickly. Tomorrow morning, we will clear away the ashes and scatter them on the Hill at the place where the witches meet. Marigold will never be forgotten. Not by us.

The women form a circle round the fire. They stretch out their arms to create a psychic connection and begin to sing. I throw the taper into the pyre's heart.

The fire burns bright and fierce. I see the linen that is Marigold's shroud blacken and crumble. I watch sparks dance in the purple sky and think of her singing sweetly to her baby son.

'I'm not saying this is wrong, Florence, but you realise that without Marigold's body, you'll never prove that Bracken Lee is her son,' says Luna at my side. 'Even if he's found, you won't prove it. And without that connection, you'll never prove the Craftsmen murdered her.'

I share a look with Dwane and my left hand enfolds the small velvet bag, hanging on a ribbon round my neck.

'I don't think Bracken Lee will ever be found,' I say. 'But we haven't burned all of Marigold's bones. I saved one.'

Luna stares at me with something approaching horror and I hold up my left hand so that they can all see it. 'I took one of her fingers,' I say. 'Specifically, the third from her left hand. If Bracken Lee is ever brought to justice, we can claim Sally found it in one of the boxes in the attic. It will make sense. The Craftsmen took fingers from their victims.'

'You're going to carry a dead woman's finger round your neck?' Cassie asks.

'I've been missing a finger for thirty years,' I say. 'And dealing with that has been difficult. I think this will help.'

The bonfire burns on. The witches sing and cry for Marigold. In the south-east, the moon has risen and the palest crescent hangs in the sky, watching over us. The black moon is gone. For now.

# Author's Note

*The Buried* is both sequel and prequel to *The Craftsman*.

The hunt for Sabden's child-killer, leading to the arrest in 1969 of Larry Glassbrook, is explored fully in *The Craftsman*; as are the events of 10 August 1999, referred to briefly here in Abby's article in the *Lancashire Morning Post*.

Sabden is a real place, but the Sabden in this book bears little resemblance to it. Pendle Hill is also real, but no one knows the original location of Malkin Tower.

A number of 'witches' were tried and hanged in Lancashire in 1612. All references to the events in the Craftsmen series are accurate to the best of my knowledge.

# Acknowledgements

First, a huge thank you to all the readers who loved *The Craftsman* and who've been waiting patiently for the sequel. I hope it doesn't disappoint.

Sam Eades worked her usual editorial brilliance, while Sarah Benton and Anna Valentine were, as always, wonderfully supportive and encouraging. A special mention here to Rachel Neely, who swooped in at the eleventh hour, picked it up, shook it around and turned it into something so much better.

Anne Marie Doulton, Rosie Buckman and Jessica Buckman O'Connor continue to be the very best of agents, and the kindest of friends.

# CREDITS

Orion Fiction would like to thank everyone at Orion who worked on the publication of *The Buried*.

**Agent**
Anne-Marie Doulton

**Copyeditor**
Laura Collins

**Proofreader**
Jenny Page

**Design**
Nick Shah
Rabab Adams
Charlotte Abrams Simpson
Debbie Holmes
Joanna Ridley
Nick May
Helen Ewing
Clare Sivell

**Contracts**
Anne Goddard

**Marketing**
Lucy Cameron

**Editor**
Sam Eades
Rachel Neely

**Editorial Management**
Georgia Goodall
Jane Hughes
Charlie Panayiotou
Tamara Morriss
Claire Boyle

**Production**
Claire Keep
Fiona McIntosh

**Rights**
Susan Howe
Krystyna Kujawinska
Jessica Purdue
Ashley Kinley
Louise Henderson

**Publicity**
Alex Layt

**Sales**
Jen Wilson
Victoria Laws
Esther Waters
Frances Doyle
Ben Goddard
Georgina Cutler
Jack Hallam
Anna Egelstaff
Inês Figueira
Barbara Ronan
Andrew Hally
Dominic Smith
Deborah Deyong
Lauren Buck
Maggy Park
Linda McGregor
Sinead White
Jemimah James
Rachael Jones
Jack Dennison
Nigel Andrews
Ian Williamson
Julia Benson
Declan Kyle
Robert Mackenzie
Megan Smith
Charlotte Clay
Rebecca Cobbold

**Operations**
Jo Jacobs
Sharon Willis
Lisa Pryde

**Audio**
Paul Stark
Jake Alderson

**Finance**
Nick Gibson
Jasdip Nandra
Rabale Mustafa
Elizabeth Beaumont
Ibukun Ademefun
Afeera Ahmed
Levancia Clarendon
Tom Costello

## THE FAKE WIFE

### She's not who you think she is . . .

When a beautiful stranger appears at Olive Anderson's dinner table, telling the waiter she's her wife, Olive is immediately unsettled. But the stranger wants to talk, and isn't this what Olive wants on this lonely winter night? To vent to a perfect stranger? She's too ashamed to tell her real friends the truth – six months into the marriage they all warned her against, her life is a living nightmare.

Perhaps Olive should have asked the fake wife who she's really married to. Perhaps she should have known this chance encounter had something to do with her secretive husband.

Because there is a string of missing women connected to Mr Anderson, and by the morning, Olive will be the latest…